PRAISE FOR

Jen Stephens

"Stephens's debut story about the redemption of heartache took me to a place where the important things of life were made important again. Her writing is a reflection of the story-telling characteristics of the Creator: not what the characters expected or prayed for, but what brought real love and value in the end."

—Rebeca Seitz, author of the Sisters, Ink Series

"The Heart's Journey Home is a heartwarming story and a witness to how God works in the lives of the faithful who wait patiently for Him to reveal his purpose."

—Diane Black, Tennessee State Senator

"A wonderful story that is sure to touch the hearts of romance readers, *The Heart's Journey Home* is a sweet tale of healing and love."

—Kathleen Fuller, best-selling author of *A Man of His Word*

"In her debut novel, author Jen Stephens bursts on the literary scene with a warmth and charm that shines through her writing right into the reader's heart. With down-home candor and skilled word-weaving, Stephens allows her story to unfold through believable characters, drawing readers in right from the beginning and carrying them on a pleasant journey with enough twists and turns along the way to maintain interest to the very last page. Congratulations on a great first novel, and I certainly expect to see more from this author in the future!"

THE

Heart's
Journey
HOME

JEN STEPHENS

Charlotte, Tennessee
37036 USA

Published by Sheaf House®. Requests for information should be addressed to:

Editorial Director
Sheaf House Publishers, LLC
3641 Hwy 47 N
Charlotte, TN 37036
jmshoup@sheafhouse.com
www.sheafhouse.com

Library of Congress Control Number: 2009942135

ISBN 978-0-9797485-5-4 (softcover)

Scripture quotations are from The Holy Bible, New King James Version, copyright © 1982 by Thomas Nelson, Inc.

Cover and interior design by Marisa Jackson.
Map by Jim Brown of Jim Brown Illustrations.

10 11 12 13 14 15 16 17 18 19—10 9 8 7 6 5 4 3 2

MANUFACTURED IN THE UNITED STATES OF AMERICA

Acknowledgments

I LEARNED SOMETHING VERY IMPORTANT while I was writing *The Heart's Journey Home*. Writing, like life, isn't meant to be a solo journey. I might've written the words on these pages by myself, but the fact of the matter is that you wouldn't be holding it in your hands without the help and encouragement of many, many people. I wish I could thank everyone who has supported me along the way, but there just isn't enough room. Still, there are several whom I must recognize here.

First, and above all else, I'm eternally grateful to my Lord and Savior, Jesus Christ, for the many, many gifts he's given me but mostly for loving me, imperfections and all, with an amazing, unconditional, incomprehensible love. My heart's deepest desire is to write stories that will bring glory and honor to You, my Rock and my Redeemer.

A very heartfelt thank you goes to my husband, Chris, who sacrificed more than anyone else to make this dream a reality. Your love and support mean everything in the world to me, and I wouldn't want to share this moment with anyone else but you, the love of my life. To my two beautiful daughters, Alison and Olivia, nothing can ever compare to the joy of being your mother. I'm so incredibly proud of you both, of all you're learning and accomplishing day by day. I love you girls so very, very much . . . all the way to heaven and back.

To the staff at Sheaf House, especially Joan and Joy, thank you so much for taking a chance on me and making my wildest dreams a very beautiful reality. Also, to the other Sheaf House authors, thank you for your support and encouragement. I feel so blessed to be a part of such a wonderful, talented group of writers.

To Terri Petitt, who shot the perfect cover photo, you're not only an amazing photographer, you're also a great friend. Thank you! To Carie Lawyer and Eva Grace Felts, my gorgeous models, thank you both for bringing my characters to life. To Marisa Jackson for tying the whole cover together in a pretty (pink) bow, Jim Brown of Jim Brown Illustrations for the absolutely stunning map of Harvest Bay, and Cindi Clemmer for your brilliant work on my promotional material, thank you all so much! Your vision and creativity are awe inspiring.

I'm also so grateful to all those who took the time to read this book and then write such lovely endorsements for it. Your words of encouragement were an incredible blessing to me, and I just can't thank you enough.

To my mom, Donna Otto, there's nothing in this whole world like a mother's love. I know that now that I'm a mother, and I'm so thankful to have been brought up under the shelter of your love. It was there that I found the courage to sprout my wings. I especially want thank you for making sure we were in church every Sunday. It provided me with the sturdy foundation on which I've built the rest of my life. I also want to thank my step-parents, Shirley Dominick LaVoie and Tom Otto. I never knew life without you, and though I know I didn't always make it easy, I want to thank you both for the role you played in making me exactly who I am today.

To Bonnie Fellows, Julie Roeder, and Karen Pantaleo, thank you for not just being my sisters, but also my most precious friends. I love the three of you so much! I especially want to thank Bonnie for all the help with anything and everything in this book regarding the medical profession. I really couldn't have done this without you. Julie, thanks for insight into the drama that goes on in the ER. My most emotional scene was made better because of you. And Karen, thanks for never hesitating to keep my girls so that I could write. They adore their Aunt Kiki—almost as much as I do! Also, to my brothers-in-law and my nieces and nephew, you complete our family, and I love you all.

Thank you, Granny and Grandpa Moltz and Grandma Dominick, for the legacy of love that you've bestowed on our family. You've given me the roots I needed to confidently become who I am today. I'm so proud to be your granddaughter.

To all of the family that I received when I married Chris, but especially to Russ and Susie Stephens, thank you so much for always loving me like your own. You are an amazing family, and I'm so blessed every day to be a part of it.

To Patty Smith, my best friend since high school who's taught me about the true meaning of faith. You've inspired me time and time again. You're one of the strongest women I know, and I love you like my sister.

To the wonderful faculty of Christian Community Schools, thank you for your constant support and encouragement. A special thanks to Beth Johnstone for always believing in me as a teacher and a writer; Shelly Carlson for patiently answering all of my grammatical questions; Daon Johnson for providing me with insight on issues of the mind, body, and spirit; Peter Stratton for your assistance with my Web site and video; Janie

Thornton for all of your prayers for me and the success of this book; Amanda Rowley for supporting me as a writer, teacher, and parent, but more important, for helping me give my baby a strong educational and spiritual foundation; my fellow elementary teachers and cherished friends, Patty Burris, Evelyn Stevenson, Rita Crain, Connie Roy, Connie Trovillian, and Marsha Boak for all of the precious moments that were spent sharing life experiences and Christian beliefs. You all have greatly impacted my life and are actively changing the lives of my girls, and I love you for it.

To all of my St. Timothy family, but especially Interim Pastor Bob Maier, Pastor Emeritus Paul Frank, Vicar Matt Steinhaur, Sue Peterson, Kristin Dineen, Kristi LaPointe, and Melissa Luther, my family is so blessed to worship with you on Sunday mornings and I'm deeply grateful for the encouragement you always give me.

To my friends and fellow writers at MTCW, especially Kaye Dacus, Tamara Leigh, and Ramona Richards, who willingly helped me when this book was in its earliest stages, thank you all for the prayers, support, and encouragement when I needed them the most. Also, thank you to my new friends at ACFW and NCWA. I look forward to getting to know you all better in the years to come.

To three wonderful friends who have been my cheerleaders through this process. Jana Iwanowski, Kitty Woolever, and Beth Hall, thank you for believing in me even when I didn't believe in myself. I'm so incredibly blessed to have the three of you in my life.

Last, but certainly not least, I sincerely thank you, my reader. I welcome you on this journey with me, and I pray that this story touches your heart along the way.

Congratulations to Tammy Ruthsatz who won the "What a Difference You've Made in My Life" contest. Tammy nominated her niece, Cassie D. Ground, who was a remarkable young woman, truly a rare gem in this fallen world we're living in. A special thanks to Cassie's mother, Mindy Nutter, who provided me with additional information so that I could tell Cassie's story and create her character to the best of my ability. Now, it gives me great pleasure to introduce you to . . .

Cassie D. Ground

BORN ON SEPTEMBER 19, 1985, Cassie quickly became a faithful servant of our Lord. At just three years old, Cassie sang in front of the entire congregation at Faith Memorial Church in Sandusky, Ohio. At the age of 11, Cassie was crowned Honor Star, part of a program called Missionettes Girls Club that required reading the Bible all the way through, memorizing many scriptures including some whole chapters, writing reports, and a list of other criteria. She then went on to be involved in youth ministry, where she was the worship leader for several years along with her two younger sisters, Carlie and Cristina. Cassie was also a member of the adult choir and played the acoustic guitar in the worship band. According to her mother, Cassie "sang with the voice of an angel."

Cassie was also an excellent student. She attended Bay Area Christian Academy in Sandusky through the 8th grade, and then Monroeville High School, where she graduated in June of 2003. She was working toward a degree in elementary education at BGSU-Firelands College and repeatedly made the dean's list. Cassie simply loved being in college and was so excited about accomplishing her dream of becoming a teacher.

It was during her senior year of high school that Cassie met the love of her life, Jordon Berberick, and they planned to get married on July 27, 2007. Everything seemed to be falling in place for Cassie . . . until that fateful afternoon on August 30, 2005. It had been raining heavily, and as Cassie was on her way to pick her sister up from school, she was in an accident and was killed. She never got the chance to teach a classroom full of third-graders as she had hoped to. She never got the chance to marry her true love. But I truly believe that Cassie D. Ground will spend all of eternity faithfully serving her Lord and singing "with the voice of an angel."

In *The Heart's Journey Home*, Cassie's character is a vibrant, beautiful high school senior who is highly recommended by the pastor of her church to provide child care during a newly established ministry for single parents. On several occasions, Kate, the main character, watches from a distance as Cassie sings, dances, and plays Go Fish with the children, who instantly adore her. I pray that through this story Cassie's memory is honored in the utmost way and that everyone who reads *The Heart's Journey Home* will come to know and love Cassie the way all of her family and friends always will.

Congratulations to Brenda Olien who won the "What a Difference You've Made in My Life" contest. Brenda nominated her husband, Dan Olien, a gentleman who made a difference in many lives as you will soon see. A special thanks to Dan's sister, Jenna Harris, who shared with me some additional information that helped me to tell Dan's story and create his character to the best of my ability. Now, it gives me great pleasure to introduce you to . . .

Dan Olien

DAN OLIEN WAS A RUNNER. He began running competitively in middle school and continued to run track and cross country at Newark High School and Otterbein College. As an adult, he ran the Columbus Marathon twice and qualified for the Boston Marathon in addition to running dozens of smaller races.

It was only natural that Dan would choose a career as a physical education teacher and a track and cross country coach. Although Dan enjoyed teaching, coaching was his calling, his passion. He loved his runners. He was thrilled to see them succeed and cried with them when they had a bad race. He motivated his team before each race by quoting positive sayings such as, "Go give them the business." He even designed the team's shirt each season. Dan was district coach of the year for multiple years and was a district representative for the Ohio Association of Track and Field and Cross Country. He always did his best to promote the sport of running.

The only things Dan loved more than running and coaching were his wife and his son. Unfortunately, his time with them was short. Dan and Brenda met at New London High School where they both taught. They went on their first date on December 6, 2002. On January 6, 2003, Dan was diagnosed with brain cancer. Deciding not to waste any of the precious time they had together, they married on June 7, 2003, just six months after their first date, and a little more than two years later, on September 20, 2005, Dan became a daddy. If Dan was happiest when he was coaching, he was proudest when his baby boy, Jon, was born. He would say of little Jon, "He has my profile." Dan and Brenda took Jon to his first cross country meet when he was just two weeks old, and to the state meet when he was only two months old. Dan loved to show off his little "profile."

In early 2006, Dan's health began to rapidly deteriorate. On July 6, 2006, after running a three-year race against an unseen opponent, his body finally succumbed to cancer. But Dan Olien's legacy as a loving husband, a proud father, and a dedicated coach will live on forever, as illustrated by the crowd of people who attended his viewings and funeral.

In *The Heart's Journey Home*, Dan's character is a strong, healthy cross-country coach and physical education teacher who helps Kate, the main character and a former runner, train to run her first marathon. I pray that through this story Dan's memory is honored in the utmost way: that everyone who reads *The Heart's Journey Home* will be inspired by Dan and filled with the desire to "go give them the business."

Dedication

THIS BOOK IS FOR MY DADDY, a master storyteller who believed in my writing from the very beginning. So much of who I am today is because of you, and I'm so grateful for everything you taught me about living, laughing, and loving. I wish you were here to share this with me, Daddy, to hold this book in your hands and say the five words I long to hear: "I'm proud of you, baby!" But I know in my heart you're smiling down at me from heaven, and that'll have to be good enough for now. I love you always, think of you every day, and will miss you until the day we meet again.

Frank Charles Dominick
September 8, 1949 – December 23, 2000

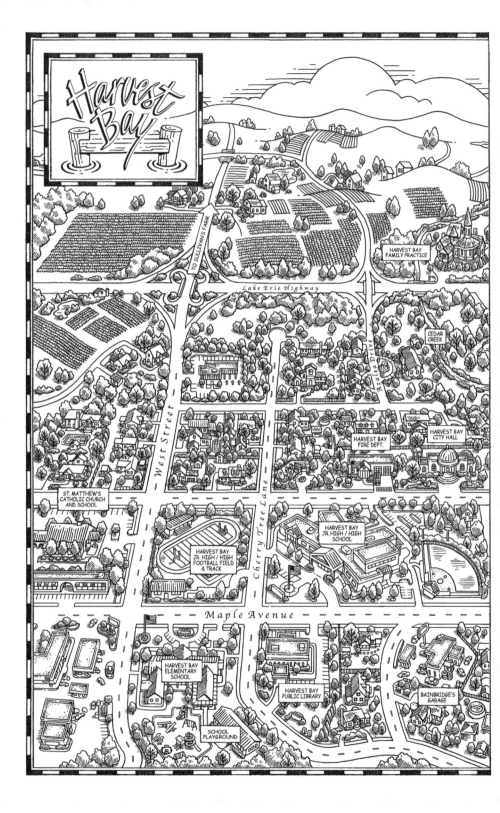

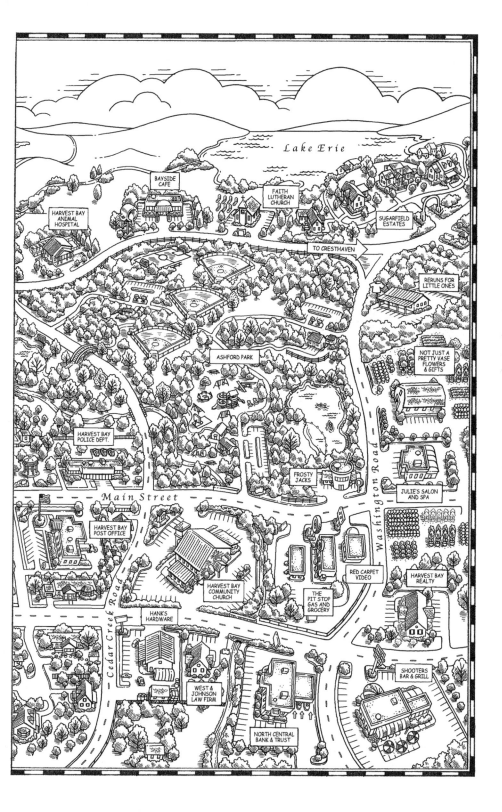

Prologue

Kate Sterling leaned against the door of her cobalt blue Explorer and sighed heavily. This morning had come quickly. Too quickly. She had always loved the Fourth of July, but now Independence Day took on a whole new meaning.

Kate's brother-in-law, Nathan, buckled her six-year-old daughter, Madeline, into her booster seat and came around the front of the vehicle to join Kate. "She fell back to sleep."

"That's good. I have a feeling this is going to be a long trip for us."

It was only an eight-hour drive from her home in Nashville, Tennessee, to Harvest Bay, her Ohio hometown situated on the bank of Lake Erie. Kate had made it a dozen times with Madeline as her only companion.

This time, though, they wouldn't be coming back.

He leaned against the Explorer shoulder to shoulder with Kate and crossed his arms. "I'm really going to miss Maddie."

A thick lump of sorrow lodged itself in Kate's throat, but she forced her words past it. "She'll miss you, too. We both will."

"Don't start doubting yourself. You're doing the right thing."

She nodded. "I know. There's nothing keeping me here now that Ryan's gone. I really need to be closer to my family, especially Grandpa Clayton."

"So then, why the hesitation?"

She shrugged. "The idea of moving 'back home' seems so foreign to me. I've lived here for so long that Harvest Bay has evolved into a vacation spot—a sleepy little town where we go to visit with family and friends. It's not home anymore."

"Does *this* feel like home?" He gestured to Kate's stately brick home.

The still-dark sky was her ally, concealing the moisture that pooled in her eyes and tickled her nose. "Not since Ryan died. I can't believe it's been three years."

Nathan turned to face her and took her by the shoulders. "It's time for you to move on and start over." His expression softened. "You know it's what Ryan would want for you and Maddie both."

"I still miss him so much," she said, her voice barely above a whisper.

He pulled her into his arms. "Me too," he murmured into her hair. "Me too."

After a moment she took a deep breath and stepped back. "I can't begin to thank you enough for everything you've done for Maddie and me since Ryan died." She shook her head. "We never would have made it through the past three years without you."

"I'll always be there for you and Maddie, no matter how far you go, okay?"

Kate only nodded, the big ball of emotion in her throat suddenly impassable.

"And don't forget to remind Pipsqueak that I'm coming up next month for her birthday."

"I'll tell her." She glanced at her watch, and then up into Nathan's face. "Well, I guess I'd better hit the road. It's not getting any earlier, and Mom and Dad will be expecting us by dinnertime." She opened the door, slipped into the seat, and started the engine.

He pushed the button to roll her window down, and then shut the door. "Just keep telling yourself there's no place like home."

She studied him, suddenly aware that once she left she wouldn't see him again for several weeks and only a few times a year after that. She reached out and touched his face as it became blurry behind her fresh tears.

"Right now I'm thinking of what Dorothy says to the Scarecrow."

"What's that?"

"I think I'll miss you most of all."

CHAPTER
One

The Sullivan farm was highly animated under the north-central Ohio sun. A dozen children ran through sprinklers, filling the atmosphere with shrieks of laughter. A handful of preteens played a game of backyard basketball on a dirt court with a hoop bolted into the side of a weathered barn.

The women were busy spreading blankets out under the shade trees and setting the smorgasbord of picnic food on a table. One by one the men came in from the field and parked their tractors in a row. There were still many acres of hay left to cut, but now it was time for a little fun.

"Hey, Uncle Adam, do you wanna play Horse with us?" the oldest of the group of preteens asked hopefully, then added, "We promise not to be too hard on you."

Adam Sullivan smiled. Of his three brothers and one sister, he'd been the one blessed with outstanding athleticism, and for that reason his nephews and nieces seized every opportunity to coax him into playing with them.

"I'm sorry. I don't know if I heard you correctly. Did you say that *you* won't be too hard on *me?*"

"Yeah, that's right. Are you game?" another nephew piped up.

"You bet!"

Adam peeled his damp T-shirt from his sweaty body and started the game by sinking a basket from outside the three-point line. It didn't take long before all five of the children had spelled out the word "horse," while Adam remained clean. He gave his nephews and nieces high fives, and then suggested that they get something to eat.

"I'll be along in a minute. There's someone I have to see first," he said while his gaze swept over his parents' large back-yard.

He spotted his sister several yards away pushing a nine-year-old girl on a tire swing, and his heart filled with pride. That was *his* nine-year-old and, good heavens, he loved that little girl! Pulling his T-shirt back on, he jogged across the yard to her.

"Hey, Chloe!"

"Hi, Daddy!" the petite girl replied, hanging onto the rope for dear life, her mane of mahogany corkscrew curls blowing in the breeze created by the high-flying swing.

"You know you're doing my job, little sis," he said to Kennedy, the youngest of the Sullivan siblings.

Kennedy grinned and stepped aside. "Just fillin' in until you got here."

He took over pushing the swing. He loved being a father, and Chloe was his shining star. He'd just never imagined that he would be raising her alone. He never in a million years would have guessed that his wife would so effortlessly walk away from him and Chloe and all they'd built together as a family.

Kennedy leaned against the tree. A long, strawberry-blonde wisp freed itself from her French braid, spiraling down her brow, and she tucked it behind her ear.

"So how are you doing?"

"Oh, we're doing great, aren't we, Chloe?"

"Sure."

"No, I mean how are *you*?"

He looked into the concerned face of his sister, the baby of the family, eight years his junior. He had spent most of this teen years watching out for her. Now it seemed as if the roles were reversed. He reached to give Kennedy's shoulder a little squeeze.

"I'm fine. You don't have to worry about me, okay?"

She shook her head. "Well, big brother, I'd love to stand here and argue with you, but I'm too hungry to think straight. What do you say we get something to eat? I can smell Mom's fried chicken all the way over here."

"You and Chloe go on ahead. I'll be just a minute."

"Suit yourself, but don't wait too long. You know the food doesn't usually last." She stopped the swing. "C'mon, Chloe."

After Kennedy and Chloe had joined the others, Adam took in the scene from a distance. His nieces and nephews gathered on blankets, some carrying their own Styrofoam plates, others receiving assistance from their mothers. Kennedy and his other sisters fussed over Chloe, but Adam sensed that it wasn't quite the same as a mother's attention. Once again, guilt twisted his stomach into a knot.

He didn't really miss Alexandra as much as he missed the role she had filled in their lives. He wished like crazy she was there for Chloe.

He wished a lot of things.

"A penny for your thoughts," a gentle voice offered from behind him.

He didn't have to look to know it was his mother. "Have you ever felt like you were living someone else's life?"

"Hmm. I think so."

"This isn't exactly how I expected my life would go."

"So what are you going to do about it?"

"What do you mean? What *can* I do?"

"Let me put it to you this way: If you went out to ride Moses one day and he bucked you off, what would you do?"

"I'd get back on him, and let him know he didn't win." It took a moment for his mother's meaning to dawn on him. "But this is different. My divorce has only been final for a little over a year."

Anna Sullivan put her hands on her hips. "True, but you were separated for almost a year before that."

"I know you mean well, but I have no plans to try dating anytime soon."

"Chloe needs to see you begin to pick up the pieces. She needs to know that life goes on."

He crossed his arms. "There's not much hope of my meeting someone new when I spend all my time either here on the farm or at school. Football practice starts in just a few weeks, and I really think that we have a chance at a state championship this year."

His mother reached up and placed her hands on Adam's shoulders. "You may not believe what I'm about to say after all you've been through, but, son, I'm proud of you, of all your accomplishments. Even though things haven't turned out for you the way you hoped, God has a plan for your life. You have to believe that."

He resisted pursuing the debate, but he couldn't meet her gaze.

She sighed. "Just promise me that you won't let an opportunity pass you by."

"I promise." He gave her a half-hearted smile. "Would you mind keeping an eye on Chloe for me? I want to take Moses out for a quick run. I won't be long."

She embraced him and patted his back. "I don't mind at all. I think it might be just what you need."

He kissed her cheek and started across the yard toward the stable that housed Moses and two palominos. When he pulled open the door and stepped inside, all three horses looked up and whinnied. He affectionately patted the palominos' necks on the way to the stall that housed his old friend.

"Hey, Bud," he called to the dark bay thoroughbred. "How about a run?"

Moses bobbed his head up and down and pawed at the ground.

Adam skillfully strapped on the saddle and bridle, and then mounted. They headed out into the open pasture at a walk, and then with a gentle prod and click of his tongue, he urged Moses to a gallop.

They cut through the humid air like a hot knife through butter. The breeze they created together felt refreshing and dried the sweat that had dampened Adam's forehead. He inhaled deeply. The fresh country air invigorated him as they raced their usual lap around the ten-acre perimeter of the pasture, temporarily leaving his worries in the dust.

⁂

Oh, please, God . . .

It was more a statement of dread than a heartfelt prayer. Kate wasn't a mechanic, but she was fairly certain what had happened by the flapping noise and the way her Explorer pulled to the right. She stopped the car on the side of the road and climbed out, then walked around to the front.

The passenger side tire was flat. In a burst of frustration, she kicked it.

From the back seat, Madeline poked her head out the window. "What happened, Mama?"

Kate fought back angry tears and took a deep breath. Walking to the back door, she tapped Madeline's nose through the window.

Lowering her voice an octave, she said, "Co-captain Maddie, we're experiencing mechanical difficulties."

Madeline giggled.

"We must make some minor repairs before we continue with our mission."

Madeline gave her a salute and a smile that revealed her missing two front teeth. "Aye, aye, captain."

Kate chuckled, and then looked down the road. Thankfully this stretch of the state highway was lightly traveled. But although there were no cars in sight, they were not in the safest place.

She turned back to Madeline and opened the door. "Sweetie, why don't you stretch your legs in that field over there while I fix the tire?"

Madeline quickly unbuckled her seat belt. "Okay!" She jumped down and ran into the open field toward a patch of wildflowers.

Kate moved to the rear of the vehicle and began unloading luggage and boxes to get to the spare tire. She heaved a large Rubbermaid container onto the grassy shoulder of the road and grabbed a suitcase in each hand.

"It can't possibly be a good thing to start our new life with a flat tire," she mumbled under her breath.

"Do you need help with that?"

She yelped and dropped the suitcases.

"Oh, I'm sorry, ma'am. I didn't mean to frighten you."

Eyebrows raised, Kate watched a man with blond hair and broad shoulders dismount from a magnificent horse. With the reins in his left hand, he extended his right hand.

"Hi. I'm . . ."

"Adam Sullivan." She accepted his hand and gave it a single, firm pump, her stomach tightening.

Bewilderment clouded the man's face as he took her in, and then recognition dawned. "Kate? Kate Marshall?"

"You remembered," she said dryly. Her memories of Adam Sullivan during their high school years included several different girls, but never her.

He nodded. "Of course. You set the school record in cross country our senior year. Wasn't it 3.1 miles in 15 minutes and 52 seconds?"

Her cheeks warmed. Avoiding his gaze, she picked up the suitcases she had dropped and set them on the grass beside the car.

"That was a long time ago."

He hooked his thumbs in the pockets of his worn, faded blue jeans. "The record still stands."

"Like I said, that was a long time ago, and you're only partially correct. I'm Kate Sterling now, and that's my daughter, Maddie."

As if on cue, Madeline skipped over carrying a colorful bunch of wildflowers. She handed the small bouquet to Kate, and then turned to Adam.

"Are you Ken?"

He looked questioningly at Kate, and then down at Madeline. "Ken?"

"Yeah. You know—Barbie's husband."

Kate had to work hard to keep a smirk off her face.

He chuckled. "Afraid not. My name's Adam, and this," he gestured toward the stallion, "is Moses."

Madeline gazed at the horse, awestruck. "Can I pet him?"

"Absolutely. He won't hurt you."

She timidly approached the large animal with her hand outstretched. Moses dropped his head to sniff her, and she burst into a fit of giggles.

"His whiskers tickle!"

Adam squatted down so that he was eye level with the little girl. "I have to tie Moses up so I can help your mom. Do you want to help me walk him over there to that tree?"

"Sure!"

Adam turned to Kate. "Is it okay with you?"

Kate tried to dismiss the way Adam's interaction with Madeline made her soften. "I don't think so. Look, thanks for the offer, but I really don't need help, so if you don't mind . . . "

"But Mama . . . " Madeline's bottom lip popped out and she crossed her arms in a huff.

At that moment a car whizzed past them stirring up a hot breeze that nearly choked Kate.

Adam patted Moses' neck. "They'll both be safer over there, and we'll be able to change the tire faster."

Kate narrowed her eyes at him. "Still not used to people telling you no, huh?"

Something that resembled hurt flashed in his electric blue eyes.

Kate glanced down at her pouting daughter and sighed. "All right, she can walk with you, but don't put her up on that animal and, Maddie, don't stand too close. He might bite or something."

Adam chuckled and shook his head. He gave Madeline one of the reins, and helped her lead the horse to a tree at the edge of the field. He tied the one he was holding to a low hanging branch, then crouched down to Madeline's level

Kate strained to hear what he was saying to her daughter.

"Now stand right here," he positioned her at least two feet away from the horse, "and hold onto him tight."

Madeline wrapped her little hands around the leather strap and grinned up at Adam.

He smiled. "Good. And make sure you don't walk behind Moses, okay?"

She nodded, and returned her concentration to the rein.

Adam strode back to where Kate was standing with her hands on her hips. "What are we waiting for?"

He grabbed two boxes, which emptied out the back of the Explorer enough to open the storage compartment and retrieve the spare, jack, and lug wrench. After changing the tire, he placed the flat and the tools back into the compartment, and then helped Kate reload the boxes and luggage. Crossing the field to Moses and Madeline, he untied the rein and helped the little girl walk the horse to where Kate stood mesmerized.

Madeline handed her rein back to him, a Cheshire cat grin on her round little face. "Wow, Mama! Did you see that? Just look at that horse! Isn't he beautiful?"

Kate couldn't remember the last time she'd seen Madeline so blissfully happy. She gave Adam a grateful smile. "You've made her afternoon."

"He has that effect on people," he said, hoisting himself into the saddle.

"Well, thanks for your help."

He tipped an imaginary hat, then turned Moses with a tug of the reins and glanced back over his shoulder at Kate. "People change. I'm not the same guy you remember."

He clicked his tongue, and Moses galloped across the field.

She watched horse and rider recede into the distance before ushering Madeline to the backseat and helping her buckle up. As she slid into the driver's seat and eased the car onto the old country highway, it occurred to her that maybe Harvest Bay wasn't as sleepy as she remembered after all.

Maybe there were a lot of things that weren't exactly as she remembered.

⁂

The office was empty and silent, with the exception of the occasional ringing of a telephone. Nathan Sterling relished the solitude. This was a different kind of quiet than he would experience at home. There the loneliness would wrap itself around him like a python, squeezing until he suffocated.

Here, at least, he felt productive. And while he worked he could glance out his window at the beehive of activity that was synonymous with Vanderbilt University Hospital and be reminded that life goes on.

He would have to go on, too, as he had after Ryan died. This time was different, though, and while he stared blankly at his computer screen, he wondered how he was going to accomplish the seemingly impossible task.

With a sigh, he pushed away from his desk and moved across his office to the large window. Placing a hand on either side, he rested his forehead on the cool glass.

"I never meant to fall in love with Kate, God. You know that. I mean, she was my brother's wife. But I did, and now I've lost her and Maddie both." He shook his head. "Lord, what am I going to do?"

"Asked myself the very same thing a time or two."

Startled, he spun around. Before his gaze landed on the receptionist's matronly figure in the doorway, he recognized the strong southern accent and relaxed.

"Hi, Alice."

Alice stepped into the room and plopped down in a chair across from his desk. "Sometimes He answers you, and sometimes He doesn't."

"How much did you hear?"

"Enough."

He shoved his hands in the pockets of his khakis and stared at his shoes. "Then you know that I have feelings for Kate?"

"Sugar, I've known that for months now."

He snapped his gaze from his shoes to Alice's plump face. "How could you have known?"

She smiled. "I guess you could say I have a knack for picking up on these things."

Nathan moved to his desk and lowered himself into his chair. "So what should I do?"

"Darlin', I reckon the only person who can answer that is you."

An exasperated breath escaped his lips. "I don't know. I just don't know. It seems hopeless."

"I don't believe my ears. We've known each other for a long time. Had lots of talks after Ryan died, remember?"

He nodded and sighed.

"We shared lots memories, a few tears, and a little anger and frustration, but I don't ever recall you giving up hope."

"This is different."

"How?"

He stood again and moved back to the window. "I couldn't have prevented my brother's death. I wasn't with him in the car that day, and even if I had been, I couldn't have predicted that the truck would run the red light—"

"But you could've stopped Kate and Maddie from leaving?"

He shook his head. "It's what's best for them—being near their family."

"*You* are part of their family."

"Yes, but everyone else is in Ohio. I alone can't give Kate or Maddie what all of their family can. Besides without Ryan, nothing was keeping them here."

Alice's expression softened. "So what's keeping you here?"

"What do you mean? *This* is keeping me here." He swept his arm in front of him. "Everything I've worked my whole life for is keeping me here."

"You mean you would sacrifice love for success?" She shook her head sadly. "I thought I knew you better than that."

"I have the privilege of working in one of the finest hospitals in the country, and I've actually developed a name for myself. How can I just walk away from that?"

She stuck her chin out, and he could see that she wasn't going to let this go. "There are fine hospitals and doctors' offices everywhere."

"It's not that easy."

She leaned forward in her chair. "And letting go of Kate and Maddie is?"

"No, of course not. My family and my career are both important to me."

She gave him her no-nonsense look. "Nathan, darlin', the time has come for you to get your priorities straight. Will you at least fancy the idea of following Kate?"

He exhaled slowly. "God will have to make it obvious if that's the path He wants me to take. I don't want to make any premature decisions."

Alice stood and went to him with her arms outstretched. "In the meantime, you know where I'll be if you need me."

"Right where you've been for the past fifteen years." He embraced the short, stocky woman, glad to have the conversation move onto a different topic. "What are you doing here this afternoon anyway?"

"Oh, I had some filing to do that I didn't want to leave for Monday morning. You know how crazy it is after a holiday weekend." She patted his back, and then took a step away. "And I wanted to invite you to a block party in my subdivision this evening."

"Thanks, but I'm planning to meet some friends from church at Riverfront Park for the fireworks show."

"Just be safe wherever you go." She moved to the doorway, paused, and glanced back at him over her shoulder. "God has a plan, but it may not be *your* plan. I'll be praying that you can tell the difference."

When she had gone, Nathan moved back to his desk, his brain swarming with questions. Was moving really an option? His medical training had conditioned him to trust facts and statistics, to proceed in a logical, sensible manner. It certainly didn't make sense to just up and leave when everything seemed to be going so well for him.

"Everyone would think I'm crazy to leave what I have here for the small town life," he whispered.

You mean you would sacrifice love for success . . . The time has come for you to get your priorities straight.

Alice's words echoed in his head. Did he really want to allow his chance at love and happiness to slip away simply because he was at a high point in his career?

But still . . .

At that moment, his cell phone rang. His pulse quickened when he checked the caller ID, and he quickly flipped it open.

"Hello?"

"Hi, Uncle Nate!"

He laughed. It wasn't the voice he expected, but it was just as nice. "Hey, Pipsqueak! How's the trip?"

"Great! Guess what. We got a flat tire, and a man who looked just like Ken—you know, Barbie's husband—came to help Mama fix it, and he had a big, beautiful horse named Moses, and I got to hold onto him by a tree!"

Nathan's smile fell slightly, though he wouldn't let the change in his expression reflect in his voice. "Wow! That's exciting!"

"Wanna talk to Mama?"

"Sure. Don't forget, I'm coming to visit next month for your birthday."

"I remember, but I miss you already, Uncle Nate."

His heart clenched. "Miss you too."

"Here's Mama."

He heard rustling, then Kate came on the line.

"Hi, Nathan."

"Hey." He focused on keeping his voice steady. "Did you make it to your parents'?"

"I just turned onto their road. We'll be there in a sec."

"How was the trip?"

"Fine, until we were within a few miles of town."

"Is that when the flat, the man, and the horse came into the picture?"

She chuckled. "You could say that, but I'll fill you in later. We're getting ready to pull in, and I can see the welcoming committee waiting on the porch."

"Enjoy your family."

Kate's soft voice floated over him like silk. "Wish you were here."

It took him a moment to find his voice, and when he did he almost didn't recognize it. "Me too."

*K*ate flipped on her blinker and turned into the driveway of her yellow, two-story childhood home. She pulled to a stop in front a vibrant Welcome Home banner that stretched from one side of the garage to the other. Before she had time to move the gearshift to park, Madeline unbuckled her seat belt, threw open the door, and jumped out.

She watched her daughter, full of excitement and unbridled joy, dash across the yard to her awaiting family. Kate's father scooped the almost-seven-year-old up in his arms and twirled her around.

Kate wished she could feel a fraction of that enthusiasm. She stared straight ahead at the banner.

Welcome home.

She sighed and turned off the engine.

We'll see.

She climbed out, stretched her tired legs, put on a happy face though her heart was incredibly heavy, and followed Madeline across the yard. Her parents met her halfway and greeted her warmly with hugs and kisses. Her father lifted her off the ground with his hug and twirled her around once, causing Madeline to squeal with laughter. By the time her sister and brother-in-law reached her, Kate felt slightly dizzy.

Grandpa Clayton gave her a wide smile and a little wave from where he sat in a rocking chair on the big front porch. Kate rushed over to gently embrace him.

"Hi, Gramps. I missed ya."

"Missed you, too, Katy," he returned, his voice gravelly with age.

"How was the trip?" Kate's mother, Rebecca Marshall, asked.

Kate opened her mouth to answer, but before she could get a word out, Madeline bubbled, "It was great! Know what?"

"What?" the others said in unison.

Kate closed her eyes, imagining the questions that were sure to follow Madeline's story.

"We got a flat tire, and a man who looked like Ken came to help Mama fix it, and he had a big, beautiful horse named Moses, and I got to hold onto him by a tree!"

All eyes turned to Kate, who rubbed a sudden pain out of the back of her neck.

"You had a flat?" Her father, Charlie, looked concerned.

"Yes, just a few miles from town."

"Everything's okay?" He stepped off the porch.

"Of course, Daddy. You were the one who taught me how to change a tire. Remember?"

He didn't respond. Instead, he headed toward the Explorer to check it out for himself, his new little shadow hot on his heels.

Kate's mother tapped her chin thoughtfully. "A man who looked like Ken with a horse named Moses, hmm?"

"That could only be Adam Sullivan," said Kate's younger sister, Elizabeth.

"It was." Kate hoped they would note the finality in her voice.

Her mother moved toward the screen door. "It's a good thing he was there to help you. I'll have to remember to thank him the next time I see him."

"For goodness sake, Mom! I had a flat. Don't make a big deal out of it. I mean, it wasn't like I was dangling off the side of a cliff or something. I could've taken care of it myself."

Her mother stopped to give her daughter a pointed glance. "The Lord sent you help whether you thought you needed it or not, and that is something to be thankful for."

As she disappeared into the house, Kate shot a what-did-I-just-do glance at Elizabeth, who returned a you-know-what-you-did-and-you'd-better-go-fix-it look.

Kate sighed and followed her mother through the house to the kitchen. She stopped in the doorway for a moment to watch her mother work at the sink, her hands moving in the sudsy water while she washed dishes.

A flood of regret washed over Kate. While she was struggling to be happy about moving back to Harvest Bay, it was almost like a dream come true for her mother. She had her daughter and granddaughter back to stay.

Kate moved across the kitchen, grabbed a towel, and sidled up next to her. "I'm sorry, Mom." She carefully picked up a wet glass and began to dry it off. "I don't know why I was so sharp with you. You know how independent I can be sometimes, and I just . . . "

She put the glass away and reached for another one, but Rebecca stopped her.

"You don't have to be sorry. We all have adjustments to make. Some are easier than others."

Kate studied her mother and noticed for the first time the weariness in her face, the dark circles under her eyes.

"How has Gramps adjusted to living here with you and Daddy?"

Rebecca began wiping down the countertops. "It was hard at first. He has his pride, you know, and naturally he didn't want to leave his home. But after the fall he took in April as a result of that mini-stroke he had, I think he understood that this is for the best. Most days are good. He's slowed down quite a bit, but for the time being he can still get around okay. And since we converted the den into a bedroom, he's right here by the kitchen and the bathroom, so that helps."

"What about his house?"

"We're working on making some necessary repairs and upgrades. To save money, your dad has been doing the work himself in his spare time. Hopefully, he'll be done in a few weeks, and then it'll probably go on the market." Her mother sighed heavily, her shoulders sagging.

Kate put the dish towel down. "What is it?"

"It's just hard to see my dad growing old. He's taken care of me all my life. Now it's my turn." Her eyes moist, she forced a smile. "I always knew the roles would reverse one day, but I still wasn't prepared for it when it happened."

Kate wrapped her arms around her. "I'm here now. I'll help in any way I can."

She gave Kate an affectionate squeeze, then let her go and continued wiping the countertop. "Thank you, sweetie. It helps just having you and Maddie here."

Kate returned her smile. Harvest Bay didn't feel like home yet, but at that moment she was glad to be back.

Her parents had planned a picnic celebration later that afternoon under the two huge maple trees in the backyard. Rebecca's sisters, Emily and Claire, came with their husbands.

Kate's father grilled seasoned chicken leg quarters, and her mother prepared two of her specialties—potato salad and apple pie. As a result, Kate ate as she hadn't eaten in three years.

"Mmm, everything was delicious!" she groaned and wiped her mouth with her napkin. "I ate way too much, and now I'm so stuffed I can hardly move!"

Her mother's face displayed a look of satisfaction. "Good. Then it shouldn't be too hard to put all the weight you've lost back on your bones!"

Kate rolled her eyes. Her mother had a new mission.

"Aunt Liz, will you and Uncle Elijah play soccer with me?" Madeline asked Kate's sister sweetly.

Elizabeth tousled her niece's hair. "I'd love to!" She turned to her husband. "How about you, hon?"

"Sure! Let's go find the ball, squirt." Elijah Truman pushed to his feet and hoisted Madeline onto his shoulders.

"Look in the garage. All the yard toys are in the cabinet closest to the door," Rebecca instructed, and then turned to Charlie. "Time to take the leftovers inside and clean up."

"Let me help," Kate offered.

"Not tonight, Katydid. You just rest and enjoy being home," her father answered. Carrying food containers in each hand, he followed her mother into the house.

Kate stretched out on the thick quilt, the lush grass providing extra cushion beneath her. Her body felt heavy, and the mini soccer match that had just gotten underway was the only thing that kept her from dozing off. Listening to her little girl shriek and giggle in sporadic intervals was sweet music to her ears.

She glanced over at her grandfather, her old buddy, who sat in a lawn chair near the blanket, and her heart clenched to know how much he had declined. Time, it seemed, was no longer on his side. His hair appeared whiter and thinner, the creases in his leathery face deeper. His steps were more gingerly just since her last visit in March, a few weeks before he fell and the doctors discovered he'd had a mini-stroke. Thankfully there had been no lasting effects. His mind was still sharp as a tack, and his eyes shined brightly behind his thick bifocals as he watched her with a happy smile.

"What are you thinking, Gramps?"

"Just that I'm glad to have you and Maddie home where you belong."

"Can I ask you something?"

"You can ask me anything."

"How have you made it all these years without Grandma?"

"Oh Katy, it hasn't been easy."

He shared the hardships he had gone through while her grandmother battled cancer, and the heavy grief he had suffered after she died. It had been twenty-four years, but his voice was still choppy with emotion.

"You're going to be okay, kiddo. Don't forget the Lord's promise in Psalms: 'Weeping may endure for a night, but joy cometh in the morning.' "

Kate felt a painful stab of guilt and quickly glanced away so he wouldn't see it in her eyes. *If only I could tell him that my faith isn't what it used to be, that I just don't have it in me to trust God's promises. Not after everything I've been through in the past three years.* Her nose tickled and her eyes stung. *Gramps would be so disappointed in me.*

At that moment, Madeline ran up and collapsed on the blanket beside her. "Hey, Great-gramps, tell me a story!"

"Yeah, Gramps!" Elizabeth chimed in, joining them on the blanket. "Tell us a story!"

"A story? Let's see here . . . did I ever tell you about the time I went fishin' for bluegills and caught a giant snapping turtle instead?"

Madeline shook her head, already enthralled.

Kate glanced at her sister, thinking of all the times the two of them had sat cross-legged at Grandpa Clayton's feet, transported to a different place and time by the master story-teller. She closed her eyes and let her grandfather take her away again.

⁂

Later that evening, Kate, Madeline, and Kate's parents met Elizabeth and Elijah at a public boat ramp, and her father helped Elijah put his bass boat in the water. After the ladies boarded at the dock, they cruised Lake Erie before finally anchoring near the beach at Cedar Point, an amusement park that put on a spectacular fireworks display every year.

It was a beautiful night. The lake was calm, and the fireworks lit up the sky for miles. Madeline oohed and aahed with her fingers in her ears. Kate's parents, sister, and brother-in-law all enjoyed the show. No one saw the teardrops slide down Kate's cheeks while she wondered what the fireworks looked like from heaven.

It was almost eleven o'clock when she walked Madeline up the stairs of her parents' house to the room she'd shared with Elizabeth when they were kids. She helped Madeline into her Disney princesses nightgown and brushed her hair while the little girl yawned.

"Did you have fun tonight, Maddie?"

"Umm hmm," Madeline responded, struggling to keep her eyes open.

"You know you are a very lucky girl."

"Why?"

"You get to sleep in the very same bed I slept in when I was your age." Kate pulled back the blankets and inhaled the familiar scent of her mother's laundry detergent on the crisp, clean sheets, thinking about the time when her biggest concern was whether to play with her Barbies or her baby dolls.

Madeline crawled into the bed and snuggled down between the sheets, hugging her favorite stuffed puppy. Kate tucked the covers in around her and kissed her on the forehead.

"Mama?"

"Yes, baby?"

"Does Daddy know we're here?"

The question sucked the air out of Kate. Taking a deep breath, she quickly gathered her wits about her as she sat down on the edge of the bed. "Yes, he does. He's here with us too. Remember what I told you? We'll keep him in our hearts and take him with us everywhere we go."

"Does Daddy miss us?"

Tears stung Kate's eyes, but she quickly dammed them up. They'd had a great day together, and she would not spoil it now.

"I'm sure he does, very much."

"But we learned in Sunday school that heaven is such a cool place that you don't cry or hurt anymore."

At that moment, Kate despised the Sunday school teachers at their Nashville church for being so good that her daughter held on to their every word. How was she supposed to give Madeline an answer when she didn't understand it herself?

"Your daddy misses you very much, but he is helping Jesus prepare a special place in heaven just for you and your mama,"

Kate's mother said, entering the dimly lit room. She knelt beside the twin bed and discreetly placed a comforting hand over Kate's.

"Really? Daddy is helping Jesus?"

"That's what I believe."

"I believe it too!"

Rebecca chuckled, leaned forward, and kissed Madeline's forehead. "That's good, honey. Now have pleasant dreams."

Madeline hugged her puppy tighter. "Okay. But Grammy?"

"Yes?"

"I don't think I want to go to heaven just yet. I wanna stay right here with you and Papa."

Rebecca got to her feet, and Kate joined her. "I'll keep you here with me as long as I can. Good night, my darling." Quietly she turned and left the room.

Kate kissed Madeline once more and followed her mother, who was waiting just outside the door with her arms outstretched. Kate stepped into her embrace as the dam burst and silent tears streamed down her face.

"Oh, Mom, I've needed you so much." It was barely more than a whisper.

"Shhh. You're home now, and everything's going to be all right." She smoothed Kate's hair and gently rocked her back and forth just as she had when Kate was a child.

For that moment, Kate believed her mother.

*W*hen Kate finally fell asleep she slept so soundly that
when she woke up, for a split second she couldn't
remember where she was. Then the heavenly scent wafting up
from the kitchen reached her and her growling stomach. No
doubt her mother had been up since the crack of dawn, hard
at work on a special breakfast. Kate slipped into her terrycloth
bathrobe and plodded downstairs.

"Morning, Mom." She kissed her mother on the cheek
and went straight for the coffee pot.

"You're up early."

Kate glanced at the clock as she made her way to the
table, carrying her steaming mug. It was half past eight. "Me?
What about you, Miss Betty Crocker? You know you don't
have to fatten me up the first week we're here."

"Of course I do, dear."

Her mother set a heaping plate of banana-berry pancakes,
scrambled eggs, bacon, and sausage in front of her. Just then,
her father walked in with the morning paper under his arm.

"You're just in time, Dad. Apparently Mom is determined
to turn me into the Pillsbury Dough Girl."

Her father chuckled and sat down across from Kate. "Is
that so? Well now, Katydid, I can't say that I'm surprised."

"May I have the classifieds?"

"Sure." He slid the section across the table. "I called Axel up at Bainbridge's Garage. He said he'd be happy to look at your tire today."

"I could have taken care of that," Kate protested.

"I know, but it's been a while since I've had the chance to take care of you, and after all, you are still my baby." He winked at her.

Kate couldn't help smiling. "Thanks." She opened the newspaper and began skimming the want ads while she ate.

"You don't have to think about getting a job yet. Just take it easy for a while."

Kate glanced at her mother, who stood at the stove flipping another helping of pancakes. Truthfully, with the money she had received from Ryan's life insurance policy, she didn't have to work. In the weeks after Ryan's funeral she had briefly considered resigning from her job teaching second grade, but teaching was her passion. It was as much a part of her identity as being a mother to Madeline was. It fulfilled her, and it kept her busy. The classroom was one place where she didn't have time to dwell on the overwhelming loss in her life.

"It doesn't hurt to look," she responded, taking another bite. "And in the meantime, Daddy, I thought I could help you finish up Gramps' house."

"I can use all the help I can get at this point."

"I'll help too." Madeline came into the kitchen, rubbing her eyes, her hair rumpled. "What are we doing?"

"Working on your great-grandpa's house." Kate wrapped her arms around her daughter and kissed her on top of the head. "Good morning, honey. Did you sleep well?"

Madeline nodded and cuddled against her.

Kate's mother began filling another plate. "How about some banana-berry pancakes, Maddie?"

Grinning, Madeline nodded again. Kate returned to the ads.

"Tutor needed for high school student preparing for SAT's. Resume and references required."

The phone rang, and her mother went to answer it.

Hmm. That's not quite my cup of tea, but just in case . . . Kate retrieved a pen from the counter and circled the ad.

"Kate, the phone's for you."

"For me?" She got up and went to the wall phone. "Hello?"

"Welcome home, Kate!"

"Jane!" She laughed out loud. "It's so good to hear from you! I was going to call you later today or tomorrow. How did you know I was home?"

"A little bird told me," Jane Garner, Kate's best friend from high school, answered.

Kate eyed her mother knowingly.

"I was just calling to see if you and Maddie have plans later this morning."

"We were going to head downtown. I have to drop my Explorer off at Bainbridge's, and while it's being looked at I thought Maddie and I could walk over to Frosty Jack's for some ice cream. Maddie wants to stop at the library, and I wouldn't mind browsing through the children's consignment shop. Why?"

"Bradley's last little league tournament game is at eleven o'clock at Ashford Park. Why don't you come and watch it, and we'll all stop at Frosty Jack's after the game?" Jane hesitated before adding, "We'd love to see you. It's been too long."

Kate heard the softness in her friend's voice. Though they kept in touch regularly with phone calls, e-mails, cards, and

letters, they hadn't gotten together since Madeline was a tod-
dler. Obviously Jane had missed her as much as Kate had
missed her best friend.

"We'll be there!"

"Great! The game will be played on the second field."

"Okay. See you then."

Hanging up, Kate turned her attention to her daughter.
"Hey, Maddie, finish up your pancakes, and then run upstairs
and get dressed. We have a baseball game to go to!"

Ashford Park was rapidly growing crowded by the time Kate
and Madeline strolled through the gravel parking lot at a
quarter till eleven.

"Wow, Mama! Look at this place!" Madeline's eyes grew
large as she took in the new sports complex Mr. Arthur
Ashford had bequeathed to the city for the children and families of Harvest Bay. The expansive complex offered several
baseball diamonds, all very animated at that moment, two soccer fields, and a huge playground that looked so fun even Kate
was tempted.

"Is this where I'll play soccer in the fall?"

"I think so, but I bet Jane will know for sure. Come on.
Let's go find her."

They hurried toward the field where the games would
soon be getting underway. When they approached the second
field, Kate spied her best friend standing in the metal bleachers, waving.

Kate waved back. "There she is. Let's hurry."

When they reached the fiery redhead, she embraced Kate
for a long moment, then finally pulled back to look her up and

down. "How do you do it? You look the same as you did the day we graduated." Jane turned her attention to Madeline. "But you, little princess, have changed so much I hardly recognize you! Do you remember me?"

Madeline looked down and shook her head bashfully.

Jane smiled and tousled her hair. "That's all right. I won't take it personally. I'm Jane, and these are three of my kids." She proceeded to introduce Madeline to nine-year-old Emma, seven-year-old Jessica, and five-year-old Samuel.

"It's nice to meet you." Madeline kept her eyes on Jessica.

"Mom, can we go to the playground?" Jessica asked.

"If it's okay with Kate."

"Sure. Go have fun, but be careful."

All four children scampered down the bleachers, little Samuel trying his best to keep up with the older ones. The playground was close enough that Kate could keep her eye on Madeline. Relaxing, she draped her arm across Jane's shoulders.

"So how've you been, Janey? I've missed you."

"Oh, you know how it is. I'm married with four kids, and I teach kindergarten. Every day is a new adventure."

Kate gave her friend a sly grin. "How's Ian doing then? I never thought he was the adventurous type."

High school sweethearts, Jane and Ian had married shortly after graduation. For the last eight years, Ian had owned Garner Construction. From what Kate had heard, the business was highly successful.

"Oh, get serious. Do you really think a man could marry me and not be a risk taker?" Both women giggled. "When he's not running the company, he's busy with the kids or working on my honey-do list." Jane winked at Kate, and they both laughed again. "Actually, he's coaching right now."

She waved toward the field where Ian was surrounded by twelve-year-old boys, evidently giving them last-minute pointers before the game started. Then she studied Kate with a concerned look on her freckled face.

"So how about you? How are you doing?"

"Maddie and I just take it day by day, but I think being near our family and friends is really going to help."

"We're sure glad to have you back!" Jane wrapped her arms around Kate and gave her a squeeze.

The game started. Keeping one eye on the playground where Madeline and the other children were playing, Kate watched and cheered along with Jane when Bradley struck out the first batter.

"That's my kid!" Jane shouted into the crowd. "Go get 'em, Bradley!"

It wasn't long before Bradley retired the side and his team came up to bat. Jane turned to Kate.

"Is there anything I can do to help you get settled?"

"Maybe. Do you know if any of the schools in the area are looking for teachers?"

Jane arched her eyebrows. "You haven't been in town for twenty-four hours and you're looking for a job? That's very ambitious."

"Let's just say I like to stay busy. It gives me less time to think about things."

"It's funny you should ask. It just so happens that one of the fourth-grade teachers at Harvest Bay Elementary went on maternity leave this spring and has decided not to return. When I found out you were moving back here, I mentioned to Mrs. Zeller that you're a teacher and that you might be looking for a job."

"And?"

"And she's expecting you to call her as soon as you get settled."

Kate threw her arms around her friend. "Oh, what can I do to thank you?"

"You've already done it. I've got my best friend back."

They were interrupted by Madeline and Jessica, who hurried up the bleachers hand-in-hand. "Guess what!" Madeline told her mother. "Jessica said she'd be my bestest friend!"

Kate glanced at Jane, and they exchanged a smile. "That's great, honey."

For the first time in a long time, Kate's heart filled to the brim with hope.

⁂

"Hey, coach, good game!" Adam congratulated his best friend after the game.

Grinning, Ian put his hand on Adam's shoulder. "Glad you could make it."

"I wouldn't miss Bradley's last game." Adam turned to Jane, who was helping her husband gather equipment. "I'll bet they heard you cheering clear to Cleveland."

"Good! Then I did my job."

Kate joined them, trailed by Madeline, Jessica, Emma, and Samuel. "We're ready for ice cream."

Jane turned back to Adam. "You remember Kate, right?"

Adam eyed Kate. "Hello again."

"Hey," she responded without enthusiasm.

"Hi, Adam!" Madeline waved. "Where's Moses?"

Adam chuckled. "In his stall at my mom and dad's farm." He turned back to Kate. "How's the tire?"

"Axel is looking at it. I'm sure it'll be fine. Thanks again for helping us out."

Uncomfortably aware of her natural beauty, Adam gave her a brief nod, determined to play it cool. Her body language made it clear she wasn't interested in him, and he reminded himself that he certainly wasn't interested in her.

"Excuse me. Am I missing something here?"

Adam glanced over at Jane. "Kate had a flat on the way into town yesterday, and I helped her out."

Jane looked from him to Kate and back again. "Uh huh. And . . . ?"

"You aren't going to win this one, Adam," Ian intervened, grinning, as he hoisted a large duffel bag onto his shoulder. "We're all going to Frosty Jack's. How about coming along and filling us in on the details there?"

Frowning, Adam said, "I'll have to leave that up to Kate. I'm heading over to the school to study game film and discuss new plays with some of my coaching staff. Two-a-day practices start in a few weeks, and I want to be ready. Besides, Chloe would have a fit if she knew I went to Frosty Jack's without her. Be sure to tell Bradley that I was once again totally impressed with his pitching."

He hurried across the park to the gravel lot where he had parked his black Silverado, rubbing the tension out of the back of his neck as he neared the truck. This was the season when he usually ran himself down, and it didn't look like this year was going to be any different. He couldn't change the fact that football season coincided with harvest time. Coaching was his passion, and he gave it one hundred percent. Farming was his duty, and he gave it everything he had left.

That left very little for Chloe, and he regretted how it hurt her. He knew she missed her mother every day, and this time of the year she missed her daddy just as much.

He climbed into his truck and started the engine. *I'll make it up to her as soon as football season is over,* he promised as he pulled out of the parking lot and headed toward the high school.

In a matter of minutes he pulled into his usual parking space and walked briskly into the building, focusing on the tasks he intended to accomplish that afternoon. Tom Ellsworth and Jonah Kelly, his offensive and defensive coordinators, would arrive at one o'clock to begin planning what was sure to be one of their best seasons yet.

He no sooner than stepped into his office and tossed his keys onto his desk when the telephone began to ring. Making himself comfortable in his leather chair, he picked up the receiver.

"Hello?"

"Hello, Adam."

He let out a silent breath and leaned his head against the chair back. "Alexandra. To what do I owe the pleasure of this call?"

It was an effort to keep the sarcasm out of his voice. He wasn't entirely successful.

"Pleasure? Oh, please, don't try to flatter me. I need to talk to you about my week with Chloe."

"Don't, Lexie."

"How do you know what I'm going to say?"

"Because you do this every time Chloe is scheduled to spend a week with you. You either move it back, shorten it, or cancel it altogether. So which one is it this time?"

"Do not speak to me that way, Adam Sullivan, and don't start laying the guilt trip on me. I have a very demanding career."

"Your daughter misses you. She desperately wants to spend time with you. Why can't you see that?"

"Listen, Mr. High and Mighty, she will spend time with me and we will have a great time together . . . but it has to be a few weeks earlier."

"How many weeks earlier?"

"Next weekend."

"How can you expect—"

"And it will only be for the weekend."

"Please don't do this!"

"One day Chloe will respect me for working hard to make something of myself."

Adam gritted his teeth. "If that makes you feel better."

"I'll reschedule the flight on Monday and overnight the tickets to you."

"What am I supposed to tell her?"

"Whatever you tell her every other time," Alexandra answered curtly and hung up.

Adam stared at the receiver for a long moment before carefully setting it on its base. Then he snatched a mini Styrofoam football from his desk and catapulted it across the small room.

"Hey, careful there! If I'd been any earlier, you'd have taken my head off," Jonah said as he walked through the door.

"Sorry."

"Let me guess. Alexandra?"

"Who else?"

"Shake it off, man. She's not worth it. After all, she's the one who walked out on you and Chloe for a better career, and then found another man before you were even divorced."

Adam winced and eyed the tall, muscular man in front of him. Jonah was young and single. How could he possibly understand the complexity of the situation, the heartache involved?

"Thanks for reminding me." He stood. "Why don't you get the first video cued up? Tom will be along shortly. I'm going to the lounge for a Coke. Do you want anything?"

Jonah hefted his bottle of Gatorade. "No thanks."

"I'll be right back."

Adam slowly walked the short distance to the teacher's lounge, feeling as if someone had taken a dumbbell from the weight room and set it on this heart. If only he could go back in time and make Alexandra stay. Even though their marriage had been far from perfect and neither of them was completely happy, Adam had been willing to work on it for Chloe's sake. But the ties were severed and the wounds ran deep. His would heal eventually, but he worried about Chloe, whose scabs were rubbed raw every time Alexandra let her down. He could already see the hurt in his daughter's eyes when he tried to explain to her that something had come up.

His mind drifted back to the day Chloe was born. He vividly remembered holding the tiny pink bundle in the crook of his arm, looking down into that sweet little face, and promising her—and himself—that he would always protect her and keep her safe.

He'd failed. Even though he wasn't the one who walked out, he'd still failed. Not just at a marriage he'd spent a little over nine years working at, but in the eyes of his little girl, who had stopped believing in fairytales. That was what broke his heart, what he couldn't get past, what he refused to see beyond.

He'd lost at a game he never wanted to play again.

CHAPTER
Four

*N*athan jogged up the front steps of his stately brick home. His hands on his hips, he slowly paced the length of the covered porch until his breaths steadied. A three mile run had never taken so much effort.

He knew it was because his heart wasn't in it. His heart was five hundred miles away in Ohio.

He sighed. Had it really been only two days? How he already missed Kate and Madeline!

That brought him back to the questions he'd been pondering nonstop since they left: What was God's plan for him? Did God really want him to leave everything he'd worked so hard for to be with the woman and little girl he loved? If so, how would he know for sure?

Wearily, he went into the house and up the stairs to his bedroom. He had an hour—plenty of time to shower, change, and get to church. Although he was certain Kate and Madeline's absence would hurt, he hoped that on this ordinary Sunday he would learn the answers to his questions while sitting in the pew he usually shared with Kate.

Maybe he would read a passage in the Bible or maybe the preacher would say something in his sermon that Nathan would know without a doubt was a message from God. Maybe

God would just whisper it in his ear or, better yet, maybe He would shout it from the heavens in His James Earl Jones voice: "Go, Nathan! Go to Harvest Bay! That is where you belong," or "You are making a difference right here in Nashville. You need to stay and let Kate and Madeline move on without you."

Or maybe he'd come home with all his questions left unanswered.

He showered and shaved, then went to his walk-in closet. While he pulled on a pair of tan Dockers, the phone rang. He crossed the room and picked up the cordless phone on his nightstand.

"Hello?" He retraced his steps to the closet to look for a shirt.

"Hey, Nathan."

"Kate! This is a nice surprise! How are you?"

"Good. Did I catch you at a bad time?"

"No. No, I was just getting ready for church." He pulled a shirt off the hanger and grabbed a white cotton T-shirt from one of the dresser drawers. "How does it feel to be back in your hometown?"

"It's been good—minus the flat tire."

"Oh, yeah. Tell me what happened."

He laid the shirts across the end of his bed and sat on the floor, resting his head against the mattress. He focused on the picture of Kate in his head while she told him briefly about the tire incident. She went on to describe the picnic at her parents', the fireworks, her reunion with Jane, and the possibility of a teaching position at Harvest Bay Elementary.

"Wow, Kate! That's great!" He put as much enthusiasm into his voice as he could while speaking around a huge lump in his throat.

"What's great is that Maddie is happier than I've ever seen her, and that makes it all worthwhile."

"I'm glad she's adjusting well."

"Yeah, but she'll be happy to see you next month." She paused. "And so will I."

His heart did a back flip. "I'm looking forward to it too."

"I hate to cut this short, but I've got to run. We're on our way to church. I'll call you again soon."

"Give Maddie a hug for me."

"I will. Bye, Nathan."

He returned the farewell and hung up the phone. He sat motionless for several minutes, his eyes growing misty as reality set in: Kate was creating a new life for her and Madeline, and although his heart filled with pride for her, it was also heavy with loneliness.

There had been a time in his life when he would have chalked this situation up as just another amicable end to what could have been a wonderful relationship. But then, he had never actually loved any of the women he dated. Before experiencing the love of Christ, the only people Nathan ever really loved were Ryan and himself.

Their mother had died when he was four years old and Ryan was just a baby. Their congressman father had been too busy being successful to raise two young boys, so their maternal grandmother cared for them as best she could. Ryan had made the adjustment well and later on in life found it easier to open his heart to the Lord and to others.

Nathan, on the other hand, struggled with relationships. For a long time he felt he didn't need anyone, and he liked it that way. He developed a hard heart and the determination of a prize fighter. He allowed no one to get in the way of his becoming successful in society's eyes until Ryan and Kate helped him to see that his status didn't necessarily make him a success in God's eyes.

Now he knew that God wanted more for him than the meaningless flings that worked out well for his career but left him feeling unfulfilled. He desperately longed to dedicate his whole life to real love, to Kate and Madeline, but as long as he remained in Nashville their life would never include him. And it could take months for the state to process the application for a license to practice medicine in Ohio.

"Lord, I know that anything is possible with You, but it's going to take a miracle to move me to Harvest Bay and back into Kate's life."

Kate sat with her family in the same pew they had occupied every Sunday at Harvest Bay Community Church for as long as she could remember. The organist played a few introductory measures, and then the entire congregation, many of whom Kate had known most of her life, lifted their voices in song until the refrain of "How Great Thou Art" reached the high, peaked beams above them.

She closed her eyes in the Spirit-filled atmosphere. She had expected to feel the same numbness she had all those Sundays after Ryan's death while sitting next to Nathan in her Nashville church, spiritually empty and just going through the motions. Most of the time, she really wanted to stay in bed, but she forced herself to go for Madeline's sake and because she knew that if she didn't, someone from the church would call the very next morning to check on her.

What exactly had changed, she didn't know, but suddenly the pain was back. Her heart ached with a longing so deep it nearly took her breath away. She wished some of the heavenly warmth would find its way into her frozen heart, filling it far beyond its capacity so that the overflow would penetrate the depths of her soul. She longed to experience a "God high" again.

Kate ran her hand over the burgundy leather cover of the Bible she held in her lap. She had been taught that it held all the answers to life's toughest questions, but it had been so long since she'd opened it that she didn't know where to begin.

Are You really there, God?

Tears stung Kate's eyes. She tipped the Bible up on its spine and let it randomly fall open. Her eyes dropped to the page, and she nearly gasped when she read Isaiah 41:10.

"Fear not, for I am with you; Be not dismayed, for I am your God. I will strengthen you, Yes, I will help you, I will uphold you with My righteous right hand."

Kate's breath quickened. Surely that was a coincidence. She closed her Bible, holding it on its spine between her trembling hands.

Okay then, God, where were You when my husband was driving home from work that day? Where were You when I had to try to explain to my three-and-a-half-year-old that her daddy was in heaven with Jesus? And where have You been since then on days when I've felt so lost and alone? You deserted me!

Again she let the Bible fall open in her lap, and her eyes fell to Genesis 28:15. "Behold, I am with you and will keep you wherever you go, and will bring you back to this land; for I will not leave you until I have done what I have spoken to you."

A tear slipped out of the corner of her eye. *Oh, God, I'm sorry. I know should've trusted more, believed harder, but how could I when in one instant I lost my husband and all our hopes and dreams for the future? Ryan was only thirty-five years old. I only got to spend eight years with him. He was such a good doctor, an amazing father, and a wonderful husband. Most of all, he was a dedicated Christian. How could You let this happen to one of Yours?*

Kate closed her Bible and indignantly brushed the lingering moisture from her cheek. *I still don't understand, and I don't think I have it in me to rely on You or trust Your promises like I used to.*

The hymn ended, and Pastor Ben made his way to the pulpit carrying his Bible and a large canvas duffel bag. He set the Bible on the podium, then deliberately unzipped the bag and set in on the floor beside him.

Intrigued, Kate glanced around her. From the looks on their faces, others in the congregation shared her curiosity.

"Grace and peace to you from God our Father." Pastor Ben greeted his congregation. "There once was a woman who seemed to have it all—an adoring husband, a great kid, a successful career, a big house, a luxury car, a clean bill of health, and a strong Christian faith. She had it all, that is, until the day her husband approached her and confessed that he'd been having an affair. He told her that no amount of counseling could change his mind and he wanted a divorce."

He pulled a brick out from under the podium and dropped it into the duffel bag with a thunderous boom that startled Kate. She leaned slightly forward, listening intently while he continued.

"One morning several months later, her child woke up gravely ill." *Boom,* went another brick into the bag. "So she had to miss work to take care of her child." *Boom!* "Days passed, but her child wasn't getting better." *Boom!* "The woman took her child to the doctor, who ran a battery of tests and finally determined that this child had cancer." *Boom!*

"The woman had no choice but to miss weeks of work while her child underwent treatment, and although the president of the company assured her she wouldn't lose her job, they also couldn't pay her for her leave of absence." *Boom!* "The bills began to pile up." *Boom!* "She was forced to sell the house . . ." *Boom!* " . . . and the car . . ." *Boom!* " . . . and many other possessions." *Boom!* "Before long she was rushed to the hospital with stress-induced chest pains."

Pastor Ben threw the last brick into the bag. He looked for a long time at the heaping duffel bag, and then gazed out over the congregation.

"Now that is a load to have to carry. Would anyone like to carry it across the sanctuary?"

People in the congregation glanced around at each other. No one raised a hand.

"Just across the dais?"

Still no volunteers.

"The woman wasn't given a choice. This was her life. This was her baggage, but because she still possessed a strong Christian faith, and knowing very well that she couldn't make it through another day with the weight of this burden on her shoulders, she cried out to the Lord for help. She said, 'I'm tired, Jesus, and I'm weak. I can't bear this burden on my own any longer.' And do you know how the Lord answered her?" He opened his Bible. "Jesus said in Matthew 11:28, 'Come to Me, all you who labor and are heavy laden, and I will give you rest.' "

Pastor Ben came out from behind the podium and stepped down into the congregation. "I don't know what you're going through in your life, but I do know that we all carry around a duffel bag. Some of you may have the weight of only one or two bricks to contend with, and it may amount to slightly more than an inconvenience. Some of you may be faced with an insurmountable burden as this woman was.

"But I'm telling you today that there is hope. You do not have to deal with the pain, frustration, worry, and fear alone. Jesus is willing to carry that load for you, and rest assured that there is no problem too great for our Lord. After all, He did conquer death, didn't He? Lay your burdens at the foot of the cross and experience freedom. The altar is open and Jesus is waiting."

The organist began to softly play "What a Friend We Have in Jesus." Several members of the congregation made their way forward to kneel at the altar.

Kate opened her Bible to the verse Pastor Ben had just read. "Come to Me, all you who labor and are heavy laden, and I will give you rest." It sounded so nice. How she longed for that rest, but . . .

She glanced down the pew and met her mother's gaze. She gave Kate a sympathetic smile. Then to Kate's surprise her parents stood and made their way to the altar.

What burdens do they have that are so unbearable?

Fresh tears stung Kate's eyes. Were they praying for her, for the healing of her broken heart? Were they praying that her faith would be restored to the fullness it had once had, that she would once again live for the Lord instead of just try-ing to make it through each day? Were they praying for Madeline's happiness and that she would thrive here in

Harvest Bay? Were they praying that Kate would join them at the altar and petition these requests for herself?

Overcome with a myriad of emotions and needing a moment alone to pull herself together, Kate grabbed her Bible and purse, slipped out of the pew, and made a hasty exit.

In her hurry she pushed through the door at the back of the sanctuary that opened into the lobby and collided with someone so hard it threw her off balance. She dropped her Bible as a strong hand encircled her arm to steady her.

"Oh! I'm so sorry!" She looked up and her jaw dropped. "Adam?"

"We meet again."

"Three times in three days. That must be a record."

Adam's lips curled slightly. "Nah, it's just life in a small town."

Gazing into his electric blue eyes, she felt her tear-stained cheeks warm and quickly shifted her gaze to the floor. Remembering her Bible, she stooped to pick it up.

"Do you always worship from the lobby?"

"I'm waiting to pick up my daughter from children's church."

"Well, it was nice running into you." She awkwardly side-stepped around him. "Er . . . I didn't mean literally running into you, of course."

The amusement dancing in his eyes only made her more flustered. "I . . . I'll see you around."

He chuckled good-naturedly. "See you."

She made her break for the heavy wooden door. Outside, the humid air didn't provide much relief for her spinning head. She sat on a nearby bench, wondering how she would begin to sort through it all.

I'm scared, God. I'm so scared to let go. For the past three years I've been just trying to make it through each day, and now I know that's not enough, but I don't know how to trust in You again. I don't know if I'll ever be able to find my way back to the faith I once knew.

"Katy? You okay?"

Kate turned to see Grandpa Clayton making his way to her with small steps, using his cane for support. She hopped up to assist him, and after he was resting on the bench, she sat back down with a heavy sigh.

"Katy?"

Kate wished she could shrug her burdened heart and withered faith off like it was nothing, but her grandfather knew her too well. "No, Gramps, I'm not okay. I wish I was, but I'm not." Her bottom lip quivered and fresh tears surfaced.

He slipped his arm around her shoulders and pulled her to him. "You questioning your faith?"

"How did you know?"

"A person can become pretty perceptive in eighty-seven years."

Kate's gaze fell to the Bible in her lap. "Are you disappointed in me?"

"Oh, Katy, don't you know by now that you could never disappoint me?"

Kate ran her fingertips under her eyes to brush away the tears. "How did you get through Grandma's death with such unwavering faith?"

"I didn't have much of a choice. Your mother and her sisters were already grown with families of their own. All I had was the Lord. There were times when I was tempted to question Him, but the Bible says, 'Trust in the Lord with all your heart and lean not on your own understanding.' See, Katy, in this lifetime we will never know the reason why Grandma and Ryan had to leave us so soon, but that's not for us to know. What really matters is that we can rely on the promise that if we have faith we will be reunited with them again one day."

"But some days a lifetime seems like so long to wait."

"Take it from this old man; it's not." He gave her a little squeeze. "And in the meantime, try to make something good come out of it. Concentrate on your relationship with Maddie. Give her as many happy memories as you can. It's what I tried to do with you and your sister."

"Thanks, Gramps."

By now people were beginning to trickle out of the service. It didn't take long before Kate's parents emerged with Madeline in tow and came to join them.

"Everything okay, honey?" her mother asked.

Kate gave her a weak smile. "Everything's fine."

"Children's church was great, Mama!" Madeline crawled up onto the bench, and Kate put her arm around her. "We sang songs and learned about a boy named Joseph. He had a really pretty coat and some really mean brothers. I'm glad I don't have any brothers. And then we colored this paper bag, and when we were done, Miss Rachel cut it and made it into a coat!"

"It's a beautiful coat. You did a fantastic job, and I'm so glad you had a good time."

"Come on, Maddie," Kate's father said. "Let's go get the van and pull it up for Gramps."

"Oh, no you don't, Charlie. I can walk. I need my exercise."

"How about we compromise? You can walk right there to the curb." He pointed to a spot about five feet away.

Grandpa Clayton waved him away, pretending to be annoyed.

Madeline kissed Grandpa Clayton on the cheek and gave him an earnest look. "It's okay. Most of the time, I don't get to do what I want either." Then she hurried off with her grandpa.

Kate and her mother stifled a giggle. Kate gathered her purse and Bible, glad to be going home.

"I'll walk with you, Gramps."

"Just a minute, honey," her mother said.

Kate turned. "What is it?"

"Pastor Ben was hoping to see you this morning. He has a few minutes before the next service starts. Why don't you run in and say hi?"

"Can I see him next week?"

"It'll just take a minute. We'll wait for you."

Seeing that she wasn't going to win the argument, Kate agreed as graciously as she could and went back inside the church, hoping that Adam had already left. She didn't know if she would recover from the humiliation that would certainly engulf her if she were to come face to face with him again.

To her relief he was nowhere in sight, and she made her way down a short, narrow hallway of offices on the opposite side of the building from the sanctuary. If she remembered correctly, Pastor Ben's office was the last one on the left. She peered through the doorway and saw him sitting at his desk, poring over some paperwork. When she tapped lightly on the open door, he looked up with a welcoming smile.

"Good morning, Kate!" He rose and came around his desk. "Please come in."

"Mom said you wanted to see me."

He closed the door behind her. "I was just wondering how you're doing."

"I'm fine." Kate could see that he didn't completely believe her.

"Grief can be a hard thing to work through. Just know I'm always here in case you need anything."

"I'll keep that in mind."

Can you join me for a moment?"

He gestured toward a sofa and chair in a corner of the office. Kate knew that area was his "counseling corner." Engaged couples preparing to marry, married couples on the brink of separation, blended families that couldn't seem to blend all worked toward a hopeful future in that corner. She sat on the sofa, her posture rigid, while Pastor Ben took the chair.

"I know you have a lot on your mind right now, and by no means do I wish to add to it, but I want to talk to you about something."

"Okay."

"Over the last few years I've noticed a significant increase in the number of single-parent families in our community. More recently I've been considering how we as a church family can best minister to these families, and I've decided to start a weekly support group for single parents in the fall. We'll run it on a trial basis, and then reevaluate it after a few months."

Kate relaxed. "I think that's a great idea!"

"Good. Now I just need someone to lead it, and I was thinking that you might be the perfect person."

Stiffening, she said, "Oh, Pastor Ben, I'm sorry. I don't think—"

"I don't want you to answer right now. We've got a few months so there's no rush. But please pray about it, okay?"

She stared at him, wanting to say no, absolutely not. For goodness sake, she was in the midst of a faith crisis! It had been so long since she'd had a heart to heart with God she didn't know if she'd even remember how, but if she did she had a mile-long list of things she needed to pray about. Pastor Ben's proposal was too much to take in.

Still, how could she say no to his simple request that she pray about it? She thought the world of her pastor. He had been a spiritual leader in their community ever since he came to the church twenty-five years ago when she was almost ten and very impressionable. He was enthusiastic and understood the importance of building a strong Christian foundation in children. Still a mentor for the youth, he created a bond with many of them that could not be easily broken.

Like the bond he had formed with Kate long ago.

"All right. I'll pray about it, but I can't promise anything."

"That's all I ask." He gave her an encouraging smile. "I believe this ministry could make a world of difference for some of our families."

She rose and moved to the door. "I don't mean to rush out of here, but my family is waiting."

"Have a good week, Kate, and let me know if there's anything I can do for you or Maddie."

She opened the door but suddenly stopped and turned back. "Why me?"

"You don't know?"

She shook her head.

"Search your heart. You'll figure it out."

CHAPTER
Five

The next afternoon Kate stood on a ladder, rolling paint onto the walls in the kitchen of the ranch-style home Grandpa Clayton had lived in for nearly sixty years. Kate's father had already installed new cabinets and countertops and updated the appliances. The pretty pale yellow paint would finish the room with a touch of cheer.

Kate climbed down, took a long drink of her lemonade, and surveyed her progress. *Two walls done.* As she looked around, the transformation in progress couldn't prevent the memories from rushing back to her—early, foggy ones of baking cookies with her grandmother and recent, vivid ones of joyfully preparing Thanksgiving feasts and Christmas dinners with her mother, sister, and aunts.

One day soon another family will be making memories in this kitchen. The thought made her suddenly nauseated.

"Katydid!" her father called out from the foyer.

"In the kitchen!"

He emerged through the archway, dressed in his work clothes. "How's it coming?"

"Good, I think. Is it three o'clock already?"

"A quarter after. I'm going to run home and change. Then I'll be back up to do some landscaping. Do you need anything?"

"Will you check on Maddie for me? Make sure she's not driving Mom crazy already. You know, talking her ear off or anything like that."

Her father grinned. "Sure thing. Be back in a jiffy."

Kate followed him out and waved as he backed out of the driveway and headed down the quiet residential street. She leaned against the railing of the small front porch, alone with her lemonade and her memories.

Their tire swing still hung from the thick branches of the old oak tree. Kate laughed out loud as she remembered twisting the rope as tight as she could make it with Elizabeth in the tire, then letting go and watching Elizabeth spin wildly until she was so dizzy she couldn't stand up.

From where she stood, she couldn't see the willow tree on the other side of the house by the little creek that ran along the property line, but she knew it was there. Kate had loved to play behind its whip-like branches that nearly hung to the ground like a long hula skirt. The cornfields that flanked the property on both sides and in the back always beckoned to be explored, and in the early spring when they were still barren they were perfect for flying kites.

Looking around her for what might be one of the last times, Kate sighed, drained her glass, and went back inside.

She refilled the paint tray, climbed back up the ladder and continued with the task at hand while more tidbits of her past floated back to her like cottony clouds in the breeze. Some memories made her smile, like the time she and Elizabeth had planned to camp out in the backyard when they were around the ages of twelve and eight. Grandpa Clayton had told them a ghost story that was so scary they were too frightened to sleep in their tent, so they sneaked into the house and crawled in bed with him instead.

Some of the memories brought tears to her eyes. Ryan had stayed in this house the night before their wedding. She remembered standing on the front porch, kissing him good-night before she went back to her parents' house. The next afternoon after the ceremony was over, she had learned that he had stayed up until two o'clock in the morning, playing cards with Nathan and Grandpa Clayton in the very kitchen she was now painting.

She placed the roller in the paint tray, climbed down from the ladder, and sat on the linoleum floor where the table had once been. Like this house, her life was changing so rapidly. Some things were missing, some things were being replaced, but the core of her being was still the same. Now more than ever she needed to cling to something familiar, something that would strengthen her true identity instead of redefine her. Something like this house.

When her father walked in ten minutes later and found her on the floor, her eyes brimming with tears, he rushed to her side. "Katydid, what happened? Did you fall? Are you hurt?"

Kate smiled up at her father. "Good news, Daddy. I just may have a buyer for this house."

❦

By the time they finished working that evening, Kate was so exhausted that she didn't mention her idea of taking over ownership of Grandpa Clayton's home to him or her mother. She had no idea what kind of reaction to expect, and she was way too tired for a question-and-answer session, so she kept it between her and her father.

The next morning, after breakfast and before she headed back over to Grandpa Clayton's house to finish the land-scaping—and before she lost her nerve—she dialed the number for Harvest Bay Elementary.

"Hello, Ms. Sterling. I've been expecting your call," the principal, Margaret Zeller, said. "Are you available for an interview this afternoon? Say one o'clock?"

Kate's jaw dropped. *This afternoon? There's no way I'll be prepared by this afternoon!*

Still, she really wanted to teach at her alma mater, and if Mrs. Zeller could meet her this afternoon, she'd make it work. She pasted on a smile that she hoped oozed through the phone lines.

"That'll be perfect. I look forward to meeting you."

At ten till one, she sat in the office waiting for Mrs. Zeller, her nerves operating in overdrive. She glanced over her resume one last time, double checking the dates and spellings of her employment history. She flipped through her portfolio, making sure her sample lesson plans and corresponding photos were in order. Then she studied her newly polished pale pink fingernails.

Five more minutes and I'm going to start nibbling.

"Ms. Sterling?" A sandy-haired, fifty-something woman with kind eyes and a warm smile approached.

Kate rose to her feet. "Please call me Kate."

"Hi, Kate. I'm Margaret Zeller." The principal of Harvest Bay Elementary School firmly shook Kate's outstretched hand. "I'm glad you could make it this afternoon."

"Thank you for seeing me." Kate's frazzled nerves calmed slightly.

"Let's go back to my office where we can talk."

They made their way through the administrative part of the building, an L-shaped hallway of offices and conference rooms. Once inside her office, Mrs. Zeller motioned for Kate to occupy one of the two chairs at a small, round table near the door. Kate laid out her resume and portfolio, while Mrs. Zeller grabbed a legal pad off her desk, and then came to join her.

"Why don't you tell me a little about yourself?" she said.

An hour later, they retraced their steps through the hallway. Kate felt upbeat and confident, certain the interview had gone well.

Reaching the school's main entrance, Mrs. Zeller turned to her. "I'll be in touch within a week regarding the vacant fourth-grade position."

"Thank you."

Now all Kate could do was wait . . . and wait . . . and wait. Between the house and the job, it was almost too much for her to bear.

She was so grateful when Jane called to invite her and Madeline to a pool party at her house on Saturday afternoon. It would be a welcome distraction.

As expected, the Garner house was buzzing with activity when Kate pulled up. Madeline jumped out of the Explorer and rushed her mother along.

"Hurry up, Mama! I hafta go find Jessie!"

Kate recognized a few of her former classmates along the way, and much to Madeline's dismay, she chatted for a few minutes with each one.

"Hey, Kate! Hi, Maddie! Glad you could make it," Ian greeted them when they finally reached the large deck at the back of the house. His swimming trunks were dripping, and a towel hung around his neck.

"Hi, Ian! Thanks for inviting us."

"Wouldn't have it any other way. I've got to fire up the grill here in a minute, but Jane is down by the pool with the kids and my sister, Ava. Just make yourself at home."

Madeline saw Jessica in the pool, waved enthusiastically, and started down the steps of the deck. By the time Kate reached the pool, her daughter had already kicked off her flip-flops and was easing down the ladder into the water.

"Where's your suit?" Jane demanded from the pool, where she was helping Samuel, her five-year-old son who was not yet a strong swimmer.

"It's in my bag."

"Then get it on. You're missing out on the fun."

Ava, involved in a serious game of water tag with Emma and some older girls, waved at Kate. She smiled and waved back.

"You can change in the bathhouse over there." Jane motioned to the other side of the pool, where there was a small shed-like building with two circular windows covered by nautical-themed curtains.

"Will you keep an eye on Maddie?"

"Sure, I'll watch her. She'll be fine."

Kate hurried off to change. She rejoined the party minutes later in a flattering black tankini speckled with tiny fuchsia, emerald, and royal blue flowers.

She no sooner than sat on the edge of the pool and dangled her legs into the refreshingly cool water when Madeline and Jessica approached. Madeline held a huge, multi-colored beach ball.

"Mama, wanna play Monkey in the Middle with us? Pretty please?"

"Okay. Who's the first monkey?"

"Me! Me!" Jessica eagerly volunteered. She moved between Kate and Madeline and easily caught the ball when Madeline attempted to throw it to her mother. "You're in the middle now," she informed Madeline.

"I know." Madeline moved into the middle, her face puckered in a pout that quickly transformed into a grin when the game resumed.

Jessica heaved the ball with all her might. It sailed past Kate's head onto the patio. As she pulled her legs out of the water to retrieve it, a voice stopped her in her tracks.

"Nice throw, Jessie. Looks like you've inherited your brother's arm."

Kate glanced up as Adam Sullivan strode to the edge of the pool, the beach ball under his arm. She wasn't surprised to see him since he and Ian were such close friends, but she hadn't expected that his presence would cause something to stir inside of her.

He looked down at her with a friendly smile. "Hello again."

Kate's throat felt like the Sahara, and she wondered if it had something to do with the heat that crept up her neck to settle in her cheeks. "Hi."

"Mind if I join in?"

"Yeah! Come on, Adam!" Jessica invited.

"Oh, yeah! This'll be fun!" Madeline piped up, splashing around enthusiastically.

Adam held Kate's gaze.

Kate shrugged, hoping she wasn't as transparent as she felt. "Majority rules."

Adam hopped into the pool. Soon both girls were in the middle, shrieking and splashing happily while they tried their hardest to capture the ball Adam and Kate threw back and forth.

While they played together, Kate's inner turmoil gradually subsided, and an easiness set in. She not only grew comfortable in Adam's presence, she felt strangely comforted by his nearness.

After a while Madeline and Jessica grew bored with the game, mostly because they couldn't get the ball away from Kate or Adam. They decided to go play Marco Polo with the bigger kids and Ava.

"You're no fun," Adam called after them, coming to the side of the pool.

He tossed the ball onto the patio and hoisted himself onto the edge beside Kate. "There's nothing like a good, old-fashioned game of Monkey in the Middle."

Kate laughed. "That's true."

"How is it that we keep running into each other?"

"I don't know, but thankfully this time there wasn't an impact."

They both laughed, and the door of her heart opened a crack.

Just then, Jane waded over with Samuel hanging on her back. "Hey, guys, Sam wants to go play on his swing set, and I'm going to help Ian with the food. Will you keep an eye on Jess for me?"

"Of course," Kate replied.

Adam nodded. "Absolutely."

"Thanks! Now will one of you help me get this monkey off my back?"

Adam stretched his arms out. "Come here, Sammy."

Little Samuel fearlessly leaped to him, and Adam's seemingly natural ability with children impressed Kate. By the time Jane climbed out of the pool, wrapped a towel around herself, and headed up the deck steps toward the house with a quick wave, Samuel had already scurried off to the backyard play equipment.

"So . . . " Kate and Adam said simultaneously. They laughed, and then Adam motioned for Kate to proceed.

"I was just wondering what the quarterback of our high school football team is up to these days. I mean, besides rescuing women and children stranded alongside the road."

Adam chuckled softly. "I'm the head coach of the football team, and I teach junior high health and wellness classes."

"Really? You're a teacher?"

"You sound surprised."

"Well, as I recall, you weren't well-known for your studious behavior."

"Yeah, those were the good old days." Adam grinned.

"And you have a daughter now?" Kate said, recalling their brief conversation in the church lobby.

She instinctively glanced at his left hand. Not finding a wedding band, she quickly decided to stay away from that subject. It was none of her business, and she certainly didn't care whether he was single or not.

"Yes, I do." His rich, warm eyes twinkled at the mention of his daughter.

"Is she here?"

"Unfortunately, no." Adam sighed. "Chloe's mother lives in Chicago, and she's spending the weekend there."

"Oh. Then I guess you won't have to hide out in the church lobby tomorrow." Although Kate smirked, she felt a stab of disappointment that alarmed her.

"That's correct."

"If you don't mind my asking, why wait in the lobby instead of participating in worship?"

Adam shrugged. "Just a matter of preference, I guess."

There was an awkward silence. "I'm sorry. I didn't mean to—"

"What about you?"

"Excuse me?"

"I just told you my stats. So what are yours?"

"Well, you know, I have Maddie."

"Yes. Occupation?"

"I'm a teacher too."

"What grade?"

"Elementary. I taught second grade for eleven years in a suburb of Nashville, but I just interviewed with Mrs. Zeller on Tuesday for a fourth-grade position."

"So you're here to stay then?"

"That's right. It's been three years since my husband . . . " She still tripped over the words. " . . . passed away, and I guess I figured it was time for Maddie and me to get on with our lives."

"Sometimes moving on can be harder than living with the pain."

Adam's voice was so gentle Kate's eyes became misty. "Yes."

In the silence that followed, she found the focus of her sorrow shifting to him. What had he been through to give him such insight?

She forced a smile and patted his knee. "Now that we've gone and spoiled our cheerful mood, what do you say we get a bite to eat?"

He nodded, stood, and held out his hand. She accepted it and got to her feet, trying to ignore the warmth of his touch.

"Maddie! Jessie!" she called as she wrapped a beach towel around her waist. "Let's take a quick break and eat."

"I'm not hungry!" Madeline called back.

"Me either!" Jessica added.

Kate planted her hands on her hips, slightly self-conscious under Adam's watchful eye. "I'm not asking if you're hungry. I'm telling you that we are taking a break to eat."

"Yes, ma'am," Madeline answered.

She and Jessica climbed out of the pool in a huff. Kate ushered them toward the deck steps, and they followed the deliciously smoky aromas from the grill to the table full of picnic food.

By the time they got there, both girls were commenting on how hungry they were. Kate filled two plates, carried them to an umbrella-shaded patio table with Madeline and Jessica following close behind. Adam brought the girls each a cup of lemonade. Seeing that they were settled, Kate and Adam filled their own plates.

Kate's stomach was growling by the time she sat down next to her daughter. She almost had her hamburger to her mouth when Madeline interrupted her.

"Aren't we gonna pray?"

Kate shot a gaze at Adam, whose chewing quickly slowed to a stop. She placed her burger back on her plate and tried to come up with an excuse.

"Well, honey . . . I just . . . I mean . . . "

Adam put a fist to his lips, swallowed hard, and cleared his throat. Then, to Kate's astonishment, he folded his hands.

"Of course we are. Would you like to lead us, Maddie?"

Madeline nodded. "Uh huh." She folded her hands, shut her eyes tight, and began to sing a little prayer she had learned in Sunday school.

Kate caught his eye from across the table and mouthed, "Thank you."

He winked.

It was a simple gesture, but it caused Kate's heart to skitter, and for the first time that afternoon she wondered what was really taking place inside her. Could she actually be feeling something for him? The mere possibility frightened her. She wasn't ready for that part of the moving-on process, and certainly not with Adam.

Madeline finished with an enthusiastic "Amen!" and wasted no time digging into her food. With her mouth full of half-chewed hotdog, she turned to Adam.

"Is Moses here?"

"No, silly. We don't have a place to park him," Jessica answered matter-of-factly.

Adam chuckled, wiping his mouth on his napkin. "I'm afraid she's right, Maddie. He's in his stall on the farm."

Madeline snapped her fingers, but since it was a skill she was still learning to master, the motion was bigger than the sound. "Rats!"

"Tell you what, you and your mom can come visit Moses anytime you want." Adam shifted his gaze to Kate, and the furnace in her cheeks kicked on again.

Madeline squealed. "Really?"

Adam returned his attention to the little girl. "Really. Moses loves having visitors, and there are lots of other animals that would enjoy the company too."

"Didya hear that, Mama? When can we go?"

Kate stared at Adam, who appeared pleased with himself. "I'm not sure."

"Tomorrow?"

"No. We have plans after church with Grammy and Papa."

"The next day?"

"Some day. We'll go some day, okay?" Kate's tone rang with finality.

"Okay."

After that they ate and made light conversation, mostly revolving around the girls, and their plans for the rest of their summer vacation mixed with their excitement over the new school year. Emma and Samuel joined them long enough for each of them to scarf down a hot dog and a few chips, but Ava sat down with her plate and visited with them for a while.

The longer Kate visited with Adam and watched him interact with Madeline and Jessica, the more she realized he really wasn't the same shallow, careless boy she remembered from high school. He was sensitive and insightful, and he seemed to relate to her in a way no one else had for a long time. The door of her heart inched farther open.

Adam looked up and brightened as Bradley and two other boys approached. One of the unfamiliar boys juggled a toy foam football from hand to hand.

"Hey, guys! What's up?"

Kate got the impression Adam knew what was up before Bradley even opened his mouth.

"We're gonna play some football, and we just thought it would be cool if you'd be the quarterback."

Adam turned to Kate, an undeniable spark lighting up his eyes. Obviously his love of football hadn't changed over the years.

"Will you excuse me?"

Kate quickly hid the sharp disappointment that squeezed her heart. "Oh, sure. No problem. Maddie, Jessie, and I will be heading back to the pool in a little bit anyway."

"All right then." Adam stood and held out his hands. Bradley's friend tossed him the ball. "Let's go play some ball."

The boys pumped their fists. "Yes!"

Kate had to consciously keep her gaze from following Adam and his young protégés as they headed across the yard. She was beginning to realize what he meant to Harvest Bay. And despite her reservations, he was beginning to mean something to her too.

⚜

An hour and a half later, the sinking sun cast lavender and fuchsia strokes across the western sky, softening the edges of what had been a sizzling summer afternoon. Ian had built a bonfire, and the adults gathered around it to make S'mores, talking, laughing and visiting with one another while the children ran barefooted in the dew-moistened grass playing Ghosts in the Graveyard or chasing lightning bugs.

Adam stood off to the side trying to gather his thoughts, a task that was difficult with his head spinning. He watched Kate from a distance. She sat in a lawn chair next to Jane and Ava, laughing at something Jane was saying, and he wondered about this effect she had on him.

In the glow of the fire she looked like an angel with her honey-blonde hair falling around her shoulders and a smile lighting up her beautiful face, and his defenses began to crumble. His heart tapped a light, happy beat instead of thumping the same old monotonous rhythm that did little more than sustain life. He was actually *feeling* again.

And advancing toward dangerous territory.

He had to be very careful and not allow himself to get too close, though he seriously doubted it would come to that. It was obvious that Kate didn't see him the way he now saw her. To her he was still the crazy, immature boy she knew in high school, only now he was divorced with a daughter, with shards of shattered dreams all around him.

And to seal the deal, there was the God thing. Her attendance at Sunday worship made it obvious she was a Christian. Adam, on the other hand, didn't know what to believe in anymore.

He'd been brought up in a Christian home, had gone to church as a child, learned the Bible stories, and sung the songs. And he had believed all of it. When he became a teenager, however, he had begun to question the validity of Christianity.

In college, when he lost his biggest dream, and then his grandfather, the frayed ends of his faith unraveled past the point of repair. At the time, Alexandra had helped ease that utter disappointment. He put his faith in her, and out of their relationship came his greatest blessing, Chloe. But in the end he was left even more lost and alone than before.

His mother's words from a little over a week ago came back to him. *Just promise me that you won't let an opportunity pass you by.*

No, Kate wasn't an opportunity, but that didn't mean that she couldn't be a friend.

Fronting a casual attitude to cover up the chaos taking place inside him, he made his way over to the women. When Jane finally noticed him he held his breath, waiting for a sarcastic remark. That would be typical of her, and most of the time what he loved about her. They had fun joshing each other—she could take just as much as she dished out—but he didn't think his rattled nerves could handle it right now.

To his surprise she brightened. "Hey, Adam! Come sit down!" She gestured to an empty chair on the other side of Kate. "We were just reminiscing."

He thought about turning on his heel and walking away on that note. He didn't need Kate to remember who he was back then. He wanted her to get to know who he was now. Hesitantly, he moved to the chair and took the seat. He rested his forearms on his knees, and rubbed his hands together.

"Oh, yeah? About what?"

"About how much has changed since high school," Kate answered."

A refreshing wave of relief washed over him, and it felt so good that he had to restrain himself from laughing out loud. Instead, he simply nodded. "I was just thinking the same thing."

Jane sighed and shook her head. "But there are some things that will never change." She swatted Ava on the arm, nodding toward Ian who had gotten out his guitar and was playing an old Eagles hit while the others helped him sing. "Will you look at your brother?"

Ava gave a little shrug. "I still say he was adopted."

Adam, Kate, and Jane laughed. Ava, the typical introvert, never had much to say, but on the rare occasion that she did, it was usually witty.

Adam sat back in the chair. "Come on, Janey. He's not *that* bad."

"Yeah, you're right. And he's mine, so if you don't mind, I'm going to go make a fool of myself with my husband. Come on, Ava. I'm going to need some moral support." Jane grabbed her sister-in-law's arm and the two of them headed toward the circle of people surrounding Ian, leaving Adam and Kate alone.

Kate raised an eyebrow. "Do you get the feeling we've been set up?"

"I wouldn't put it past Jane. Her intentions are good, though. She wants everyone to have what she and Ian have."

Kate watched Jane climb up to sit on the picnic table, while below her on the bench Ian began to strum the first unmistakable measures of "I Got You, Babe."

"They've always been a cute couple."

"I guess a love like that comes along once in a lifetime."

"I think it happens more than that, but people are too scared to embrace it."

He gazed at her, wanting to ask what she meant, but before his mouth could form the words, she said, "Tell me about your daughter."

Somehow she'd found his one weakness. His defenses were suddenly gone, melted away to a goo that sank clear to his toes. Yes, he was vulnerable, but at the moment he didn't care.

"Chloe is a great kid."

"What sports does she play? I mean, I can't imagine any child of yours not being involved in something that includes a ball."

He chuckled. "She plays soccer in the fall and softball in the spring."

"Maddie's really into soccer too, and she'd love to have someone besides me to play with. We should get them together sometime."

He stared at her, wondering if she really meant what she said. "That . . . that'd be great."

Kate gave a nod. "Good. So tell me more. How old is Chloe?"

"Nine."

"She must be going into the fourth grade then."

"Yes, and she's an excellent student—one of those kids school just comes naturally for." He paused. "If I remember correctly, kinda like you."

She laughed. "Is that so? Then she must be a good kid."

"She's amazing." He rubbed his hands together, afraid to be so susceptible, and yet increasingly comfortable with Kate. "I don't know how I got so lucky."

She reached over and touched his arm. "I do." Her voice was so gentle he had to look at her to make sure she hadn't sprouted wings and a halo. "It's because she has you."

Adam could barely breathe.

"I watched you interact with Maddie and with Jane's kids this afternoon. I saw how those boys adored you when you played football with them. They hung on your every word. If you are that good with other people's kids, how much better must you be with your own?"

Their gazes met. He wondered if she felt the same electric current he did.

"What I'm saying is I don't have to meet your daughter to know that you are a wonderful father."

That sucked the last bit of air out of his lungs. *You are a wonderful father.*

The words repeated themselves over and over in his head in the matter of a few seconds. Kate could not have had any idea what those five words meant to him. He hid his insecurities well, but the truth of the matter was that his confidence left him when he came off the football field.

"Thanks." It was all he could manage to push through his tightened throat.

His spirit soared. And he began to fall.

CHAPTER

Six

A mere two-and-a-half weeks later, the newest teacher at
Harvest Bay Elementary School spent the day moving
heavy boxes and furniture out of storage and into her new
home, assisted by her parents, sister, and brother-in-law. By
five o'clock they were all famished.

"How does pizza sound to everyone?" Kate's father asked.
After receiving a unanimous thumbs-up, he turned to Kate.
"If you call in an order, I'll pick it up. We can spread out a
blanket and eat right out here on the lawn."

"Yeah! Did ya hear that, Great-Gramps? We're having a
pizza picnic!" Madeline cheered from the tire swing.

With her feet through the tire's hole, she ran as far as the
rope would allow, pulled her feet up, stretched out her arms,
and sailed back and forth until her momentum slowed. Then
she did it all over again.

Grandpa Clayton watched his great-granddaughter in
amusement from his lawn chair under the old oak tree.
He'd graciously given Kate his blessing in purchasing the
home and had been a spectator most of the day, but she
knew it couldn't be easy for him.

It was harder for her than she expected. Even though
she had signed the papers, she still thought of it as his

house, and she suspected the change would take some getting used to for everybody.

Elizabeth followed Kate inside to order the pizzas, then
snatched her hand and dragged her to the master bedroom.

"Liz, what's going on?"

Shutting the door behind her, Elizabeth joined Kate on
her bed, a giddy expression on her face. "I need you to do me
a favor."

"Sure. Anything. Just name it."

"Pray for me."

Kate stared at her sister. "You've got to be kidding." She
moved to her dresser and busied herself unpacking the small
box on top of it, muttering, "First Pastor Ben and now you."

Too late, she realized what she'd done. She turned to
Elizabeth, her heart falling with her sister's smile. She
returned to the bed and scooped up Elizabeth's hands.

"I'm so sorry. I shouldn't have reacted like that. Of course
I'll pray for you. What should I pray for?"

"Well . . . Elijah and I are trying to have a baby."
Elizabeth's grin rivaled the Mississippi River's size.

Kate gasped, covered her mouth to stifle a scream, and
then leaned forward to embrace her sister. "I'm going to be an
aunt?"

"Not yet. That's why I want you to pray. We've just started
trying, but I'm so anxious I can hardly stand it."

"That's fantastic news! And you'll be a wonderful mother."

"Thanks." Elizabeth hesitated. "So you'll pray?"

"I'd do anything for you, sis."

"Why did you sound so upset then?"

Kate shrugged. "Because Pastor Ben asked me to pray about
something and . . . " she sighed, "I just don't think I can."

Elizabeth's brow knitted in bewilderment. "What is it, Kate?"

Kate picked at a chipped nail. "He wants me to lead a single-parent support group in the fall."

"That sounds like a great opportunity for you. Why won't you pray about that?"

Kate stared at Elizabeth for a long moment. She didn't want to admit to her sister what she'd already confessed to her grandfather, but she couldn't go on running from the truth either. She dropped her gaze to her lap.

"I'm not as strong in my faith as I once was. How can I lead a group of people if I don't have it all together myself?"

Elizabeth shook her head. "I don't know, but I think that sometimes leaders who are willing to grow with their group take them farther on their journey than those who have it all together."

Kate pondered her sister's words. "I just don't think it's the right time. A year or two down the road maybe, but I have too much going on right now."

"Think about it some more. Pray about it and when you get tired of praying, I'll pray for you."

"Thanks."

"Hey, that's what sisters are for."

⁂

That evening Kate developed a fever and ended up spending the next day in bed with cold symptoms. Her parents picked Madeline up for Sunday school and kept her most of the day so Kate could rest, but by the next morning, she wasn't feeling much better. At her mother's urging, she made an appointment with Doc Brewster.

Easing her Explorer into a spot in front of the huge, reno-
vated Victorian home, she got out and headed up the walk to
the large, welcoming covered porch. When she pushed
through the front door, a bell chimed. At the desk behind the
check-in window, the medical receptionist looked up and
smiled.

"Hi, Kate! It's been ages. How are you?"

"Hi, Denise. Not too well today, I'm afraid." Kate coughed
hard, and then sniffed.

"Land sakes! That is some cold!" Denise Golden laid a
pen on the sign-in sheet and pushed it toward Kate.

Another young and very pregnant receptionist looked up
from the paperwork she was filing. Giving Kate a sympathetic look, she retrieved a box of tissues and set it on the
window ledge.

Kate signed her name, helped herself to a couple tissues,
and blew her sore, red nose.

Denise passed a clipboard that held a form and a pen to
Kate. "I'm going to have to get you to fill these out for me
because your information has obviously changed since you
were here last. Do you have your insurance card on you?"

Kate pulled her wallet out of her purse, found the card,
and handed it to Denise. "I'm covered under this company for
now, but it will change when I start my new job."

"That's fine. We'll just change the information the next
time you come in." Denise flashed Kate a smile and went to
the copier.

Denise had graduated a year ahead of Kate. Everyone in
school knew she was by far the most energetic cheerleader on
the squad. Kate could see not much had changed. Still as
pretty as ever, her friend had tied her sandy brown hair in a

bouncy ponytail, and only a few faint lines fanned out from the corners of her sparkling topaz eyes.

Kate cleared her scratchy throat. "How's Daryl doing?" She remembered what a perfect couple Denise and her high school sweetheart had been.

Denise's bright smile faded as she returned to her seat behind the window. "Daryl and I divorced two and a half years ago. He remarried and has a new life with his new family." A smile returned to her face, smaller than before but sincere, and she handed Kate her card. "The boys miss him, but I'd say all-in-all we're doing just fine."

"I'm so sorry. I wish I would have known."

"Actually, I'm relieved to know that you didn't. Daryl's affair had the whole town talking. It was pretty embarrassing, not just for me but also for Griffin and Greyson."

"Your boys?"

Denise put a hand over her heart. "My whole world. Griffin is fourteen and Greyson is twelve." She sighed. "They are great kids, but I never imagined how hard being a single parent would be."

"I've thought the very same thing many times."

"Oh, forgive me. Here I am going on about my troubles after all you've been through. Is there anything I can do for you?"

Kate gave her a heartfelt smile. "Maybe we can be there for each other."

Denise appeared to be next to tears. "That sounds great." She paused. "Now you'd best get these forms filled out. Doc Brewster will be ready for you in a few minutes."

"Right. I'll be on the porch." She took the clipboard and another tissue and went out to wait on the comfortable, white wicker porch swing.

She had just finished filling out the last sheet when a nurse opened the door and stuck her head out.

"We're ready for you, Kate."

She gathered her things and followed the nurse, pausing briefly by the check-in window to hand the clipboard and pen to Denise. She waited to make sure Denise noticed the slip of paper she'd tucked under the clip that had her new address and phone number on it.

Denise looked up with shining eyes.

Kate smiled. "Call or stop by anytime."

"Thanks. I'll do that."

Kate hurried to fall into step behind the nurse. After she weighed Kate, she showed her to an examination room, took her temperature and blood pressure, and recorded the information.

Flipping the file closed, she said, "Doc Brewster will be with you shortly." She stepped out of the room.

In the silence Kate shivered. *I never imagined how hard being a single parent would be.*

Just as she did with Adam, she and Denise had more in common now than they ever did in high school. Kate made a mental note to drop off an invitation to Madeline's birthday party for Denise and her boys first thing in the morning.

A light rap on the door caught her attention, then Doc Brewster walked in.

"Well, hello, Kate. It's nice to see you again. It's been a while. How are you?"

"I'm all right. A little under the weather today."

"I see that." He studied her chart. "It looks like you're running a low-grade temp. What other symptoms are you having?"

"A nasty cough and a runny nose."

"Um hmm. Well, let's take a look at you and see what we can find." He looked in her ears and down her throat, felt the glands in her neck, and listened to her chest and back. Then he pressed gently but firmly above her cheeks with his thumbs.

Kate winced.

"It appears that you have a sinus infection. We'll treat it with an antibiotic, but more than anything you'll need to rest."

She thought of the unpacking she still needed to do before Madeline's birthday on Friday. "For how long?"

"At least a few days." He sat on a stool and jotted some notes in her file. After a moment, he turned to her, his brow creased with concern. "Now, how are you really doing?"

"What do you mean?"

"According to our records you weigh twenty pounds less than you did at your last visit thirteen years ago, and you were on the low end of average then."

Kate hung her head.

Doc Brewster moved to her and put his hand on her shoulder. "I know you've been through a lot, but you have to take care of yourself. Have you had any counseling since your husband's death?"

"I talked with the pastor of my church in Nashville a few times."

"Grief can be a hard thing to work through. I can give you the name and number of an excellent Christian counselor if you need someone here to talk to."

"Thanks. I'll keep that in mind."

"I do think you made a wise choice by moving back here to be near your family."

"Me too."

"I'm sure your mother will waste no time fattening you up a bit." He smiled.

Kate chuckled. "It's been her mission since day one."

"And how is your little girl?"

"Maddie seems to be doing great. She loves being here with her Grammy and Papa."

He reached into the pocket of his white lab coat for his prescription pad. "There is a great pediatric practice in Cresthaven," he told her, referring to a larger neighboring town. Opening his pad, he scratched something on it, tore out the small, square paper, and handed it to Kate. "This is the number to the office. Ask for Dr. Pearson. My grandkids see her. She's an excellent pediatrician."

Kate took the paper and looked at the number. She had been so preoccupied since arriving in Harvest Bay that she hadn't even thought of finding a pediatrician and probably wouldn't have until she had a sick, irritable child on her hands.

"Thank you."

He nodded. Leaning his tall, sturdy body against the sink, he began to scribble on the prescription pad again.

Kate coughed and blew her nose. "So how have you been? Still running three miles a day?" It had always been a common denominator between them.

"I wish, but I had to slow down a few years ago after I had knee replacement surgery. Don't feel too bad for me, though. I started walking with Nancy, and sometimes I believe I'm getting a tougher workout than running!" Grinning, he finished writing and looked up.

"And how is your lovely wife? Still taking good care of all the pets in Harvest Bay?"

Nancy Brewster had been the town veterinarian for twenty-five years, practicing in the small animal hospital right next door to Harvest Bay Family Practice.

"For now—though she's been hinting at retiring in order to be a full-time grandma."

"You aren't thinking of retiring, are you?"

He laughed. "That is the plan eventually, which is why I'm expanding my office."

"What do you mean?"

"Let's face it. Someday I'll be too old to run this practice. It's already becoming more than I can handle on my own, so in October I'm planning on bringing in another physician, possibly another nurse, and a temp during Maggie's maternity leave."

"Wow, more has changed around this town than meets the eye."

"Change is a good thing, Kate. Lots of people hate it, refuse it, and fight it tooth and nail, but if everyone stayed content inside their comfort zone, too afraid of the unknown to try something new, we'd live in a mediocre society." He paused thoughtfully. "If we never had the courage to take a leap of faith, we'd be cheating God out of a chance to mount us up with wings like eagles and watch us soar."

Kate nodded, meditating on his words.

"I can't explain it, but I just have this strange feeling that this expansion will impact people's lives in ways that I can't even imagine."

"Well, congratulations! I'm very happy for you, although I should wish you good luck in trying to get the citizens of Harvest Bay to see another doctor. You know—that accepting change thing and all. He will have to be a pretty special person." Silently Kate added, *Like Ryan was*.

"I'll just pray and trust that the Good Physician will send me the right doctor." He ripped the prescription off the pad and handed it to her. "We'll try you on Amoxicillin. Take one capsule three times a day for ten days. If you don't notice a significant improvement in a week, come back in."

"Got it." She slung her purse over her shoulder and hopped off of the table, the paper crinkling beneath her.

He put an arm around her shoulders. "And if you need any-thing, call, even if it's after hours. I always have my pager on."

"Thanks. I'll remember that."

Kate headed down the short hallway to the waiting room. Denise was on the phone, so Kate waved and went outside to her Explorer. When she was on the way to the drug store, the thought struck her that there was a lot about her appointment that she would remember.

CHAPTER
Seven

*N*athan stood off in a corner of Kate's festively decorated living room, watching while Madeline eagerly opened her birthday presents. Kate hovered around the excited little girl, taking pictures and helping her read the cards. Both were beaming. It was a wonderful sight; one that he'd missed, one that he wanted to go on watching forever.

Was that what God wanted too?

He still didn't know. He'd hoped that being here with Kate and Madeline would give him an indication, but it only made him more confused. Standing there in a room full of Kate's family and friends, he felt a sense of belonging and, at the same time, strangely out of place.

Nathan closed his eyes. *God, please give me a sign so I can finally have some peace of mind.*

A soft tap on his shoulder interrupted his prayer. He turned to see a sandy-haired woman smiling up at him.

"You must be Kate's brother-in-law."

"Yes, I'm Nathan Sterling." He stuck his hand out politely, and she shook it.

"I'm Denise Golden. It's nice to meet you."

"And you." He thought her last name suited her, just a shade or two from the color of her light brown eyes.

"So have you met everybody yet? Kids' birthday parties can get pretty crazy. I have two older boys, but I remember their parties when they were little very well."

He chuckled, a welcome ease finally setting in. "I know Kate's family, but that's it. I'm sure she'll introduce me to her friends after all the excitement dies down."

She brushed his upper arm. "There's no need to wait for that. Come on. I'll make the introductions."

He followed her across the room to where a small cluster of friendly looking people had gathered.

"Hey, Denise!" a woman with short red hair and fire in her eyes said. "Who do you have here?"

"This is Nathan Sterling, Kate's brother-in-law." Denise turned to him. "That is Jane Garner."

"It's nice to meet you. I've heard a lot about you."

"Only believe about half of it." Jane winked, her lips curled in a mischievous smile.

"This is her husband, Ian."

Nathan nodded and received a nod in return.

Denise continued around the circle. "This is our town's librarian, Ava Garner, who happens also to be Ian's sister."

The tall, slender woman pushed her wire-rimmed glasses up higher unto the bridge of her nose and shyly waved hello.

"And this is Adam Sullivan, our high school football coach."

Adam and Nathan shook hands, and Nathan scanned the faces around him. "Kate's lucky to have such good friends."

Jane cocked her head. "We're lucky she came back to us."

Denise turned back to Nathan. "How long will you be visiting?"

"Until Sunday afternoon."

"Do you have any plans?" Jane asked.

"I'm not sure."

"Our harvest festival starts tomorrow morning. Surely Kate will bring you to that," Jane said.

"Oh, definitely! What a great way to show you around town! Everyone will be there," Denise added.

Nathan couldn't help but smile at her enthusiasm. "Okay."

"Hey, yeah, Nathan, we can use you on our softball team, or we won't stand a chance at winning the tournament," Adam broke in. "Do you play?"

"I haven't in years, but I attended Florida State on a baseball scholarship."

Ian turned to Adam and scratched his goatee. "I thought we had everyone in place."

"Tom had to go out of town for a wedding, and my brother Owen has to cover a shift at the fire station."

"Oh, man."

Both men turned to Nathan.

"So what do you say? Are you up for a few games of softball?" Adam asked.

"I . . . I didn't bring any equipment."

Ian patted Adam on the back. "Oh, don't worry about that. Adam, here, has everything you'll need."

"Okay, then."

"It's time for cake and ice cream!" Kate called, starting for the kitchen with Madeline racing ahead. She stopped beside Nathan and linked her arm through his. "I see you've met everyone. Sorry I didn't introduce you sooner."

"Oh, that's all right."

"We were just talking about the harvest festival downtown tomorrow," Jane explained.

Ian tapped the face of his watch. "You'll need to have him at the ball diamonds by eight A.M. on the dot."

Kate looked at Nathan, her eyebrows arched in astonishment.

He shrugged and gave her a small grin. "They needed another guy."

She giggled and playfully elbowed him in the side. "And to think I was actually worried about you fitting in."

"Mom-meee!" Madeline's voice rang through the house.

"Come on, guys. We can't keep the birthday princess waiting."

Nathan followed the group of friends into the kitchen thinking that, in all his thirty-eight years, he'd never looked so forward to birthday cake.

⚜

Beads of perspiration already formed on Kate's brow at a quarter past eight the next morning. She sat in the metal bleachers, watching Nathan interact with Ian and Adam and reveling in this connection of her past with her present.

Adam walked a baseball mitt over to Nathan, who slipped his hand in, punched at it a few times, and nodded at him. When Adam smiled, it felt as though someone suddenly set a hundred Monarchs free inside her chest. It had happened several times the night before at Madeline's party too, and she was beginning to realize what it meant.

She crossed her arms over her chest and hugged herself tightly, willing the fluttering to settle. Then she closed her eyes and instinctively did something that surprised her. She prayed.

God, my heart is changing before I'm ready. I know Doc Brewster said that change is good, that if we don't take a leap of faith it cheats You out of the chance to mount us up on wings like eagles. Well, I'm not ready to jump. I'm scared. I still desperately love my husband, and though I know I can't have him, I can't let go of him. I don't want to let go of him.

I know I haven't been able to put my trust in You since Ryan died, and I still don't know if I can, but if you're really there and listening, I'm asking You to please remove these feelings from my heart. Please, God. I'm just not ready yet.

She opened her eyes to find Jane standing in front of her, eyeing her curiously. Kate blinked and forced a smile.

"I'm sorry. Did you say something?"

"I asked you if you were sleeping. I think I got my answer."

"I wasn't sleeping, just deep in thought."

Jane plopped down next to her, and stuck her purse securely in between them. "So, whatcha thinking about?"

"Oh, it was nothing. Really."

Jane ran a hand through her stylishly unkempt, short red hair. "I'm sorry we're late. Sometimes it takes forever to get my kids out the door."

Kate glanced over at the playground equipment several yards away where Bradley pushed Samuel on the swings and Emma climbed to the top of the jungle gym, then grinned at her friend. "And you didn't even have all four of them this morning. Thanks again for letting Jessica spend last night with Maddie. It made her birthday extra special."

"Jessica was equally thrilled."

"Elizabeth is staying at the house while they sleep in. She'll bring them up here in a few hours."

"That's fine. There's not much to do this early, but in a couple of hours they'll be dragging us from the pony rides to the face painting tent to the children's theater at the library. I don't know about you, but I'm enjoying this little bit of R and R."

Kate turned her attention back to the field. By this time, the whole team of twelve men had assembled and participated in relaxed warm-up exercises.

"Looks like Nathan survived his freshman initiation. The guys must not have been too hard on him, huh?"

Kate watched while Nathan skillfully executed his part in a drill. "I think he's made a decent impression on everybody, don't you?"

Jane nodded. "It's a shame that he could only be here for the weekend."

Kate's expression sank. "Yeah."

She propped her elbow on her knee and rested her chin in her palm. In an attempt not to dwell on the fact that after tomorrow they probably wouldn't see him again until Thanksgiving, she focused on the activities on the field . . . and inevitably on Adam.

She didn't know which was worse—thinking about Nathan leaving or this crazy attraction she seemed to have developed to Adam. Both were equally disturbing. The difference was that she expected the disappointment that was sure to come the following afternoon. She'd already begun to prepare her heart for telling her brother-in-law good-bye. But she never expected to be so drawn to Adam.

"Let's bring it in, guys!" Adam called to his team

As if Kate were a living, breathing lightning rod, his voice traveled to her, sending an electric jolt through her that prickled her skin and caused her heart to beat in an erratic rhythm that could have been mistaken for a distress call in Morse code.

"Hey." Jane gently elbowed Kate. "Are you bringing Nathan to the Sullivans' barn dance tonight?"

"Oh, well, I . . . I hadn't really thought about it," she lied, rubbing the goose bumps on her arms.

Realistically, Kate knew that eventually someone somewhere along the journey she was on would move her, offer her a second chance at love. However, now that it was really happening, especially so soon after her return to Harvest Bay, a big part of her wanted to crawl back into her shell where she was safe and live off memories.

She chewed the inside of her cheek, wondering what to say. As much as she loved her best friend, Jane would never be able to understand the turmoil in her heart.

At that moment a voice called out. Denise hurried toward them, waving.

"Hey there, gals! I thought I'd find you up here."

Kate breathed a sigh of relief at the temporary distraction, while Jane happily patted the metal seat beside her. "We were just talking about the barn dance. Are you coming?"

"Wouldn't miss it."

Kate's stomach turned over. Her reprieve had expired.

Jane stared at her. "So?"

Kate glanced at Jane, then Denise, and then down at her hands folded in her lap. She sighed again. What could she say? Everyone went to the Sullivans' barn dance. She opened her mouth to state the obvious when Denise reached across Jane to lay her long, slender fingers on Kate's knee.

"Are you afraid of missing Ryan?"

Stunned, Kate looked up into her friend's compassionate eyes and blinked twice, consciously keeping her bottom jaw in place. "You could say that, but how did you know? Is it that obvious?"

Denise withdrew her hand and shrugged. "I can recognize the signs. I've been there. Maybe it isn't exactly the same, but heartache is heartache."

Kate leaned in closer. "So how did you get past it?"

"I relied on God's promises that there is a time to weep, and a time to laugh; a time to mourn, and a time to dance." Denise tipped her head to the side. "And there is a time to begin to live again."

Moisture filled Kate's eyes. When she spoke again, her voice barely rose above a whisper.

"Does living again mean forgetting?"

Now Jane had tears in her eyes, and she wrapped her arm around Kate's shoulders.

Denise shook her head. "Of course not. As much as I'd like to sometimes, I could never forget Daryl because I see him every time I look at Griffin and Greyson. Ryan will live forever in Maddie, in her children, and even her grandchildren."

Kate smiled and quickly wiped away a tear. "Thank you."

Denise winked at her. "That's what friends are for."

Jane sniffed and nudged Denise. "Hey, when'd you get to be so smart?"

Denise put a finger to her lips. "Shh. Don't tell. It's a well-kept secret."

The three of them giggled, and the mood lightened considerably.

"You know, if it's too much for you to go to the barn dance, we could just have a small get-together at my house this year," Jane suggested gently. "It wouldn't be that big a deal."

"Thanks, Janey, but I suppose it wouldn't be right for Nathan not to get the entire Harvest Festival experience."

"Including the barn dance?"

"What's the Harvest Festival without the barn dance?"

Jane gave a whoop that turned a few heads, and Kate and Denise laughed. After a moment, Denise leaned across Jane's knees.

"Thanks again for inviting me to Maddie's birthday party last night. I had a great time."

"I'm so glad you came, and thank you for taking Nathan under your wing like you did."

"It was my pleasure. He's a super nice guy." Denise lowered her voice in mock seriousness. "Ian and Adam haven't run him off yet, have they?"

Chuckling, Kate answered, "Not yet, but there's still time. They're just getting ready to start the game."

CHAPTER
Eight

For some reason, playing in the Harvest Festival softball tournament had been even more fun this year than in years past, and winning the championship was the cherry on top. But Adam had really been waiting for this night.

Standing at the refreshment table, he scanned the growing crowd with eager anticipation. He'd never in his life looked forward so eagerly to the dance his parents held in their largest barn every August. In fact, for several years he had only made an appearance out of obligation and left at the first opportunity.

But this year was different. This year there were Kate, Madeline, and feelings that he didn't think he'd ever experienced before, not even with Alexandra. Maybe, just maybe, this was an opportunity after all, and if it was, he would absolutely not let it pass him by.

"Congratulations on winning the tournament championship, though I can't say I'm surprised."

He turned to see Kennedy standing behind his right shoulder. "Thanks! We had a great team this year."

"You can say that again." She cracked open a Coke and took a long drink. "The new guy made some nice plays. Who is he?"

"You wouldn't know him. He doesn't live around here."

She shrugged, causing her strawberry-blond corkscrew curls to spill over her shoulders. "I'm just curious."

"Do you remember Kate Marshall?"

She tapped her chin. "Oh, yeah. She set the school record in cross country your senior year, right?"

"That's right. The new guy's name is Nathan. He's her brother-in-law."

"Brother-in-law? So she's married?"

He shook his head. "Her husband was killed in an accident three years ago. You were finishing up your student teaching at Ohio State at the time."

Just then he spotted Kate, Madeline, and Nathan strolling through the big barn door, and he—and his pulse—perked up.

Kennedy followed his gaze. "She looks great."

"That's just the beginning of how beautiful she is."

When she didn't respond, he glanced down to find his sister watching him with a sly grin on her face. "You like her, don't you?"

"No. No, of course not. I mean, sure, as a friend, but not like *that*."

She put her hand on his arm. "Adam, it's okay to love again."

He put his hand over hers. "But I don't think it's okay with her." He cocked his head to the side. "Come on. I'll introduce you."

By the time they wove their way through the crowd, Kate, Nathan, and Madeline had already found Jane, Ian, and the rest of their friends.

Madeline was the first one to notice Adam, and she waved enthusiastically. "Hi, Adam! Guess what!"

Kate turned to him with a dazzling smile, and he had to stop for just a second to catch the breath that had escaped him. He recovered quickly and grinned down at Madeline.

"What?"

"Mama said this is your mama and daddy's farm, so can I see Moses?"

He got down on one knee so he was on the little girl's level. "He's been waiting for you to visit him. We'll go a bit later, okay?"

"Okay!" She leaned in to whisper into his ear, "Who is that pretty lady?"

He chuckled and stood up. "Maddie, this is my sister, Kennedy."

Kennedy stuck her hand out. "Nice to meet you, Maddie."

Madeline put her small hand in Kennedy's and looked up at her in awe. "You're pretty."

"So are you."

Madeline beamed. "Thanks." Spotting Jessica, Emma, Samuel, and Chloe out on the designated dance floor hopping, wiggling, and spinning around with Denise, she begged, "Mama, can I go?"

"Sure, honey. Just stay close to Denise."

Eager to join her friends, Madeline started off before Kate finished, calling over her shoulder, "I will!"

When Kate turned back to him, Adam finished introducing her and Nathan. "It's nice to meet you both." Kennedy shook their hands, and then turned to Nathan. "You did a great job on the field today."

Adam relaxed." Looks like your days at Florida State came back to you," he agreed.

"Yeah, after I knocked the rust off a little," Nathan said with a laugh. "Thanks for inviting me to play. I had a lot of fun."

Seated at the picnic table, Ian shook his head. "Rusty or not, I don't think Owen could have played that well, and I know Tom couldn't have. Without you, we would have been out of the tournament three games into it."

"Yeah, thanks a lot, Nathan. Now we're going to have to listen to every detail of this victory for a whole year."

Everyone laughed at Jane's lighthearted sarcasm.

Adam locked gazes with Kate, and he felt his mouth go dry. He should say something. He knew he should. But the words got lost somewhere between his brain and his mouth.

And then the moment was gone.

She looked past him, brightened, and waved, then turned to Nathan. "I'm going to go say hi to Mom and Daddy, and then grab a drink. Do you want anything?"

"I'll have whatever you're having."

"Two Diet Cokes coming up." She floated out into the sea of people.

Strike one, Adam thought.

As the evening wore on and the gravitational pull toward the dance floor strengthened, the designated area grew to encompass the entire middle of the barn. The picnic tables were pushed to the walls, and a few were moved outside to make more room. Although Kate, Jane, and Kennedy had joined Denise, the kids, and dozens of others on the dance floor, Adam continued to occupy their picnic table, visiting with Ian, Nathan, and Ava and trying to devise a new game plan.

Patience was essential. Every good football coach knows that sometimes you just need to wait—for a block to open up a gaping hole for an explosive tailback, for a defensive end to bust through for a fourth-quarter sack, for a last second Hail Mary pass to spiral out of the sky into the hands of a waiting receiver for the winning touchdown.

For that one magical moment.

Eventually Kate would have to come off the dance floor, and when she did he'd be ready to execute the perfect play.

Before long the upbeat song ended, the first few notes of a ballad floated to the rafters, and the dance floor thinned out. Adam looked up when Kate and Kennedy neared the picnic table, his pulse quickening with each step they took.

"Where's Jane?" Ian asked.

"She's dancing," Kate answered.

"With?"

Kennedy's shamrock-green eyes twinkled. "A very handsome young man who reminds me a lot of you."

He stood begrudgingly. "That's just great. Bradley's showing me up! I'd better get out there and dance with Emma or I won't hear the end of it."

Kate smiled. "Oh, Emma's spoken for too. She's dancing with Greyson."

Ian's eyebrows arched high over the rims of his glasses, and he picked up the pace. "You mean Denise's twelve-year-old? Now I've really got to get out there."

"Oh, come on," Kennedy called after him. "Greyson is a good boy."

"Yeah, but he's a boy," Ian shouted over his shoulder, and Kate and Kennedy both giggled.

Kennedy rubbed her stomach. "I'm starving. Ava, do you want to grab a bite to eat with me?"

Ava nodded and slid out of the bench seat.

Kennedy linked arms with her and gave Adam a wink over her shoulder as they walked away.

Adam glanced at Kate, who was happily watching her father and her daughter dance, and took a deep breath. Just as he opened his mouth, Nathan stood up.

"Come on, Kate. Why don't we go join them?" He offered her his hand.

She slid her gaze to Adam.

He needed to say something, do something. So, he gave her his best smile and said, "Don't keep the man waiting."

Watching the woman of his dreams make her way to the dance floor with someone else, he tried to ignore the pain in his heart.

Strike two.

Frustration burned inside him. He was not one to throw in the towel. Typically he would fight until the very last second if he had to. But a woman was different than a football game, and he had battle wounds left from Alexandra that reminded him that losing a woman could be much more devastating than a loss on the field.

He stood up and moved to the big open doorway decorated with multi-colored lanterns. He leaned heavily against the strong wooden beam and sighed deeply.

What was he doing thinking he was ready for another relationship? It was still too soon after his divorce, and he had to think about Chloe's feelings. Not to mention that he couldn't possibly start dating at the beginning of football season. He'd be way too busy. It was just bad timing.

Still, the disappointment stung. He'd begun to feel something special for Kate, something real, but he had to let this opportunity go and walk away with his dignity. Maybe somewhere down the road, circumstances would be different and things could work out for them. Maybe.

He had a sudden urge to go see Moses. Turning, he stepped out into the night.

"Leaving so soon?"

He froze in his tracks, though his heartbeat quickened. He turned, holding his breath for fear of it leaving him again. There, framed in the doorway like a pretty picture, stood Kate. Instantaneously, a glimmer of hope returned.

She crossed her arms. "Well?"

He took a step toward her. "Uh, no. No, I'm not leaving. I mean, I was, but I'm not." He rubbed his neck and grinned bashfully at her. "I needed some fresh air so I was going to walk over and see Moses."

"Without Maddie?"

"She was dancing." He glanced at the ground and back at her. "I thought you were too."

"The song ended. I needed a break, and Denise was happy to take over."

He bobbed his head and took another step toward her.

She slipped her hands into her pockets. "I don't remember your parents' barn dances being this much fun."

He took one more step until he stood close enough to smell the fruity scent of her shampoo mixed with the floral fragrance of her perfume. The combination was intoxicating.

"To tell you the truth, neither do I."

They stood together silently for a long moment. One song ended and another one began. He peered through the doorway at the dance floor, relieved to see Denise and Nathan still swaying, but a song only lasted three or four minutes. Time was not on his side. Once again he fumbled for the right thing to say, to do, but he was drawing a blank.

Kate's gaze locked with his for the second time that evening. "I guess you'd better go see Moses."

He shifted from one foot to the other. "Do you . . . do you want to come with me?"

She glanced over her shoulder. "I'd love to."

He smiled as Kate stepped in line with him. Maybe, just maybe, somewhere down the road was right here after all.

⁂

"So, Nathan, what do you think of our little town?" Denise asked as she and Nathan fell into a comfortable rhythm on the dance floor.

"Is that a trick question?"

"Not at all. I imagine it's quite a bit different from a big city like Nashville."

"That it is. But to answer your question, I think Harvest Bay is an ordinary town filled with extraordinary people." He glanced over to where Kate stood talking with Adam and wondered what he was doing on the dance floor with Denise when the whole reason he'd come to Harvest Bay in the first place was to be with Kate and Madeline.

Denise nodded. "That's what I've always loved about Harvest Bay too—the people."

"How long have you lived here?"

"All my life."

"Have you ever wanted to move on, experience bigger and better things?"

"No. Never. Sure I'd like to visit different places, see the famous landmarks—you know, the Empire State Building, the

Lincoln Memorial, the Golden Gate Bridge, things like that—but I'm a country girl through and through. Everything I know and love is right here in Harvest Bay." She glanced down the space between them. "Besides, it would kill my boys to be too far away from their dad."

George Strait nicely wrapped up his song, and the first few chords of another slow country love song floated through the barn, signaling the end of his commitment. His steps slowed.

"One more song?" she requested.

He turned his gaze toward Kate. He wanted nothing more than to go to her, but . . . what was one more song? After all, Denise had been genuinely kind to him since he'd arrived.

"Sure." They picked up the pace to keep time with Alan Jackson.

"Okay, enough about me," Denise prompted. "What about you? Have you always lived in a big city?"

"For the most part. My father was a congressman, so I spent most of my childhood near Washington, D.C. I went to college at Florida State, where I majored in pre-med. Then I attended medical school at Vanderbilt, and I've been there ever since."

"And you've never wanted to move on, experience something more simple and personal?"

Nathan pondered the question. "You know, if you'd asked me the same question two months ago, I would have said absolutely not. I like the challenges of a big city. But I'm beginning to see that a small town has challenges of its own."

She cocked her head to the side. "What's changed in two months time?"

Kate is what changed, he thought, but he shrugged and simply answered, "I'm not sure."

"I think I know."

"Oh, yeah? Enlighten me."

"You are a country boy at heart. I knew it from the moment I met you."

He chuckled. "You might be right."

"You said you went to medical school at Vanderbilt. You're a doctor then?"

"Now that's an accurate guess. I'm one of five physicians in our family practice."

"You don't say. Well, that's something we have in common."

He eyed her curiously. "You're a doctor?"

She burst into laughter. "No, but I work for one. I'm the office manager for Harvest Bay's family physician."

"Then he's a very lucky man."

The words were out before Nathan could stop them. The last thing he wanted to do was say something that might send her the wrong message, but Denise didn't seem to read more into it than was intended.

She shook her head. "I'm the lucky one. Doc Brewster is a wonderful, kind-hearted man, and a very generous boss." She paused. "Would you like to meet him?"

"He's here?"

She smiled warmly and nodded toward the opposite side of the dance floor. "He's been two-stepping with his wife all night."

She led him over and introduced him to the doctor and his wife. While they visited, Doc Brewster shared his intent to expand Harvest Bay Family Practice. And the more he learned, the more Nathan began to suspect that God was revealing His plan for Nathan's future bit by beautiful bit.

He didn't see Kate walk out of the barn and into the warm August night with Adam by her side.

❦

There is a time to dance. There is a time to dance.

Kate repeated the words over and over to herself throughout the evening, taking turns stressing "is", "time", and "dance". *Heaven knows I've spent enough time mourning. Denise was right. There is a time to begin to live again.*

As she walked across the dewy grass with Adam, she felt more alive than she had in months. They followed a wooden fence, making the most meaningless of small talk while the energy of their togetherness revealed a significance that couldn't be put into words.

When they reached another barn, smaller than the one they had left, he pushed open the door, flipped on the lights, and gestured for her to step inside. The sweet, earthy scent of hay engulfed her, and she gasped in delight at the sight of two pretty Palominos.

"Oh, Adam! They're beautiful!" She hesitated. "Can I pet them?"

"Sure."

She went up to the adjoining stalls and stretched out her hand. They each sniffed her, the whiskers on their leathery muzzles tickling her palm, and she giggled. Adam came up beside her, so close that their arms were touching, and she was certain he could hear her heart banging in her chest like a bass drum in the high school marching band.

She scratched one of the horses between her big brown eyes. "What are their names?"

"That's Dixie." He patted the other one on the neck. "And this is Dolly."

"Do you ride them?"

"Kennedy does most of the riding on these girls. She shows Dixie and has won a couple first place ribbons with her."

She raised her eyebrows. "First place. That's quite an accomplishment."

He nodded. "Chloe wants to start competing in horse shows. I think she's still a little young, but she started training with Dolly under Ken's supervision, and I have to admit she looks great. She'll probably be ready next summer."

"Wow! That's amazing!" Kate patted Dixie's neck. "Do you show Moses too?"

"No. We raced Moses for a few years, but he's retired now. These days he's the stud of the farm."

"Oh, I see." Heat crept up her neck and set her cheeks on fire.

A low whinny came from the other end of the barn, and Adam cocked his head to the side. "Come on."

He took her by the hand and led her down a short row of empty stalls, though his touch made her so light-headed she wondered if her feet touched the ground.

As they neared the last stall, Moses stuck his head over the gate. Adam went to affectionately run his hand from the white patch between the horse's eyes down to his velvety nose.

"He's more beautiful than I remembered." Kate cautiously approached and allowed Moses to sniff her.

"You don't have to be afraid. He is very gentle."

"And rather intimidating."

"Have you ever been riding?"

She reached up and stroked Moses' neck. "You mean besides the pony rides at the festival when I was a kid?"

He laughed and nodded.

"No."

"I could take you out sometime . . . I mean riding, that is. You and Maddie both."

She glanced at him, and then back at Moses, the corners of her mouth tugging into a smile. "Maybe we can work something out."

He returned his attention to Moses.

In the silence that followed, she went to sit on a bale of hay a few feet away, wondering if he was as unsure of what to say or do next as she was. She put her hands together and slipped them between her knees, feeling like a high school girl again, uncertainties and all. Doubts began to roll in like a thick fog.

Technically, Denise had been correct. There was a time to begin to live again. But time was the variable, and she was having second thoughts about whether or not this was her time.

Adam turned and leaned against the stall, crossing his arms. "You know, if someone had told me that afternoon when I helped you fix your flat that we'd be here together now, I never would've believed them."

She laughed. "Me neither." She took a deep breath. "I want you to know I've been thinking about what you said to me that day right before you rode off. Do you remember?"

He rubbed his chin. "I think it was something to the effect of I'm not the same guy you remembered."

"That's right. And I understand what you meant. Life has a way of changing people."

He snorted. "Yeah. Sixteen years ago, I was heading off to Ohio State on a football scholarship with a very good chance at going pro."

"I didn't know that. What happened?"

"In my third year, I tore my rotator cuff during a game. It healed, but my throwing arm wasn't the same after that. It blew any chance I had at entering the draft. A few months later, my grandfather died leaving this farm to my dad, and with the NFL no longer in my future, I finished my teaching degree and moved back to help out when I could." His gaze fell to his boots. "Alexandra wasn't too happy about it. She's a big city girl, and though she tried to make a go of it, she never quite adjusted to small town life. After we had Chloe, I thought she'd finally be truly happy, but . . . "

Compassion filled Kate to overflowing. "I'm so sorry for all you and Chloe have been through, Adam.""

He stuffed his hands in his pockets. "In case you're wondering, I don't spill my guts to just anyone. But I thought you'd understand."

Her heart thudded so wildly in her chest it echoed in her ears. "So I'm not just anyone?"

He gazed at her intently. "Far from it."

He moved from the stall to where she was sitting and knelt in front of her. She caught a hint of his cologne and it went straight to her brain. He took both of her hands in his, palm-to-palm, and intertwined his fingers with hers.

"I want to kiss you." He spoke in a low voice, his face inches from hers.

Her breath quickened. "I know."

His stare dropped to her lips. "Are you ready for that?"

Her answer was barely a whisper. "I don't know."

He leaned in and softly caressed her lips with his.

The sweet passion touched Kate to the core, leaving her breathless. She hadn't been so close to a man since Ryan died, and the longing for the intimacy she had lost was intense.

Ryan.

That stab of guilt returned with a new sense of betrayal that physically hurt. The loneliness for her husband scrambled her thoughts and feelings until nothing made sense.

As he pulled back, a tear slipped out of the corner of her eye. He reached out and wiped it away.

"Are you okay?"

She shook her head and whispered, "I'm sorry."

"Shhh." He wrapped his strong arms around her and held her for just a moment.

She leaned back and swiped her fingertips along her lower lashes. "I guess I'm not as ready to move on as I thought I was. I didn't mean to lead you on."

He stood and stuffed his hands in his pockets. "No. I'm sorry, Kate. I shouldn't have been so forward."

She got to her feet and gathered herself together. "I'll have Jane or Denise walk Maddie down here to see Moses, and then I think we're going to leave. We have to get up early for church."

He nodded. She began to walk quickly down the rows of stalls, hurrying to the stable door to escape, to flee the emotions that overwhelmed her.

"Kate!"

She stopped and glanced back at him.

"I'm not going anywhere."

Forcing a weak smile, she slipped out the door.

The tears came as soon as she hit the safety of the night, sliding down her cheeks in rivulets. She pressed her lips together as the memory of Adam's kiss made them tingle. How could she have developed such strong feelings for him when she still didn't have it in her to let go of Ryan? Why hadn't God answered her prayer and removed her attraction for him altogether? She cursed herself for not trusting her first instincts.

She shouldn't have come tonight. It was just too soon.

Yes, Denise was right. There is a time to begin to live again. But for Kate that time hadn't come yet.

"Do you think I'm crazy?" Kate asked Denise as they walked up the sidewalk in front of the best little restaurant in town.

The question plagued her the entire week after the barn dance. She knew she could count on Denise, the one person who might be able to understand the turmoil inside her heart, for an unbiased opinion. Fortunately Daryl had the boys for the weekend, and Kate's mom was more than happy to keep Madeline for the afternoon so the two women could spend a few uninterrupted hours together.

"No. I think you're normal." Denise opened the glass door to the foyer of the Bayside Café and held it for Kate.

She stepped through and returned the gesture with the door into the small restaurant. "How can I have these intense feelings for Adam and yet be so incredibly lonely for Ryan? It doesn't make sense."

"It's all a part of the moving on process."

The two women claimed a table in a deserted corner of the dining room. Kate silently opened the menu stowed between a napkin dispenser and the wall and stared blankly at the selections.

"Everything seemed so right, so natural with Adam. I thought I was ready."

"Beginning to live again doesn't necessarily mean getting involved in another relationship right away." Just then the waitress approached their table, and Denise gasped. "Maggie!"

Kate glanced up to see the young, pregnant medical receptionist she had met at Harvest Bay Family Practice.

The raven-haired young woman smiled shyly. "Hola."

"You work here?" Denise asked.

Maggie nodded. "Sí, on weekends." She placed a hand on her protruding belly. "I have to save money for de baby."

Denise's concern was obvious. "It's no wonder why your lower back has been bothering you lately. You have to rest."

"I do. At night." Maggie retrieved her pen and pad from a pocket in her red and white checked apron. "I can take your order now?"

Denise looked at Kate, who nodded, and then back at Maggie. "Sure."

When both women had ordered, Maggie waddled back to the kitchen to bring their drinks. Denise watched her go with worry in her topaz eyes.

Kate folded her hands on the table. "Everything okay?"

Denise shook her head sadly. "It's just another story of heartache and pain."

Kate waited, but Denise didn't elaborate. Instead, she turned her attention back to Kate. "Everyone has a story. Each chapter is unique, but the underlying themes of heartache and loneliness are universal."

Kate's eyes fell to her freshly painted fingernails. It was all she could do not to pick at the polish.

"I feel like I'm between chapters. I can't go back, but I can't turn the page either."

"I know."

"So how am I going to get out of this rut?"

"I think the first thing you have to do is accept the fact that your life has changed and will never be the same again."

Even though Denise spoke gently, her words stung and Kate winced. "I thought that's what I did when I moved back here."

Denise reached across the table and grabbed Kate's hand. "You took a huge, very courageous step when you moved, but that was just one step in a journey. You can't stall out now. You've got to keep moving, even if you have to crawl sometimes."

Kate nodded. "I understand."

Maggie returned, carrying two tall glasses of iced tea. "Your sandwiches will be out soon."

Denise grinned up at her. "*Gracias.*"

Maggie returned the warm smile. "*De nada.*" She moved on to another table.

Denise took a long drink of her tea, but Kate only stirred hers with the straw for several moments. Finally she took a quick sip and looked at Denise.

"You seem so confident, like you've got it all together, yet you've only been divorced for two and a half years. How long did it take you to reach this point in your journey?"

"I am only now getting to the point where I feel like I'm doing more than just putting one foot in front of the other." Denise chuckled. "And if you ask Griffin and Greyson, they'll tell you that more often than not I still don't have it all together."

"Really?"

"Really. When Daryl left me for another woman, he took every bit of my self confidence with him. I would lie awake at night, wondering what was wrong with me and why wasn't I enough for Daryl? What did she have that I didn't have? Wasn't I pretty enough or smart enough? What could I have done to have been a better wife and mother? I've had to learn to love myself again before I could learn to live again."

Kate put a hand over her heart. "Oh, Denise."

She quickly raised her hand. "No. Don't feel bad for me. I'm thankful for what I've been through. My faith has grown deeper and more meaningful. I'm stronger now than I have ever been. I appreciate the people in my life—my boys, my family, and my friends—more than I ever did before. And I'm starting to really like what I see when I look in the mirror. When you can see the love of God through your struggles and you don't need another person to fill a void, you're in a pretty good place."

"Okay, so how do I get to that place?"

"I did a lot of journaling and meditating on scripture. I printed up some of my favorite scripture passages and encouraging phrases and taped them at key places in my house like my bathroom mirror, my refrigerator, and even in my checkbook. I surrounded myself with people who really loved and supported me, especially my boys. Kids are so intuitive, you know? Maddie is probably more in tune with you than you are right now."

Kate felt like she should be taking notes.

Denise looked thoughtful for a moment. "I remember that you used to love running. You might try getting back into it, if you haven't already, or try a new hobby altogether. Maybe you could volunteer your time with an organization you feel passionate about. Sometimes by helping others in need you'll find you're healing yourself."

Kate soaked it all in, feeling hopeful, but slightly overwhelmed. The mixture of emotions must have shown on her face because Denise reached across the table and patted her hand.

"Just take it one step at a time. You're on a journey, and as long as you're moving, you're making progress."

"It's hard to be patient."

"I know. Believe me, I know, but Psalms 27:14 says, 'Wait on the Lord; be of good courage, and He shall strengthen your heart; wait, I say, on the Lord!' I recite that verse to myself daily."

Kate repeated the verse to herself as Maggie approached their table once again, this time carrying a plate in each hand. She hesitated a moment, a pained look on her face, and then set the women's orders on the table in front of them.

Denise reached out to her. "Are you okay?"

She forced a weak smile. "*Sí.* De baby just kicked. Maybe he will play *fútbol.*" She looked from Kate to Denise. "Can I get you anything more?"

Kate shook her head, and Denise said, "We're fine, but maybe you should go sit down."

"*Sí,* I will. Right after I clean that table." She turned slowly and cautiously moved toward a table in another corner of the dining room.

Denise watched her go, and then picked up her chicken salad croissant. "There's one more thing you need to know."

"What's that?"

"When it comes time for a relationship, don't miss out on what's right under your nose."

Kate swallowed a bite of her turkey club. "I'm sorry. You lost me."

"Maybe Adam isn't the one."

"Then who are you talking about?"

"Nathan."

Kate nearly choked. "Nathan is my brother-in-law. I can't think of him romantically."

"Well, he certainly thinks of you that way."

"Excuse me?"

"Last weekend when he was here, it was written all over his face. Besides, why else would he consider leaving his practice at Vanderbilt to join Doc Brewster?"

Kate blinked. "What did you say?"

"Didn't he tell you? Oh, no. Maybe it was going to be a surprise. He faxed his résumé to our office early Monday morning, and Doc Brewster already scheduled an interview with him in two weeks over Labor Day weekend."

Kate stared at Denise in shock. She didn't know whether to be happy at the idea that Nathan might be moving to Harvest Bay, angry that she had to hear this good news from Denise, or appalled that Nathan might be interested in her romantically.

Suddenly a huge crash sounded from the other side of the dining room. Kate and Denise looked up in time to see Maggie hunched over, holding her belly. A puddle of liquid formed on the floor beneath the skirt of her baby doll dress, and broken glasses and dishes lay scattered around her feet.

"Maggie!" Denise stood up with such force her chair tipped backward. She rushed to Maggie's side with Kate right behind her.

"What in the world is all the commotion?" Audrey Valentine, the stout, platinum-haired owner of the café, ran out of the kitchen, wiping her hands on a towel.

"Maggie's water just broke. I'm going to take her to the hospital. Will you page Doc Brewster? He'll want to know." Denise recited Doc Brewster's pager number from memory.

"Oh, my goodness! Oh, my goodness! We're having a baby!" the North's version of Paula Deen half screamed as she grabbed the phone.

Denise put one arm around Maggie, and Kate flanked her on the other side. "I'm coming too."

Maggie looked at Kate and then at Denise with fear in her young eyes. "It's too soon. My baby cannot be born yet."

Denise spoke calmly, soothingly, while they moved toward the door. "Babies born six weeks early can be perfectly healthy. You've got a very good doctor who will know just what to do to keep you and your baby safe, and I promise I'll be right there with you. I won't leave you through this, okay?"

Maggie nodded, and they slowly made their way down the sidewalk. "Is there someone we should call?" Kate asked, feeling helpless.

Denise shot her a sad look over Maggie's head. "No."

Suddenly all Kate's troubles seemed unimportant compared to Maggie and her unborn child. She hurried ahead to open the car door, praying over and over, *Please, God, let Maggie and her baby be all right. And help me to know what I can do to help them.*

⁂

Several hours later, Kate gently rocked the tiny bundle snuggly wrapped in a blue receiving blanket, while Denise dozed in a recliner. She moved the blanket away from the baby's ruddy little face.

"Oh, Maggie, he's so precious."

Maggie smiled wearily from her hospital bed. "Gracias."

"What's his name?"

"Justin Armando Martinez."

Moisture formed in Kate's eyes. "I think that's perfect."

Earlier, Denise had pulled her aside and quickly briefed her on Maggie's situation. The baby's father, Justin McGregor, died serving in the military in Iraq. He'd never even known about the baby. Maggie's father, Armando Martinez, didn't hide his disappointment that his daughter was an unwed mother, but supported her as best as a migrant worker could.

As Kate stared down into baby Justin's angelic face, she wondered what the future held in store for him. Would he be a soldier like his daddy? Or work the land like his grandpa? With a mother like Maggie, he could accomplish anything he set his mind to, Kate believed, and she was determined to help them both in any way she could.

"Do you have everything you need—diapers, formula, clothes?"

"*No sé.* It is such a surprise that he's here already, but he's healthy. That is all that matters."

"Don't hesitate to ask if something comes up, okay? You're going to be a great mother, but you don't have to do it alone."

"*Muchas gracias.*"

Kate could almost see the weight coming off Maggie's shoulders. It was at that moment that she realized what she had to do, not just for Maggie, but for Denise, Adam, her community, and for herself.

She wasn't exactly sure how encouraging she could be to others when she still wasn't completely comfortable with her own situation, but she had to try. Maybe they would all help each other. And maybe along the way, as Denise had suggested earlier, Kate would become whole again.

CHAPTER

Ten

$\mathcal{N}$athan stood at the sink in his large kitchen, washing the few dishes he'd dirtied at supper. Of course he had a dishwasher, the best make and model money could buy, but it would have taken him days to fill it all by himself. He gazed out the window at the sun, now dipping low at the horizon.

"Maybe my days of eating supper alone are numbered." He shook his head while he rinsed a small sauce pan and set it in the rack to drain. "Maybe my days of talking to myself are numbered too."

He couldn't believe how things were turning out. He grabbed a dish towel and started drying the dishes in the rack, still marveling at the series of events that were surely revealing God's plan.

Just then the phone rang. He dried his hands, picked up his cordless, and checked the caller ID. Recognizing Kate's cell phone number, he fumbled with the phone as he pressed the talk button.

"Hello?"

"Hey, Nathan."

"Hi, Kate. What's up?"

"Why don't you tell me?"

He noticed the sharpness in her voice, and his smile faded slightly. He cleared his throat.

"Nothing's up. Why?"

"That's funny. It seems to me that moving to Harvest Bay and joining Doc Brewster's medical practice should be something."

He exhaled slowly. "You found out."

"Why would you want to keep something like this from me?"

"I swear I never meant to. I just didn't want to jump the gun."

Her tone softened. "I still wish I would've heard the news from you first."

"You're right. I'm sorry."

"And I'm sorry I snapped at you. I've been on an emotional rollercoaster ride today."

He pulled out a bar stool and made himself comfortable at the counter. "Why? What happened?"

She proceeded to recap her afternoon. "So Denise and I were getting ready to have lunch, and Maggie's water broke right in the middle of the Bayside Café!" She filled him in on Maggie's situation. "My heart went out to her. I felt like I had to do something for her and all of the other single parents in our community, so I made the decision to lead that single-parent support group I told you about."

"That's great!"

"I'm a little nervous. I mean, teaching children is one thing, but leading a support group for single parents is an entirely different ballgame. But as long as Pastor Ben goes for it, Denise has agreed to be a co-leader, which takes some of the pressure off."

"Co-leader or not, you'll be great."

"And you are a great brother-in-law."

Was it his imagination or did she just put extra emphasis on "brother-in-law"?

"Thanks for listening and for your vote of confidence. I'm really glad you might be moving to Harvest Bay. It'll be great to have you right up the road again."

"I hope it all works out."

He could already imagine being close to Kate again, able to see her and Madeline on an everyday basis. He eagerly anticipated the holidays—spending time with Kate and her family, making her see that he was the one who could help her learn to love again.

It would happen. It was all just a matter of time.

⁂

Kate fidgeted in her pew. Was it just her or did Pastor Ben seem to have an extra long sermon this morning? She glanced around her to see if anyone else had lost interest.

Nope. Just her.

All she could think about was Maggie, baby Justin, and the program she and Denise had spent several hours planning in Maggie's hospital room while cuddling the sleeping mother's infant son. Still somewhat unsure of her abilities as a leader, Kate bubbled with uncontainable enthusiasm at the possible difference it could make in their community.

"Let's look in the book of Galatians, chapter six, verse two."

Pastor Ben's voice cut into her thoughts. She obediently flipped her Bible open as he began to read.

" 'Bear one another's burdens, and so fulfill the law of Christ.' Ladies and gentlemen, this is what Christianity is all about. God never intended for us to walk this world alone, and Christ did not die for us to keep His love all to ourselves."

Kate reread the passage. *Bear one another's burdens, and so fulfill the law of Christ.* She swallowed the lump that was beginning to rise in her throat while the black words on the thin ivory pages morphed into images of Maggie, Denise, and Adam—all single parents who had quickly impacted Kate's life.

"In that same chapter, Paul goes on to say, beginning at verse nine, 'And let us not grow weary while doing good, for in due season we shall reap if we do not lose heart. Therefore, as we have opportunity, let us do good to all, especially to those who are of the household of faith.' "

He looked up from his Bible and scanned the congregation. "There are opportunities all around us, folks, on the other side of the world, in our own neighborhoods, and every place in between. The question you have to ask yourself is what kind of a harvest do you want? I encourage you this week to seek out opportunities to share the love of Christ. You will never regret it."

Two hymns and several prayers later, the service ended, and people began filing out. Kate knew Pastor Ben would be tied up for several minutes greeting the congregation.

"Can we count on you and Maddie for lunch today, honey?" Kate's mother asked when they stood to leave.

"Of course! I wouldn't want to break our new tradition. And actually . . . "

"What is it, Katydid?"

"Would you mind taking Maddie home with you? I'll be right behind you. I have to talk with Pastor Ben for a few minutes, and I don't want her to have to wait on me."

Kate's mother grinned. "We'd be happy to. It's no trouble at all. Take as much time as you need."

"Thanks, Mom. I'll go get her from children's church and walk her out to your van. By that time Pastor Ben should be in his office."

As she had guessed, he made it back to his office before she got there. She timidly tapped on the wide open office door.

He looked up from his computer. "Well, hello, Kate! This is a nice surprise. I wasn't expecting you this morning."

"I know. I'm sorry, but this will only take a minute."

He stood and came around his desk. "It's okay. Come on in. What's on your mind?"

She took a few steps into his office. "The single-parent support group."

"I see." He pulled his office door shut and motioned for Kate to have a seat. "Have you made a decision?"

"I have." She took a deep breath. "Something happened yesterday afternoon that has made me want to give it a try." She related Maggie's story.

He leaned forward in his chair. "First of all, does Maggie have any immediate needs that you know of?"

"I really don't know, but I can find out. I don't think she'll be up to cooking for a while."

He nodded. "I'll make a few phone calls this afternoon. I'm sure some of our ladies will be more than happy to provide daily meals until she gets back on her feet."

That would be great!"

"Now back to you."

Kate's wide smile faltered.

"Are you sure you want this leadership role?"

She thought a moment, then her lips curled into a mischievous smile. "This is my opportunity. I'll regret it if I don't take it."

He laughed. "At least I know someone listened to my sermon." Then he sobered. "This is your opportunity, and you'll be blessed by it."

"I just have one request."

"I'm listening."

"I'd like to have a co-leader."

He rubbed his chin. "I think that would be fine. Do you have someone in mind?"

"Yes. Denise Golden, the medical receptionist at Doc Brewster's office. I've already talked to her, and she's agreed to do it."

He chuckled. "Then I guess it's settled. I've already started spreading the word in our congregation, but we'll need to start advertising around town. We want to reach the entire community, which includes those in other denominations as well as the unchurched."

"Denise attends Faith Lutheran. She can advertise it there. I'm sure Dalila Styles and Ava Garner will be more than happy to put up fliers at the flower shop and the library. Also, I can ask my best friend, Jane Garner, what the school board's policy is regarding promoting an organization unrelated to school."

"That's a start. Let's make plans to meet next weekend to pin down the fine details."

"That sounds good."

"Shall we close this meeting in prayer?"

"Definitely."

Kate bowed her head and folded her hands, and while Pastor Ben prayed God's blessings upon her and their efforts to serve their community, she felt a familiar warmth, one she hadn't felt in a long time, radiate through her body and concentrate in her heart.

Leaving his office, she practically floated down the hallway of the administrative wing, but nearly crash landed when she reached the lobby and her gaze fell on Adam. It had been a week and a day since the barn dance debacle, not enough time for the humiliation of the way she left—or the memory of his sweet kiss—to begin fade. He strategically stood between her and the exit, so dodging him and making a break for it was out of the question.

"Hi." He took a step toward her.

She worked her mouth into something of a smile. "I see you're waiting for Chloe."

"Nope. She's outside on the playground." He dropped his gaze. "You're the one I've been waiting for."

In some death-defying, acrobatic feat, Kate's heart plummeted to her stomach, and then catapulted into her throat, making it impossible for her to even squeak a response.

"I want to apologize for what happened last Saturday night."

She swallowed hard, forcing her heart back to its place in her chest. "I—I'm the one who should apologize."

He shook his head. "I never meant for it to go that far, and I certainly never meant to upset you. But I want you to know you're the only one I've been this close to since Alexandra."

"You don't have to tell me this."

He shoved his hands in his pockets. "Doesn't everyone deserve the truth?"

She eyed him, careful not to linger too long on his amazing midsummer-cloudless-sky-blue eyes, for fear of getting lost in the depths of them, never to be recovered again. "Maybe." Her gaze fell, right along with her spirits. "But that doesn't mean that everyone is ready to deal with the truth." She shrugged. "I think sometimes things are better left unsaid."

"Oh." He studied her a moment longer. "In that case, I guess I'll just see you around."

She watched him turn and stride away. She ached to go after him, but what good would it do? Her brain agreed with Denise, even if her heart didn't. She had to get reacquainted with herself before she got involved with anyone, and Adam would just be a distraction.

She clutched her purse to her side and lifted her chin as she started for the parking lot. It was settled. She had to avoid him for as long as it took. After all, out of sight, out of mind.

CHAPTER
Eleven

"It seems as though fate has brought us together yet again." Adam leaned against the doorway of Kate's classroom, his hands shoved in the pockets of his warm-up pants to hide his sweaty palms.

"Hello, Adam." She laid her pen on the paper she was grading and sat back in her chair. "What can I do for you?"

He moved farther into the room, leaned on one of the student desks, and crossed his arms. "I should be asking you that question since you're my daughter's teacher this year."

"Funny how things work out, isn't it?"

He nodded. "Who'd have thought?" Actually, he'd almost laughed out loud when he received Chloe's class assignment a couple weeks earlier.

Worry creased her brow. "You aren't here to get her, are you? I received a note that said Chloe was to go home with her Aunt Kennedy every day during football season."

"That's right. I practically live in my office at this time of year."

"That must be hard on Chloe."

He shrugged. "I suppose."

"So are you here for a report?"

"A report?"

She cleared her throat. "Chloe had a great week. Of course, I think it helps that she and Emma are together, but regardless, she will be a wonderful student."

"Thanks. That's good to know. So how was your first week?"

"Hectic, but good. Fourth grade is quite a bit different from second. What about you?"

"Busy. I only have three classes this semester, but we've got a tough football schedule that I'm trying to prepare for."

"Speaking of which, don't you have a game to get ready for?"

"We're ready for tonight, and the boys don't have to report until five-thirty on game night."

She stood, came around the front of her desk, and leaned against it. "If you don't mind my asking, why are you here?"

He forced himself not to ogle her, but in her black slacks and pink short-sleeved sweater, she was more beautiful than the last time he saw her at church three weeks ago. He shifted his attention to his running shoes to better concentrate on the matter at hand.

"I saw you run by the football field after school the past couple of days."

"I guess you could say I'm trying to get back in a routine."

He glanced back up and got pulled in by her jade eyes. "I thought I'd join you today. I mean, that is, if you don't mind."

She returned to her place behind her desk and began straightening a few papers. "Sorry, but I'm taking a day off today. I've got to leave shortly for the airport."

He tried to hide his disappointment. "Are you and Maddie going somewhere for Labor Day weekend?"

"No. I'm picking Nathan up. He has an interview with Doc Brewster on Monday. He might be moving to Harvest Bay. Isn't that great?"

Adam felt like he'd been hit in the chest by Muhammad Ali. Sure he liked the guy . . . when his permanent residence was five hundred miles away. It didn't take a genius to figure out what would happen if Nathan ended up moving to Harvest Bay.

"Wow. Yeah. That's great. Just great."

Kate eyed him questioningly.

"How about tomorrow? Will you be running tomorrow?"

"Probably at some point, though I can't say when. Maddie's first soccer game is at eleven o'clock, and later on we're having supper with Mom and Daddy."

"Maybe next week then."

She slid the papers into her bag and looked up at him. "Why the sudden urgency to go running?"

He shrugged. "Just thought you'd like some company. You know, they say you get a better workout with a buddy."

She raised her eyebrows at him. "And you think you can keep up with me, buddy?"

He grinned. "I guess we'll have to wait and see."

Their gazes locked for a moment, and he searched for a sign that he wasn't the only one experiencing an emotional surge. But she was a closed book.

"Well, I'll let you get back to work. It won't be long and you'll have to go meet Nathan." He started toward the door.

"Hey, Adam?"

He turned. "Yeah?"

Kate took a few steps toward him. "I'm going to be leading a single parent support group on Tuesday evenings at church. It's open to all single parents in the community. I just wanted you to know."

He stared at her for several moments, wondering what exactly she was trying to tell him.

Isn't a support group for people who have a problem? So I'm not a candidate for Father of the Year. So what? Big deal. Chloe and I are doing just fine . . . aren't we?

He narrowed his eyes slightly. "You told me I was a wonderful father."

"You are, but even the best parent can use a little help every once in a while."

"Thanks, Kate, but I've got a pretty full plate right now as it is."

"Just in case you change you mind, the first meeting is next Tuesday at seven o'clock, and we'll have child care, so you can bring Chloe."

"Like I said, I think I'll pass."

"Would you mind spreading the word over at the high school?"

"Sure. See ya."

The walk down the hall, across the street, and through the high school to his office seemed to take a fraction of the time the walk over had taken. He sank into his chair and replayed their encounter in his mind as if it were game film that he needed to study and analyze. Trying not to dwell on his obvious inadequacies as a father, he gently squeezed his temples with the thumb and middle finger of his left hand.

A support group? I don't have time. I have to come up with a fail-proof game plan and quick. I'm not about to lose Kate.

⁂

It was a beautiful day for a soccer game—slightly overcast with a faint breeze. Not only was it ideal weather for

Madeline's debut with her new team, but with the temperature topping out in the mid seventies, it was cool enough for Grandpa Clayton, who couldn't tolerate the summer heat like he once could. He sat in a lawn chair next to Kate's.

"I'm glad you're here." She reached over and placed her hand on his.

He squeezed her fingers and winked at her from behind his bifocals as the breeze rustled his thinning white hair.

She glanced past him at her mom, dad, Elizabeth, and Elijah. Everyone was there . . . except for Ryan. The dull ache in her chest returned. She was beginning to understand that no matter how much time had passed, or how much her heart had healed, she would always long for Ryan at every special event in Madeline's life.

"Thinking of Ryan?"

She turned to see Nathan watching her, a tender expression on his face. "How'd you know?"

"Because I am too."

Her lips curved upward appreciatively, and when she turned her attention back to the field, her mind drifted to her conversation with Denise.

"*He certainly thinks of you that way . . . it was written all over his face.*" She shook her head. *Denise is way off base.* She glanced sideways at Nathan to find him watching her with a subtle gleam of affection in his eyes. *Isn't she?*

She refocused her attention on the group of seven to nine-year-old girls warming up on the field. Madeline, Jessica, Emma, and Chloe had formed a square and were passing the ball lightly back and forth.

She had to admit, having Nathan there was almost like having Ryan with them. It comforted and soothed her, almost like a Band-aid on a wound that would never completely heal. She hugged herself tightly. *Maybe . . .*

"Hey, guys! Sorry I'm late," a voice called from a few yards away, and the hair stood up on the back of Kate's neck.

"Hey, Adam," Jane responded from Nathan's left. "It's about time. Ian started sweating bullets five minutes ago. He dreads the thought of coaching without an assistant again this season."

Kate's eyes widened. "Assistant?"

Adam grinned. "Ian should know by now he can count on me." He turned to Nathan. "Hey, man, it's good to see you again."

Nathan stood and shook his hand. "Great game last night. You've got some talented players."

Adam glanced down at Kate. "You came?"

Her heart banged wildly in her chest, but she wouldn't let him get to her. "Who in Harvest Bay doesn't go to the game on Friday night?"

"Oh. Right. Well, I'd better get out on the field." He jogged a few steps onto the field, then turned. "What do you say? Ice cream at Frosty Jack's after the game?"

"Count us in," Jane answered before Kate could even open her mouth.

Adam smiled and dashed to Ian's aid. From across the field Kate heard Chloe shout, "Daddy!" and Madeline and Jessica called in unison, "Hi, Adam!"

He gave Chloe a big hug and tousled Madeline's hair, unknowingly tousling Kate's heart as well.

As the soccer game got underway, Kate forced Adam to the back of her mind and concentrated on her daughter. Kate came out of her chair, hands high in the air, when Madeline scored the first goal of the game, and her heart soared when she heard the praise her little girl received from Ian, her team-mates, and especially from Adam.

Forty-five minutes later, sitting at a picnic table at Frosty Jack's, Kate silently watched Madeline interact with her new teammates and coaches.

"She looks really happy," Nathan observed from his place on the bench beside her.

She nodded, wishing she could experience the same joy, but it just wasn't that easy. Nothing was easy anymore.

She glanced at Adam wondering how she was going to keep her distance from him now. Obviously the out of sight, out of mind concept wasn't working.

Teaching his daughter was one thing. Chloe was a good girl and, from what Kate saw so far, an excellent student. She could feasibly keep communication to a minimum. However, now she had no choice but to see him every Saturday for the next nine weeks. And what was even worse was that she would have to watch him bond with Madeline.

Kate sighed. Thank heavens he wouldn't be going to the single-parent support group.

Nathan wanted to arrive at least ten minutes early for his eleven o'clock interview with Doc Brewster. He checked his Rolex as he ascended the porch steps of the converted Victorian home. A quarter till. He was doing better than he'd thought. He turned the handle and stepped through the front door of Harvest Bay Family Practice.

"Hello, Dr. Sterling. You're early," Denise greeted him warmly from her place behind the window.

He grinned, his nerves calming momentarily. "Hello, again, Denise." He rested his arms on the windowsill and leaned in slightly. "Working on Labor Day?"

"Since Maggie started her maternity leave early we don't have a temp yet, and the paperwork piles up. But I'll be out of here before lunch."

"Kate told me about Maggie. How's she doing?"

"Pretty good, I think. We had a shower for her last Sunday, and she got a ton of stuff—all the necessities plus some. And several of the ladies from Kate's church are still bringing her meals, so from what I can tell she doesn't have too much to worry about besides adjusting to motherhood."

Nathan nodded. "Glad to hear it."

She reached over to pick up the phone's receiver, nestled it between her ear and shoulder, and punched a three digit extension. "I'll let Doc Brewster know you're here."

It was then that Nathan noticed the two boys sitting in the clerical office with her. He thought he recognized them from the barn dance. After she hung up the phone, he tipped his head toward them.

"These must be your boys."

She nodded. "That one over there with his nose in the book is Griffin, and this one playing the portable playstation is Greyson."

" 'Sup?" the boys responded in unison, giving him a nod.

Denise rolled her eyes. "Please excuse their bad manners. They aren't thrilled to be here with me on their day off." She leaned in closer and lowered her voice. "Plus they just came home from spending the weekend with their father, who apparently doesn't reinforce appropriate behavior."

"Sorry, Mom," Greyson said looking up from his hand-held video game. He shifted his gaze to Nathan. "Nice to meet you."

"You, too. What game are you playing?"

"Madden '08."

"Cool game."

"Way cool. Wanna take a look?" Greyson started to get to his feet, but Nathan held up his hand.

"Maybe after I see Doc Brewster." He evaluated the stocky preteen. "So do you play football?"

Greyson puffed his chest out a little. "Harvest Bay junior varsity."

"He's one of the few seventh-graders to make the team," Denise added a tone of pride in her voice.

"Really? What position?"

"Fullback."

Nathan smirked. "Are you any good?"

"Coach Sullivan says I could be starting varsity in a couple of years."

"Keep working hard, and I'll bet he's right."

Greyson went back to his portable playstation, and Nathan turned to the quiet older boy. "What are you reading?"

Griffin didn't look up. *The Odyssey.*

Nathan arched his eyebrows. "School assignment?"

Looking mildly annoyed, Griffin closed the book using his finger to mark his place. "Ninth grade honors English. Our semester project is to read *The Odyssey*, then write an essay comparing and contrasting it to the movie *O Brother, Where Art Thou?*"

Nathan's eyes shot to Denise, who was watching her son affectionately, then turned his attention back to Griffin. "I'm impressed. Hasn't school just started?"

Griffin shrugged, his longish bangs falling into his eyes. "Yeah, so? I wanted to get ahead."

"So he can spend the rest of the semester working on his biology grade. He already made a D on a quiz," Greyson interjected, not looking up from his video game, where his thumbs where going a mile a minute.

Griffin threw a wadded up piece of paper at his brother. "Shut up!"

Denise grabbed the paper ball before Greyson could launch it back. "Enough, boys!"

Sensing Denise's frustration, Nathan stifled a chuckle at the display of brotherly love. He guessed that it wasn't easy sharing parental duties with someone in a separate house, living a separate life. He was pretty sure it wasn't easy on the boys either, moving back and forth from one set of rules and expectations to another.

He cleared his throat. "Don't let it get you down. Biology is tough."

Griffin snorted and returned to his book. "Easy for you to say. You're a doctor."

"Now I am, but when I was your age I was tutored for a semester in biology . . . and algebra."

Griffin's eyes widened. "Nuh uh."

Nathan glanced at Denise, who seemed interested in this new information, while Greyson pretended not to care.

Nathan nodded. "It's true. People automatically think that in order to be a doctor you have to be some sort of a brainiac, but more than anything else you have to have the drive and determination." He paused. "It's sounds cliché, but it's true. You can accomplish anything you want to, but that's the key. You have to want it."

Griffin stared at him for a few moments, and Nathan thought he saw a spark of hope in the young teenager's eyes. But then he turned back to his book, and it was gone.

"It's not that easy."

Nathan held Denise's gaze for a moment before she gave a tiny shrug and silently returned to her paperwork.

He decided to reach out one last time, mostly because he really did owe Denise after the way she'd been so kind to him, but also because, for some strange reason he couldn't explain, he felt a connection to this kid. Maybe he recognized the pain of not having a dad around all the time. Maybe he could see a little of himself in Griffin. Or maybe he saw Griffin as a challenge, and he loved a good challenge.

He looked at his watch. Five till. Doc Brewster would be out any second.

"Tell you what. If this interview goes well and I end up moving here, I'll tutor you in biology."

Griffin snapped his head up.

"Maybe study for a while, and then shoot some hoops. You do have a basketball court in this town, right?"

Griffin looked from his mom to Nathan. "What's in it for you? You don't even know me."

Greyson had stopped playing his portable playstation and was intently following the conversation.

"I don't have to know you to know that you're worth it."

Doc Brewster stepped into the waiting area. "Dr. Sterling."

Nathan shook his hand. "Hello. Thanks for seeing me on a holiday."

"Don't mention it. It was convenient for me too." Doc Brewster turned and motioned for Nathan to follow. "My office is down the hall. I'll give you a tour on the way."

Nathan took a step forward, but then quickly turned and found Denise's golden brown eyes. "It was great seeing you again and meeting your sons."

Denise smiled. "You, too, and thanks."

He moved away from the window to follow Doc Brewster but was still within earshot when Griffin muttered, "I'll bet we never see that guy again."

As they made their way through the building, those words fueled Nathan determination to get this position.

Entering his office, Doc Brewster motioned to a leather chair and, while Nathan made himself as comfortable as his nerves would allow, moved around his desk to sit across from him. He picked up a pen and positioned it over a legal pad.

"Tell me a little bit about yourself, Dr. Sterling."

Nathan detailed his academic and professional history.

Doc Brewster studied him for a moment. "And your family?"

Nathan looked down. What if Doc Brewster wanted a family man for his practice?

"Kate and Maddie are really the only family I have."

Doc Brewster rubbed his chin. "Seems like a young, single guy like yourself would have it made in a successful, big city practice like Vanderbilt. I certainly can't pay you Vanderbilt money."

Nathan nodded. "I realize that. This isn't about the money." He cleared his throat. "I hope I'm not being too forward, Doc Brewster, but are you a Christian?"

Doc Brewster set the pen on the legal pad and folded his hands on top of the desk. "Yes."

"Then hopefully you will understand that, as unreasonable as it sounds to make this move, I feel very strongly that God is leading me here."

Doc Brewster nodded, picked up Nathan's resume, and scanned it. "Well, there's no doubt you're qualified." He looked across the desk at Nathan. "Tell me why I should hire you."

Nathan had known this request was coming. It was a standard interview question, and he was prepared with an elaborate, rehearsed statement about how his experience and work ethic would prove to be an asset to this practice. But when he opened his mouth to answer the words wouldn't come. He stared at Doc Brewster, very aware that he could still blow this interview.

And then Griffin would be right. He exhaled. *God, give me the words to say.*

"Dr. Sterling?"

Nathan swallowed. "I've spent the past ten years treating illnesses, and that used to be enough. But now I want to treat people." He searched Doc Brewster's face for a sign that he understood what he was trying to convey.

A knowing gleam danced in Doc Brewster's eyes. "That's why I started this practice twenty-five years ago. It hasn't always been easy, but I wouldn't have it any other way."

Nathan couldn't keep his lips from curling upward. "If you hire me, I believe we could be an answer to each other's prayers."

An answering smile tugged at the corners of Doc Brewster's mouth. "Is that your professional opinion?"

Nathan nodded. "It is."

Doc Brewster's smile widened. "Well, Dr. Sterling, I think you may be right."

Twelve

Kate arranged the chairs in one of the adult Sunday school rooms, battling the questions that had tormented her all day.

What if this support group doesn't go over well?

Everyone she had talked to thought it was a great idea and no doubt needed in their community. But what if the people who would really benefit from it already had a full plate, like Adam?

Or what if we get an overwhelming response, and we need different accommodations?

She smiled. That would be a good problem, but with the next thought her smile fell.

Worse yet, what if we get a room full tonight, the meeting flops, and no one comes back next week?

Her shoulders drooped. She glanced at the clock on the wall. It was a quarter after six. Over the course of fifteen minutes, she'd arranged the chairs, gone over her material, rearranged the chairs, laid out some refreshments on a table in the corner of the room, and finally rearranged the chairs again, settling on the typical circle formation.

She took a deep breath in an attempt to calm her frazzled nerves. Denise would be there soon, and that would help. In the meantime, she spontaneously decided to do the only other thing that could possibly help her.

She left the Sunday school room and headed down the education wing. Nearing the end of the corridor, she could hear Madeline's laughter mingling with music in the large recreation room, and she paused for a moment at the double doors. Cassie Ground, the high school senior who had been highly recommended by Pastor Ben to handle child care, was doing a silly dance to a fun Bible song. Madeline tried to follow along, but kept collapsing in fits of laughter.

Kate stood there only a moment before Madeline spotted her, jumped up, and ran over to give her a hug. "Hi, Mama!"

"It looks like you're having a good time."

"I am. Miss Cassie is so fun, and she's really pretty too. Can she babysit me at home?"

Kate looked up as Cassie strolled over to them, her brown ponytail swinging, a friendly spirit flowing from her. Kate smiled down at her daughter.

"Maybe someday, but for now you can play with her here, okay?"

"Okay. C'mon, Miss Cassie! Let's dance some more!" Madeline raced off to where the CD player sat.

Kate turned to Cassie. "Thanks again for being here. I'm sure there are plenty of other places you'd like to be on Tuesday evenings."

"It's no problem. I love kids. After I ~~graduation~~ graduate, I want to go to college and major in elementary education." There was a twinkle in her in her eyes, a spark of ambition that Kate recognized.

Kate smiled. "I'm sure you'll be a great teacher."

"Thanks." Cassie turned and hurried over to Madeline.

Kate watched the pair a moment longer, then continued around the corner and down the hall to the sanctuary.

She pulled open a door, slipped inside, and walked up the aisle in the eerie silence. The late afternoon sun streamed in through the large stained glass windows, and two spot lights illuminated the mammoth cross that hung just behind the altar.

She slid into the first pew and just sat there, staring at the cross. The burdens it represented were so great in comparison to hers, and yet at the moment she was so overwhelmed she couldn't even think straight.

She stayed there for what seemed like a long time, perfectly still, waiting for peace to shower down around her like a gentle rain, but the worry and fear never faded.

"I . . . I need Your help tonight. I don't know if I can do this without You." She sighed deeply. Her shoulders sagged. "I came here to find You, but I still feel alone."

"Maybe you're looking in the wrong place."

She nearly jumped out of her skin. She put a hand over her racing heart and turned as Pastor Ben side-stepped into the pew behind her. "You scared me."

"Expecting someone of a . . . " he glanced heavenward, then back at her with a light expression, adding, "higher stature."

She offered a weak, lopsided grin, which fell along with her gaze a second later. "No. Hoping, maybe, but not expecting."

He leaned forward and rested his forearms on the back of Kate's pew. "Sometimes we can see God all around us, everywhere we look. And sometimes we have to search deep inside ourselves."

She stared at him. She didn't want to admit to him what she had confessed to Grandpa Clayton and Elizabeth, but the time had come for her to be honest with her pastor. "I don't think I'll find Him there either."

"Are you sure? Because I found Him there."

She scrunched her brow in confusion. "I don't understand how. It's kind of been a while since I've experienced a close relationship with the Lord." She paused, then quietly added, "Or any kind of a relationship at all."

"So you still haven't done what I told you to do the day I asked you to consider leading the support group."

"What do you mean? What haven't I done?"

"Search your heart. He's there, Kate. You can ignore Him, try to run and hide from Him, even convince yourself that He's not there, but He promised us that he would never leave or forsake us." He tipped his head to the side. "Kind of like how you promised not to leave Maggie when she was going through labor. Maggie still had to go through it. You couldn't take the pain away, but you were there to hold her hand, to encourage her, to make sure she knew she wasn't alone. And when it was all said and done, something beautiful came out of what she endured."

Kate pondered his analogy, tears of understanding filling her eyes.

He watched her with an expression of deep compassion. "I know it's hard when things don't make sense and you have so many questions, but you just have to trust Him, Kate, and you will end up with something beautiful, too."

She swiped at a tiny tear that had managed to escape over the ledge of her lashes. "Like this support group?"

"I think this is just the start of the blessings you'll receive."

She gave him a small smile. "Thanks."

"Anytime, and I mean that. I'm always here for you."

She nodded and gathered herself together. "I guess I'd better get back to the Sunday school room. Denise is probably already here and wondering where I am." She stepped out of the pew.

"Call or e-mail me tomorrow and let me know how it went. I'm sure it'll be great."

"I will, and I hope so." She hurried down the aisle and out the back doors. Retracing her steps through the building, she poked her head into the recreation room. Madeline and Cassie were playing a card game with Greyson, while Griffin sat a few feet away reading.

"Go fish!" Madeline shouted, bursting into a fit of giggles when Greyson grudgingly drew a card from the "fish pond."

Kate grinned and moved on. Reaching the designated adult Sunday school room, she found Denise sitting with her women's devotional Bible open in her lap, poring over the page, yellow Post-it notes sticking out here and there.

"Sorry I wasn't here when you came in. I guess you could say I was trying to acquire some last-minute inspiration."

Denise stood and embraced her. "It's okay. I was doing the same thing, actually. Is everything set?"

"I think so," Kate answered going over her mental checklist for the umpteenth time. "How about on your end?"

"All set. Information packets are on the table next to the nametags."

"Hola, chicas."

They turned to see Maggie coming through the doorway with a diaper bag slung over her shoulder and pushing a stroller.

"Hola, Maggie! How's that angel boy?" Kate hurried across the room to take a peek at the now three-and-a-half-week-old, while Denise gathered a nametag, a stapled packet, and a pen for Maggie.

Maggie gave Kate a weary grin. "*Muy bien*. Sleeping much better, *gracias a Dios*."

"May I?" Kate held her hands poised above the stroller ready to snatch the baby up, and the young mother nodded. Kate reached in, lifted Justin out of the stroller, and positioned him in the crook of her arm. "He must be eating well. He's a little bigger every time I see him."

Maggie looked adoringly at her baby. "*Sí*, he is."

Kate turned her attention to Maggie. "What about you? How are you doing?"

"*Bien*. I am learning."

Denise handed Maggie her paperwork. "Don't feel bad, sweetie. My boys are twelve and fourteen, and I'm still learning."

Kate kissed the top of Justin's soft little head, inhaling his sweet baby scent. She could have spent the rest of the evening cuddling him, but just then an unfamiliar man appeared in the doorway, reminding her that she had a bigger job to see to.

"Are you here for the single parent support group?" she asked and the man nodded. "You're at the right place. Come on in. Denise will get you a nametag and some other information to fill out." Kate handed Justin back to Maggie as two more ladies filed in.

A few minutes later, at seven o'clock, no more guests had come. Kate couldn't help feeling bitterly disappointed when she glanced around the room at all the empty chairs, wondering if she'd made a mistake committing herself to leading the support group. A little sigh escaped her lips. Hoping no one noticed, she quickly cleared her throat.

"Good evening, and welcome. I'm so glad you came tonight, and I pray that you are blessed by the time we spend together."

She had practiced this introduction over and over in front of her bathroom mirror, and now she was afraid it sounded too rehearsed. She had a seat facing the doorway and tried to relax.

"Let's start by going around the circle and introducing ourselves. Tell us your name, how many children you have, and anything else you feel comfortable sharing with our group. I'll go first."

Her gaze swept around the circle and froze when it reached the doorway. There stood Adam.

He wore a T-shirt, warm-up pants, and an expression of uncertainty. "Sorry I'm late. Practice ran over."

She could only stare. Her brain was going a mile a minute, zooming right past the exit for vocalizing thoughts. She had been nervous before, when she thought he wouldn't come. Now her nerves had shifted into overdrive.

What if this support group failed? Adam would witness the whole thing. Nausea set in and Kate swallowed hard.

After an awkward moment, with no relief in sight, Denise jumped to her feet and went to him. "It's okay. We were just getting started. Did you bring Chloe with you?"

"No. She's with my sister."

"All right." She gestured to the pens, packets, and nametags on the table beside the door. "Take one of each of these and find a seat. It's good to have you."

"Thanks." Stealing a quick glance at Kate, he gathered up the items and moved to the closest chair, which just happened to be directly across the circle from her.

Her stomach twisted, knowing that every time she looked up she would see the face of the man she was trying to avoid, a feat that seemed more and more impossible with each passing day. Finally she managed to find her voice.

"Back to introductions. I'm Kate Sterling, and I'll be leading our meetings each week. I have a seven-year-old daughter named Maddie, and we just moved back to Harvest Bay two months ago after living in Nashville, Tennessee, for ten years. I'm teaching fourth grade at Harvest Bay Elementary, and I'm a member of this church." Then she passed the imaginary baton off to her left where Denise was sitting.

"I think all of you know me." She looked down at her nametag and smoothed it with her hand. "I'm Denise Golden, and I'll be assisting Kate with leadership duties. I have two boys. Griffin's fourteen and Greyson's twelve. I'm the office manager at Harvest Bay Family Practice." She looked over at Maggie and winked. "And I attend Faith Lutheran down the street." She turned to the woman on her left, signaling that it was her turn.

The middle-aged woman cleared her throat and sat up a little taller. "Hello. My name is Kim McDoogle. I have three children—a son who's a sophomore at Kent State, a daughter who is a senior in high school, and another daughter who is a freshman. We're new to the area so I don't have a job or a church yet. I suppose it's irresponsible to move without having something in place first, but we couldn't stay where we were any longer." Her voice wavered. She looked around the small group and whispered, "Sorry."

"Don't be. That's why this group was created. Pastor Ben, the pastor of this church, saw a need for single parents in this and neighboring communities to meet and work through their struggles together."

Kim nodded, and Kate turned her attention to the next person in the circle.

"I'm Matt Johansen. I have twin daughters who just turned four. They live with their mother, but I get them on

Wednesdays, Thursdays, and every other weekend. I am a lawyer with the firm West and Johansen. Our office is just up the street. And I attend this church . . . occasionally."

"Hi, everyone. I'm Adam Sullivan."

Feeling heat rise in her cheeks, Kate dropped her gaze to her lap.

"I have one daughter, Chloe. She's nine and she's in Kate's class this year."

She looked up and forced a smile, hoping no one noticed the goose bumps that had popped out on her arms at the sound of him saying her name.

"I teach junior high health and wellness classes, coach our varsity football team, and help out on my parents' farm when I can." He bent to rest his forearms on his knees and rubbed his hands together. "And I don't go to church. Chloe comes here, but I don't."

Kate tipped her head to the side. She thought she heard regret or shame or some combination of the two in his voice. She met his gaze and noticed that storm clouds darkened his eyes' brilliant blue.

Suddenly, as if she'd been slapped across the face, she realized the selfishness of her behavior, and it stung. She studied Adam from across the room, aware of her attraction to him, but reflecting that this was no longer about her. She had agreed to lead this support group to help the single parents in the community, and that included Adam. She would somehow have to set her feelings aside, box them up and put them away in a closet in her heart. It was more important now that she fulfill her new role in her community.

I need Your help, God. Please let me know that You are here.

"I guess it's my turn," said the woman on Adam's left.

Kate redirected her attention and smiled at the woman encouragingly.

"My name is Letisha Jackson, but all my friends call me Tish. I have two beautiful babies—five-year-old Andre and three-year-old Mercedes. Of course, most of you know that I'm a realtor with Harvest Bay Realty. I'm also a member of this church, where I sing in the choir and am active in the children's ministry. In fact, if you don't mind, Kate, this past Sunday our children learned a memory verse that I would like to share."

"By all means."

"Psalms 46:1 says, 'God is our refuge and strength, a very present help in trouble.'"

Kate sucked in a breath. "Can you say that verse again?"

"Sure. 'God is our refuge and strength, a very present help in trouble.'"

In a voice that was barely audible, Kate repeated, "A very present help in trouble." Unable to keep the tears from welling up, she folded her hands in her lap, looked at Letisha through her blurred vision and said, "Thank you."

Letisha's smile was brilliant white against her red lipstick and dark skin. "Oh, you're welcome, sugar." She had no way of knowing that Kate was also thanking the Lord.

Kate smiled, this time easily, her spirit lifting, and she turned to the last person in the circle. "It's your turn, Maggie."

"*Me llamo* . . ." Maggie shook her head. "My name *es* Maggie Martinez. I have *uno niño*." She peeked into the stroller at her sleeping baby. "I work with Denise as a receptionist in Doc Brewster's office, but I will be home for eight more weeks with Justin." She looked at Kate and shrugged. "I guess that's it." Justin started to squirm, and she gently rolled the stroller back and forth a few times.

"Okay. Now that we're all acquainted with each other, who would like to lead us in a word of prayer?"

"I will," Denise volunteered, and everyone bowed their heads.

As Denise began to pour her heart out, Kate glanced up at Adam. Still leaning forward with his hands folded, he hung his head heavily, and she wondered about the burdens he was carrying around on those broad shoulders.

" . . . and, Jesus, if there is anyone here tonight who doesn't know You or is struggling in his or her relationship with You, Lord, I ask that You make Yourself known to them. Touch their hearts in a way that only You can, Lord, so that they will know a peace that passes all understanding, and, Father God, help us all to remember that You are a very present help in trouble. I ask all this in Jesus' name. Amen."

That was when it happened.

The peace Kate had been looking for earlier in the sanctuary descended on her like the pixie dust in Madeline's cartoons, making her heart soar and her cup overflow with emotion. She inhaled deeply, and her lungs filled with a fresh, invigorating oxygen. It was the first "God high" she'd experienced in a very long time, and it felt so incredibly wonderful that she wanted to laugh and cry and dance, but she couldn't . . . at least not for another forty-five minutes.

She quickly got a grip on her emotions, turned to Denise, and said with more feeling than she intended, "Thank you."

Denise gave her a little wink.

"Tonight's topic of discussion is You Are Not Alone. Letisha gave us a perfect illustration of God's constant assistance in our lives, but God didn't intend for us to live without human support. A few weeks ago, Pastor Ben quoted a scripture passage in his sermon that really spoke to me. It was Galatians 6:2, and it says . . . "

From that moment on, the meeting took on a spirit-filled life of its own, and before Kate was ready for it to be over, the hour was up. Everyone mingled for a few minutes, but by ten minutes after eight, Kate, Denise, and Adam were the only ones left.

Denise glanced at Adam, and then at Kate. "I'm going to get the boys and head out. Would you like me to have Cassie walk Maddie down here on her way out?"

"That'd be great, and thanks for your help tonight."

"You're the captain. I just toot the horn every now and then." Denise beeped an imaginary car horn in front of her twice, and then slipped out the door.

Kate continued tidying up the room despite the weight of Adam's presence.

"Hey, Kate, I just wanted to thank you for inviting me to come tonight."

She turned, relieved yet equally disappointed by the space he kept between them. "I didn't think you'd show up."

"Me either."

Her mouth curved upwards slightly. "I'm glad you did."

He met her gaze with an intensity that nearly knocked her over. "Me too."

⚜

The boxes had been accumulating in the basement for years. Adam had no idea how he was going to find what he was looking for, but he knew it was down there—it had to be—so he kept on searching.

As he went through each box, his mind remained on the single-parent support group meeting. He still didn't know what made him go. It certainly wasn't Kate. In fact, she was his reason not to go. He didn't want her to see his flaws, his failures as a father—and in a church of all places! Even so, after football practice had ended, he had pulled out of the high school parking lot, making a left instead of a right, and a few minutes later parked his Silverado in the church parking lot.

During the meeting something moved deep down in the cold, unreachable pit of his soul, something warm, rich, and satisfying. When Denise prayed and Kate read that Bible passage about carrying each other's burdens, it was as if he'd been handed the state championship trophy, but couldn't remember playing the game.

He could literally feel weight lifting off his shoulders—his banished NFL dreams, the loss of his grandfather, his failed marriage, and his inadequacies as a single father. For the first time in a long time, he felt . . . hope.

After he'd gone through about half of the boxes, he stretched and checked his watch. Half past ten. He'd been searching for over an hour with no luck, and it was getting late. Then a thought occurred to him. Pray.

No. It's crazy to pray about something like this . . . He glanced around him and rubbed the back of his neck . . . *even if it's needle-in-a-haystack status.* He sighed heavily and sat down on the basement steps.

"Besides, God wouldn't listen to me. Why should He?" Then he looked up at the strong beams above him. "But if You are listening to me, You know what I'm looking for, and I need Your help to find it."

He shook his head, got up, and went back to the boxes. As he opened one, frustration erupted inside him.

"Why bother? What's the point?"

He turned sharply intending to go back upstairs, crawl into bed with his remote control, and fall asleep watching ESPN. But in his haste, he bumped the box, knocking it off the stack and spilling its contents on the basement floor.

He cursed under his breath, stooped over to pick up the mess he'd made, and froze. He rubbed his eyes to make sure they weren't playing a trick on him in the dimly lit basement.

There, lying on top of the pile, was what he'd been searching for—his grandfather's Bible.

He reached out and ran his fingertips over the dusty leather cover. His grandfather's name was printed in gold lettering on the bottom right corner of the cover.

"Jacob Adam Sullivan III," he whispered, surprised by how much emotion it stirred up in him. That name was part of his heritage, part of who he was today.

He gingerly reached out and picked up the Bible as if it were a newborn baby, dusted it off with the hem of his T-shirt, and then opened the front cover. His eyes misted when he recognized his grandfather's familiar chicken scratch filling in the family tree and other records on the first few pages.

Documentation of weddings, births, and deaths sprawled out over two pages, with lines connecting them all to each other. He found his name under the names Jacob Adam Sullivan IV and Anna Rose (Kennedy) Sullivan, but the lines under his name were blank. His grandfather never knew Chloe.

"Daddy?"

He jumped and turned. "Chloe! What are you doing up?"

"I heard a big crash. I couldn't find you, and I got scared."

"Oh, honey." He placed the Bible gently in the box and went to the bottom of the basement steps, where she stood in her pajamas. He wrapped her up in his arms.

"A box fell, and I'm cleaning it up. That's all. Everything's fine. Go back up to bed and I'll come tuck you in."

Obediently, she started up the steps, and he returned to tidying.

"Daddy?"

"Yes?"

"What were you looking at a minute ago?"

That was the $64,000 question. If he told her the truth, more questions would surely come, and at the moment he had plenty of questions of his own that he had to figure out the answers to.

He exhaled slowly. "A book that belonged to your great-grandfather. Now go back upstairs. I'll be up in a minute."

She took two more steps, and then turned again. "That meeting you were at tonight, did you go because you and mom got divorced?"

He ran a hand through his hair. "Yes."

"Is it going to help you find another wife?"

He shook his head. "No. It's going to help me be a better daddy."

"Oh, Daddy, you're already the best!" She ran back down the steps and jumped into Adam's arms.

He held her, smoothing her hair and knowing that nothing was more important at that moment than giving his daughter the comfort and security she needed. He carried her up the stairs of the old farmhouse to tuck her back into bed, leaving his grandfather's Bible and all of his unanswered questions behind.

⁂

Kate couldn't sleep. She didn't know why she even bothered trying. She looked at her bedside alarm clock. 11:03. She threw her covers back, swung her legs over the side of the bed, and plodded out into the hallway.

At the first door she came to, she popped her head in to check on Madeline, who was snoring lightly in her bed. Then she headed to the kitchen to brew a pot of coffee. She'd need a strong cup in the morning, but still feeling the effects of her earlier "God high" was well worth the price she'd pay tomorrow.

She quietly opened her front door and stepped out onto the small porch. It was a beautiful early September night. The cool air caused goose bumps to pop out on her arms, and she pulled her flannel housecoat tighter around her.

The black sky was a sea of stars, and a perfect crescent moon made it look like someone in Heaven was smiling down on her. She fancied the idea that it was Ryan or maybe her grandmother. Maybe it was even God.

She walked out into the yard, her bare feet becoming wet with dew, and she began to twirl and sway and spin just as she used to when she was Madeline's age and pretended to be a ballerina. She put her arms out and spun around and around until she collapsed on the ground, laughing. Lying in the wet grass of the same yard she'd played in as a child, she could begin to see God's hand in her life.

"The Bible says that all things work together for good to those who love You. I still don't know how good can come out of Ryan's death because I miss him so much, but . . . " Kate's voice trembled. "I trust You." The dam burst and she began to weep. "I trust You . . . I trust You . . . I trust You . . . I trust You . . . "

When her alarm sounded at six the next morning, she awoke with a start. She couldn't remember going back inside and crawling back in her bed.

The following Friday, Kate stopped by her parents' house after school, picked up Grandpa Clayton, and took him home with her and Madeline for a visit. Approaching ominous clouds hovered low over the horizon when she pulled into the drive. She had no sooner than eased the Explorer into the garage and hit the button to close the door when the first raindrops splattered on the ground outside.

She assisted Grandpa Clayton out of the Explorer and up the three steps that led to the kitchen, while Madeline ran to her room to change out of her school clothes.

"Would you like some coffee, Gramps?" Kate went to the kitchen counter while he hobbled to the table and shakily sat in a chair.

"Love some."

She got filters and coffee down from the cupboards and went to work. "So what do you think about what Daddy and I have done with the house? It's not too different, just a little more modern."

He looked around him and nodded, his bottom lip protruding a little. "It's nice. I think your grandma would love it, especially the dishwasher. She hated doing dishes. Loved to cook, but hated dishes."

Kate moved over to the table and sat in a chair next to him. "I remember her chocolate chip cookies. I can almost smell them sometimes."

"Mmm. Me too."

There was a far away look in his eyes, and she let him have a minute with his thoughts. The rain began to come down in buckets, beating hard against the windows.

Madeline came into the kitchen. "Wow, Mama! Look at it pour! Are we going to the football game tonight?"

A loud crack of thunder shook the house. Kate thought of Adam and felt that familiar pull in her chest. "No, sweetie. Even if the game hasn't been cancelled, we still aren't going."

"Rats! I like watching Adam tell those big boys what to do."

"Why don't'cha tell me about the support group meeting last Tuesday, Katy?"

Kate returned her attention to Madeline, who stood with her nose pressed against the window, watching the rain. "It was . . . good."

His white eyebrows arched high over the rim of his glasses. "Just good?"

She eyed her grandfather. Knowing that she had a long road ahead of her, she'd only told Pastor Ben and Nathan about the miracle that had happened in her heart. How did Grandpa Clayton know then?

She averted her gaze back to her daughter. "Maddie, do you have homework?"

"No, not on Fridays."

"Well, since you can't go outside to play, you can watch something on the Disney channel."

"Okay." She scurried off to the living room and moments

later was dancing and singing to the *Hannah Montana* theme song.

The coffeemaker stopped sputtering and hissing, so Kate got up, retrieved two mugs, and poured the steaming liquid. A flash of lightning filled the sky, followed by a boom of thunder so loud it startled her, causing her to almost spill the coffee as she carried the cups to the table. She set Grandpa Clayton's in front of him and, keeping a cautious eye on the window, took a sip of hers.

Sitting back in her chair, she turned her attention to her grandfather. "It was better than I expected."

He stared at her, waiting, his hands trembling as he lifted his coffee cup to his lips.

A smile spread across her face. "I found the Lord again, Gramps." Her voice was low, just loud enough that she knew he could hear it with the help of his hearing aids.

He stuck his bottom lip out and nodded again. "That's good, Katy. Real good."

She gave him a sideways glance. "You already knew, but how?"

He took another shaky swallow of his coffee. "You've got that glow."

She felt warmth radiate from the core of her being that she knew was more than the coffee.

"So how's Maggie?" He was one of a number of people in Harvest Bay consistently checking up on Maggie and baby Justin.

A crack of thunder sounded, and the lights flickered. From where she sat on the floor in the living room, Madeline looked at Kate with a worried expression.

"It's okay, sweetie. It's just a thunderstorm."

Satisfied for the moment, Madeline turned back to the TV and Kate to her grandfather.

"Maggie's doing pretty well, I think. When we introduced ourselves, she didn't say anything about attending church. That kind of has me concerned, especially now that she has the baby. She really needs a church family."

"She's been through a lot at such a young age. You know firsthand how that can affect a person's faith." He took another sip, watching her over the rim of his mug. "And how's Adam?"

She hoped her wise old grandfather wouldn't detect the effects of the mini bonfire suddenly burning in her cheeks, knowing full well he would. "He's fine, I guess. He seemed to enjoy the meeting. He said he was glad he came."

"How did you feel about him being there?"

"Listen, mister, I know what you're trying to do, and I can tell you one thing: You are not a matchmaker. You're my gramps, so let's leave it that way, huh?"

He laughed jovially, and Kate joined in. She couldn't help it. She adored this man and cherished the time they spent together.

"Hey, what's so funny?" Madeline shouted from her place in front of the TV.

"It's nothing, honey." Kate waved her away, which only served to attract Madeline's attention more.

She wandered out to the kitchen, curiosity oozing out of her pores. "What'cha laughin' at then?"

"It was just something your mother said." Grandpa Clayton calmed enough to take another drink of coffee.

Madeline scrunched up her brow. "But Mama's not funny."

This caused another burst of laughter, which was quickly stifled by an ear-splitting crack of thunder that rattled all their nerves. Madeline crawled up on Grandpa Clayton's lap.

"Would you like a snack, sweetie?"

The little girl nodded, her chocolate eyes round with fright.

Kate got up, went to the pantry, and returned with a package of Oreo cookies. "Oreos make everything better."

Before she could lay the package on the table, Madeline was diving in. "Mmm. Oreos are my favorite!" She twisted the top off a cookie and scraped the white filling off with her teeth.

"Mine too." Grandpa Clayton grabbed a cookie and did the same thing with his.

Kate smiled, thinking that someone needed to do a study on the role genetics played in Oreo cookie consumption. "How about some milk, Maddie?"

"Yes, please."

Kate started for the refrigerator just as the telephone rang. She picked up the cordless lying on the counter and, without bothering to check the caller ID, punched the talk button.

"Hello?" She grabbed the carton of milk and shoved the fridge door shut with her foot.

"Hi, Kate."

"Hey, Nathan!" She swiped a cup from the cupboard and began to pour.

"I wanna talk to Uncle Nate!" Madeline shouted across the kitchen with her mouth full of Oreos and black crumbs speckling her lips.

Kate carried the cup of milk to Madeline. "In a minute."

"Is this a bad time?"

"Not at all. We're just sitting at the table with a package of Oreos, and I was telling Gramps about the support group meeting last Tuesday." She went back to the counter and leaned against it. "You sound like you have something on your mind."

"I do, as a matter of fact."

"Is everything okay?" Thunder sounded again, loud and strong. If it was anybody besides Nathan she would have asked if she could call back later.

"Doc Brewster called me this morning and offered me the position."

"Nathan, that's great!" she said joyfully, but then paused. "You don't sound like you want to take it, though."

"I've already accepted it."

"Oh. Are you sure that's what you want?" He was silent for so long, she wondered if they'd been cut off. "Nathan? You there?"

"I'm here."

"What's wrong?"

"I have to tell you something."

The rain was coming down harder than before. She thought it sounded like hail. At that moment, she didn't know what she was more frightened of—the storm outside or the storm that was obviously brewing in Nathan's heart.

"What is it?"

Another pause. Finally he cleared his throat. "Kate, I need to tell you that I . . . "

At that moment a powerful bolt of lightning struck, followed very closely by a deafening clap of thunder. The power went out.

She stared at the dead phone. *That just figures.*

She decided she would wait a few minutes until the worst of the storm passed, and then try to call him back on her cell phone. For the time being there were more urgent issues to take care of, such as finding flashlights, candles, and matches.

As she searched for the items in the dim room, Madeline clung tighter to Grandpa Clayton, and said in a trembling voice, "Great-Gramps, please tell me a story."

⁂

" . . . love you." Nathan stared at the phone in his hand until the blaring dial tone prompted him to hang it up. With no where to land now, his words floated heavily in his office atmosphere.

He'd felt like he should confess his feelings for Kate before he made this life-altering move, but maybe it was for the best that the two most important words he might ever speak were trapped in his office with him. Maybe he needed to wait until he got to Harvest Bay to sweep Kate off her feet.

Regardless, he now had a chapter of his life to close before he could open a new one. He'd never used the word *bittersweet* before, but there was no other word to describe how he felt.

He loved this life he'd built for himself. Being part of a successful family practice in a top-notch hospital had been a dream come true. But things change, and now he loved Kate and Madeline more than his career. While starting over was a frightening concept, he was even more afraid of not following what was clearly God's plan for his life.

Taking a deep breath, he picked up his phone and dialed a three-digit extension, which was answered almost immediately. "Can I see you in my office right away, Alice?"

"Sure thing. Be right there, hon."

True to her word, two seconds later, she tapped lightly on his office door and poked her head in.

"Come on in and have a seat."

She slipped in, shut the door behind her, and sat in the leather chair across from his desk. "What can I do for ya, sugar?"

"Well . . . " Nathan hesitated. Once he voiced his intention to leave this practice, this city and state, this life, he wouldn't be able to take it back.

For I know the plans I have for you, declares the Lord, plans to prosper you and not to harm you, plans to give you hope for the future.

He silently repeated the verse from Jeremiah that he'd come across the night before. It served as a source of comfort today. He looked at the sweet southern woman who perched on the chair, watching him curiously.

"I, uh . . . " He tapped his pen on his desk. "I took your advice. I got my priorities straight, and God has made it obvious to me that I need to be with Kate and Maddie in Harvest Bay."

She looked as if he had just told her that she'd won the lottery. "Well, as I live and breathe! What happened?"

"Long story short, I went to visit and ended up being introduced to the town doctor who's expanding his office."

"And?"

"I had an interview with him this past Monday."

"And?" Her voice jumped up an octave.

"He called this morning and offered me the position."

"And?" One more octave, and he thought she'd break a glass.

A small grin crept onto his face. "I accepted it."

She threw her hands in the air. "Oh, praise the Lord!"

"Geez, Alice, can you wait until I'm gone before you throw a party?"

"Darlin', I've been prayin' mightily for you. I know you've been lonely for a good while now, and that's been harder to watch than you leaving to be with Kate and Maddie will be."

He nodded. "I'll turn in my formal resignation on Monday. My last day will be September the twenty-sixth. That's three weeks from today. What I need for you to do is make sure I don't have any new appointments scheduled. Any of my patients scheduled after the twenty-sixth will have to be rescheduled with Doctors Parker or Houser. They are both accepting new patients, and I'm confident they'll make it a smooth transition. I'll continue to see patients who already have appointments until then."

"Got it. I'll make sure it gets taken care of."

His expression softened and his heart began to swell. "Thank you for everything."

"Believe me, sugar, it has been a pleasure." She got to her feet and headed for the door.

"Oh, and Alice?"

She turned. "Umm hmm?"

"Keep this between us until Monday morning when my resignation is official."

She winked at him. "My lips are sealed." She stepped out of the room.

It was done. He'd activated his words, made them come alive. He was really moving to Harvest Bay in three short weeks, and his list of things to do between now and then was growing to monstrous proportions.

He clicked his computer to life. After he checked the status of his Ohio medical license online, he would try to get back in touch with Kate to see if she knew a good realtor. He didn't have a moment to lose.

The storm passed before the scheduled kickoff time, and it was determined that the football game would be played in spite of the continuing light rain. In the locker room just minutes before the start of the game, with his players and all six of his assistant coaches gathered around him already soaked to the bone from the pre-game warm ups, Adam was relieved they didn't have to cancel. This game wouldn't be fun.

Tonight it wasn't about the crowd, which would most likely be only a fraction of their devoted fans. It wasn't about the lights or the smell of popcorn in the soggy air. This would be a game of willpower and determination, stamina and perseverance.

He needed this kind of game tonight.

His world had been slightly tilted ever since Kate showed up in Harvest Bay, but this past week, after a seed had been planted at the support group meeting, it seemed as if his world had been turned upside down. To get his head back on straight he needed the kind of focus a game like this would take.

His gaze swept the musty-smelling cinderblock room. His team watched him, waiting for their pep talk, but he needed one himself.

He took a deep breath. "Guys, I don't have to tell you what this game means to everyone in this locker room, and all of you know what the conditions are like on the field. Having fun out there is half the battle. Don't let the elements get in the way of that. If we have a miscue, stay positive. Maintain composure. Be opportunistic. Force fumbles. Play smart and pounce on our opponents' every mistake."

He shoved his hands into his damp pockets. "That's it. We have a game plan in place. Carry it out and let it develop. You can do it!"

"Yeah! Let's go Falcons!" one of the captains stood and shouted with his helmet raised high in the air.

As all the other players joined him shouting, pumping their helmets above their heads, slapping each other on their shoulder pads and mentally preparing for battle, Adam could feel the adrenaline rush through his veins like the mighty Mississippi. Yes, this was what he needed.

They filed out of the locker room, jogging and jumping, and when Adam started to follow them, he nearly tripped over the quarterback. Kyle was down on one knee with his head bent.

Suddenly, as if he'd been hit by icy arctic air, Adam froze. The adrenaline he'd enjoyed just a moment before evaporated. His blood drained from his face. Right there in front of him was a picture of exactly what he was trying to get out of his head—his lack of any kind of a relationship with God.

He didn't understand it. He had always been just fine without making God a priority in his life. But suddenly, while he watched this young man on bended knee, he wondered what he was missing. How had this high school senior developed a faith so strong he felt confident praying in front of his peers?

A small part of Adam, the part where that seed had been planted, wanted to ask. But his proud side not so gently reminded him that *he* was the coach, and that this boy looked up to him for guidance and direction.

And besides, I don't have time for any relationship—not with Kate . . . he paused, examining the hairline cracks in the cold, hard, cement floor, thinking that it bore a close resemblance to his heart . . . *and certainly not with God.*

"Amen." Kyle rose to his full six-foot frame. "Oh, hey Coach."

"Your teammates have already left. They're probably half way to the field by now."

"Right. Better go catch up then." Kyle grabbed his helmet and started for the door.

"Kyle, wait." The words were out before Adam could stop them.

"Yeah, Coach?"

Adam's heart and brain were deep in battle, and between the two of them he had no idea what to say. So he made a fist and, keeping it close to his body, shook it as a fighter would.

"Go get 'em out there!"

The boy gave him a winning smile and shoved his helmet on. "You got it, Coach!" Then he rushed out of the room to join the others.

Adam knew he should hurry out behind Kyle. Kickoff would be in just a few minutes, and his boys would need him—all of him, his brain and his heart. He couldn't dwell on what was missing in his life, on that giant void that even his immense love for Chloe couldn't completely fill.

But he needed time to pull himself back together. And so he stood stock still for several moments, staring at the open door.

CHAPTER
Fourteen

A few clouds still lingered that first Saturday in September, and dry warmth with an occasional refreshing breeze replaced the steamy summer heat. Autumn was just around the corner, and Kate was ready for the change.

Madeline hopped out of the car and rushed to the soccer field to warm up with her team. Kate followed, toting her canvas lawn chair, which she set up in the space between Jane and Grandpa Clayton.

She sat down just as Adam gave Madeline a high five for completing her part of the drill. The gesture tugged on Kate's heart. Although deep down she wished it could be Ryan there with Madeline, she was suddenly very thankful for Adam.

The thought frightened her. It wasn't the right time for her to get involved with anybody. But her heart kept gravitating toward him, with no way to stop it. She was being pulled in.

Nothing is impossible for God.

She believed it, trusted it, but she had already turned this over to God. Why wasn't He taking care of it?

"Have you heard from Nathan lately?"

She turned her attention to Jane, grateful for the distraction. "Yesterday afternoon. He called to tell me that Doc Brewster offered him the position."

Jane took a sip of her Coke. "That's great! Doc Brewster really needed another physician in his office."

Kate thought about the bizarre telephone conversation she'd had with Nathan, and she hoped beyond all hope that he'd made the right decision.

At that moment two referees came onto the field, and one blew a whistle. "Looks like I'm just in time," a voice from behind them said.

Kate turned to see Kennedy Sullivan, who just happened to be Madeline and Jessica's teacher this year, walking up with a lawn chair.

"Are you coming to watch Chloe? Or did Jessie and Maddie twist your arm into coming to watch them?" Jane scooted closer to Kate to make room for another chair.

"Both." Kennedy flashed them a smile before moving closer to the sideline. She caught the girls' attention and waved.

Madeline and Jessica waved back, and then skipped over to Adam, talking and pointing animatedly, while Chloe ran over to give her aunt a quick hug. Kate could tell there was a special bond between the two.

After a moment, Madeline, Jessica, and three other players took their positions on the field. A referee blew her whistle to start the game, and one of Madeline's teammates, a tall, stocky girl, charged in and got the ball. She dribbled it a few feet, and then passed it to Madeline, who skillfully ran with it to their goal and gave it a swift boot, only to have it blocked by the other team's goalie.

Kate could hear Adam applauding Madeline's efforts from his place beside Ian. "It's okay, Maddie! Get to the ball and try it again! You can do it!"

Jane and Kennedy and her parents were all shouting their encouragement to Madeline too, but they didn't register in Kate's brain the way Adam's voice did.

The other team got the ball and worked on shuffling it down the field, but before they got within scoring distance, Jessica swiped the ball away, dribbled it halfway down the field, and then passed it to Madeline. Madeline moved the ball a few feet closer, then kicked it as hard as she could.

It sailed right past the goalie's head into the net. Kate came out of her chair with her hands high in the air.

Madeline jumped up and down several times. She waved at Kate, and then ran straight to Adam who picked her up off the ground with his hug.

In that moment Kate felt herself fall. She knew that Madeline was becoming attached to Adam too. She was walking on thin, dangerous ice. She had to find a way back to safe, solid ground.

Before she knew it, the ten-minute quarter was over, and Ian had swapped out some players. Chloe was running up and down the field now, while Madeline sat on the bench cheering for her. Kate watched Chloe with special fondness, wondering whether she needed a female role model in her life as much as Madeline needed a male role model . . . and as much as she knew deep down in her soul that she and Adam needed each other. The thought crossed her mind that they could be everything for each other. The four of them could be a family.

A family.

She sucked in a breath. The idea made her tingle all over. It had been just her and Madeline for so long that the thought of being part of a family almost made her giddy. Sure the blending might take some time, but in the end maybe none of them would be lonely anymore.

Or maybe it would end up being a disaster. Maddie and Chloe have been through too much already. I can't risk having their hearts broken again . . . I can't risk having my heart broken again. It would never heal.

That was the bottom line. She wasn't as afraid of falling in love as she was afraid of that love falling apart. Kate studied Adam, hoping God would instantaneously answer her ongoing prayer regarding her feelings for him. But He didn't.

Or did He?

You are the answer, aren't You, God? Adam isn't a Christian, and I can't get involved with a nonbeliever, especially when I'm just now finding my way back to You.

Kate nodded once and crossed her arms, ignoring the way her heart sagged in her chest. It was final. She had a very legitimate reason not to think of Adam as anything more than a friend.

She just hoped this reason held up better than the out of sight, out of mind idea.

Frosty Jack's was already hopping by the time the soccer team flooded in for victory ice-cream treats. Adam gave Chloe a couple dollars and watched her flow into the small building with the river of blue jerseys. Then he found a nearby picnic table to wait for her.

"You're not getting ice cream? Are you feeling okay?"

Without having to look, he knew that teasing tone. He'd heard it from the moment his kid sister learned the art of sarcasm nearly twenty years ago.

"I'm fine, just not hungry."

"I'm not hungry either, but that's not keeping me from enjoying two scoops of Chocolate Espresso Bliss."

Adam laughed. "Okay. I'll have what you're having." He slipped his wallet out of his back pocket, pulled out a ten, and held it out to her. "And it's on me."

She pushed it away. "I've got it, big brother." Kennedy's expression softened, and she gently placed her hand on his forearm. "After last night, I'd say you deserve a treat."

His gaze fell to her hand for the brief moment before she turned and headed toward the building. Kennedy knew him better than any of his brothers did, maybe even better than Jane and Ian did. But this time she had no idea what turmoil churned inside him. Of course, he was disappointed that Harvest Bay had lost the football game by a field goal in over-time. He wanted to win every game; he didn't coach to lose.

Today the fact that he was sitting the bench in another game, magnified the letdown. He'd rather play in a losing game than sit the bench because there was always a chance he could throw a miraculous pass to shift the momentum of the game. At this point in his life he felt he needed to let a Hail Mary fly into the awaiting grip of a reliable receiver, but he was help-less. He had to get in the game, but he didn't know how.

He wondered if the "Coach," forgiving and merciful as He claimed to be, would even want him after he'd missed so much of the game. Adam wanted to learn more about the specific stipulations for playing on God's team, but he was ashamed to ask anyone.

He looked up in time to watch Kate and Madeline come out of the building and join their family at a picnic table a few yards away.

Madeline caught his gaze and waved, a wide, chocolatey grin on her face.

He brightened and waved back, hoping Kate would look his way, but she didn't. He briefly thought about asking her to help him understand Christianity, but what if she thought he was using that as a means to get closer to her. Just a week ago, when his main goal was to win her over, that might have been something he'd do. What exactly had changed in one week's time, he didn't know, but watching her now he only wanted her happiness . . . and his.

He wanted the joy his mother and father knew. He was skeptical that it was solely a result of knowing Christ, but what if it was? What if that was the foundation everything else was built upon? He could feel his shoddily built life gradually become rickety, but he had no idea how to make it stronger while keeping the crucial areas intact.

"Don't worry, buddy. I'm right here."

He looked up questioningly to see Ian settling into the bench across from him. "Excuse me?"

"You look like you've lost your best friend. I was just letting you know I haven't gone anywhere."

Adam shook his head, a small grin on his face.

"So, what's up?"

Adam scrunched his brow. "Nothing. Why?"

"You look like you have a lot on your mind."

Adam shrugged. "Football, I guess."

"You can't fool me, bro."

"I'm not—"

"Jane said that Chloe made a comment when she spent the night last night about you acting weird. That little girl is worried about you . . . and so am I."

A hunk of Adam's heart cracked off and fell to the pit of his stomach. He never wanted Chloe to worry about him. He tried his hardest to hide his true feelings from her.

Looking into his best friend's face, he saw the concern in his eyes. His gaze fell to his folded hands on the table top.

"You own the most successful construction company in the area. How do you fix a shaky foundation?"

Ian stared at him for a minute. "This is about your house?"

"Not exactly, but I have to know."

"Okay. There are several different methods, but basically you would have to drill holes around the house with an auger, place steel bars or pilings in the holes, and pour concrete into the holes. After that cures for several days, the home has to be jacked up and leveled, and then all the voids under or around the foundation are filled. That's the simple version."

"So it's possible to strengthen a foundation without destroying everything you've already built on it?"

"Sure, but the sooner you fix it the better. A weak foundation is nothing you want to mess around with."

Adam nodded, filled with a sense of urgency. "Thanks. I'll keep that in mind."

"Keep what in mind?" Kennedy asked, approaching the picnic table carrying two ice-cream cones.

Adam looked at Ian with pleading eyes, willing him to not say anything. Apparently he didn't get the message.

"Adam's foundation issues."

"You're having foundation issues?" Kennedy stared at her brother as she handed him his ice-cream cone. "Do Mom and Dad know about it?"

Adam should have guessed Kennedy would ask that question. His farmhouse used to belong to their parents before they inherited his grandfather's big brick home, the heart of the farm.

"No, and they don't need to. It's not a big deal." He nonchalantly took a bite of his ice cream, though his insides were now churning violently.

"Oh, foundation issues are a big deal all right. Trust me. You want to get it looked at right away." Ian pulled out his wallet, retrieved a business card from inside, and held it out to Adam. "Call these guys. They'll do a good job for you."

Adam put his hand up. "Thanks anyway, but I really don't need that. There's no issue. I was just asking a question." He turned to Kennedy and spoke very deliberately. "The house is fine. There's nothing to tell Mom and Dad."

She looked from him to Ian and back again, obviously puzzled at the strange conversation. Ian appeared just as flabbergasted.

"Okay," they said simultaneously.

"Thanks for the ice cream, but Chloe and I need to go. I have to study game film from last night."

Adam started to get up, but Kennedy reached out and stopped him. "Why don't you let Chloe hang out with me today? I'll take her up to the barn and work with her on Dolly for a while."

He hesitated, Ian's words coming back to haunt him: *That little girl is worried about you.*

It certainly wouldn't help Chloe to sit at home while he holed up in his den, reviewing every little move his team had made the night before. He knew that Chloe loved being on the horses almost as much as she loved being with her Aunt Ken.

"Have her home in plenty of time to take a bath before bed."

"Seven o'clock okay?"

He nodded. "I'm going to go tell her the game plan." He turned to Ian. "Good game today, Coach."

"Couldn't have done it without you."

Without another word, Adam strode away to find Chloe.

Less than an hour later he sat in his den, staring blankly at the video of last night's game playing on his big-screen TV. He forced himself to focus. After all, it was his duty as a head coach. But his discontented spirit was a difficult opponent, and before he even realized it, his mind was wandering again.

Determined to win this battle, he got out of his recliner and stood in his typical coach stance—feet shoulder-width apart and arms crossed. Watching the game with deliberate intensity, dissecting every play out loud, he made it through the first quarter without his focus wavering.

Two minutes into the second quarter, however, Harvest Bay scored the first touchdown of the wet, sloppy game, and the cameraman got a close up of Kyle, the quarterback, pointing heavenward.

Adam grabbed the remote and pushed the pause button. Slowly he sank back into his chair. There was a picture of a boy half his age acknowledging God in front of not just his teammates and coaches, but also the whole town. Granted, the whole town didn't attend this particular game, but Adam was confident that Kyle would have done the same thing had the stands been packed.

Adam tossed the remote aside, got up, and paced the floor. He could hear Ian's voice in his head. *A weak foundation is nothing you want to mess around with.*

"But how do I make it stronger?" He pushed his fingers through his hair, hopelessness surrounding him like a heavy fog.

Then he remembered his grandfather's Bible.

Leaving Kyle frozen on his TV, he sprinted out of the den, through the quiet house, down the basement steps, and straight to the box where he remembered leaving it earlier in the week. He reached in, pulled it out, and stared at it, wondering if it really contained the answers he was looking for.

Finally he tucked the book under his arm and carried it upstairs. In the length of time he'd been out of the room, the pause had expired and the tape was rolling again, but suddenly Adam wasn't interested in critiquing his coaching techniques or that of his assistants. He'd become more concerned with what his team could learn from young Kyle—and what he could learn from him too.

For a long time Adam just held the Bible, moving it from hand to hand. It wasn't fancy, just black leather with the words "HOLY BIBLE" in capital letters across the front and his grandfather's name at the bottom. Still, he knew all it stood for and all that stood between him and the promises inside.

It became vividly clear to him that he had reached a critical point in the game of his life, and he must decide once and for all if he really wanted to take the field. As long as he was merely surviving on the sidelines, he was safe from blame, accusation, and heartache. But the champion that remained somewhere deep down in him knew that, if given the chance, he could win this game and maybe even experience great joy in the process.

He flipped through the Bible, glancing at the names of some of the books and skimming a couple random verses. He was on the fringes of feeling comfortable with it in his hands, almost as though it were a football he'd thrown a dozen times.

Oddly, just by holding it, he felt stronger than he had in a long time.

Yes, he wanted to get in the game, to have the opportunity to turn his life around, but he had to learn the playbook first. And there was only one person who could coach him.

Kate sat alone in the adult Sunday school room relishing the solitude. Madeline was safe in Cassie's care, and if the faint strains of laughter that sporadically floated down the hall were any indication, she was already having fun. The chairs were arranged, the handouts and refreshments set out, and she was actively preparing her spirit by poring over her Bible.

For the past week, since she handed her life back to the Lord on her dew dampened front lawn, she had spent every quiet moment in the Word. She recognized that she was still weak, and she craved the strength that God's promises provided. She'd always found an extra dose of comfort in the book of Psalms, and this evening she was meditating on Psalm twenty-seven.

"The Lord is my light and my salvation: Whom shall I fear?" she read, her voice nearly a whisper. "The Lord is the strength of my life: Of whom shall I be afraid?"

She tipped her face upwards with her eyes closed. She inhaled deeply and exhaled slowly.

"There are so many things I'm scared of, but I'm trusting You, Lord, to be the strength of my life. Help me to not be afraid of living . . . or loving again."

Feeling renewed, she lowered her chin, opened her eyes, and gasped.

Standing in the doorway wearing an uncharacteristically timid expression was Adam. "I didn't mean to startle you."

"I . . . I didn't hear you come in." She forced smile. "You're early."

He moved into the room a few steps. "Tom and Jonah took over the last few minutes of practice." He glanced at the floor, and then back at Kate. "I was hoping to catch you alone."

Her pulse kicked into overdrive. "Well . . . " she swept her arm in front of her, indicating the empty room, "your wish is granted." She added quickly, "But Denise should be along any minute, so . . . "

He moved quickly to take the chair next to hers. "I need your help."

He clutched an old, weathered Bible in his hand. She glanced into his face and found desperation in his eyes.

Realizing she was putting her heart in the line of fire again, she swallowed and said, "Okay. What's up?"

His gaze fell, and silence engulfed them. He leaned forward, resting his forearms on his knees while he turned the Bible over and over.

In growing concern, she reached out and touched his arm. "Adam?"

He glanced fleetingly at her, and then held his Bible up. "Help me understand this."

She stared at him in disbelief. "Your Bible?"

He hung his head, his shoulders slumped.

She hesitated for a moment, then asked gently, "What exactly do you want to know?"

He ran a hand through his hair. "What it's all about. You know, what's the big deal?"

"That would take more than just an afternoon."

"I know."

"And I can't . . . "

Her gaze drifted up to his eyes. She saw hope shining through the desperation, and she couldn't finish. She didn't have it in her to admit to him that she was only just becoming reacquainted with the Bible herself.

She eyed him briefly wondering about his motives, but knowing that, regardless, she couldn't deny him the chance to study God's Word. "What is your schedule like?"

"It's busy, but I have some time to spare on Saturdays."

Saturday. Nathan was coming on Saturday. He'd made an appointment with Letisha to look at a few properties, and Kate had promised to go with him. She heard noises down the hall and figured Denise had arrived with Griffin and Greyson.

Making a quick decision, feeling confident that Nathan would understand, she said, "Plan on coming over to my house this Saturday after the girls' soccer game, okay?"

His smile melted her heart. "Okay."

A moment later Denise breezed into the room, talking a mile a minute while rummaging through her purse. "Hey, Kate. Sorry I'm running a few minutes late. I got held up at the office." She looked up. "Oh. Hi, Adam."

A remnant of his bright smile remained on his face. "Hey."

Denise applied a thin coat of the lip gloss she'd pulled from her purse. "I didn't mean to interrupt."

Kate stood and walked over to greet her friend. "You didn't."

"Okay. Then we'd better get our nametags on and make sure we have everything in order. Several patients who came in last week asked for information on this group, and a few stopped me after church on Sunday."

"Really?" Kate nearly squealed. She self-consciously glanced back at Adam.

He got to his feet and crossed the room to join them. "Word spreads fast in a small town, especially when there's something worth talking about."

Denise wrote her name across the white nametag in her beautiful cursive, peeled the backing off, and smoothed it onto her chest. Then she handed Kate and Adam each a tag and a pen. "I expect a big turnout this evening."

She'd made an accurate prediction. In just one week the small group of seven had become a group of twelve. As Denise began the meeting with a word of prayer, Kate was beyond elated at the ministry's early success. Her heart soared when she thought about the possibilities for the upcoming months, and she couldn't wait to start planning.

What she could wait for, however, was Saturday. She stole a glance at Adam, who appeared to be earnestly in prayer with Denise. Why, of all people, did he have to come to her? How could she, who was using his lack of faith as a valid reason to keep him at an arm's length, embrace his request? But how could she neglect it?

She needed to seek advice from someone who understood the delicacy of the situation, and an image of the perfect mentor formed in her mind. She smiled, relief washing over her.

Maybe she wasn't what Adam needed, but she knew exactly who was.

Fifteen

There was no sign of autumn that Saturday. The bright morning sunshine streamed through the kitchen window and splayed out on the table. Tiny dust particles that had managed to escape Kate earlier in the week floated in and out of the rays. She leaned against the counter, sipping a cup of coffee and fighting the urge to grab her dust rag and rid her house of them once and for all.

She narrowed her eyes in the direction of the rebellious specks. "I'll get you next time."

"Is that a threat or a promise?"

She nearly jumped out of her skin. She set her cup on the counter and pulled her flannel housecoat tighter around her lounge pants and T-shirt clad body.

"Good morning, Nathan. I didn't hear you get up. How about some coffee?"

"Sounds great." He took a seat at the table.

She poured him a cup. "How'd you sleep?"

"Like a rock." He gave her a small grin. "I especially liked the glow-in-the-dark stars on the ceiling."

She laughed. "Liz and I stuck those up there when I was in junior high. I meant to take them down and never got around to it." She topped off her cup, carried both steaming mugs to the table, and took a seat in an adjacent chair.

He tipped his head to the side. "Think I can find a house with as much character?"

She laughed. "Not a chance. But I'm sure you'll find one that's perfect for you, with or without glow-in-the-dark stars."

"So when do we meet your realtor friend?"

Her happy expression faltered. "Oh, well . . . there's been a slight change of plans."

Concern crossed his brow. "What do you mean?"

She took a deep breath. He deserved an explanation, but she didn't want to tell him too much. "A friend approached me about wanting to learn the basics of the Bible, and this afternoon was the most convenient time."

He stared at her for so long that she wondered if he was waiting for more information. At last he nodded slowly.

"Okay then. What's Plan B?"

"Denise is going to meet us at the soccer field, and after Maddie's game she'll go with you to look at the properties Letisha picked out for you."

He sipped his coffee silently.

"Are you disappointed?" She chewed on her bottom lip, wondering if she ought to postpone the Bible study with Adam until the following weekend.

"A little, but we'll have this evening."

Without thinking, she reached out and took his hand. "Thank you for understanding."

He gave her hand a little squeeze. "It won't be long, and we'll be together again."

Her eyes dropped and her stomach twisted at thought of Denise's words from over a month earlier. *It was written all over his face.*

She slowly slid her gaze up to his face, afraid of what she'd find. But when she reached his eyes she found Ryan's, and she felt something stir in her soul. It wasn't the breathtaking, knee-weakening spark that she experienced with Adam. This sensation more closely resembled her grandmother's chocolate chip cookies—warm, comforting, and familiar.

She and Nathan had a connection that was stronger than an intense attraction. They had lost someone they both deeply loved. Now that sweet softness in her heart oozed throughout her body as she realized that together they could keep Ryan alive for each other and for Madeline.

She squeezed his hand back, her lips curling upwards. "We're looking forward to it."

"Looking forward to what?" Madeline came into the kitchen, carrying her favorite stuffed puppy.

Kate snatched her hand back and gave Madeline a smile that was too bright to be natural, hoping a seven-year-old couldn't tell the difference. "Your soccer game today."

It was a safe, believable answer. She held her arms out, and the little girl crawled up onto her lap. She smoothed down Madeline's rumpled chestnut bob.

"Did you sleep well?"

"Uh huh. I like having Uncle Nate here."

Kate glanced at him over Madeline's head. "That makes two of us."

⁂

"Are you ready to go house hunting?"

Nathan studied Denise's friendly face, pondering the question. Was he ready?

Lord, forgive me for not trusting You enough, but please give me just one more sign that I'm doing the right thing—that moving here will be worth leaving Vanderbilt.

He glanced over his shoulder at Kate. She had her lawn chair in one hand and assisted her grandfather with the other. Their eyes met, and she gave him a smile so warm it melted his heart. The puddle forming at the bottom of his chest cavity was enough of a sign for him.

He turned to Denise with renewed confidence. "Ready."

She looped her arm through his and gave a gentle tug. "What are we waiting for? Let's go!"

Kate giggled. "Good luck!"

The first property Letisha showed them was a stately brick home in a newer, upscale subdivision catty-corner from the park and just down the street from Harvest Bay Family Practice.

"Based on the information Kate gave me, this particular listing is a close comparison to the home you're selling in Tennessee." Letisha punched the MLS ID number into the bulky gray lock on the door handle, and they stepped inside.

It was slightly smaller, but with the open floor plan, high ceilings, and several additional amenities, it was similar. As a bonus feature, it had a great view of the lake.

Letisha showed him two other properties, one of which was a rustic log home sitting on ten partially wooded acres. The other was bigger than the first one, but with a much smaller lot. Nathan scratched his head wondering if a swing set would even fit in the backyard.

"I have the information on a few more listings. Do you want to take a look?" Letisha asked when they walked to the cars.

"I don't think so."

She perked up. "Do you want to make an offer on one of these three?"

"Not quite yet." He really wanted Kate to see the house before he made a final decision.

She nodded. "Just let me know when you're ready." She got into her pink Lexus, carefully backed out of the driveway, and sped off.

He turned to Denise and slipped his hands into his pockets. "Thanks for hanging out with me today."

She leaned against the side of her Camry and folded her arms. "Did I do okay filling Kate's shoes?"

His typically eloquent tongue suddenly became tied at the unexpected sound of Kate's name. "Oh . . . well, yeah . . . sure . . . I mean, of course."

She laughed wholeheartedly and opened her car door. "Come on, Pinocchio. You and your growing nose owe me a piece of homemade apple pie for that."

Without another word, he slunk around to the passenger side, got in, and buckled up.

She backed out of the driveway and started down the road. While they made the smallest of small talk, his blazing cheeks returned to their normal temperature and skin tone.

As they coasted into town, he cleared his throat. "Mind if I ask where we're going to get this piece of pie?"

She pulled her car into a curbside parking spot right in front of a friendly looking diner with a red and white awning, and turned off the engine. "Right here."

He read the sign above the door. "Bayside Café."

"Yep. Come on." She joined Nathan on the sidewalk. "Audrey, the owner, makes all of her pies from scratch every morning, and, believe me, they're the best around."

"Sounds good." He held the glass door open for her, thinking that what really sounded good was going back to Kate's and spending the rest of his short trip with her and Madeline.

But how long will it take to eat one piece of pie? He figured he owed her that much after he'd taken up part of her Saturday afternoon.

The café seemed fairly busy, but there were several tables open, and they found a booth in an unpopulated corner. A waitress arrived before Nathan had a chance to open his menu, and Denise took the liberty of ordering two slices of apple pie a la mode with two cups of coffee. After the waitress retreated to the kitchen, Denise turned to Nathan.

"You liked the first one, didn't you?"

He nodded. "The log home was nice, but I'd rather be in town."

"That was my reasoning for buying a house in that subdivision."

He arched his eyebrows. "You live in Sugarfield Estates?"

"Don't look so surprised. Just because I'm an office manager doesn't mean I'm broke. I was married to a CPA for thirteen years. I learned real quick how to manage my money."

"Point well taken."

"So do you think you'll like it here?"

He sat back, somewhat surprised by how quickly he was growing comfortable with her. "It'll be an adjustment, but, yeah, I think I'm ready for something a little more . . . how did you put it at the barn dance? Simple and personal."

Her eyes twinkled. "See? I knew it all along. You are a country boy at heart."

He chuckled and put up his hands. "I don't know if I'd go that far."

"I think you'll fit in just fine."

"Thanks. And thanks again for looking at those houses with me today. I'm sure there are plenty of other ways you'd rather be spending your Saturday afternoon."

"No, not really." Denise's topaz gaze dropped to her hands folded on the table top. "Daryl has the boys this weekend so my alternative would have been cleaning or laundry." She glanced back up and gave him a crooked smile. "This was much more fun."

The waitress reappeared with their order. Denise added creamer and sweetener to her coffee while he dug right into the pie.

"And how are those fine young men of yours doing?"

She took a sip of her coffee. "They're good."

Her response was less than enthusiastic. She traced the rim of her mug with her fingertip. After a moment or two, she picked it up, took a drink, and gave him a smile that rivaled the warmth of the coffee.

"Greyson is doing great. He's so easygoing. Everything seems to be a breeze for him—school, sports, friends."

"And Griffin?"

Her smile fell. "Griffin's having a hard time right now."

Concern creased Nathan's brow. "What seems to be the trouble?"

"I'm not sure if I can pinpoint it. He has always been a quiet kid, more so after his dad and I divorced, and now he's developed this attitude to go along with it."

"How old is he?"

"Fourteen."

"Ahh." He nodded knowingly, but she quickly shook her head.

"I think there's more to it than him being a teenager. He's in high school this year so everything is a little more challenging—academics, sports, and social issues. He's such an intense kid that I'm sure he's beyond frustrated. On top of that he never seemed to adjust to having divorced parents. He blames his dad for leaving, he blames me for letting Daryl go, and I know somewhere in that head of his he blames himself.

"How do you make a fourteen-year-old boy understand that his dad was gone long before our marriage ended? And that I want—deserve—to be married to a man who loves me." She placed a hand over her heart. "Not someone who is just sticking around because I refuse to sign divorce papers."

She shook her head. "I expressed my concern to Daryl, hoping he would talk to Griffin, but he just shrugged it off. He said it's a phase Griffin's going through." She looked pleadingly at Nathan. "I don't know what's going on with him, but that boy means everything in the world to me, and most of the time it feels as though we're on opposite sides of a battlefield."

"Listen, don't worry, all right? Let me get settled in, and I'll be happy to spend some time with him. If nothing else, maybe I can help him work on that biology grade."

Denise stared at him. "Really? You mean it?"

"Of course. I made a deal with Griffin on the day of my interview, didn't I? There are still men in this world who keep their promises."

She smiled, a hint of heartache barely noticeable in the depths of her eyes. "I'm learning that a little more everyday."

Before they knew it, they had talked away an hour. Although Nathan was eager to get back to Kate and Madeline,

he thoroughly enjoyed visiting with Denise, content in knowing he now had another good friend in this small town.

⚜

When Adam turned onto Kate's quiet street, his fingers
gripped the steering wheel until his knuckles turned white.
Every nerve in his body felt like a lit fuse, and his racing heart
warned that the dynamite stick was about to explode.

"Daddy, why are we going to Ms. Sterling's house?"

In a futile attempt to steady his racing pulse, Adam tightened his grip on the steering wheel. "I just have to talk to her
about something."

"Is it about school?"

"No."

"Soccer?"

"Strike two. One more and you're out." He glanced in his
rearview mirror and could almost see the wheels turning in
her mind from where she sat in the extended cab, but she was
quickly running out of time. He grinned inwardly as he
slowed in front of Kate's house and flipped on his blinker. He
was in the clear.

"Is it about church?"

Her question sucked the breath out of him. "Wh-what
would make you think that?"

"You go there for your meetings, don't ya?"

"Oh. Yeah." He pulled up to the garage door, threw his
gear shift into park, and shut off the engine. His stomach
twisted into a knot, he fixed his gaze on his daughter.

"Your guess is close enough. Now I really need you to play
with Maddie and mind your manners so this doesn't take any
longer than it has to, okay?"

"Yes, Daddy."

"That's my girl. Let's go." He discreetly grabbed his grandfather's Bible from under his seat, tucked it under his arm, and climbed out of his black Silverado, with Chloe trailing close behind.

When Kate appeared on the small front porch, he couldn't help but wonder if this was a mistake. What if he didn't have it in him to believe the Bible was anything more than a glorified book? He couldn't fail at something else, couldn't let down another person he cared about.

For a second he considered conjuring up a quick story, making an about face, and hightailing it back to his truck. But as gruesome as this experience might be, he had to take the risk. He had to know. He clenched his jaw and kept moving forward, closing the gap between him and Kate.

"Hi, guys!" she greeted a little too brightly when he and Chloe reached the porch. He hesitated, but Chloe bounded up the steps and embraced this new female fixture in her life. Adam's knotted stomach somehow lodged in his throat.

Kate met his gaze as she gave Chloe a little squeeze. "It's nice to see you again today. Come on inside."

They barely had enough time to step into the small foyer and shut the door behind them before Madeline raced around the corner and screeched to a halt. Adam smiled. Still in her soccer jersey, she now also wore a chocolate milk mustache.

"Hi, Chloe! Wanna come see my room? We fixed it up more since you were here for my birthday party. And then we can go outside and play. Mama and I have a secret hiding place she said I can show you."

Chloe glanced up at Adam, who nodded his approval. A happy grin spread across her face, and the two girls ran off, leaving him and Kate standing in the foyer alone. Adam fidgeted and repositioned the Bible under his arm, resenting that it was the cause of this sudden awkwardness.

"Are you ready to get started?"

He exhaled while running a hand through his hair. "As ready as I'll ever be."

She motioned for him to follow her into the kitchen. When he stepped through the doorway, an elderly gentleman looked up from where he was sitting at the table.

"Adam, have you met my grandfather?"

Adam worked on shifting gears. He wasn't planning on meeting anyone today, least of all the patriarch of Kate's family. "Uh, no. I don't think so. Not formally, I mean. I've seen him at the soccer games."

The old man stuck his bottom lip out slightly and nodded. "I've been at several of the football games too. For such a young fella, you're a darn good coach."

The words worked like a mild tranquilizer for Adam's soul, calming his frazzled nerves and setting him at ease. He moved to the man with his hand outstretched.

"Adam Sullivan."

Kate's grandfather accepted the gesture with a grip that surprised him. "Clayton Wilbanks. Nice to meet'cha."

"You too."

Kate cleared her throat and wrung her hands. "Now that you're acquainted, there's something you should know."

"What is it?" Adam tensed up again.

She hesitated. "Well . . . you see . . . Grandpa Clayton is going to be teaching you what you need to know."

His mouth gaped slightly, and something that resembled betrayal tried to snake its way into his heart.

"Before you get upset, hear me out. Gramps is much more knowledgeable about the Bible than I am, and I felt you could learn more from him."

He turned to face her. "You *felt*? Did you consider discussing your *feelings* with me?" He managed to keep his voice low and calm, but inside he was screaming. "I asked for your help in confidence."

He shook his head unbelieving. He knew this was a mistake, that he should just turn and walk out without so much as a second glance, and he would have except that he was paralyzed by her pleading stare.

She held her hands out in desperation. "I want to help you, but the truth is . . . " She hung her head, her blond hair falling over her shoulder. "After Ryan died, I got about as far away from the Lord as I could get. I've just recently returned to Him, and I'm still working on relearning the Bible." She looked at him, her jade eyes damp, her voice barely more than a whisper. "I'm sorry. I didn't mean to betray your trust, but if you're still willing, maybe we can study the Bible together."

He softened. "I'll give it a try."

She touched his arm and smiled. "You'll never regret it."

I guess we'll see about that.

"Why don't you have a seat? Would you like a cup of coffee or a Coke or something?"

He sat down in a chair that flanked her grandfather and laid his Bible on the table in front of him. "A glass of water?"

"Coming right up. Gramps, are you ready for a refill on your coffee?"

Grandpa Clayton put his hand up, palm out. "Not'chet, Katy." Then he gestured at Adam's Bible. "That your grandpa's name on there?"

Adam glanced at the name printed in gold lettering. "Yeah."

"I knew Jacob."

Very suddenly this man was more than Kate's grandfather. He provided a connection to Adam's grandfather.

"You knew my grandpa?"

"Yep. He graduated two years ahead of me. Jacob was a talented athlete back in those days. If I remember correctly, he became the starting quarterback his sophomore year and led Harvest Bay to state in back-to-back years. Came home with the trophy both times too."

"That's right." Adam was intrigued and annoyed. This man he had met just a moment ago had unknowingly discovered a skeleton that he kept neatly tucked away in his closet.

There was a brief silence before Grandpa Clayton nodded. "Jacob was a good man."

"Yes."

Kate quietly carried two tall glasses of water to the table, set one in front of Adam, and took a seat with her Bible on the table in front of her. Inadequacy once again infiltrated Adam's brain as he eyed the multi-colored post-it notes peeking out from its pages.

Grandpa Clayton lifted his coffee cup to his lips with a shaky hand. "So, Adam, how can I help you?"

"Well . . . " He laid his hand on his grandfather's Bible. "I need to know what this is all about."

"I'm not a theologian. I can only tell you what I believe based on eighty-seven years of experience."

Adam's gaze swept across the table to Kate, and then fell to the Bible partially hidden under his hand. "And I can't promise that I'll believe it."

"Think you can have an open mind?"

"I'll try."

"Fair enough." Grandpa Clayton took another swallow from his coffee cup. "What I know about the Bible is what it says in John 1." He opened his large print Bible, flipped a few pages, and adjusted his bifocals. "Verse one says, 'In the beginning was the Word and the Word was with God and the Word was God.' It goes on to say in verse fourteen, 'And the Word became flesh and dwelt among us and we beheld His glory, the glory as of the only begotten of the Father, full of grace and truth.' "

Creases formed on Adam's brow while he considered what Grandpa Clayton had said. "What exactly does that mean?"

"It means that the Bible is more than just a book of stories. It's Jesus coming to earth, fulfilling all the promises in the Old Testament, teaching us how to live in the New Testament, and finally paying the ultimate price so we can have an actual relationship with God."

Adam looked down at his grandfather's old, worn Bible. All he saw was a plain, ordinary book. Nothing special.

"That's a pretty tough concept to grasp. Logically, it doesn't make sense."

Grandpa Clayton studied the design around the rim of his coffee cup. "When a person makes the choice to believe even when it doesn't make sense, he suddenly sees things in a whole new light." He looked at Adam, his eyes gleaming from the fire burning brightly in his soul. "It's called faith."

"Faith."

The word left a bad taste in Adam's mouth. He'd experienced faith before. He had faith that he'd play in the NFL, that his marriage would last, that Alexandra would be a better mother, and each year he had faith that Harvest Bay would win a state championship. Every time he'd been let down.

"You make it sound easy." Adam knew better than that.

"Sometimes it is, sometimes it's not, and sometimes you don't have a choice because it's all you have left in the world." Grandpa Clayton paused. "Having faith is kind of like playing football."

The words caught Adam's attention.

"Making the choice to play is easy. The long practices can be tough and studying the playbook can get tiring, but you know you have to do it to become a better player. Sometimes you have to play under tough conditions. Unfair calls are made. Injuries occur. But when it's all said and done, there's nothing else you'd rather do than play football."

Adam understood that illustration perfectly. It was his life. But faith wasn't football.

"You took a big step today, Adam, and now you have a lot to think about. Spend some time reading the Bible—I think the book of John is a good place to start—and let me know if you have any more questions. The choice is yours to make, but I'm happy to help in any way I can."

"Thanks. I'll keep that in mind."

Adam and Chloe left a short time later, and Adam immediately turned his attention to spending time with his daughter, helping with chores on his parents' farm, and later reviewing game film. However, when night fell and his house was quiet, memories of the afternoon with Kate and her grandfather came rushing back to him like waves on a stormy sea.

Yes, he had a lot to think about. He glanced at his grandfather's Bible on the nightstand next to him. He suspected he would have to do some soul searching too.

He stretched out on his bed, his hands cupped behind his head, wondering if it would be worth the effort.

Sixteen

The next two weeks were pure agony. As usual, Kate saw Adam on Tuesdays for the support group meetings, Saturdays for soccer games, and briefly on Sundays after church. But he gave her no indication that he'd accepted anything Grandpa Clayton had said.

"Just give him some time, Katy. He's got to figure some things out on his own now, but he'll be back. Mark my word. He'll be back," Grandpa Clayton had said. But Kate wasn't so sure.

She still kicked herself for not being honest with him from the start. She found it nearly impossible not to dwell on the example that she'd set for a nonbeliever. After all, this was regarding his salvation, an eternal life-or-death situation.

Finally she decided she had to let it go and leave it in the Lord's hands. Sitting on her front porch steps on that cool, late September afternoon, she sighed and wrapped her light jacket tighter around her.

"I trust You, Lord, but I need to trust You more than I trust myself or even Grandpa Clayton. I'm praying that You will win Adam over in Your time and in Your way. And I'm praying that You use me as You see fit."

At that moment Madeline, still wearing her soccer jersey from her late morning game, burst through the front door. "He's here! He's here!"

Kate stood just in time to avoid a collision as the seven-year-old steamroller plowed down the steps, used the sidewalk as her race track, and came to a screeching halt at the edge of the driveway. Kate slowly followed Madeline, who was a jack-in-the-box ready to pop, waiting for the BMW that had just pulled in to come to a stop and the driver-side door to open.

"Hey, Pipsqueak! You aren't happy to see me, are you?" Nathan asked, emerging from the sleek, silver car.

Madeline leapt into his arms. "Oh, yes, Uncle Nate! I'm so happy you're going to be living here! It'll be just like before, but better."

Better. Of course, it would be better, but when Kate embraced Nathan and that warm, comforting, familiar sensation returned to her, she wondered to what degree.

He grabbed a suitcase and garment bag from the back seat, and they started up the sidewalk, Madeline running up ahead.

Kate glanced at the two bags. "Are you sure you have everything you need until you close on your house Monday?"

"As long as the movers show up when they're supposed to, I'll be fine." He gave her the same grin she'd received thousands of times before, but this time it caused a powerful jolt in her heart. "I just hope I can be settled in by Wednesday."

October first—Nathan's first day at Harvest Bay Family Practice.

"Are you nervous?"

They climbed the steps and walked through the front door, where Madeline was already waiting. "I'm gonna go pick out a game for us, Uncle Nate, okay?"

He chuckled as he set his luggage down. "You bet." As she ran to her bedroom, he followed Kate into the kitchen.

"A little, I guess. People in this town love Doc Brewster."

She reached into the cupboard for two glasses. "Don't worry. It won't be long before everyone knows and loves you like . . ." She stopped, leaving the words "I do" hanging at the tip of her tongue.

"Like?"

She swallowed and opened the fridge. "Well, like Doc Brewster, of course." She grabbed the pitcher of lemonade, filled the glasses, and handed one to him. "And if you're not completely settled in by then, you'll be close. You'll have lots of help. Maddie and I will stop by after school. Mom told me to tell you that she's available all day. Oh, and Daddy and Elizabeth can come over after their shifts."

He stared at her with humble appreciation. "Wow. Thanks, Kate."

She grinned, hoping it was genuine enough to conceal the emotions he had stirred up in her. She took a long drink to soothe her suddenly dry throat.

"Listen, I have to get some food ready and take care of a few other chores before the get-together this evening. Why don't you make yourself at home? I'm sure Maddie has a list of things she'd like you to do with her."

They both chuckled.

"Or I could help you, and then we can both spend time with Maddie." Nathan's chocolate eyes searched hers.

Kate looked away fearful of what he would find if he searched hard enough. "Okay."

Standing at the kitchen counter side by side, peeling cucumbers and cleaning celery for a vegetable tray, they chatted happily about Madeline, school, life in Harvest Bay, Alice and the doctors in the Vanderbilt practice, and, as always, their favorite memories of Ryan.

She smiled to herself, thinking that Madeline was right. It was going to be just like before. But better.

⚜

Nathan mingled half-heartedly with the houseful of guests Kate had invited. Despite the fact that they had all come to welcome him, he felt almost as out of place as he had at Madeline's birthday party. After what seemed like hours, he found a quiet corner and discreetly checked his Rolex.

Seven-thirty. He sighed. In lieu of this great party, he really just wanted alone time with Kate, to just be together and reminisce the way they had in the kitchen earlier that day.

"If I remember correctly, this is where I found you at Maddie's birthday party."

He snapped his gaze up to find Denise's dazzling smile and sparkling topaz eyes. The corners of his mouth turned up as he casually slipped his hands into the pockets of his khakis.

"I believe you're right. So who are you going to introduce me to this time?"

"Funny you should ask." At that moment, a raven-haired young woman joined them. "Nathan, this is Maggie Martinez. She's a medical receptionist in our office."

"It's nice to meet you. I've heard a lot about you."

Rosy tones colored Maggie's cheeks when she shook his hand.

"Maggie still has five more weeks of maternity leave, but we'll be glad to have her back after that." Denise winked at her.

Nathan scanned the room. "So where's this baby Kate keeps talking about?"

"Kate's *madre es* holding Justin." Maggie pointed to the other side of the crowded living room, where Rebecca cuddled and bounced a bundle of blue.

"Ah. Well, he's in good hands then."

"*Sí*, but he will need to eat soon. Who would have thought a baby could have such a *grande* appetite? Aye yi yi!"

Denise laid a hand on the young mother's shoulder and lowered her voice. "Just wait until he's a teenager."

Nathan was about to point out the benefits of raising boys, such as spending less money on clothes, shoes, and hair, when little Justin's mighty wail rang out. Maggie gave a weary grin.

"Right on time."

"I'm looking forward to working with you, Maggie."

"*Gracias*. I do too." She gave a little wave and made her way to her hungry baby.

He shifted his attention to Denise. "She seems to be doing well."

"For the most part, I think she is."

He studied her. "How about you? Things any better with Griffin?"

She shrugged, her cheerful expression fading a bit. "We have our moments. Some days go by without any fighting, but that usually means there's no talking taking place either."

"Are the boys with their dad today?"

"No. They're here. They joined in a game of backyard football as soon as we got here. I'm sure they'll be in soon, if for no other reason than to search for food."

He chuckled. "I can't wait to see them again." *Especially Griffin.*

That evening he saw the boys only briefly between visiting with guests. Greyson gave him a nod and a " 'Sup?" Griffin didn't acknowledge him. Understanding the ways of a teenager, Nathan shrugged his indifference off.

On Thursday afternoon, however, after seeing only a handful of patients in an office he wasn't the least bit comfortable in, his heart was so heavy it seemed to be resting on his stomach. He stepped into his new office, half the size of the one he'd left at Vanderbilt, closed the door, and went to his desk. Exhausted from all of the moving and organizing he'd done in two days, he sat down heavily and put his face in his hands.

"God, didn't you bring me here? Was I hearing you correctly, or have I made the biggest mistake of my life? Please, God. This can't be it. It can't be."

He didn't feel like reading, but he needed a heavy dose of inspiration to get him through the day, so he pulled his Bible out of his leather briefcase and opened it to where he'd left off the night before.

He began the fifth chapter of Romans with a lackluster attitude, but by the time he reached verse three, the heavy weight he'd been carrying all day began to disappear and his spirits lifted. He could almost hear the Lord whispering the words in his ear.

"And not only that, but we also glory in tribulations, knowing that tribulation produces perseverance; and perseverance, character; and character, hope. Now hope does not disappoint, because the love of God has been poured out in our hearts by the Holy Spirit who was given to us."

Nathan closed the Bible. He'd read all he needed to for the time being. His heart brimming with renewed hope and his soul oozing fresh determination, he decided to flap his wings a little harder. He'd taken leap of faith in moving to Harvest Bay. Now with the Lord's help, he would fly.

He was a doctor. Doctors help people. He had come to Harvest Bay to heal Kate and Madeline's broken hearts, but in the meantime there were plenty of people needing assistance, and Nathan was determined to reach them. First he would earn their trust, and then he would win their hearts just like Doc Brewster had all those years ago.

Step one would be getting out in the community. Talk with the citizens. Let them see his face and get to know him. But where would he start in a town this small?

"The Bayside Café!"

He jumped to his feet and in four long strides reached the door. Turning the knob he threw it open. And froze.

His office was right across the hall from the reception area. He had a perfect view of Denise working diligently on her computer, and the thought struck him that maybe she'd like to take a quick break for a piece of pie.

He moved into the hallway to ask her, when he heard the tinkling of the bell above the front door. A moment later he saw Griffin emerge into the area behind the front counter.

Nathan crept closer.

She looked up from her computer. "Hi, sweetie. How was your day?"

The teen flopped into a chair, snatched a book from his backpack, zipped it shut, and then threw it down. "Who cares?"

Nathan's gaze shot to Denise's crumpled face, and it took everything inside him not to shake that boy to wake him up and show him what he was doing to his mother.

She silently returned to her work.

"Oh, by the way, Greyson told me to remind you that practice is over at six tonight instead of five."

She stared into the computer screen, but Nathan got the impression that she was seeing something farther off than their patients' name and information. "That's cutting it a little close for church."

"So what?"

Nathan bit his tongue so hard he could taste blood.

"Listen up right now." Her tone was calm but firm. "You are done disrespecting me, and I won't tolerate you undermining the importance of our church." Her expression softened. "We wouldn't have made it on our own without our church family."

"Whatever."

She sighed deeply and shook her head, her topaz eyes becoming glassy. "Get started on your homework."

"I don't have any."

"You're lying. I spoke with your biology teacher today. You have a chapter review that's due tomorrow and a test scheduled for Friday."

Nathan perked up. Griffin wasn't physically sick or hurting, but he was still in need. Nathan moved in closer.

Griffin's shoulders slumped. "C'mon, Mom. What difference is it going to make? Whether I do it or not, I'll still get an F."

Nathan leaned against the doorway and crossed his arms. "Wanna bet?"

Griffin nearly jumped out of his chair, which caused a smile to return to Denise's face. "Sheez, what are you? Some kind of eavesdropper?"

"Not at all. I was just coming to see if your mother had scheduled any new appointments for me this afternoon, and I couldn't help but overhear. You weren't exactly whispering."

Denise stifled a giggle.

"So, Ms. Golden, anything new on the books?"

"No, Dr. Sterling. You have an hour and a half before your next appointment."

"In that case, I am going to walk over to the Bayside Café. I hear they have the best homemade apple pie around." *There we go. There's that dazzling smile.* He turned to Griffin. "Why don't you come with me? We can eat pie and talk biology."

Griffin remained silent, unmoving.

After a long minute, Nathan pushed away from the door. "Funny. I never knew a guy to turn down a piece of pie." He shrugged and turned to walk away. "Suit yourself."

Please, God, soften his heart before I get out the door. Not for me. Not even for Griffin. Right now he doesn't deserve it. Please, God, do it for Denise.

As he reached the front door and slowly turned the handle, he felt like he was hanging from a cliff.

Come on, Griffin. I'm reaching out to you. Reach out to me, too. Your mother needs to see that effort from you.

He opened the door, bell tinkling, and took one step onto the porch.

"Wait!"

He exhaled, suppressed a smile, and turned. "Yeah?"

Griffin came hurrying around the corner of the reception area, his backpack slung over his shoulder. "I am a little hungry. And I suppose it wouldn't hurt to go over my chapter review."

"It'll be virtually pain free. I promise." He thought he saw one corner of Griffin's mouth twitch. "Maybe you should check with your mom first, though."

Griffin dismissed the thought with a wave. "Oh, she won't care."

"I care." He stared at Griffin. "It's the right thing to do."

Griffin pondered that thought for only a second before turning around. He didn't have to go far to ask for permission. Denise had quietly followed her son out of the reception area and stood in front of the check-in window, watching with hope gleaming in her eyes where only moments before there had been tears of despair.

"Can I go, Mom?"

She nodded. "Sure."

Griffin walked past Nathan out onto the porch. Nathan glanced back at her, and she mouthed the words, "Thank you." He nodded and followed Griffin out.

As they walked down the sidewalk, making the most insignificant conversation, Nathan trod on eggshells. He had to earn Griffin's trust, but at a higher level, Nathan would have to persevere. He would also have to be realistic.

But regardless of what happened, this was a start, definitely a step in the right direction. And maybe one day Griffin would reach the place where he could glory in his tribulations, knowing that tribulation produces perseverance; and perseverance, character; and character, hope.

ate had helped Nathan get settled in his new home after school on Monday and Tuesday, but she needed every spare minute of Wednesday and Thursday to prepare for parent/teacher conferences on Friday. Her list of preparations seemed a mile long. But when the morning of conferences arrived, she was ready and even confident as she strolled into Madeline's bedroom.

"Rise and shine!" She crossed the room and opened the blinds, instantly lighting up the room.

Madeline pulled her pillow over her head, muffling her voice. "Aw, Mama! I thought we didn't have school today."

"You don't, but I do. You're going to spend the day with Grammy and Great-gramps."

Madeline pulled the pillow down just a hair. "What about Papa?"

"You'll get to see Papa when he gets home from work."

Madeline sat straight up in bed. "Yay!"

Kate laughed and tousled Madeline's already rumpled hair. "Hop up and get dressed. We've got to leave soon."

The little girl quickly obeyed, and within twenty minutes they walked out the door.

"Mama, are you going to talk to Jane?" Madeline asked as soon as Kate pulled out of the driveway.

"I am Emma's teacher so, yes, I'll talk to Jane today."

Madeline was thoughtful for a moment. "Does that mean you'll talk to my teacher too?"

"Yes." Kate glanced in her rearview mirror, amused by the Madeline's concerned expression. "Don't worry, honey. I'm sure Ms. Sullivan will have nothing but good things to say about you."

Madeline relaxed as Kate flipped on her blinker and turned onto her parents' street. A brief lull filled the Explorer before Madeline thought of another question.

"So are you gonna talk to Adam too?"

Kate felt the blood drain from her face and land in the pit of her stomach. "Yes."

But what would she say to him? It would only take her a few minutes to tell him what he needed to know about Chloe. And then what?

She guessed he would leave and begin to prepare for the football game that evening . . . unless she could hoist all her courage up from the depths of her soul and ask him if he'd considered anything that Grandpa Clayton had told him in the three weeks since their meeting. Had he studied the Bible? Prayed? She'd take anything, including the tiniest of baby steps, if it was in the right direction.

Conferences were scheduled every half hour, starting at eight and ending at six, with only a few gaps where parents had requested a conference earlier in the week due to week-end plans. Adam's conference was at four o'clock. She had to make it through fourteen conferences bearing the weight of anticipation.

Fortunately when she was in a conference she was so focused on the student, praising his or her accomplishments and offering the parents suggestions for needed improvements, that her inner turmoil only surfaced during her hour-long lunch break and the brief minute in between conferences. Unfortunately the fourteen conferences passed quickly, and before she had time to fully prepare herself mentally, Adam appeared in her doorway.

"Am I early?"

Quickly taking in his gray dress pants, pale blue Oxford shirt, and matching tie that intensified his blond hair and blue eyes, she forced a smile, hoping he wouldn't notice the furnace that had just kicked on in her cheeks. This was going to be the very first conference in which she had a tough time focusing on the student.

"Right on time, according to my clock." She motioned to the table near her desk where she had been conducting her conferences. "Come in and have a seat."

He strode over and sat down. "So how are your conferences going?"

She carried a portfolio of Chloe's work over to the table and took a seat across from him. "Great! I have some wonderful parents this year."

Adam tipped his head to the side, a smirk playing with his lips. "It's okay. You can mention Jane and Ian by name."

"Oh. Well, I was referring to all of you." She nearly gasped. "I mean, not just you . . . All of the parents . . . which, of course, includes you, but everyone else too."

She glanced up to see that his smirk had blossomed into an amused smile, which only cranked up that furnace. She fanned herself with Chloe's papers.

"Are you interested in moving this conference outside? I think I need some fresh air."

He laughed out loud, his bright blue eyes sparkling. "Sounds good to me."

As they strolled down the hallway, close but not touching, she calmed her wildly beating heart the only way she knew how.

God, Your word says that with the temptation, You will also make the way of escape. Right now, I am tempted and I need an escape. I must fulfill my role as Chloe's teacher. Please, dear God, clear my mind of everything except my student and her progress.

She repeated the silent prayer. By the time they turned a corner and headed toward the heavy, metal double doors that led to the playground, her cardiac rhythm had almost returned to normal.

"So how have your conferences been today?" she asked.

"Pretty good, but I don't see as many parents as you do even though I have more students."

"Why not?"

He shrugged. "It's different when a kid has seven teachers in a day. Health and wellness is certainly not top on the list of parents' priorities."

They walked the remainder of the hallway in silence. When they reached the door, Adam pushed through and held it open for Kate.

She stepped through to a small courtyard that opened up into a large fenced-in playground. She filled her lungs with the crisp, fresh air and became instantly rejuvenated.

They headed to a nearby picnic table in this little nook, which was one of Kate's favorite attributes of Harvest Bay

Elementary. It was partially shielded from the elements by three exterior walls of the building and far enough away from the play equipment to keep the children's attention from wandering. Every class held dozens of science experiments and other activities there each year.

"Better?" He asked lowering himself onto the bench seat.

She slipped into her side. "Much. For me, being inside all day is the hardest part about parent teacher conferences."

"I agree."

"Shall we discuss your daughter?" Her tone rang with professionalism, and she wondered if it was too brisk.

He didn't seem to notice. "Absolutely."

She turned the stapled papers around so he could read them. "As you can see, Chloe's grades are all well above average." She turned the pages of the spreadsheets, pointing out the grades she wanted to bring to his attention. "I've paired her with a student who's struggling a little in math. Chloe has such a gentle, patient spirit that she makes an excellent peer tutor."

He nodded. "That's good."

She flipped to the samples of Chloe's work. "It's quite obvious that she doesn't rush through her assignments. Her handwriting is beautiful . . . "

"Wait!" He scanned one of the assignments that she'd flipped to. "What's this?"

"That's a writing assignment we did just after Labor Day— a short essay on who their hero is and why." She paused allowing him time to read the paper. "Many of my students chose famous athletes or other celebrities. Chloe chose you."

"This is really . . . " He glanced at her, emotion welling up in his eyes. " . . . It's really something."

She impulsively reached across the picnic table and placed her hand on his forearm. "You must be very proud."

"I am," he said, his voice gruff.

She slid her hand back. "I do have one potential area of concern."

"What's that?"

"Chloe is very eager to please to the point of putting others' needs before hers. Several times I've watched her drop what she was doing because one of her classmates wanted her attention. I know it's a fine line, and in fourth grade it's not really an issue. But if this tendency is left unaddressed, she could end up getting walked on. With your help, I want to teach her that it's okay to speak up for herself, to be an individual not a puppet."

He rubbed the tension out of back of his neck. "I think she might've come by it naturally."

Her heart bubbled over with compassion. "The best way to teach Chloe is by example."

"I understand."

Silence fell between them. Kate wondered if Adam was still thinking about Chloe's essay or about his responsibility to teach her to think for herself.

She glanced at her watch. It was twenty after four, and the conference was over. If she was going to find out if he'd given any thought to what Grandpa Clayton had told him, she couldn't wait a minute longer. Just when she was about to open her mouth, Grandpa Clayton's words echoed in her mind.

Just give him some time, Katy. He's got to figure some things out on his own now, but he'll be back. Mark my word. He'll be back.

And she knew that, for the time being, it wasn't her place to question him.

She placed her hands, palms down, on the table top and stood up. "That's all I have, so unless you have any questions . . . "

"Actually, I do have a question."

"Oh. Okay." She sank back down. His confident tone had turned serious, and she braced herself. "What's up?"

He fidgeted. "You know that homecoming is in two weeks?"

She frowned. "Yeah."

"The game is on Friday and the dance is on Saturday."

"That's how it's always been."

"Well, I was asked to chaperone the dance this year and, knowing Chloe like you do, it shouldn't surprise you that I couldn't tell them no." He cleared his throat. "I know this is short notice, but I was wondering if you'd be my date."

Kate's lips slowly curled upwards, and she wondered if they would ever stop. "You're asking me to go to the homecoming dance with you?"

"Yeah . . . yeah, I am." He momentarily met her gaze and managed a timid grin.

She couldn't help laughing out loud.

His smile fell flat. "Why are you laughing?"

"We have been out of high school for sixteen years, and now you're asking me to the dance!"

He chuckled, and then sobered. "That's true, but you still haven't answered me, and I'm starting to get nervous."

She nodded. "Yes, I'll go with you."

"Great. Thanks, Kate."

Although his words were composed, his eyes sparkled like the sun shining on the ocean, nearly hypnotizing her. She could have stared into them the rest of the afternoon and into the evening, but the cognitive part of her brain reminded her that she had a job to finish.

"Sure. Now we better get back." She stood on suddenly shaky knees and checked her watch. "I don't want to be late for my four-thirty conference."

He got to his feet. "Right. And I have to take care of some last-minute preparations before we load the bus."

She practically floated back to the building. *How could this conference have gone any better?*

He once again held the door open for her. "Oh, one more question."

She sailed through. "Ask away."

He slipped his hands into his pockets. "Do you think your grandpa has plans tomorrow after the girls' soccer game?"

That's how.

Kate gave Adam a smile she was certain would have made the Cheshire cat envious. "I'm pretty sure he's free."

⁕

The short drive to Kate's house from Frosty Jack's shouldn't have given Adam enough time to think about anything in particular, but his mind was going about as fast as his truck down the country roads. Truthfully, a part of him couldn't believe he was on his way to talk to Grandpa Clayton again. Similarly, he couldn't believe that he'd actually read the entire book of John and even reread some of the chapters. And he still had a hard time believing he'd showed up at the first single-parent support group, where that seed of curiosity had been planted.

He'd had no intention of going through with any of it. His plate was comfortably full. He managed it well, but he certainly didn't need to add to it. Yet here he was once again, the magnet in his soul being supernaturally pulled toward the hard-as-steel answers to the questions that perpetually plagued him.

He supposed he could turn the truck around and go home. The attraction wasn't that strong. But he knew something deep inside of him would be disappointed, and he'd experienced enough disappointment in his thirty-four years to last him a lifetime.

He pulled into Kate's driveway, shut off the engine, and grabbed his grandfather's Bible from where he'd stashed it under the seat. Chloe sprang out of the truck and ran off to play with Madeline, who was waiting eagerly for her. Adam, on the other hand, wasn't in that big of a hurry. He spotted Grandpa Clayton sitting in a lawn chair under a sprawling oak, and since Kate was nowhere to be seen, he headed in that direction.

"Nice day, isn't it?" Grandpa Clayton said when he drew near.

"Sure is." Although the older man wore a light-weight jacket, Adam was comfortable in his T-shirt and jeans.

"Katy's in the house brewing a pot of coffee. She'll be out in a little while." Grandpa Clayton gestured at the empty lawn chair next to him. "Have a seat. Make yourself comfortable."

Adam didn't know if he could shake enough of his edginess to qualify as comfortable, but he took a seat anyway.

Grandpa Clayton patted the arm of the chair with the palm of his hand. "That was a good game last night."

"Thanks." Then astonishment hit him over the head. "You mean you were there?"

"Nah. I listened to it on my old transistor radio. I don't make it to too many away games anymore."

"The boys have been working hard. They really want to win a state championship." Adam really wanted it too, but he left that side note out.

"Think you'll bring home the trophy this year?"

Adam was silent for a moment. He wished he could confidently say yes, but he just didn't know.

"We still have to clinch playoffs." He shrugged. "Our team is good, but there are a lot of good teams in our division this year."

Grandpa Clayton nodded, his bottom lip protruding just a bit. "Well, I'm guessing you didn't come over here to talk football."

Adam leaned forward, resting his forearms on his knees, and rubbed his hands together. "You're right. I didn't." He took a deep breath and decided to jump right in. "The last time I was here you said that faith is when a person makes the choice to believe even when it doesn't make sense."

"That's it in a nutshell."

"I need to know more about that."

"Got your Bible?"

Adam held it up.

"Turn to Hebrews 11:1."

Adam opened the front cover, skimmed the table of contents until he found Hebrews, and then flipped to the page number. Finally finding chapter eleven, he began to read. "It says, 'Now faith is the substance of things hoped for, the evidence of things not seen.' "

"In other words, faith is made up of what we hope for and believe in but can't see with our eyes." Grandpa Clayton tapped on his chest. "Faith is kind of like seeing with your heart."

"Simple as that." Adam shook his head.

Seeing with your heart? How is that even possible?

"I suppose for some it's as simple as that." Grandpa Clayton looked at Adam. "But everyone I know has had their struggles."

"Including you?"

"Oh, sure. Surviving the attack on Pearl Harbor made me question a lot of things."

Adam stared at him in awe. "You were at Pearl Harbor?"

" 'Fraid so."

Adam sat on the edge of his seat, not wanting to pry, but hoping the old man would share some of his experience.

After a few minutes, Grandpa Clayton cleared his throat. "I was a young man in 1941, not that long out of high school, full of myself and empty of the Lord—though I was raised in a church-going family, mind you. Well, I arrived in Pearl Harbor just after Labor Day, and I was assigned to the *Vestal*, a little repair ship. Our job was upkeep of all the other ships. Not a fancy job, but I was proud of the *Vestal* and the crew I was a part of."

He wore a reminiscent grin. "By the time my buddies and I finally crawled out of bed that Sunday morning, it was somewhere around a quarter till seven. I wasn't feeling too well. A late night ashore will do that to a fella." He elbowed the air near Adam and chuckled. "So I skipped breakfast. While I made my way very slowly to the bathroom, I remember thinking that with the time zone difference, if I'd been here at home with Mom and Pop, we'd already have been to church and home by then. I knew Mom would've been disappointed that I was headed to the bathroom to sober up instead of cleaning up for church."

Adam nodded. He understood the pain of disappointing one's family all too well.

"About an hour later, just before eight o'clock, we heard the alarm sound general quarters, but we didn't think much of it. We just thought, odd as it was, that someone was holding a drill . . . until I heard the planes flying unusually close. When I looked out my porthole and saw a big red ball on one of the planes' wing, I knew it wasn't just a drill."

Adam sucked in his breath. "What did you do?"

"We'd all trained for this, but for a minute or two no one really knew what to do until our commander started shouting orders. 'Man your stations! Man your stations!' The station I was responsible for was the three-inch gun. The other gunners and I got to our stations lickety split, trying to prepare ourselves for what was about to happen. We didn't have long to process it. Right about the same time we began firing our weapons we felt the ship shudder and rise out of the water just a bit."

"You were hit, weren't you?"

"Yes, indeed. Twice. Once on the port side and once on the starboard side. We were taking on water fast, and I knew there were men hurt, maybe even dying, below the decks." Grandpa Clayton let out a little sigh. "But I couldn't think about that. I had my own problems. After firing three rounds, our gun jammed. The commander barked at me to go get more ammo while the rest of the crew worked on clearing the jam. I followed his orders without question." Grandpa Clayton shrugged. "That's just what you do in the service. But I had a lot of questions after it was all said and done."

Adam thought if he sat any closer to the edge of his seat, he'd fall out of it. "Why?"

"Well, you see, the *Arizona* was moored inboard of us, and as I was heading back to my station, a bomb hit her in one of her magazines. That explosion ignited adjacent magazines and resulted in a blast so powerful it blew our commander and my fellow gunners right off our ship!"

Grandpa Clayton's boney shoulders fell. "I saw the whole thing. Despite the intense heat, I ran to the side of the ship. Oil had leaked into the water and was burning. There was no way any of them could've survived. I had permanent hearing loss from the explosion, received some burns, and a few cuts and scrapes." His gravelly voice wavered. "But that didn't compare to the pain I felt for my shipmates."

Emotion rose in Adam's throat, and he swallowed hard. "I'm so sorry."

"I was too, not just for my crew and me, but for all of the men on *Arizona* and the other ships moored on Battleship Row. Over two thousand men died, eleven hundred on the *Arizona* alone." Grandpa Clayton wiped a hand over his mouth and down his clean-shaven chin. "I sure got a glimpse of hell that day."

"Is that when you turned to God?"

"Nope. No, I turned farther from Him. For a while I questioned whether God even existed because in a young man's mind it didn't make sense how a loving God could allow such devastation and destruction to happen."

"I can understand that." After a brief moment of silence, Adam said softly, "But your faith seems so strong now. How did you get from there to here?"

Grandpa Clayton slid his gaze over to Adam. "The love of a good woman."

Adam glanced at the house just as Kate emerged carrying a steaming mug, and all his senses involuntarily came alive.

"My Bonnie was a nurse at the hospital on the base. I finally went to get checked out when the ringing in my ears wouldn't stop. She asked me if I minded if she prayed for me. The foolish boy that I was told that pretty young thing that she could do whatever she wanted, that it was still a free country for the time being." Grandpa Clayton chuckled as Kate approached and handed him his cup of coffee. "Thanks, Katy." He took a cautious sip.

Adam hopped up. "Here, Kate. Take my seat."

"That's okay. I'll get another chair from the garage. Be back in a jiffy." She turned and headed back toward the house.

Adam couldn't keep himself from watching her go.

Grandpa Clayton cleared his throat. "As I was saying, when my Bonnie laid her hand on my shoulder and earnestly prayed for me, a stranger, my soul stirred. Despite all the death and destruction, there was a sweet little glimmer of hope. After about two weeks I finally got up the nerve to ask her out on a date." He smiled, staring off into space. "She told me yes, but she would have to pick the time and place." He turned to Adam with a twinkle in his eye. "Do you know where we went on our first date?"

Adam shook his head.

"We went to a young adult Bible study that she was leading at her church, and then out for coffee afterwards."

Adam grinned. *That sounds just like Kate.* But then his expression fell slightly.

"So you became a Christian for your wife?"

"No-o. No, no, no. You can't become a Christian for some-one else. I became a Christian for me, but it was because of Bonnie. Sometimes the Lord brings people into your life who will very gently take your hand and lead you to Him."

Adam redirected his gaze to Kate, who crossed the lawn with a chair to join them. "I'm beginning to see that."

"That's good. You're seeing with your heart. That's a start." Grandpa Clayton looked thoughtful for a moment. "You know the old saying, 'Everything happens for a reason?' "

Adam nodded.

"Well, it's true. The Bible promises us that God uses all things for our good. All things. As terrible as that December day was, there was good that came out of it—in our nation, in the world, in my life. Because of what happened, I met Bonnie, and the forty-two years I spent with her were the best years of this old man's life. It took a long while, countless evenings of Bible study, and a whole lotta prayer, but she helped me grow to have a solid relationship with the Lord."

Grandpa Clayton's eyes became misty, and Kate laid her hand over his. "And when He called her home twenty-four years ago, I still had that relationship to bring me peace and comfort. If ya ask me, that's what faith is about."

Adam's gaze fell to his beaten, worn tennis shoes. He could never have a faith like Grandpa Clayton's, and he couldn't stand the thought of letting Kate down, not to mention Chloe and the rest of his family.

Kate leaned forward. "Just take it one step at a time. It's a journey, Adam. A marathon, not a sprint."

He looked at her, suddenly very aware that she hadn't entered his life by some crazy coincidence. Driving from Nashville, she'd had five hundred miles to have a flat tire, yet it happened just a few yards from his parents' house. Was that God?

The corners of his mouth turned up. "One step at a time, huh? I think I can do that."

CHAPTER
Eighteen

*S*unday brunch at the Marshalls was unlike anything Nathan had ever experienced but had always dreamed of. At the soccer game the day before, Rebecca had invited him to join them. He happily accepted, unable to keep from remembering the family gatherings of his past.

He, Ryan, and their grandmother would sit at the little, round kitchen table in the old, musty-smelling house that had been the setting of most of his childhood. His sweet grandmother, a wonderful cook, always had a cheery disposition, but it did little to soothe the loneliness that constantly weighed down his young heart.

Occasionally their father would join them, but his attention was constantly on whoever was on the other end of the phone line. That had fueled Nathan's anger and bitterness and hardened his heart so it had taken twenty-five years for anything to penetrate that impossible barrier.

Now as he sat at the Marshalls' long, oval dining room table with Kate, Madeline, and their family, his heart once again grew heavy, but this time with sadness for his father. *Does he even know what he's been missing out on all these years?*

Kate's grandfather said the blessing, and immediately after everyone at the table said "Amen," they began to visit.

Nathan caught bits and pieces of three different conversa-
tions surrounding him. He answered when directly spoken to,
but mostly he just took it all in. Although the food was amazing, it paled in comparison to the warmth that filled his once
stone-cold heart. He had come to Harvest Bay for Kate and
Madeline, never expecting to inherit a whole family.

"Hey, Uncle Nate, will you come outside and play soccer
with me?" Madeline asked when the meal neared its end.

"Sure, but you'd better check with your mom first."

Madeline looked pleadingly up at Kate, who laughed and
touselled her daughter's chestnut bob. "Go on, but grab your
jacket."

"Yay!" Madeline scooted back from the table with one
mighty shove and ran for the door, swiping her jacket off a
chair on the way.

By the time Kate and Nathan came outside, she was
already kicking the soccer ball against the thick trunk of a
huge shade tree. They ran around the yard for quite a while,
playing a version of Keep Away in between fits of hysterical
laughter. Finally, Elizabeth and Elijah appeared with two tall
glasses of iced tea and a plastic cup of water.

"Water break!" Elizabeth shouted.

Madeline raced to quench her thirst, while Kate and
Nathan strolled over and gratefully accepted the refreshments.

"Thanks," Kate said after a long drink. "We needed that."

"I thought you might. Why don't you two take a breather?
Elijah and I are ready to see if we can take on this little soccer
machine."

"You're on!" With that Madeline thrust her empty cup at
Kate and took off with the ball.

Elizabeth shrieked. "Get her, Elijah!"

Elijah tried unsuccessfully to swipe the ball. "I could use some help!"

Laughing, Kate and Nathan walked over to the covered swing near the house. It was such an intimate moment in what had been a special morning that he considered taking her hand. It seemed only natural, but he resisted the temptation. It was still too soon. They sat together in silence for a moment, the only sound coming from the soft squeak of the swing's hinges.

She angled toward him. "How was your first week in Harvest Bay?"

He caught a hint of her perfume, and it went straight to his brain. "It just keeps getting better." He shifted his gaze away from her hoping she didn't detect the depth of his words. "Each day I see a couple new patients, so even though I'm no Doc Brewster, I think people are getting used to me."

She pulled her knees up to her chest while the cool breeze fingered her hair. "It's still hard for me to believe that you've actually moved here."

"I've had to pinch myself a couple of times too."

"Do you regret it?"

He watched a leaf float to the ground. "No. I think it's what Ryan would want."

She leaned into him a little. "You mean for us to be surrounded by people who love us?" She smiled sweetly. "You're absolutely right."

He worked hard to maintain his cool, confident attitude, but he was sure the giddy sensation in the core of his being was popping out of his pores like daisies on a warm April afternoon. He crossed his arms, hoping to contain his emotions.

"So tell me about your week. How were your conferences?"

Her smile fell slightly, and she sat up straighter. "They went well. I always enjoy meeting and talking with my students' parents, but they never fail to surprise me."

His interest grew. "What happened this time?"

She forced a laugh. "Actually, it was the funniest thing. I got asked to go to the homecoming dance in two weeks. Can you believe that?"

He quit moving the swing and stared at her. "One of your parents asked you to go to the homecoming dance?"

She nodded.

He turned his head to look out over the yard, slowly digesting this information. He didn't have to wonder who it was, but he asked anyway.

"Was it Adam?"

"He needed a date. I'm doing him a favor."

Of course, Nathan couldn't blame him. What man wouldn't want to show up at a dance with Kate? Besides, Adam didn't know that it was God's plan for Nathan to move to Harvest Bay, begin a life with Kate and Madeline, and become a part of their incredible family.

"But I'm going to have to cancel. Mom and Elizabeth both have plans so I don't have anyone to watch Maddie. I'm sure Adam will understand."

Her words were drenched with disappointment. It was a tone that he'd do anything to change.

"Don't be silly. Go to the dance. I'll watch Maddie." The words tumbled out before he could stop them.

She stared at him. "Excuse me?"

He closed his eyes and inhaled deeply. "Don't go back on your word just because you can't find a sitter. Maddie and I will have our own special date. Just tell me what time to pick her up."

Sweet affection lit up her face, and he was sure it was the closest he'd ever come to seeing an angel this side of heaven.

"Um, five-thirty?" Then she added with a grin, "And her curfew is nine." At that moment, her radiance rivaled the sun's. She placed her hand on his forearm. "Thanks, Nathan."

He put his hand over hers. "It's all right."

And it would be. He would make sure of it.

⁂

Autumn was at its peak by the time homecoming arrived. Rich shades of red, orange, and gold accented the tree-lined streets through town. The temperatures dropped from slightly nippy to severely chilly, and the earthy scent of decaying leaves floated in the breeze with the billowy clouds in the early evening sky. It was the kind of setting that could make even a non-fanatic crazy about football, and homecoming heightened the excitement.

Adam grinned, visualizing the scene that would be awaiting his team when they trotted out of the locker room and took to the field. The lights would illuminate the field with such wattage that the glow could be seen on the other side of town. The smell of popcorn and other concession snacks would drift into the packed stands and weave through the spectators lined along the fence. And the atmosphere would be charged with competitive energy, a sensation he would never grow immune to.

Somewhere in that crowd would be his family—his parents, brothers, sisters-in-law, nieces and nephews, Kennedy, and Chloe. They were a constant support, and he hoped he would make them proud tonight.

But there would also be Kate, Madeline, and Grandpa Clayton—three people he'd grown to care very deeply about and believed were helping him to become a better person. Most likely he wouldn't be able to see any of them from the field, but he'd know they were there and that was enough. It was probably better that way. Once the game started, even the often deafening roar of the crowd equated to nothing more than background noise while his total concentration during those four twelve-minute periods was on winning the game.

He stepped into the musty-smelling cinderblock room lined with lockers and benches. His team had suited up and was now preparing mentally by listening to their iPods. Some were stretching. A couple of linemen were taping their fingers. Kyle was wrapping his knee. Tom Ellsworth and Jonah Kelly, the offensive and defensive coordinators, were going over plays with their key players.

"Hey, guys." He moved further into the room, closing the semi-circle of uniform-clad guys and half a dozen coaches. "I don't have to tell you that this is a big game. Yes, it's homecoming, but winning tonight will also clinch our spot in the playoffs." He shifted his weight. "And if any team deserves to be in the playoffs, this one does. You boys understand the meaning of the word team. I've seen it over and over again so far this year. You work together and you get the job done. And I am proud of you. No matter what happens out there tonight, I'm proud of you."

He cleared his throat, a powerful, unknown force pushing him forward. He assumed his "coach" stance—feet firmly planted shoulder-width apart, arms crossed.

"Recently I started studying the Bible, and I read last night in the book of Matthew about a father who took his sick son to see Jesus."

His gaze swept the room as he took in the team's reactions. Most looked bewildered, a couple disinterested. But Tom's and Kyle's triumphant grins provided enough motivation for Adam to plunge forward.

"The father told Jesus that the disciples tried to heal his son and couldn't so Jesus went ahead and healed the boy. Later, in private, the disciples asked Jesus why they weren't able to heal the boy. Do you know what Jesus told them?"

Everyone except for Tom and Kyle returned blank stares.

"He told them that they didn't have enough faith." Adam slipped his hand into the pocket of his Dockers and pulled out a notecard he'd scrawled the verse on, wishing he could just pull it from his memory like Grandpa Clayton did. "Jesus said, 'If you have faith as a mustard seed, you will say to this mountain, "Move from here to there," and it will move; and nothing will be impossible for you.' "

He looked at his team. "*Nothing* will be impossible for you. Not this game. Not playoffs. Not a state championship. Believe in yourselves like I believe in you, like He," Adam pointed heavenward, "believes in you, and you will always be victorious."

The locker room fell silent. Through the heavy concrete walls Adam could hear the faint rhythmic sound of the marching band parading up the street to the field. They would need to take to the field soon.

"Kyle, will you lead us in a word of prayer?"

"Be glad to."

"Anyone who doesn't want to participate can wait for us outside the locker room."

Adam waited but no one moved.

As Kyle began to pray fervently for safety and good sportsmanship, Adam grinned inwardly. Because of this moment, no matter what happened on the field, they had already won.

And it turned out to be an unbelievable game. From kick-off until the clock wound down the last seconds, the boys played with a fiery determination that he hadn't seen before, not even from this talented team. They ran harder, blocked stronger, and executed plays with more precision. They scored their first touchdown within the first two minutes and held off the tough Cresthaven Knights until the last two minutes of the game.

The final score was 28 to 7. Their homecoming victory was made even sweeter by ensuring them a trip to the playoffs.

He wondered if his pep talk had made the noticeable difference, had spurred some underlying energy and revived the true spirit of the game. Maybe it was Kyle's prayer, though Adam still had a hard time believing that prayer really made that big of a difference. Still, it was possible that it gave the boys' attitudes a boost.

But was it worth it?

An uncomfortable twinge tightened his gut as he reminded himself that he could get in big trouble for giving a Christian message, and then concluding with prayer in a public school. That thought had crossed his mind the night before while he was working through the section of Matthew. He'd almost completely dismissed the idea of sharing it with his team, but the message was powerful and the tug at his heart unrelenting. He reasoned that if he was going to lead this group of young men, it ought to be down the right road. He wouldn't force them to come along, but he'd lead them.

And maybe, just maybe, it would make a difference in all their lives.

CHAPTER
Nineteen

The next morning, soft, rhythmic tapping on her roof and against her window roused Kate gently out of a peaceful sleep. She lay there, lulled by the rain, cozy and warm in the cacoon of her blankets.

She closed her eyes, willing herself to doze off and return to the blissful dream she'd been having. Some of the details were obscure, as was the case with most of her dreams, but it was very clear that she was in Ryan's arms, dancing, and it was simply wonderful. They moved together with an elegance that came from being someone's partner for eight years. She anticipated each of his steps and easily followed his lead.

She wanted to tell him so many things, mostly about Madeline. And there was so much she wanted to ask him about heaven. She wanted to know everything.

But when she opened her mouth, there was no sound. There was no noise at all, not even music. It was just her, Ryan, and the beating of their hearts . . . the soft, rhythmic tapping that stayed with her while he gradually faded away and reality crept back.

She would have lain there all morning, next to tears, longing for him. But the very next minute, Madeline burst through her bedroom door and took a flying leap onto the queen-sized bed.

"Wake up, Mama! I hafta go play soccer, and then we hafta get our hair and nails done. And we hafta put our pretty dresses on. And—"

Kate moaned and pulled the covers up over her head. She didn't want to think of dressing up and going to the home-coming dance, not after the dream she'd just had.

Madeline tugged on the covers. "Come on, Mama!"

Kate poked her head out and watched Madeline through bleary eyes, wondering how it was possible that her child could wake up containing a whole day's worth of energy. "Hold on a second, firecracker. First things first. How about some breakfast?"

"Banana berry pancakes?"

Kate sighed, threw off her covers, and held out her arm. "Go on and twist it."

Madeline giggled. She pounced on Kate, attempting to grab hold of her arm, but Kate swept it around her waist, pulled the little girl up close, and proceeded to tickle her, a challenging feat with the way Madeline kicked and thrashed about in hysterics.

Kate finally stopped when Madeline screeched, "Stop! I can't breathe!"

Madeline lay next to Kate, breathing heavily. Her big, happy grin showed off the pearly, white buds where the gaps in her smile had been. She reached out, wrapped an arm around Kate's neck, and gave her a little peck on the lips.

"I love you, Mama."

Kate smiled. The urge to cry had disipated, and the ache in her heart was not quite as acute as it had been moments ago.

"And I love you, pumpkin, very much." She sat up, ready to start the day. "Now, what do you say we go make those pancakes?"

They had a fun morning in the kitchen making pancakes together and were just finishing up breakfast when the phone rang. "Please carry your dishes over to the sink, and then go get dressed," Kate told Madeline as she rose to retrieve the cordless handset.

"In my fancy dress?"

"Not yet." Kate grabbed the phone and punched the talk button. "Hello?"

"Hey, Kate. It's Ian."

"Oh, hey, Ian. I wondered if you'd be calling. Is the game cancelled?"

" 'Fraid so. The soccer fields are too soggy with the rain we've gotten overnight and this morning."

"Will we be able to make it up?"

Madeline noisily deposited her plate, cup, and silverware in the sink and stomped off to pout in her room. Kate, however, breathed a silent sigh of relief. It was one less thing for her to worry about on an already busy, very exciting day.

"I'm not sure yet. Hopefully I'll find out before Thursday's practice."

"Okay. Well, thanks for letting us know."

"You bet. And, hey—"

"Yeah?"

"Have fun tonight."

She could almost see Ian wiggling his eyebrows through the phone. "It's not like that," she protested.

"If you say so. Talk to you later."

They both said good-bye, and she hung up the phone.

The rest of the morning was busy with playing Barbies, two games of Candyland, and watching back-to-back episodes of Madeline's favorite cartoon. After lunch the rain stopped, but the afternoon was still cloudy and damp. They snuggled on the sofa under an afghan with one of Kate's favorite childhood books, *Charlotte's Web*. By the time Kate finished reading the first chapter, Madeline was softly snoring.

Kate slid out from underneath her, leaving the little girl to nap on the sofa while she went to unwind in a bubble bath. She made the sweet-smelling water as hot as she could stand it, and when she cautiously lowered herself into the tub, the tension in her muscles melted away.

This is going to be a fun evening.

She sighed. She'd repeated the thought several times over the past two weeks and at least as many times just since breakfast that morning. She'd been thrilled to have the opportunity to go to the dance and relive her high school years for a night, but as much as she longed for those carefree days again, she wasn't a teenager anymore. Neither was Adam. Relationships were no longer simple. That's why she was glad this was just a casual date. And she would keep telling herself that until she actually believed it.

It's completely casual, no big deal. Just two friends going to a dance together.

She kept that thought in the front of her mind where it was easy to grab hold of when her heart tried to start whispering to her. She meditated intensely on it later that afternoon while she and Madeline had their hair, nails, and makeup done at Julie's Salon and Spa, using it to battle her inner romantic. She smiled at the pure joy that radiated from Madeline like morning sunshine while Julie Donahue applied tastefully light shades of makeup to Madeline's eyes, cheeks, and lips.

"Do I look like a princess, Mama?" Madeline batted her eyelashes and puckered her lips.

Kate laughed, instantly grateful that Nathan was making a big enough deal about his "date" with Madeline that they could share this special moment. She would have to remember to thank him.

"You sure do, with and without makeup. Look out, Cinderella! Here comes Princess Maddie."

Madeline giggled and clapped her hands, careful of her freshly polished pearly pink nails.

Kate wondered when girls outgrew the love of playing dress up. Sitting in the salon chair and looking at her reflection in the mirror, with her hair all done up and her makeup perfect, she realized she still hadn't outgrown it.

Back at home, Kate calmed her little bundle of energy down long enough to pull Madeline's tights on her and slip the pretty burgundy taffeta dress she'd found at the children's consignment shop over her head, careful not to touch a single hair. She tied the wide sash in the back and straightened the netting under the skirt.

"There. Now go find your shoes and get them on. I can help you buckle them if you need me to."

Madeline gave her a clumsy little curtsey and happily twirled and danced out of the room.

Kate took a deep breath. *I guess it's my turn now.*

She crossed the room to her closet and pulled out a dress from all the way in the back. It had been a long time since she'd worn the simple but elegant black chiffon dress, and she prayed it still fit. The memories that came it with were too numerous to count, all of them including Ryan, but she believed that the time was right for her to wear it again.

She slipped into it. The soft fabric against her skin was like a healing touch. She zipped it up, went to her full-length mirror, and evaluated what she saw. The modest halter neck-line added an extra dose of femininity, and the satin shawl a touch of class, while the smocked satin waist and tea-length hemline accentuated her figure.

"It's perfect," she whispered.

A single tear slid down her cheek, but she smiled. She was moving on.

"Wow! You look pretty!"

Madeline dashed to Kate's side, half tripping over her unbuckled shoes, to examine her mother more closely. She spotted the moisture on Kate's cheek. A crease formed in her forehead and her mouth turned slightly downward.

"Why are you crying, Mama?"

Kate led her to the bed and sat beside her to buckle her black leather shoes.

"Are you sad?" Madeline asked.

One shoe fastened, Kate started on the other. "Maybe just a little."

"Why?"

She wasn't about to discuss something a seven-year-old heart couldn't possibly understand. Thinking quickly, she said, "Because I don't think I look like a princess."

Madeline nodded emphatically. "You do, with and without makeup. Look out, Cinderella! Here comes Princess Mama."

Kate laughed and hugged her daughter tightly. "Thanks, kiddo. I feel much better now."

She went to the dresser and opened her jewelry box. Madeline didn't move from her place on the bed.

"Mama?"

Kate turned. "Yes?"

"Are you and Adam going on a date?"

Kate's heart fluttered. "Yes, but it's just casual," she said hastily. "Adam and I are only friends."

"Ohh." Madeline dragged the word out.

Kate chuckled and returned to picking out her jewelry.

"Mama?"

Preoccupied with untangling the gold chain of a black onyx pendant, Kate said, "Yes?"

"Do you think you'll ever get married again?"

The question sucked all the air out of Kate's lungs, and it took a minute for her to recover. She immediately forgot about the pendant and returned to sit on the bed beside Madeline.

"I don't know. I have no idea what the Lord has in store for us, but I'm certainly not thinking about marriage right now." She wondered if her date with Adam had affected Madeline more than the little girl let on. "Why do you ask?"

Madeline fingered a pink flower embroidered on the bodice of her dress. "I miss Daddy."

Kate pulled her close, fighting back tears. "Oh, baby, I do, too. Every day."

"But Adam and Chloe make my heart feel not quite so sad." Madeline looked up at Kate with her big, chocolate eyes. "Do you think that's okay?"

A small grin played on Kate's lips, and her eyes glistened with tears. Madeline was moving on too. A lump of conflicting emotions lodged in Kate's throat so she could barely squeak out a whisper around it.

"Yes, I think that's okay." She tucked a stray wisp of hair behind Madeline's ear. "Daddy wouldn't want you to be sad."

"Yeah, I know. He wouldn't want you to be sad either."

Madeline hopped off the bed and twirled in front of the mirror, watching her skirt float around her. As Kate watched, she replayed Madeline's words in her head.

"Adam and Chloe make my heart feel not quite so sad."

The truth of the matter was that they were having the same effect on Kate.

At that moment the doorbell rang. "Uncle Nate's here!" Madeline cried. "Go get the door, Mama! I wanna surprise him."

Kate chuckled. "Okay, okay. You stay here." She hurried to the front door and threw it open just as Nathan raised his hand to push the bell a second time. "Hey, Nathan! Sorry to keep you waiting."

"Typical first date." His broad smile tickled her insides.

He stepped inside and greeted her with their usual brief embrace. Then he backed up, took her hand, and gave her a twirl, while letting out a low whistle. "You look amazing. Adam is a lucky guy tonight."

His words caused a strange cyclone of emotions to spin in her soul. Somewhere along the line the love she felt for her brother-in-law had turned into something more significant than mere brotherly affection. But her attraction to Adam had never been more intense, especially now that he was seeking the Lord. The conflicting rush of emotions made her dizzy.

She cast her gaze to her freshly painted toenails in an attempt to prevent Nathan from catching a glimpse of her inner turmoil. "You are too." Brightening, she turned toward the hallway. "Come on out, Maddie!"

"Psst." Madeline poked her head around the corner.

"You're 'posta say, 'Introducing Princess Maddie,' " she instructed in a loud whisper.

Kate stifled a giggle. "Oh, sorry," she whispered back. She cleared her throat and dropped her voice an octave. "Introducing Princess Maddie." She swept her arm in Madeline's direction.

Remarkably poised for a seven-year-old, Madeline came toward them, taking very deliberate steps. She stopped a few feet in front of Nathan and twirled around.

He bowed low in a chivalrous manner and pulled out a square box from behind his back. "A gift for my lady." He removed the lid to reveal a dainty silver tiara embedded with crystal and pale pink pearlized beads.

Madeline gasped in delight. "Oh, Mama, look! A Cinderella crown! Now I really am a princess!" She looked up at him pleadingly with her hands folded in front of her. "Can I wear it, Uncle Nate? Please, please, please?"

He chuckled. "Of course." He carefully took the tiara out of the box and situated it on top of Madeline's head.

Watching this ceremony of sorts, Kate couldn't help being moved. The fact that Nathan would go to such lengths to make Madeline feel extra special caused the river of her emotions to crest above flood stage, the excess welling just beneath her eyelashes.

"There. Your mom might need to adjust it a little."

She took a step closer and examined it. "Nope. It looks perfect to me. Well done, Sir Nathan."

"I'm gonna go look in the mirror!" Madeline disappeared around the corner.

Kate met his gaze and held it. "Thank you. For everything."

"My pleasure. It's always been my pleasure." His chocolate eyes twinkled, sending an electric spark straight to her heart that made her tingle all over.

Madeline zipped around the corner again, but this time she didn't stop until she tackled Nathan around his waist. "I love it, Uncle Nate! Thank you!"

"You're welcome, Pip—" He shook his head. "I mean, Princess Maddie." He straightened and shifted his gaze to meet Kate's. "I guess we'd better be going."

She nodded, her heart suddenly as heavy as the raindrops that had fallen that morning. She wished she was going with them, that the three of them could spend the evening together. As she and Madeline had with Ryan.

He bowed low again and swept his arm toward the door. "Your carriage awaits, Princess Maddie."

Madeline clapped her hands and squealed. She dashed to the door and peered out expectantly. Instantly, her smile fell flat, and she turned to him with her hands on her hips. "There's no carriage out there."

"You're seeing with your eyes. You need to use your heart and a little imagination. After all, wasn't Cinderella's carriage a pumpkin?"

Kate was using her heart and a little imagination. *That's something Ryan would say.* At that moment, the fat little raindrop inside her chest let go and began to fall.

⁂

Adam glanced at the digital clock in his dash and eased off the accelerator. He was overly anxious, he knew. His mother hadn't helped matters any when he dropped Chloe off by reminding him yet again not to let an opportunity pass him by. He knew she meant well, but now he had a very short amount of time to calm his nerves.

Kate's not an opportunity to be had. She's not ready for a relationship, and I don't have time for one. She's a friend and that's it.

He almost had himself convinced by the time he parked in her driveway and headed up the walk to her front door. When he reached out to ring the bell, however, his nerves started to twist into knots again. It had been so long since he'd been on a date. What if he did something wrong?

He glanced at the small box he absentmindedly shifted from hand to hand as if it were a football. What if he was too old-fashioned for a modern woman like Kate?

He glanced at his watch. Ten till six. Kate wasn't expecting him for another ten minutes.

He turned and went to the edge of the little porch. Leaning against the railing, he looked out over the yard. The fine mist in the air softened the lines and edges of the scene, making it look so much like a dream that he considered pinching himself.

He shook his head. If this was just a dream, he'd be confident, with a normal, steady heartbeat.

"I wonder if the Bible says anything about being nervous on a first date," he said, his voice barely above a whisper. Silently he added, *It seems to have the answers for everything else.*

"I was wondering the very same thing."

He spun around as Kate stepped out unto the porch. Drinking in the sight of her, he opened his mouth to tell her how stunning she looked, but nothing came out. His words must have escaped along with all the air in his lungs.

She pulled her satin shawl around her shoulders. "The only thing I could come up with was 'Peace, be still.' Jesus calmed a terrible storm with those three words."

He dropped his gaze to his black dress shoes. "I guess I don't know that one."

"How about if I tell you about it over dinner? I'm starving."

He grinned, his heart rate returning to a somewhat regular rhythm. "Sounds good." At that moment he remembered the box he'd been holding. "I know it might be old fashioned, but Mom would've killed me if I hadn't gotten you a corsage."

It was partly true. She'd asked him a couple times if he'd picked one out and never seemed to be satisfied with a simple yes.

Kate giggled. "I'd hate for that to happen."

He opened the box with trembling hands and presented her with a simple but elegant cluster of small red roses accented with ivy and soft red ribbon.

"Oh, Adam. It's beautiful!"

He slipped the delicate arrangement onto her wrist. As if someone had plugged him into an electrical outlet, he felt a sudden surge of courage.

"It pales in comparison to you."

She gently touched a petal. "Thank you."

"Shall we go? Our reservations are for six-thirty, but I'm sure it won't hurt to get there a little early."

"Okay. Let me just grab my purse and lock up."

A minute later, they were on their way. It was a half-hour drive to his favorite restaurant. Located in larger town than neighboring Cresthaven, O'Dell's Steak House sat right on the lake, providing an ambiance like no other. Within just a few minutes they were seated at a table for two by a large window with a lake view, and their waiter took their order for drinks and an appetizer.

"I'll put this in and be back for your dinner order in just a few." The waiter spun on his heel and headed off toward the kitchen.

Adam shifted his attention to the best view in the restaurant—the beautiful woman across from him, staring out the window at the lake. He fought hard against the urge to take her hand. It would have felt completely natural in this romantic atmosphere except for the fact that this date was supposed to be no big deal. She was really just doing him a favor.

He fiddled with his linen-wrapped silverware, trying to come up with an engaging topic of conversation, but his mind was a blank slate. He was about ready to settle for this peaceful lull when something his mom often said emerged from the clouds that had encircled his head the minute he laid eyes on Kate.

"A penny for your thoughts."

She shifted her gaze to meet his. "Oh, it was nothing. I was just thinking about something Maddie said earlier this evening."

He nodded, waiting, wondering if she was going to elaborate. But it was a dead end.

Time for a U-turn.

"You know, back on your front porch you piqued my interest, and then you left me hanging."

Her mouth gaped slightly. "Excuse me?"

Puzzled by her reaction, Adam frowned while he considered his words. When the dawning occurred a small gasp escaped his lips and he quickly clarified. "I was referring to the story you mentioned about how Jesus calmed the storm."

"Oh. Right." Kate sat a little straighter in her chair. "Jesus was teaching a large group of people by the Sea of Galilee. After a while He kind of needed a break, so He and His disciples took a boat out onto the lake. Jesus fell asleep, and a fierce storm suddenly came up. The waves crashed over the sides of the boat, filling it with water and causing it to start to sink. The disciples were afraid for their lives and woke Jesus up. So He got up and simply said, 'Peace, be still!' Just like that," Kate snapped her fingers, "the storm stopped and everything was calm."

Adam looked out the window at Lake Erie, choppy from the rain earlier that day, trying to imagine the scenario. "Impossible."

"Yes, for anybody else." She paused. "When you talked with Gramps about faith a couple weeks ago, didn't he tell you that everyone has their moments of doubt?"

He nodded. "Something like that."

"It was true even of the disciples, and Jesus was right there with them."

"My whole life has been a moment of doubt."

"Jesus can calm those storms too." Positive energy, radiated from her like rays of golden sunshine, warming him to the center of his being.

His smile came automatically, involuntarily. He couldn't have prevented it if he tried.

"I understand that better and better every day." He glanced back out the window at the rough water, his smile fading a bit. "Now I just hope the boys on my team get it."

She stared at him with curiosity. "What do you mean?"

The waiter appeared at their table with two glasses of iced tea. "Your appetizer will be out in a minute." He hurried on to another table.

Adam took a drink, then set the glass down. "Last night before the game I shared something I'd read from the Bible with the team. It was the passage in Matthew that says if you have faith like a mustard seed nothing will be impossible for you."

Her face lit up. "Very appropriate."

He nodded. "I thought so too, though I debated for quite a while about whether I should share it."

Kate took a sip of her tea. "Why?"

He shrugged. "There could be serious repercussions. I don't think there will be, but it's always a possibility."

"And you shared it anyway?"

"Yeah. I can't really explain it. I just . . . "

"Felt led to?"

He nodded.

"That was the Holy Spirit. You were being tested and you passed." She laced her fingers together and brought them up under her chin. "Congratulations."

His heart overflowed with more emotions than he could identify, but he felt a sense of accomplishment. He was making this journey. Slowly but steadily.

"Thanks."

The waiter swung by with a platter of sliced French bread and asiago artichoke dip that filled the air between them with a rich aroma. Adam's stomach growled.

She tipped her head to the side. "Would you like to pray or shall I?"

Still uncomfortable praying silently, let alone out loud, he motioned for her to proceed before folding his hands and bowing his head. While she softly spoke a blessing over their food and their evening, Adam silently added one heartfelt sentence: *And thank You for bringing Kate into my life.*

CHAPTER
Twenty

$\mathcal{N}$athan and Madeline walked into the Bayside Café. Spotting their reserved table right away, he smiled. *Perfect!*

In the few short weeks he'd been in town, he had become a regular patron of the little restaurant. He'd told the owner his ideas for this evening, and Audrey Valentine instantly made it her mission to see his plan through.

She'd gone above and beyond the call of duty, draping a lone table in the far corner in a white linen tablecloth instead of the usual red and white checked cloth. On it, the small flame of a red votive candle flickered and danced, while a pretty flower arrangement added a special touch. Classical music softly played from a CD player nearby.

A young waitress with a swinging ponytail met them at the entryway. She seemed pleased to play a part in this make-believe enchanted evening.

"Good evening, Lady Maddie and Sir Nathan. Welcome to the Bayside Ballroom."

Madeline looked up at Nathan and giggled.

"Your table is right this way."

Madeline followed the waitress with a prim and proper demeanor, but then crawled onto her chair and sat on her knees like a typical seven-year-old. She leaned forward to sniff the flowers and closely examine the candle, then rested her chin in her hands.

"Why is everyone acting so silly, Uncle Nate?"

"Don't you like it?"

"Yeah. Lots. It's really fun, but it's kinda weird."

He chuckled. "I guess you're right." He shook his head. "What can I say? You're a very special little girl to me, and I wanted you to have a fairytale evening."

"You mean like Mama?"

His stomach turned at the thought of Kate having a magical evening with another man. "Sort of."

The waitress appeared with a white towel draped over her arm and carrying a pad of paper and a pencil. "May I take your order, madam?"

"Do you have chicken fingers and French fries?"

"But of course." The waitress jotted the order down. "Anything else?"

"Umm . . . " Madeline rubbed her chin, and then pointed her index finger high into the air as if an imaginary light bulb illuminated above her head. "A strawberry milkshake!"

"Excellent choice." The waitress made another note, and then turned to Nathan. "And for you, sir?"

"I'll have what the princess having."

"Very well. I'll go place this order, and it'll be just a few minutes." The waitress bowed and hurried off to the kitchen.

Nathan sat back in his chair and propped his ankle up on his opposite knee. "Was your mom excited about going to the dance tonight?" He wasn't one hundred percent sure he wanted to know the answer.

She gave an exaggerated shrug. "I dunno. She was crying before you came."

"Why was she crying?"

"She said it was because she didn't feel like a princess, but I told her she did. That made her feel better."

"I'll bet. She's lucky to have you."

She twirled a strand of hair that had somehow managed to escape from the rubber band and bobby pins. "Yeah, I know."

He tipped his head to the side. "But you're a pretty lucky little girl yourself."

She gave a big nod. "I know that too."

He grinned at his niece. "Sounds like you know a lot. School must be going well for you, huh?"

"Oh, yeah! My very best friend, Jessica, is in my class and at recess we play . . . "

He only half listened while she gave a report of every game she and Jessica played on the playground, listed all her classmates with a brief description of each one, and gave a rundown of her school subjects in order from greatest to least favorite. He nodded and added an occasional, "Oh, really?" but in his mind he went back to her earlier comment about Kate.

"She was crying before you came . . . She said it was because she didn't feel like a princess, but I told her she did."

What truth had Kate tried to cover up with a fib that would pacify Madeline? It had to be one of two things: She was either extremely happy or terribly grieved to be going to the dance with Adam. He prayed with all his might that it was the latter.

God, You brought me here to be with Kate and Maddie, didn't You? I thought I heard You loud and clear, but now I'm not so sure. Regret came rolling in like a raging storm. *Why did I ever leave Vanderbilt?*

"Excuse me, sir. Can you tell me how I can get a table like this?"

He was so deep in thought the voice didn't register until he looked up into Denise's bright, smiling face. He stood to greet her and Greyson.

"This is a surprise. What are you doing here?"

"Do you really have to ask? We came for a piece of pie, of course."

"Right." He wondered if there was a soul on Earth with a prettier smile. "Where's Griffin?"

"We just dropped him off at a friend's house. He's going to his first high school dance tonight."

"So is Mama," Madeline piped up.

"Yes, I know. You're mama told me, and she told me that you were going to have a very special date too." Denise looked over at Nathan and winked.

Madeline nodded emphatically. "I am! I get to be a princess today. See my crown?" She tipped her head slightly and pointed to her tiara.

"It's lovely. I had one just like it when I was the home-coming queen."

Madeline's eyes widened. "You were a queen?"

"Just for a day, and it was a long, long time ago." Denise's smile faded a bit, and Nathan guessed she was thinking about Daryl and life before heartache. She turned to Greyson and ruffled his hair. "Well, bud, should we go find a seat?"

"Sure."

Suddenly, not wanting to lose her cheerful company, Nathan said quickly, "To answer your question, this is the only table like this in the restaurant. Sorry."

She sighed dramatically. "I guess an ordinary table will have to do then."

"Unless we push these tables together." Nathan indicated the table beside them. "The tablecloth is long enough to cover both, and we can share the candle and flowers."

Denise crouched down until she was at eye level with Madeline. "Would you mind if Greyson and I joined you on your special date with your uncle?"

Madeline considered her thoughtfully for a moment. "Will you sit by me?"

Denise's sunshiny smile returned. "Absolutely!"

In less than a minute they transformed the table for two into a table for four, taking nothing away from the elegance of it. The waitress was thrown off only for a second when she brought out Nathan's and Madeline's food.

"Okaaay. Can I take your order?" she asked first Denise, and then Greyson. Despite Denise's protest, Nathan instructed the teenaged girl to add their order to his bill.

"Yes, sir. Whatever you say." Again their waitress hurried off to the kitchen.

Nathan and Madeline were almost finished eating by the time Denise and Greyson got their meals, but they kept right on visiting. It never even crossed Nathan's mind to get up and leave until Denise finished the last few bites of her chicken salad croissant.

Then he pushed away from the table. "Well, Maddie, I guess it's time to go." His spirits fell with Madeline's expression.

"Aw. Do we have to?"

"Hey," Denise said and wiped her mouth with her napkin. "Greyson and I rented a couple movies for tonight. Since you shared your table with us, why don't you let us share our movies with you?" She turned her attention to her son. "Is that okay with you, bud?"

"It's cool with me."

"Can we, Uncle Nate? Pretty please?" Madeline folded her hands and turned on her puppy-dog eyes.

He chuckled. "How can I say no now?" His exuberance surprised him, but he quickly shrugged it off.

Why shouldn't I be happy about spending time with Denise and Greyson? This will be a lot better than going back to Kate's house and thinking about her being with Adam all night.

Thinking fast, he snagged their waitress and, with a quick glance at Denise, ordered two pieces of apple pie to go. When the desserts arrived at the table, he paid for their meals, leaving the waitress and Audrey a generous tip for their time and trouble. Then they strolled outside into a cold drizzle.

Madeline shrieked and tried to cover her head with her hands. "Uncle Nate! It'll ruin my crown!"

He picked her up and dashed to his car. After he helped her get buckled in the backseat, he straightened and shouted to Denise, "I'll follow you."

Denise waved and slipped into her Camry. As she carefully pulled out onto the street, Nathan followed right behind her.

A few minutes later he stood in Denise's foyer, holding two to-go containers of apple pie and marveling at how his plans had changed. Suddenly his evening didn't seem quite so miserable.

He swiped his shoes well on the rug, and slipped out of his damp jacket. Madeline had already discarded her coat and shoes and disappeared, leaving her belongings in a heap on the floor.

Hanging his jacket on the coat rack, he chuckled. "I guess she feels right at home, huh?"

Denise hung Madeline's coat next to Nathan's and placed her shoes neatly on the rug against the wall. "I think so. She's been over a couple of times when Kate and I were planning for the support group, but I have a feeling Maddie would feel at home just about anywhere."

They both laughed and moved into her tastefully decorated great room, where Madeline already occupied an oversized beanbag chair and Greyson had taken control of the TV remote.

"Hey, Grey, why don't you start the movie? I'll go get the popcorn started."

"Okay, Mom." Keeping one eye on the game he'd turned on, he moved at tortoise speed to the entertainment center, took the DVD out of its case, and put it in the player.

Denise put her hands on her hips. "There's no rush. Make sure to take your good ol' sweet time."

Nathan could hear the teasing in her voice and he smiled. But when she turned around, there was a hint of weariness in her demeanor.

She sighed. "At least you listen."

She spoke so softly Greyson couldn't have heard her over the television. But Nathan heard her loud and clear. He followed her into the open kitchen.

"You have a beautiful house."

"Thanks." She pulled two packages of microwavable popcorn out of the cupboard. "Sometimes I think it's more than we need." After tossing one of the packages into the microwave and hitting the start button, she added, "And then there are times I'm glad we have some extra space."

Nathan pulled out a bar stool at the end of the island and sat down. "Things still aren't better with Griffin?"

She gave a little shrug. "You've only spent two afternoons with him. That's hardly enough time for a transformation."

He silently considered her comment while she scooped coffee into a filter. He wasn't sure if it was her words or her defeated tone that bothered him more.

"Do you think I'm going to give up on him?"

"No."

"Does he?"

She filled the coffeemaker with water and turned it on. "Probably."

The microwave beeped, signaling that the popcorn was ready. Denise quickly pulled out the inflated bag, opened it, and dumped the contents into a big plastic bowl.

"You have to understand. In his eyes, the two people he thought he could always count on gave up on our family. You're barely more than a stranger to him. It'll take a while to earn his trust."

"I do understand." He took a deep breath. "My mother died when I was four. My congressman father was too busy to raise two young boys. We rarely saw or heard from him."

She set the bowl of popcorn aside and leaned against the island. "Who raised you?"

"My grandmother. She did about as good as any grandmother could do, but it wasn't easy. It took a long time for me to trust anyone but my brother." He folded his arms on the countertop and shifted his gaze downward. "It took me even longer to learn to love."

Denise tipped her head to the side. "Does she know?"

Creases formed in Nathan's brow. "I'm sorry?"

"Does Kate know that you love her?"

For several moments he stared silently at the pattern in the marble countertop. Denise had a way of catching him off guard, and each time the recovery time lengthened. Thankfully, Madeline wandered over in search of the popcorn that filled the kitchen and great room with its buttery aroma.

"Well?" Denise pressed when Madeline walked back to her beanbag chair with the bowl of popcorn.

"I don't know. I've never told her, if that's what you mean."

"Is Kate the reason you moved here?"

"Originally I thought it was." He sighed heavily. "But to tell you the truth, now I'm not sure why the Lord led me here."

"Are you sure He led you here?"

Uncertainty flooded his heart, but his pride dammed up vulnerability. "Of course I'm sure. I wouldn't have left a very successful career in a Vanderbilt practice otherwise."

"If He led you here, He'll keep right on leading. If you misunderstood Him, it's okay. He'll take over as soon as you give Him the controls."

Before Nathan could reinforce his levee, the uncertainty began to leak out again. "What if it doesn't turn out the way I want?"

She placed a reassuring hand on his arm. "It'll turn out how God wants, and that's all that matters."

CHAPTER

Twenty-One

A wave of nostalgia washed over Kate, carrying her back to simpler days when her biggest worry was maintaining a grade-point average that would guarantee her the honor of graduating as salutatorian. As she stood with Adam at one side of the festively decorated gymnasium, watching the growing crowd of teenagers, memories started coming back to her in a steady stream.

He glanced down at her. "Thinking about old times?"

"Old? It feels like only yesterday. And these past few years seem more like a lifetime ago." She shifted her gaze to him. "Does that sound crazy?"

He shook his head. "Not at all. I feel the same way, especially on Friday nights when we're in the locker room getting ready for a game. There's a part of me that still thinks I should be suiting up with the boys, until I look at them and see how young they are. There's so much they don't know about life." He dropped his voice with his gaze. "So much I hope they never have to experience. It's then that I understand the importance of my role on the team." He gave Kate a lopsided grin.

She placed her hand on his arm. "You're doing a great job with those boys." Feeling the strength through his sleeve set the butterflies inside her abdomen to flight.

His smile broadened. "Thanks."

He placed his hand over hers, causing her heart to begin dancing with the butterflies. She could have stayed just like that for the rest of the evening.

"Hey, Coach!" Two older-looking boys approached them.

Adam dropped his hand, so she removed hers and put several inches of space between them.

"Hi, there, Brady, Kyle." Adam nodded at both of the guys. "How are you two doing this evening?"

"Good," they said in unison.

Brady took a step closer. "Coach, I just wanted to say thanks for what you said in the locker room before last night's game. It made me feel good inside and kinda got me thinkin'. I talked some with Kyle about it after the game, and I've decided to go to church with him tomorrow, you know, to see what it's all about." The teen shrugged. "That's all. I just wanted to say thanks."

Adam cleared his throat. "I think you made a wise decision, one you'll never regret. I'm proud of you."

Brady beamed. "Thanks."

"Hey, Coach, will we continue to have prayer before our games?" Kyle asked.

Adam rubbed the back of his neck. "I'm not sure, but if we do, can I count on you to lead us on occasion?"

"Yes, sir!"

"That's the way to be a team player." Adam folded his arms. "Now you two go have fun."

"Yes, sir!" the two boys answered again in unison. They walked off and were quickly flanked by two pretty girls.

Adam watched them go in silence before turning to Kate. "What just happened?"

"I think you planted a seed. You certainly got Brady thinking." She smiled. "It feels good, doesn't it?"

A bright sparkle lit up his eyes. "Amazing."

"I'll tell you what's amazing," an unfamiliar voice said.

They both turned quickly to see a man not quite as tall as Adam but similarly built, with thick, dark hair and a contagious smile. "The fact that they actually roped us both into chaperoning again this year," the man chuckled.

Adam laughed and patted him on the back. "That's not amazing. That's a miracle." He turned to her. "Kate, this is Dan Olien. He teaches phys ed and coaches track and cross country."

"Really?"

"He was named district coach of the year the past two years," Adam added.

Kate arched her eyebrows. "Impressive."

Dan shook his head. "Not really. I just love running."

She stuck her hand out. "Hi. I'm . . . "

"Kate Marshall, the 1993 cross country state champion," he finished, shaking her hand. "Your record is still hanging in our trophy case. Now that is amazing."

Her cheeks were blazing. "Not really. I just loved running."

He tipped his head to the side. " 'Loved'? I've watched you run after school, and I wouldn't put it in the past tense."

"I've been away from it for a long time, but I'm finally starting to get back into a routine."

He grinned. "That's what I thought. And I was thinking something else too."

She glanced at Adam, who appeared just as curious as she was, and then returned her gaze to Dan. "I give up."

"You would make an excellent assistant coach for our cross country team."

If she'd been drinking something, she would've sprayed it all over the gymnasium. "Are you serious?"

"As a heart attack. What do you say?"

"Think of all the teens you could mentor," Adam piped up.

She stared at him through narrowed eyes before turning to Dan. "I'm honored, but I don't think so."

She sighed as she felt herself softening. Helping to coach Harvest Bay's cross country team was something she'd really love to do . . . someday.

"I just can't. At least, not right now."

"Maybe next year then?"

"We'll see." She hesitated, not sure if she wanted to share something so personal with someone she just met, but she sensed that Dan would understand better than anyone. "I started running again to rediscover myself. I can't coach anybody until I'm confident in who I am."

He nodded. "I've been there a time or two."

"How did you find yourself?"

"I entered races. I've run dozens of races, including the Columbus marathon twice. I promise you that nothing will help you learn more about yourself than training for a race." He paused. "Tell you what. I just registered for the Cleveland marathon, held in mid-May. The course is flat and fast, which makes it a good race for runners who are new to the sport or getting back into it. Think about it and if you decide to go for it, I'll be happy to train with you."

She considered this for a moment. Training for a race sounded fun and exciting and was exactly what she needed. If she decided to enter a race, it would be another commitment, but it would essentially be a commitment to herself.

But still, a marathon? She was thirty-four years old and hadn't run competitively for over fifteen years. How could she even fancy the idea of running a marathon?

She shook her head. "I don't know if I have it in me to compete again."

He stuffed his hands in the pockets of his pants and gave a little shrug. "At this point, I don't think it's about the competition as much as it's about just running the race."

The words she had said to Adam a few short weeks earlier regarding his faith journey floated back to her. *It's a marathon, not a sprint.* A dawning occurred in her heart and awakened her spirit. *Life is a race, and what matters most isn't when a person crosses the finish line, but how strong they've grown along the way.*

She glanced up at Adam who was watching her expectantly. She'd encouraged him to run a marathon of sorts. What kind of example would she set if she didn't at least give it a try?

A rush of adrenaline coursed through her veins, and she turned back to Dan. "When do we get started?"

A satisfied grin spread across his face. "I'll give you a call at school on Monday so we can coordinate our schedules. Sound good?"

She nodded. "That'd be great."

He took several steps back. "I'm going to patrol the dance floor for a while, keep the hanky panky in check. Wish me luck."

She giggled, and Adam raised his hand in a parting gesture. "Good luck," they both said.

Kate stared after Dan until he blended into the crowd, her brain processing the past few minutes. Reality quickly set in.

Heart-soaring excitement wrestled with gut-wrenching fear, knotting her insides until she could hardly move, barely even breathe.

"I can't believe I just agreed to train to run a marathon. I must be out of my mind."

"Why do you say that?"

She pressed her fingertips to her temple. "It's a marathon, not a 5K or even a 10K. The training is bound to be intense. It's not something I was planning on." Looking up, she found a tender expression on Adam's handsome face.

"Sometimes I think life's greatest blessings are unplanned."

"That's very insightful."

Kate thought about Maggie and Baby Justin. What a precious gift he was! She thought about how she hadn't planned to lead the single parent support group, and it had turned out to be a huge blessing to all of the participants, including her. She never planned to move back to Harvest Bay and, although she wished it was under different circumstances, it had been a blessing as well. She began to see that training to run a marathon could quite possibly be a wonderful experience.

The music slowed, and Adam moved closer to her, their arms brushing together lightly in the process. "Did you plan on dancing with me tonight?"

"No." She shyly dropped her gaze to the shiny hardwood floor. "But I was hoping to."

He gave her a smile that melted her heart. "Come on."

He took her by the hand and led her to a less crowded area of the dance floor. Holding her right hand against his heart, he pressed his free hand firmly against the middle of her back.

The warmth of his touch brought back the memory of the Sullivans' barn dance, and she cautiously kept him at arm's length, resting her hand on his shoulder as they began to sway in time to the music.

"Sorry if I step on your toes. Dancing's not really my thing." He paused, his vibrant blue eyes clouding over. "Alexandra always said I had two left feet."

She glanced down the narrow gap between them, and then looked up to meet his gaze. "I see a right foot."

The affection she glimpsed in his eyes took her breath away. He released her hand, wrapped his arm around her waist, and gently pulled her to him.

And suddenly she didn't want him to let her go. She slid her hands up around his neck and rested her head against his shoulder, allowing herself to become so lost in the comfort of his embrace that she barely noticed when one song ended and another began.

"Are you okay with this?" His breath caressed her cheek.

Was she okay? She loved Ryan and would always love him, but she didn't want to live the rest of her life alone. She deserved a second chance at love, to love and be loved in return. And standing there in Adam's arms, she thought that maybe, just maybe, there was enough room in her heart for two men.

She tipped her face upwards, just inches away from his. "Yes." She watched a smile play with his lips. Her breath quickened as she remembered the way they felt on hers.

"That's good." He leaned in then and kissed her gently on the forehead.

It was a sweet gesture, but she couldn't help wondering why he didn't deposit it a little further down her face. She guessed it was probably because he was at school. Maybe he was being extra careful with her after the episode at the barn dance. Either way, the song ended, the tempo picked up the pace, and the moment was over. But when he led her off the dance floor, her feet never touched the hardwood.

She was still floating on air three hours later when Adam walked her up to her front porch, their fingers entwined.

"Thank you for coming with me tonight." He stroked her thumb with his.

"Thanks for inviting me. I had a great time." She paused. Goosebumps popped out on her arms though she suspected that it wasn't entirely because of the frigid, damp night air. "I hate to see the evening end."

"Me, too." He moved in closer.

She caught a hint of his cologne on the faint breeze, heightening the intimacy of the moment. All of her senses were awakened, standing at attention.

"I was wondering if you and Maddie have plans next Saturday after the soccer game."

"I don't think so. Why?"

"I want to make good on my offer to take you and Maddie riding."

"Don't you have to get ready for the playoffs?"

"I can spare a couple hours on Saturday. Besides, it would make Chloe's day."

She gave him a teasing grin. "Then for Chloe's sake, we accept your offer."

"Okay, great! I'll see you next Saturday then." He leaned in.

Her heart was in her throat and her was stomach in a knot, but the core of her being was on fire. He brushed his lips against her cheek, and then began backing down the walk.

"Wait! Won't you be at the support group?"

"Probably, but it'll depend on practice. We've got to start getting ready for the playoffs, ya know?" He winked at her, turned, and hustled to his truck.

She stood on the porch watching him back out and drive off. She touched the place on her cheek where his lips had been and smiled blissfully. He was being careful with her after all, and it made her feel special, cared for . . . loved.

"So how was it?"

The voice behind her effectively acted like an emotional emergency brake in her brain. She turned to see Nathan bathed in the glow of the porch light, and she sucked in a breath. If she hadn't known better, he could have passed for an apparition of Ryan. A chill ran through her.

"You're shivering." He shifted to the side. "Come in out of the cold."

She moved past him and stepped into her small foyer. Bracing herself against the wall, she slipped off her shoes and gave each tired foot a quick rub.

"Would you like a cup of hot cider?"

"No, thanks. I'm going to head home. It's late, and I'm sure Maddie will want to tell you all about her night."

She straightened against the weight of disappointment and offered him a warm embrace. "I don't know how to thank you for going to such extremes for Maddie tonight. It meant a lot to her to spend a special evening with you." She gazed into his deep, dark eyes noticing for the first time an unbridled emotion. "And it meant a lot to me, too."

He held her closer, tighter than he ever had before and tipped his face down to hers. "Don't you know by now that I'd do anything for you and Maddie? Anything."

Anything. Including leaving a career in a successful Vanderbilt practice for a small town office five hundred miles away. Her breath caught in her throat while her heart nearly pounded out of her chest at the realization that Denise had been right after all.

He loved her.

He cupped her face in his hands and brushed her lips lightly with his. The moment lasted no more than a second, and when he released her she wondered if she'd just imagined his kiss. The lingering sweetness provided all the clarification she needed.

He opened the door and stepped out onto the porch.

"Will we see you tomorrow at church?" she asked from the doorway.

"I'll be there." He started down the steps.

"And you know you're invited to Sunday brunch at Mom and Dad's."

He looked over his shoulder and smiled. "I'll be there too."

She watched him drive away, yet he remained closer to her than ever. She touched the spot on her cheek where Adam had kissed her moments earlier and wondered if there was room in her heart for three men.

Twenty-Two

As the days passed, the temperatures fell with the last of the leaves. Harvest Bay saw the first few snow flurries of the season during the second week of November, and while every aspect of life seemed to slow down, Kate's schedule was busier than ever.

Truthfully, a significant part of the planning overload was intentional. The busier she stayed between Halloween and New Year's Day, the less time she had to dwell on the past. She suspected that being in Harvest Bay with her family and friends would make the holidays easier this year, but she didn't want to take a chance.

School was going great. It didn't take her long to establish a genuine camaraderie with the rest of the faculty, and she was having a blast with her group of fourth graders. After she fell into a workable routine, the planning became less tedious.

When the lesson planning dropped off, planning for the single-parent support group picked up in a major way. In just ten weeks their original group of seven had grown to thirty plus. The fact that single parents came from Cresthaven and other neighboring towns in search of hope and healing humbled Kate, and it made her that much more determined to provide a solid, Scripture-based program.

She could have stopped there and been plenty busy, but she volunteered to direct the children's Christmas program at church. Practices were held every Wednesday evening and Sunday afternoon beginning the last week in October.

At about the same time Kate began training for her first marathon. In the beginning the runs weren't much more challenging than what she'd already been doing, but Dan promised they'd gradually become tougher.

She thought about that on the afternoon of the third Tuesday in November as she tied the laces of her tennis shoes and stretched her muscles. She walked for a few yards, and then took off at a comfortable pace. Typically she listened to her iPod when she ran, but since starting training she meditated on scripture.

"Do you not know that those who run in a race all run, but one receives the prize? Run in such a way that you may obtain it. And everyone who competes for the prize is temperate in all things. Now they do it to obtain a perishable crown, but we for an imperishable crown."

She silently repeated the words over and over. The verses were the lyrics to her personal anthem. The pounding of her feet on the pavement provided the rhythm and all her muscles worked together harmoniously. Within just a few minutes she reached her zone and became lost in each breath, in and out, filling her lungs with the fresh, brisk air, and then forcing it out of her body. Her blood merged with her adrenaline and flowed through her veins like a raging river. She was alive, and her spirit was revitalized.

She could feel herself growing stronger physically and mentally. She was learning more about herself in this phase of her life, redefining her hopes and dreams, and experiencing the Lord's amazing grace with each stride. She discovered that she could count her blessings during a run and still have a list left when she reached her cool-down stretch. Despite all she'd lost, she was blessed.

Two miles into her run, Kate had become so focused that she almost collided with a pedestrian in front of Harvest Bay Family Practice.

"Oh! I'm so sorry! I wasn't watching . . . " As she worked on slowing her pulse and steadying her breathing, she shifted her focus to the tall, dark near-casualty. A sheepish grin crossed her face.

"Uh . . . hi, Nathan."

He chuckled. "I wondered if I'd see you this afternoon. Didn't expect you to almost plow me over, though."

She burst out laughing and swatted at him. "Stop that or next time I won't stop."

He held his hands up in surrender. "I don't have my running shoes, but I'll walk with you a ways."

"Okay."

They started down the sidewalk together, close but not touching.

He slipped his hands in his pockets. "I see you're training solo today."

"Dan is at a cross country meet about an hour away, but I know our training schedule so it's no big deal."

She pressed her middle and index fingers to her neck to check her pulse. It was still slightly elevated, and she had a feeling it was more a result of their encounter than an ineffective cool down.

"What about you? Calling it a day a little early, aren't you, Dr. Sterling?"

"Not without a good reason. I didn't have any patients scheduled after three o'clock so I'm meeting Griffin at the high school. We're going to hit the books, and then shoot some hoops. Denise knows to call my cell phone if something comes up, and I'll be back later on this evening to finish up my paperwork."

She glanced at him sideways. "How are things going with Griffin?"

He sighed and rubbed the back of his neck. "I don't know . . . baby steps, if that. He's put up a pretty tough wall, and I have to wonder if I'm ever going to get through. Denise said that he's surprised her a couple time at home with a positive attitude and his biology grade on his report card was a C, which is . . . okay, I guess." He shrugged. "Maybe I'm expecting too much."

Kate stopped and placed her hand on his arm. "The wall around Jericho was a tough one too." She searched his eyes. "Keep doing what you're doing and it'll come down, even if it's one pebble at a time."

As he nodded she felt a sense of intimacy begin to set in, but this was the worst possible place and time. Quickly she switched gears.

"And I'd better keep doing what I'm doing or I'll be late to the support group this evening." She started off on a jog, then turned and ran backward a few steps. "I'll call you later on tonight."

"Sounds good." He put his hand up in a farewell gesture.

She found it difficult to get back into her zone. Seeing Nathan had thrown her off, and getting back on track was like trying to right a derailed freight train. She made it to the end of Lake Erie Highway and turned left onto West Street.

By then she had a stitch in her side. Her breathing was all off. She'd lost her rhythm. She had to find it again or the rest of the run would be torture. She repeated her special verse again and again and gradually slipped into somewhat of a groove.

Up ahead off to the left she could see the fence surrounding the high school track and football field. The closer she got, the easier it was to make out the football players in their practice jerseys performing various drills in their small groups. An assistant coach was with each group according to their positions.

And then she spotted Adam.

He looked up from his place on the field and waved his hand high in the air.

She returned the gesture. *He's running a marathon too.*

Pride filled her heart, causing it to skip a few beats, and then came a powerful surge of adrenaline. With the sudden shift of focus, she knew she would finish strong. Lately, just the thought of him seemed to have a way of pushing her on. She couldn't explain it, and she didn't want to try. She just wanted to enjoy this journey they were on together.

She closed in on four miles and started cooling down. She slowed to an easy jog and stretched out her upper body muscles, wondering if Adam would be at the support group later on. She was surprised he hadn't missed one yet, with his practice schedule intensifying the further Harvest Bay advanced in the playoffs. If they won on Friday, they would be heading to the state championship.

She knew he'd worked so hard for a chance at that title. She also knew that the Lord was working hard for the title of his heart, and she sent up a prayer that both championships would be won in God's perfect time, according to His will.

Reaching the elementary school, she walked over to a bench, propped her right foot on the seat, and leaned forward to stretch her hamstrings. Glancing up, she recognized Nathan's BMW parked in front of the high school, and she prayed that he would also be victorious, not just for Griffin's sake, but for his own.

⁂

"Okay. Let's review. How many systems does the body have?" Nathan passed the basketball to Griffin.

Griffin shot the basketball and missed. "Eleven." His voice was flat, defeated.

Nathan rebounded the basketball and took a shot. It went through the hoop with a swish. "Name them."

Griffin rolled his eyes and grabbed the basketball. He bounced it with every system he ticked off the list. "Circulatory, respiratory, digestive, immune, nervous, skeletal, muscular, reproductive, excretory, endocrine, and . . . " He paused. " . . . and . . . " He looked up at the high ceiling of the gymnasium as if hoping to pull the last system out of thin air.

Come on, Griffin. You know this. We just went over it.

After just a minute the frustration set in. Griffin slammed the ball hard onto the gymnasium floor causing it to bounce way over his head.

"I don't know it, okay? I'm never gonna get this stuff so you might as well stop wasting your time." He stomped to the bleachers and plopped down.

Nathan grabbed the ball as it bounced toward him. "Is that what you think? That I'm wasting my time?" He strode over to the bleachers and stood in front of Griffin, the ball wedged under his arm. "I've been working with you for eight weeks, but it only took a minute for me to figure out what the real problem is here."

Griffin glared up at him. "Are you gonna tell me or do I have to name that too?"

Nathan snorted. "It's your attitude."

Griffin rolled his eyes. "Not you too."

Respecting Griffin's space, Nathan sat down a few feet from him. His voice was gentle but firm when he finally spoke. "Listen, I'm not wasting my time because I can see all your potential. Your mom sees it too. That's why she gets so frustrated when you don't try."

"I am trying!" Griffin nearly screamed the words.

Nathan remained calm. "You try until it gets too challenging and the fear of failure sets in."

"What are you? A shrink or something?"

"Nope. Just an ordinary guy who's been in a similar boat."

Nathan hesitated wondering if he really wanted to open up to a boy who couldn't seem to care less about him. He inhaled deeply. This was his chance to bring down the walls of Jericho.

"My mother died when I was really little. I guess my father had a hard time dealing with being a single parent because my brother and I never saw him. He worked and left my grandmother to raise us. It's different from what you're going through, but I understand all about feeling abandoned and lost, not having a place to belong." He watched Griffin closely. "Any of that sound familiar?"

"Yeah." It was barely more than a whisper.

"It took a long time for me to figure out that it wasn't doing me any good to feel sorry for myself. I certainly wasn't making my mark in the world by having my own pity party, and when I was finally honest with myself, I realized it didn't make me feel any better to dwell on what I couldn't change. In fact, it only made me feel worse."

"It's hard for me to get past it, ya know?"

Nathan nodded. Was it his imagination or did he hear a sound like a trumpet blast? Was that stone he heard crumbling? He wasn't sure . . . yet.

"We were so happy for so long—Mom, Dad, Grey, and me. I didn't even know anything was wrong. Then one day, out of the blue, we came home from school, and I could tell that Mom had been crying. I asked her what was wrong, and she said we'd talk about it after Dad got home from work. That evening my dad told Greyson and me that he and Mom had some differences they couldn't work out and that he was going to be moving out." Griffin stared out across the gym. "And just like that everything changed. I felt so helpless. All I could do was watch my family get torn apart."

He glanced at Nathan quickly, and then back to the other side of the gym. "I never talked to anyone about this before."

"Sometimes it helps."

Griffin nodded. "The worst part is that no one is happy any more. I mean, Greyson . . . well, he's just a dork. Dad has his new wife and baby so he works extra hard to provide for them and us. And Mom always looks like she could cry at the drop of a hat."

"I'm not sure, but I think a part of it is that she's worried about you."

Griffin's shoulders drooped. "I know. I'm afraid to talk to her about this because I don't want to hurt her feelings." He turned to Nathan. "But I'm hurting her anyway, aren't I?"

"I don't know, Griffin," Nathan lied, "but I do know this: When things in your life change, you have to change with it.

There's not much of a choice in the matter. Being an outsider looking in, I think your mom is trying to change with it, but she sees that you're stuck."

"So . . . how do I get unstuck?"

"I think this is a good start." Nathan smiled at Griffin and actually got one in return. Yes, that was rock he heard crumbling! "And you should probably work on your attitude toward school. Yes, it's tough. It gets tougher every year, but if you just believe in yourself the way your mom, I'm sure your dad, and I believe in you, you will accomplish everything you set your mind to."

"All right. I get it."

"Griffin, do you get that the Lord has a plan for you, for your life? And everything that you are going through now is preparing you for His purpose."

"I know that in my heart, but sometimes it's hard to think about anything besides my next biology test."

Nathan chuckled. "In that case, did you think of that last system yet?"

Griffin let out a groan and ran his hands through his hair. "I remember that the major organ is the skin and its function is to prevent the body from drying out and help protect the body from bacteria and viruses."

"That's right." Nathan tossed the ball to Griffin. "Come on. Nothing will jog the memory like a little one on one."

They played a tough game of basketball for twenty minutes straight. Nathan quickly discovered that Griffin could be a fierce competitor. It was a beautiful sight because he knew it was possible for such a passion to spread to other areas of Griffin's life, and he made that his specific prayer for the teen.

As if putting an exclamation point on Nathan's unspoken prayer, Griffin dropped back behind the three point line, took aim, hurled the ball through the air, and sank the shot.

Nathan rebounded the ball. "Look out LeBron James!"

The sound of clapping reached them from the direction of the big, metal double doors on the other side of the gym. They both snapped their attention toward the sound.

"That was an awesome shot," Denise said walking over to join them.

"Thanks," Griffin mumbled.

"How's the biology coming?" She held her hands up to catch the basketball, and Nathan passed it to her.

"Good." Griffin's voice contained none of the sincerity Nathan had heard just moments ago.

No, Griffin! Don't start stacking rocks back up on that wall. Your mother needs to see that you want to change.

She dribbled over to the free throw line. "I'll make you a deal. If I make this basket, you have to cook an appreciation dinner for Nathan on Saturday."

"Oh, you don't have to do that. Really," he objected thinking of the time he'd be missing out on with Kate and Madeline.

She continued as if not hearing. "If I don't make it, then I'll do the cooking."

"Okay. It's a deal." There was a hint of interest in Griffin's voice.

She aimed and shot the ball. It hit the rim and bounced off. She turned to her son.

"Looks like I'm in the kitchen again." She shrugged good-naturedly. "Oh, well. What else is new?"

She motioned to where Griffin's backpack sat on the bleachers. "Gather your books up and come on. Your brother will be out of football practice in a few minutes. We need to grab a quick bite to eat, and then head over to Kate's church for the support group meeting."

Griffin took a step toward his mother. "Hey, Mom?"

"Yeah?"

He suddenly became fascinated with his sneakers. "Um . . . well, I was just thinking that maybe we can make supper for Nathan, you know . . . together."

She shifted her gaze to Nathan, her brown-gold eyes wide with amazement. She turned back to Griffin.

"I think that's a great idea."

A lump began to form in Nathan's throat, and he swallowed twice in an attempt to dislodge it. "I guess since my dinner plans have just been decided for me, I need to know what time to be there."

"Six o'clock sharp."

"Looking forward to it."

A minute later, alone in the gymnasium, he stared at the doors that Denise and Griffin had just walked through, letting it all sink in. It was hard to believe that in just an hour and a half Griffin had not only emerged from his shell but had also reached out.

"He actually reached out." Nathan fell to his knees. Tears slid down his cheeks. "Thank You, God! I know he has a long road ahead of him, but there is hope. There is finally hope for this family."

The gymnasium doors banged open, and he scrambled to his feet, wiping away the residual moisture on his face. Griffin stood in the doorway breathing heavily, as if he'd sprinted a mile. Nathan jogged over to him, his heart beginning to pound with the fear that something had happened to Denise or Greyson.

"What is it? What's wrong?"

Griffin shook his head. "Nothing. Mom told me to hurry. I just had to tell you . . . "

"What?"

"I remembered the last body system. It's the integumentary system."

"See? I knew you'd get it. I'm proud of you, Griffin."

"Thanks."

"Now don't keep your mom waiting."

"Oh, right." And just like that he was off, flying down the hallway and around the corner to his awaiting mother.

⁂

At seven o'clock all thirty of the seats were filled in the adult Sunday school room. By five after they had to add a chair. Thankfully it was a big room, but at this rate they'd outgrow it soon. Kate made a mental note to talk to Pastor Ben about making other arrangements.

Denise opened the meeting with a word of prayer, which had become the routine, but Kate was only listening with one ear. She was also silently making her own personal plea.

Sweet Jesus, be by my side. I have a feeling I'm going to need your help this evening.

"Amen," Denise said, and the others shifted their attention to Kate.

Her gaze quickly swept the large circle. Adam hadn't made it and, although she understood why, she really missed his support and gentle strength.

She cleared her throat. "First, I want to let you all know that Denise and I have been working on planning outings and events for us to participate in as a group with our children."

A murmur of interest passed around the circle, prompting her to elaborate.

"Right now, with everyone's busy schedules, we are aiming at one outing per month. Some events will be right here in Harvest Bay, but others will involve some travel time. We are making every effort to plan the whole year out so you have plenty of time to make arrangements if you share custody of your children. I intend to have a list of the events, along with dates and times, finalized and ready for you by our first meeting in December, but in the meantime I can tell you that in January we will be heading to Detroit for a Redwings game."

The room brightened with excited smiles and nods, and Kate took a moment to respond to them. When it came time to move on, however, a knot of dread formed in her stomach. The topic of the day was the very reason she kept herself so busy. She prayed that good could come of the discussion.

She retrieved her Bible from a nearby table and held it in her lap, hoping to absorb some divine strength through it. None came, but she had to get on with it anyway, so she cleared her throat.

"Today we are going to focus on the approaching holidays and what we can do individually and as a group to get through the next month and a half. The holidays are traditionally viewed as a time to celebrate family and togetherness, but for some it can serve as a reminder of all we've lost—relationships, hopes, dreams. While others are busy making memories with their loved ones, I've just been busy. Does anyone else ever feel like that?"

If the exasperated nods were any indication, most of those in the circle had similar experiences.

"But the Lord doesn't want us to muddle through these special holidays emotionally unattached. He doesn't want us to go through life that way either. I want to read a verse I came across in Second Corinthians."

Kate opened her Bible to where she had it marked. "It's in the first chapter starting at verse three. 'Blessed be the God and Father of our Lord Jesus Christ, the Father of mercies and God of all comfort, who comforts us in all our tribulation, that we may be able to comfort those who are in trouble, with the comfort with which we ourselves are comforted by God.' " She closed her Bible and looked up. "I don't know exactly why our group has grown so much over the past few weeks except for the fact that there is a great need for comfort and support, especially during this time of year."

She returned her Bible to the nearby table and gathered her thoughts and courage. "Last year was very difficult for me, probably the most difficult holiday season since Ryan died. Reality set in hard. I was trying to keep things as normal as possible for Maddie, but nothing was normal anymore."

She noticed some nods and murmurs of understanding.

"We had already made plans to move back here so I knew it would be the last Thanksgiving and Christmas in our house, the house that contained all our happy family memories. I didn't want to leave it, but it was getting really hard to stay there too. My life, like many of yours, was like a broken vase. During that time, it was easier for me to sit and stare at the pieces and remember what it had once been than to try to put it back together, knowing that it would never be the same vase again. Does that make sense?"

Several people nodded.

"But I'm a pretty practical person, and I realized that eventually I'd have to try to put those pieces back together. The broken pieces of a vase are basically useless, and even though I didn't want something new, I had to have *something*. I didn't want my little girl to watch me just exist."

More nods.

"So I picked up all the pieces, and we moved back here near our family and friends. We began to get involved in the community, but my life was still a broken vase, and I was still carrying around the pieces." Kate's voice wavered. "It was a heavy load, and I was so weary. Then a friend who had found comfort in the Lord during her time of trial comforted me." She glanced at Denise and a tear escaped over her lashes. "She helped me carry those pitiful pieces of my life to the Lord. He took my burdens, comforted me, and handed me back a new, different, but equally beautiful vase."

She sniffed. "And that's what I want for all of you this holiday season. I realize that all of us have different circumstances, but, regardless, the Lord didn't make us to walk this road alone. Be comforted and comfort others, and you might find that you receive a new, different, but beautiful vase."

She dropped her gaze to her hands folded in her lap. *Please, Holy Spirit, move in this room. Stir up the hearts of these hurting people so they might find comfort and healing in the Lord. Please, Holy Spirit, please.*

Before she could finish forming the last "please" in her brain, Matt Johansen, the father of four-year-old twins, cleared his throat. "I hate to admit this, but I'm having a hard time forgiving my ex-wife. I mean, I know I'm not blameless. I work a lot of long hours, which often left her at home alone with the girls. But why couldn't she see that I was only trying to provide a comfortable life for my family? Now my family is torn apart."

"I'm having a hard time forgiving myself," Letisha Jackson confessed. "When DeWayne and I separated, I thought it would only be temporary. I mean, surely he wouldn't leave me to raise a two-year-old and a newborn on my own, right?" She shook her head. "After a year and a half I gave up hope. I went ahead and filed, but every single day since our divorce was final over a year ago I've wondered what would've happened if I'd hung on just a little while longer."

"I watched helplessly while my husband of twenty-three years lost a two-year battle with cancer," Kim McDoogle tearfully shared. "I don't know how to find comfort after that, and I don't know how to help my three teenagers deal with their loss."

"Well, I was never married," Chad Remington, a newer member, shared. "I was young and careless. My girlfriend and I planned to get married someday, but when she got pregnant everything changed. She said she had to 'figure things out,' and I wasn't ready to be a dad yet. I mean, we made a mistake, but my son has to suffer because of it. I'm having a hard time dealing with that."

Maggie sniffled. Tears fell from her long, dark lashes and soaked into the fleece blanket that swaddled baby Justin.

Kate closed her eyes and racked her brain. There had to be a Bible verse that would apply to Chad's and possibly Maggie's situations. She didn't know of any other way to comfort these young parents.

You comforted me, oh God, so that I can comfort others. Help me know what to say.

"I had a hard time dealing with the disappointment of failure too."

Kate's eyes flew open at the sound of the very familiar voice behind her. She turned and looked up into Adam's face.

He gave her a weary smile. "Sorry I'm so late."

She shook her head. "Your timing is perfect."

He pulled up a chair and turned his attention back to Chad. "Everyone has expectations of how their life will go, and no one hopes to become a single parent. Something that I learned from a very wise friend is that God uses all things for His good. *All* things. He can turn our mistakes into blessings if we let Him. At first, I didn't believe it." He met Kate's gaze. " But I do now."

Kate's breath caught in her throat as she stared at him with questions in her eyes. Then the floodgates opened wide, and sharing she couldn't have predicted took place in the group. A wonderful feeling of satisfaction came over her.

Maybe this would help some of them heal, but, regardless, these men and women understood that they were not alone during the holidays or any day of the year. She glanced at Adam. Because of him, she'd accomplished her goal for the evening and then some.

Their hour was up all too quickly. The members said good night to one another, and before long, Kate, Denise, and Adam were the only ones left.

"That was a great meeting, Kate," Denise said gathering a few leftover papers and pens. "I think it was just what these folks needed, especially at this time of year."

"Thanks. I hope you're right."

"Well, I'm going to get my boys and head home." She paused, her smile working its way across her pretty face. "Maybe I'll even enjoy a nice, quiet conversation with Griffin before the night is over."

"You mean . . . "

Her smile broadened. "I'll fill you in on the details later." She shifted her gaze from Kate to Adam. "You two have a good night." She swung her purse onto her shoulder and, with a final wave, slipped out the door.

Kate turned to Adam, her heart so swollen she thought it might burst. "I didn't think you were going to make it tonight."

"Yeah. Practice ran over."

She dropped her gaze. "About what you said . . . "

"Yes."

She eyed him. "Yes?"

"I believe."

Without realizing that she'd been holding her breath, she exhaled, closed the small gap between them, and threw herself into his arms. He gathered her against him.

"So do you think your grandpa has plans on Saturday?"

Kate wondered if her smile was as big on the outside as it was on the inside. "I think his schedule is wide open."

Five minutes later, on her way home, her heart filled to capacity with a joy she hadn't known for three years, a tiny sliver of fear pricked Kate's brain. At first, it was barely noticeable but it quickly began to fester. And as she lay in bed a few hours later, it made her so uncomfortable that she couldn't fall asleep.

"What will I ever do if this new, different, but beautiful vase gets broken?"

CHAPTER
Twenty-Three

As Adam turned into Kate's driveway Saturday morning, his mind juggled three simple facts: In two short weeks his football team would be playing in the state championship. Over the past two and a half months he'd discovered the true meaning of faith, strengthening his foundation in the process. And, at some point between July and November, he'd managed to fall in love again.

He suspected that these facts were all intertwined, and somehow they lifted him so high he was sitting on top of the world. He didn't ever want to come down.

Chloe wasted no time hopping out of the truck and dashing toward Kate's front porch. Adam cut the engine and grabbed his grandfather's Bible off the passenger seat, ready to follow suit, when his cell phone rang. He picked the phone up, checked the caller id, and winced. He still needed to work on applying God's grace to this area of his life.

After taking a deep breath, he pushed the green talk button. "Hi, Lexie. How are you?"

"I'm good, and you?" Her sweet-as-sugar voice put him on alert.

"Just fine, thanks, but I'm kind of busy right now. Can this wait?"

"It won't take but a second. I wanted to let you know that I'm coming to visit in a couple weeks."

Adam's brows scrunched involuntarily. "To spend time with Chloe?"

"Yes, of course." She paused. "But I also need to talk with you."

Adam's eyes narrowed. "About?"

"Oh, I'm not going to get into it over the phone. Besides, you're busy, aren't you?"

"Well, yeah, but . . . "

"Just keep your calendar open, okay?"

"Okay, but . . . "

"Ta tah," Alexandra said in a sing-songy voice, and then there was silence.

"Lexie . . . Alexandra?" He could have called her back, but he wasn't sure he wanted to know the purpose for her visit right then, especially if it had anything to do with his custodial rights. What would it do to Chloe if they went back to court to fight over her custody? The thought made him shudder.

He heard a tap on his window. He glanced over to see Kate's beautiful face smiling at him, and his tension immediately started to ease.

She pulled open the door, and then put her hands on her hips. "Are you gonna stay in there all day or what?"

"Sorry. I just got a call." He held up his cell phone.

She frowned. "Is everything okay?"

"I hope so." He looked at her and managed a smile. Tucking the Bible under his arm, he climbed down from the truck and slipped his arm casually around her shoulders. "Come on."

Inside, Kate had a cozy fire burning in her fireplace, and the rich aromas of chocolate and coffee wafted in from the kitchen. Grandpa Clayton gently rocked in the recliner, and Madeline and Chloe's voices floated to Adam from where they were playing down the hall. It felt like home in so many ways.

"I made hot chocolate for the girls and put a pot of coffee on for Gramps. Which would you like?"

He gave her a boyish grin. "I can't remember the last time I had hot chocolate."

"Hot chocolate it is then. Coming right up." She motioned toward the living area. "Go on in and make yourself at home."

Adam went into the room, shook Grandpa Clayton's hand, and took a seat at the end of the sofa nearest the recliner.

"Good to see you again, Adam."

"You, too."

"Looks like you're takin' your team to state, eh?"

Adam rubbed the back of his neck in an effort to tamp down the excitement bubbling up in him. "Guess so."

"Your grandpa would be real proud of you."

Adam worked hard to keep his emotion in check. He ran his hand over his grandfather's Bible. "I hope so."

Grandpa Clayton stopped rocking and leaned forward a little. "Believe it."

The corners of Adam's mouth turned up slightly. "Thanks."

Grandpa Clayton went back to rocking. "So, what brings you by today?"

Adam's palms began to get clammy, and he rubbed them together, feeling beads of perspiration forming on his brow. "I've been sharing some things that I've read in the Bible with my team."

Grandpa Clayton's eyebrows arched high over the frame of his glasses. "Oh?"

"Yeah, and I think they're really listening."

At that moment, Kate entered the living room with two steaming mugs. She handed one to Grandpa Clayton, the other to Adam, and sat on the opposite end of the sofa from him, tucking her feet up under her.

Grandpa Clayton took a cautious sip and cleared his throat. "I remember a young man I helped lead to Christ. I was somewhere in my mid forties but had only been a true Christian for about ten years, and this nice young man showed up on my doorstep right over there," he gestured toward the front door, "to take Kate's mother to a school dance." He waved his hand, palm out. "Oh, they were just friends. Rebecca was already dating Charlie, who was away at college, but she was still my little girl, our firstborn, so I had to sit this fella down and ask him a few questions."

"What did you ask him?"

Grandpa Clayton chuckled. "Oh, this old memory isn't what it used to be. I can't recall everything we talked about in those few minutes, but I do remember that I asked him if he was a Christian."

"And what did he say?" Kate asked.

"He told me that he believed there was a God but he didn't attend church or anything like that, so I knew that he had no idea who God really was." He shook his head sadly. "Later on, Rebecca confided in me that this young man didn't have the best home life. If I remember correctly, he lived with his mother and four or five other siblings. His father was an alcoholic who'd left them before he was even born. His mother worked two jobs just to make ends meet while his oldest sister took care of them.

"While his friendship with Rebecca grew, he started spending more and more time over here. My Bonnie and I, we understood that this young fella needed us so we welcomed him. Eventually he began staying late enough to be involved with our family evening devotions, and gradually our devotions took on the theme of salvation. A month and a half later, this young man dedicated his life to Christ. He started attending church with us and began ministering to his family. Last I heard, his mother and all but one of his siblings became dedicated Christians."

"That's awesome." Adam fancied the idea that he could one day help bring about such a change for a lost family.

"Do you know what became of that boy, Gramps?"

"He had intentions of going to law school, but after he experienced the love of Christ, he changed his plans and went to seminary instead."

"He became a pastor?"

Grandpa Clayton glanced at Adam. "Yep. Pastor Ben Andrews."

Kate's jaw dropped. "The boy you and Grandma led to Christ is *our* Pastor Ben?"

Grandpa Clayton laughed out loud. "The very one."

"That would explain his desire to help the single parents in our community and in the surrounding areas."

Grandpa Clayton nodded, then turned to Adam. "You just never know what kind of difference you can make in this life."

Adam stared at his mug. "But to make a difference you first have to set an example, don't you?"

Grandpa Clayton rubbed his chin. "I've never had too much luck talking the talk without walking the walk."

"I think I'm ready to become a Christian, but . . . " Fear gripped his heart. "What if I mess up? What if I let Him down?"

"Do you have your Bible?"

Adam held it up.

"Look up Romans 3:23."

Adam remembered that the book of Romans was in the New Testament, but he still couldn't quite pinpoint where so he scanned the table of contents until he found it, and then quickly flipped to the verse. "It says, 'for all have sinned and fall short of the glory of God.' "

"*All* have sinned, Adam. You wouldn't be the first to mess up."

"Then what's the point? Why even try?"

"Because of Romans 5:8."

Adam turned the page. "It says, 'But God demonstrates His own love toward us, in that while we were still sinners, Christ died for us.' " He reread that verse silently. "Wow," he breathed.

Grandpa Clayton nodded. "Wow is right. It's even more powerful when you read Romans 6:23."

Adam hurriedly skipped over to the passage. " 'For the wages of sin is death, but the gift of God is eternal life in Christ Jesus our Lord.' " He swallowed a lump of emotion that suddenly formed in his throat and looked at Grandpa Clayton. "It seems impossible."

"To a human mind, yes, but that is where faith kicks in. The Bible tells us that nothing is impossible for God. I made a choice to believe that promise and the promises you've just read. I won't lie. Sometimes I'm faced with doubt, but the commitment I made to trust in the Word of God covers me every time."

Adam fell silent. For as long as he could remember he'd been afraid of letting down and disappointing those he loved the most, but what he just read told him that God loved him so much that He'd already made arrangements to not only cover all his mistakes, but also to bless him.

"For the wages of sin is death, but the gift of God is eternal life in Christ Jesus our Lord." He looked at Grandpa Clayton with damp eyes. "Is it selfish of me to want a gift that I don't deserve?"

"Not if the One giving it wants you to have it even more."

Silence fell again while Adam reflected on his life, specifically the past seventeen years. During his senior year in high school, his spiritual downward slide had accelerated after he threw an interception that ended up costing Harvest Bay the state championship. That had left him with a heavy burden he carried around for a decade and a half. He was a failure. When he entered his freshman year of college, his heart became cold, hard stone. It was easier to deal with the pain of his mistakes on and off the field that way.

But recently he'd noticed a thawing sensation inside, a sweet warmth as if the hot chocolate he'd just enjoyed had worked its way through his veins, leaving behind hope and happiness. Was that his faith growing, spreading? He didn't know for sure, but it felt good.

"What . . . " His voice cracked and Kate scooted closer to lend her support. "What do I have to do?"

Grandpa Clayton smiled. "Just read Romans 10:9."

Adam flipped a few pages, found the passage, and read it. " 'If you confess with your mouth the Lord Jesus and believe in your heart that God has raised Him from the dead, you will be saved.' " He snapped his gaze up to meet Grandpa Clayton's. "That's it?"

"That's it." Grandpa Clayton held his hands out. "Just say it and mean it."

Kate slipped her hand under his and laced their fingers together. She looked up at him with misty eyes.

"Would you like me to pray with you?"

A new sparkle flickered in Adam's damp eyes. "Yeah."

That morning, Adam's life changed forever. He saw his relationships and experiences through new eyes—the eyes of his heart—and he recognized the traces of God's love in each instance. His stone cold heart was suddenly ablaze with the Holy Spirit.

But he was under no illusions. He understood that it wouldn't always be easy. He knew enough to know that he would experience trials and tests, but he made a choice, a commitment, as Grandpa Clayton once had, to trust God's promises, and he was confident that would get him through. He also knew this wasn't the end of his journey.

It was only the beginning.

⚜

Nathan pulled into Denise's driveway at five minutes until six o'clock. He turned off his engine and sat there for a moment, stuck in the middle of a tug-of-war match between his emotions.

On one end of the imaginary rope was the excitement of seeing how much progress Griffin had made just since Tuesday. Denise had reported that she had a long talk with Griffin on Tuesday night. They'd cried some, laughed a little, and come to an understanding: They were both at fault, and they were both going to try to bend in each other's direction a little. Griffin's attitude was showing signs of improvement overall, and Denise was trying to give him the space he needed to figure some things out on his own.

Nathan gave all the credit to God for reviving this relationship. He felt privileged to have played even a small part in God's plan for Denise and Griffin.

On the other end, pulling just as hard, was the disappointment of not being able to spend this evening with Kate and Madeline. In the five weeks since the homecoming dance, the bond between them had grown stronger, more intimate, and though neither he nor Kate had verbally declared their love for each other, he thought for sure they were in the beginning stages of becoming a real family.

"It's God's plan for us. I know it is." His voice was barely above a whisper but still filled up his small BMW.

He settled the battle of emotions by promising himself that he'd take a drive out to Kate's later that evening, but first he resolved to have an enjoyable dinner with Denise and her boys. So he got out of his car and headed up the cobblestone walk to the front door. He raised his hand to push the doorbell, but before it made contact, Denise swung the door open.

"Hey! You're right on time. Come on in."

Although the sun had almost completely set that late fall evening, a bright ray of sunshine was standing right in front of him, and he couldn't help but smile as he stepped inside. Immediately a rich, garlicky aroma hit him, and his stomach growled loudly.

Denise laughed. "Sounds like you're hungry."

He hung his jacket on the rack by the door. "Who wouldn't be? It smells fantastic. Mind if I ask what's on the menu?"

She led the way into the great room that flanked the kitchen. "Not at all. We made Griffin's favorite—lasagna— and Greyson's favorite—chicken fettuccine alfredo. I also threw together a salad and baked a loaf of garlic bread. Oh, and for dessert we made my favorite—chocolate fudge brownies a la mode. Sound okay?"

He was stunned. "It sounds like a lot. You really didn't have to go to all that trouble."

She stopped and turned to him. "Look, I don't know what you did or what you said in the gymnasium the other day, but you gave me my son back. Oh, he still has his moments like any other teenager, but all in all this has been the best week we've had in a long, long time. There's nothing I can do to repay you for that." She turned away quickly and gave a little snort. "Besides, with these two boys there won't be much left over. Believe me."

Nathan chuckled and followed her into the kitchen. "Is there anything I can do to help?"

"Nope. Everything's ready. I just need to know what you want to drink." She rattled off a few choices.

"I'll just have water, thanks."

She was filling a glass with ice and water from the dispenser in the freezer door when Griffin walked in.

"Mom, everything's ready in the dining room." He turned to Nathan then and put a hand up. "Oh, hey."

It was all Nathan could do not to gawk. The boy even looked different—happier maybe. "I hear you've been slaving away here in the kitchen."

Griffin chuckled and gave a quick shrug. "Nah. Mom ended up doing most of it. I baked the garlic bread and set the table."

"And don't forget you'll be helping your brother clean up," Denise reminded with a wink.

"Riiiight." Griffin backpedaled a few steps, then turned and high-tailed it into the dining room.

Denise threw Nathan a see-what-I-mean look. He nodded nonchalantly, though he inwardly praised God for what appeared to be a near miraculous transformation. She handed him his glass of ice water, and they joined the two boys at the table in the adjacent dining room.

"Shall we pray?" Denise asked

"I'll do it, Mom," Griffin volunteered.

A beautiful mixture of joy and pride danced in Denise's eyes as she motioned for her son to go ahead. Nathan folded his hands, bowed his head, and listened intently while Griffin prayed.

"Lord, thanks for all this food and for my mom who fixed it and who does lots of stuff for my brother and me that we don't appreciate. Thanks also for bringing Nathan here to help me understand biology better," Griffin hesitated for just a second, "and to remind me that You have a plan for my life. Help us all to follow Your plan for our lives. Amen."

"Amen," they all echoed.

Denise reached over and placed her hand on Griffin's giving him a grateful grin

"He didn't thank God for me," Greyson pointed out.

"And your point is?" Griffin teased.

The playful banter between the boys intertwined with the casual conversation for the duration of the delicious meal. Nathan thoroughly enjoyed the evening, and by the time he swallowed his last bite of brownie a la mode, he was completely satisfied.

"That was an amazing meal. I'm tempted to have more, but I know I'd be miserable if I did." He patted his belly.

"I told you there wouldn't be many leftovers, didn't I?"

When Denise flashed him a smile, something stirred deep inside Nathan's heart that he tried to ignore.

"Okay, Mom, we're done," Greyson reported, coming back into the dining room.

Griffin stopped in the doorway. "The dishes are loaded in the dishwasher and leftovers are in the fridge. Can we go upstairs and play the Wii now?"

"Yes, but please get along."

The boys were out of the room before she said the word *along.*

She sighed and shook her head while she watched them go. "There's never a dull moment with those two." She stood and carried their dessert plates into the kitchen.

Nathan followed and leaned back against the counter while Denise found a spot in the dishwasher for the two small plates. "What were they like when they were little?"

"Oh, about the same. Griffin was more of the introvert, like his dad, and Greyson was our social butterfly."

"Like you."

"Guilty as charged." She held her hands up. "Still, considering how different as they are, they've always been buddies." She hesitated. "Until about a year ago."

"What happened?"

"Griffin's world was changing faster than he was prepared for. He turned thirteen and a month later his dad and new step-mom had a baby, while he was still trying to adjust to having a family in two separate households. The first person he pushed away was the one he was closest to—his brother— and it really hurt Grey."

Leaning against the counter around the corner from him, she crossed her arms and dropped her gaze to the tile floor. "That's what most people don't understand about divorce. When kids are involved, it's not just the end of a marriage and it doesn't just hurt the spouse. It completely changes a child's life. Sure, they learn to make the adjustment, but even in the best-case scenarios, it's still the end of a family."

"I'm so sorry you've been through so much."

As far as Nathan could see, there wasn't anything about Denise that wasn't . . . well, wonderful. Why Daryl would want to throw away a life with such an amazing woman and hurt two great kids in the process was beyond him.

She shrugged. "I'm really okay. I mean, what other choice do I have? I'm not one to wallow in my heartache. I grieved for a while, but I had two boys who needed me, and I decided I had to pick up the pieces and find a way to move on. I started going to a Bible study, and the Lord worked a miracle in my heart. He helped me to see myself the way He sees me—priceless—instead of the way Daryl saw me. My relationship with the Lord has grown in ways I never imagined."

She glanced heavenward. "He's my best friend, and for that I'm thankful for all I've been through. But I still hate what it's done to my boys. I hate that they get shuffled back and forth, that we have to split holidays and vacations. There's just always something missing, ya know? I've prayed for God to fill that gap with whatever would help them heal.

"Greyson was easy. He found football and, at this point in his young life, that's enough. Griffin needed someone. I tried to talk him into seeing a counselor, and that made things worse. He didn't talk to me for days." She blew out an exasperated breath. "It's so frustrating to not be able to help your own child, but the more I tried the further he slipped away from me. So I just prayed. I begged God to send someone who could really help him."

Her chin quivered, and tears pooled behind her thick lashes. "And He sent you."

Nathan's heavy heart melted. *She thinks that God sent me to them, but He didn't . . . did He?* His mind flashed through the string of events that had led them to this moment—Madeline's birthday party, the barn dance, his interview with Doc Brewster, house hunting with Denise, homecoming night, and it just kept going on.

"*Help us all to follow Your plan for our lives,*" Griffin had prayed earlier. Nathan had questioned whether or not he was following God's plan for his life. Had God really led him to Harvest Bay?

But suddenly, gazing at Denise as she brushed away the tears trickling down her cheek, he questioned *why* God had led him to Harvest Bay. What if it wasn't for Kate and Madeline after all, but for Denise and her boys—especially Griffin?

The idea was ridiculous. *Of course* he was here for Kate and Madeline. They were his family. He loved them.

He shook his head. "I'm sorry, Denise. I don't think God brought me here for Griffin."

She nodded and wiped the moisture from her cheeks. "I know what you think." She shrugged as fresh tears surfaced. "I just don't know how else to explain the change in my son. My heart won't let me believe anything else." A sob escaped, and she covered her face with her hands.

Nathan closed the gap between them and wrapped his arms around her, vividly remembering how she'd befriended him just three and a half months earlier when he stood alone in a corner at Madeline's birthday party.

She clung to his shirt as if it were a lifeline. "You don't understand the hurt, Nathan," she said, her voice muffled. "You can't possibly understand the pain of losing your spouse and being so afraid that you're going to lose your child too. I prayed so hard for so long for someone who could reach my son before he was too far gone." She hiccupped and tipped her face upwards. "You are the answer to my prayer. Can't you see that?"

Holding her so close and gazing down into her beautiful face streaked with liquid emotion gave him a new perspective. He bent his face closer to hers and whispered, "I can now."

In the next heartbeat, his lips were on hers in a kiss that was so magical it touched the depths of his soul, revived his spirit, and awakened his senses.

She pulled back slightly, but staying well within the boundaries of his embrace. "This could get complicated."

He had to catch his breath. "I know."

It wasn't until he was on his way home two hours later that the full impact of the situation hit him like a left hook from Smokin' Joe Frazier. He loved Kate. That hadn't changed, but he was now falling in love with Denise, and both of them had children he adored. They'd all had their hearts broken, and none of them deserved to be hurt again.

Yes, this could get very complicated.

Twenty-Four

On that first Saturday afternoon in December, Adam stood at the entrance to Fawcett Stadium in Canton. It wasn't the biggest stadium he'd ever been in, but with over twenty-two thousand seats it was significantly bigger than what his boys were used to playing in. The NFL Pro Football Hall of Fame game was played there to start each pre-season. This, however, was his team's Super Bowl.

He vividly remembered the thrill of playing in the state championship . . . and the gut-wrenching anguish of defeat. How many times had he wished that he could turn back the clock and re-attempt that intercepted pass? How many times had he wished for just one more play? He had finally returned for a state championship game, but this time his role on the field was different, and, even more drastically, his priorities had changed.

He was a Christian now, and he learned more and more every day how special that was. Studying God's Word and developing a relationship with God had recently become his top priority. He had to admit it was a bit of a challenge when it seemed as if his everyday life kept trying to shift his focus to worldly things, and he struggled to get over disbelief that God actually wanted to have a relationship with him. But he continued to read his Bible every night and was growing in his prayer life. When he'd been at Kate's for Thanksgiving dinner, he was able to sneak an undisturbed moment to ask Grandpa Clayton a few questions.

He'd already begun to reap surprising benefits. A constant joy filled his being, a joy like that of a child who'd been accepted into the cool kid's club. Acceptance was a wonderful gift. He'd underestimated how important it was to be accepted and loved for who he was, not for who he thought others expected him to be.

Now that he'd made the commitment to live his life for God, he'd also made the commitment to strive to be a better father. He'd lost count of how many games of Trouble he and Chloe played during the past two weeks. He'd taken her to the farm several times to work with her on Dolly, something he'd always left up to Kennedy.

Best yet, they'd begun having bedtime devotions together every night. It was the best time of his day. Chloe was a very close second on his list of priorities.

He pondered how the role football had played in his life had changed. He still loved the game. He'd played it since he was old enough to hold a football. It was a part of who he was but no longer the most important part.

He still wanted to win the state championship, but mostly for his seniors. They were a good group of boys and didn't deserve to feel the agony of defeat the way he had. While he stood there, he silently prayed that God would protect this team, that they would play a memorable game, and that they would be able to savor every moment of this trip to the state championship.

"It goes by way too fast," Adam said softly.

"It sure does." Tom Ellsworth, the offensive coordinator, came up beside him.

Adam turned. "How are the boys doing?"

"They're ready to play the biggest game of their young lives. What about you?"

Adam watched the people stream into the stands on both sides of the stadium. "I've waited a long time to get back to the state championship and now that I'm here . . . " a slow grin eased its way across his face, " . . . it feels even better than I remember."

"That's because this time it's not about you."

Adam nodded and shoved his hands into the pockets of his Dockers.

"Listen, I want you to know that it took real guts to bring faith into this ball club like you did, and most of those boys have really been listening. You and I both know by now that football games will come and go, but our faith is forever. You've set the example that it's okay to put your hope in something besides the scoreboard, and that's something these boys will take with them wherever they go."

Adam placed a hand on Tom's shoulder. "Thanks, man. I appreciate it. So now that I've had my pep talk, what do you say we go give one to these boys?"

Tom gently slapped him on the back. "Now you're talking!"

The two men walked down the short tunnel together and stepped inside the locker room to find the usual pre-game rituals taking place. Adam cleared his throat, and the boys turned to him expectantly.

"We made it!" As the locker room erupted in a cheer, Adam held his hands out, palms down, quieting the energized players. "And no one deserves to be here more than you guys do. You've come together as a team and worked hard to earn this chance at the state championship. I've told you before and I'll tell you again, I'm proud of you. I'm proud of what you've accomplished this season individually and as a team."

Making sure to keep his emotions in check, he made eye contact with his seniors. "For some of you, this is it. Four twelve-minute quarters is all you have left in those jerseys, and then you'll go on to college or maybe the workforce or some of you might join the military. But the bottom line is this: This is not your defining moment. It's a moment. All I'm asking from you right now is that you go out there and play like you love this game. If you promise me, yourself, and each other to put forth your very best effort, have fun on the field, and have faith like that mustard seed . . . well, gentlemen, I'm confident that there isn't any team anywhere that could beat us."

Another cheer erupted and some of the players pumped their helmets in the air. "Now before we go out there and play the game of our lives," Adam continued, "would anyone like to lead us in prayer?"

Finally a hand went up. "I'll do it, Coach."

Adam smiled. "Go right ahead, Brady."

Brady nodded uncertainly and cleared his throat. "God, thanks that we get to play in the state championship game. Please, keep us all safe out there and help us to have good sportsmanship, um, no matter what happens. Amen."

They all jogged out to the field with confidence despite the fact that their opponent, Cincinnati Bishop Hadley, bigger in just about every way possible, had made an appearance in the playoffs for five years running.

Against all odds, the Bulldogs fumbled the opening kickoff on their own eleven yard line, and Harvest Bay recovered it.

Knowing he needed to take full advantage of the error, Adam called a trick play. Brady accepted the handoff from Kyle, took three strides to the left, luring Bishop Hadley's intimidating defense with him, then abruptly stopped and lofted an easy pass into the corner of the right end zone. Only one person had a chance to catch it. With no one around him, Kyle gracefully caught the ball for an easy six points. Kicking the extra point, Harvest Bay started out with a 7-0 lead.

Getting on the scoreboard first was crucial since that set the tone for the first half. Bishop Hadley continued to make uncharacteristic mistakes, fumbling two more times and throwing an interception just before the end of the half. Still, Adam knew that a 13-7 lead at halftime wasn't good enough. While excited chatter filled his team's locker room, he had a sick feeling that the Bulldogs were getting chewed out thoroughly by the coaching staff and preparing to return to the field on a mission. In his gut, he secretly feared the outcome.

It's in Your hands, God.

He must have repeated those words in his head a hundred times before addressing his players. In his half-time speech he focused on building his team up by driving every positive he could think of from that beautiful first half into their heads and not mentioning the missed opportunities.

"Give me that same dedication, that same heart and soul this second half, and we're walking outta here with the trophy, boys!"

Cheers went up, and the captains wasted no time leading them back onto the field. Adam brought up the rear silently chanting, *It's in Your hands, God.*

But just as he'd feared, the momentum shifted. Harvest Bay received the kickoff, and the offense quickly sputtered like an engine needing a tune-up. After three failed running plays they were forced to punt . . . to First Team All Ohio wide receiver, P. J. McKay. McKay drifted back and caught the punt on his own forty-five yard line, then easily avoided the first Falcon in pursuit with just a sidestep to his left. He then changed direction again and found a gaping hole.

Adam fought hard against the urge to throw his clipboard to the ground. When McKay crossed the fifty yard line and moved into Harvest Bay territory, he turned on his jets and within seconds was standing in the end zone doing a little victory dance. Adam shoved his fingers through his hair. He glanced up at the scoreboard, though he knew what it would say. After kicking the extra point, Bishop Hadley had the lead, 14-13.

It should have spelled the beginning of the end for the Falcons. But every player on the roster seemed to reach deep inside for the strength to keep pushing forward, for the faith to keep believing in their team and the One who had brought them that far. At the beginning of the fourth quarter, with the score unchanged, Harvest Bay received a Bulldog punt at their own twenty-two yard line and gained several yards. Kyle followed it up nicely by leading a drive straight into enemy territory. On the fourth down, with six minutes and twelve seconds left in the game, Adam called a time out.

"What was Jeremy's longest field goal of the season?" He asked Paul Blackstock, his special teams coach.

"Thirty-two yards, but he's hit from forty-one during practice," Paul reported.

Adam looked Paul in the eyes. "Do you think he can make a thirty-seven yard field goal?"

Paul nodded. "He's a talented kid."

"Wait a second," Tom interjected. "Kyle just moved the ball all the way down the field. At this point, a touchdown would give us complete control of the game, but even if we don't make it into the end zone, just an additional eight to ten yards would increase our odds for a successful field goal attempt."

Adam chewed on his thumbnail, knowing he had to make a quick decision. "Okay," he finally said. "This is what we're going to do . . . "

His stomach was in a knot as he watched Kyle race back out to the field with orders to execute a bold play. The second the center snapped the ball, the Bishop Hadley defense exploded through Harvest Bay's offensive line causing complete and total disruption. Kyle backpeddled, unable to locate Brady with the two biggest Bulldogs breathing down his neck and, in a desperate attempt to get rid of the ball, heaved a looping pass in the general direction of where he knew Brady should be waiting. The pigskin sailed through the air, slightly off its mark, and right into the hands of an awaiting Bulldog.

Adam's heart dropped to his toes, and suddenly he didn't feel like a different person at all. He was that same boy who lost the state championship for his whole school sixteen years earlier. Urgency rose in his chest. He looked at the clock. Three minutes and twelve seconds. It seemed impossible, but Kyle had to have a second chance, the second chance Adam never got.

With determined effort, Harvest Bay stopped the play at mid-field. While the offense was on their way in and the defense was heading out, Adam stopped his best linebacker.

"Cody, I know you boys are tired, but I need you to give me all you've got on that field, one hundred percent and no less. Can you do that?"

"I'll give you a hundred and ten percent, Coach," Cody responded in his deep baritone as he strapped his helmet on.

Adam patted the big guy's helmet. "That's my boy! Go get 'em!"

Cody took his place with the others at the line of scrimmage. Bishop Hadley set the play in motion with a pass to McKay, who snatched the pass cleanly out of the tension-filled air, turned, and ran straight into an on-coming torpedo. Cody's helmet drilled the ball loose on the 17 yard line for anyone to pick up. With the roar of the Harvest Bay crowd in the background, Brady swooped in, scooped the ball up and ran with a speed and agility that Adam had never seen before.

"It's a miracle," Adam whispered, and then laughed out loud, whooping and hollering with the others on the sidelines.

The Bulldogs finally caught up to Brady and tackled him at the thirty-seven yard line. Adam couldn't believe it. Except for the fact that the clock on the score board now read fifty-eight seconds, it was as if time had been turned back. He swallowed a lump that was attempting to form in his throat.

Thank You, God, for giving us all a second chance.

Kyle took his place at the line of scrimmage, called a play, and the ball was snapped. He dropped back, found his target, and once again let the ball fly. This time Brady easily caught the ball in the end zone for a touchdown. Jeremy added a chip-shot field goal for a 20-14 lead with only twenty-one seconds left on the clock.

Harvest Bay had won the state championship!

The Harvest Bay fans poured onto the field to congratulate their team and celebrate the victory. Adam's heart nearly burst with pride when a couple of the guys hoisted Kyle onto their shoulders. This moment was worth waiting sixteen years for.

"Daddy, we won! We won!"

Adam turned as Chloe ran up to him and threw herself into his arms. Holding his daughter and watching his new state champions, he believed completely that the Lord was with them, always with them. There was only one thing that could have made it any sweeter—having someone special in his life to share it with. Someone very special.

"Congratulations, Adam."

He turned . . . and froze.

CHAPTER
Twenty-Five

"Alexandra, what are you doing here?" Adam's arms instinctively tightened around Chloe.

She gave her thick raven mane a toss. "Do you really think I'd miss the highlight of your career?"

Her words rang with a condescending tone and left a bitter taste in his mouth.

"Besides, I told you I was coming."

Then he remembered the cell phone conversation he'd had with her in Kate's driveway. "Oh, right. You needed to talk to me. So, talk."

Alexandra laughed and playfully swatted at him. "Not here, silly. Go enjoy your win. Chloe and I will be waiting for you at home."

His blood began to simmer. He wanted to remind her that she had walked out of their home and made her home in Chicago, but he bit his tongue. He stared at her, surprised by the amount of resentment he harbored in his new heart. When he'd turned his life over to Christ, shouldn't that have disappeared?

Chloe wiggled free from Adam's grip, ran to Alexandra's side, grabbed her hand, and looked up at her pleadingly. "Ya mean it? You're coming home?"

"For a while . . . if your daddy lets me, that is." Alexandra shifted her gaze to Adam, her full, pink lips forming a little pout.

His shoulders drooped. He glanced at the crowd on the field. While everyone else celebrated, he had to return to a mind game he didn't want to play anymore. The very thought of matching wits with Alexandra brought on a tidal wave of exhaustion. He didn't know if he had the energy to fight anymore, so he had to trust that with God's help he'd be victorious.

"All right. I'll see you at home." Watching Chloe walk off hand-in-hand with her mother, he knew the nine-year-old now had new hope for a happily ever after. He sighed and shook his head, already dreading the heartbreak that was sure to come.

After they had disappeared in the sea of people, he turned to the field. He really didn't feel much like celebrating, but his team had just won the state championship and no one could take that accomplishment from him. No one.

He enjoyed the moment, but during the long bus ride back to the school, his spirit became troubled. What could Alexandra possibly want? He rested his head against the back of the seat, shut his eyes tight, and quietly mumbled the only four words he could think of.

"Please, God, not Chloe."

⚜

The sun had already set by the time Adam arrived home and parked his truck beside the unfamiliar car in his driveway. He took a deep breath and headed up the walk, mentally preparing himself for battle. He stepped inside his front door, looking around as he slipped out of his coat. The lights were dim in the living room. A faint sound came from the other side of the house.

"Hello?" he called.

"In the kitchen," Alexandra's voice returned.

He kicked off his shoes and slowly made his way toward the kitchen, his apprehension building with every step. Reaching the doorway, he stood there and watched her pour two cups of coffee, adding cream and sugar to both.

"Where's Chloe?"

"Upstairs taking a bath." She carried a steaming mug to him. "I think I remember how you take your coffee."

He took a sip. "It's fine." He set it on the counter and crossed his arms. "You said you needed to talk."

She nodded and leaned against the counter, staring at the coffee cup cradled in her hands. "I've been given the opportunity to do a story that could really put me on the map as a journalist."

"You came all this way to tell me that?"

She turned to him. "It's in Iraq, Adam. I'm covering our troops during the holidays."

He stared at her, unsure of how to react. Relief began to flow through him. If he understood her correctly, she didn't want to fight him for Chloe after all, but he kept his guard up.

After a moment, she gave a humph. "Gee, I knew you'd be happy for me, but I didn't think you'd be speechless."

He looked away. "Are you sure about this, Lexi? I mean, it could get dangerous over there."

"It's a chance of a lifetime. Of course, I'm sure." She grinned mischievously. "Besides, have you ever known me to turn my back on an adventure?"

One corner of Adam's mouth twitched. "That's true." He shook his head. "But that was before you had a daughter who loves and needs you. How are you going to tell her that you're going to be half a world away for Christmas?"

"I already did."

"What?"

"She was a little disappointed, but I promised I'd bring her back some really cool stuff."

Adam's blood boiled. "Do you honestly think that's good enough?"

"Of course not. I also promised her that when I got back after the New Year we'd spend some time together as a family."

"You did what?!" He shoved his hands through his hair. "Lexi, how could you?"

Her gaze fell. Her voice barely more than a whisper, she said, "Because it's what I want, too."

He put his hands up, palms out. "Whoa. Stop right there. We quit being a family the day you left us."

She exhaled. "I made a mistake, and I'm sorry, but I'm not the only one to blame." She met his gaze. "I never stopped loving you, Adam, and I know you still love me too."

Adam clenched his jaw. He wanted to argue, to tell her he didn't love her, but he couldn't.

She closed the gap between them. "Everyone deserves a second chance."

He stared at her, his heart beginning to soften. The Lord gave him a second chance. Shouldn't he do the same for her?

After a moment, he shook his head. "I'm not the same guy you remember."

"What do you mean?"

"I . . . I'm a Christian, Lexi. I've dedicated my life to Christ, and though I've made a lot of mistakes in my past, I'm going to do the right thing now."

"And you don't think that us getting back together is the right thing?" She moved close enough to him that he caught a whiff of her high-dollar perfume. "What about Chloe? Doesn't she deserve to have her mother and father together?"

His shoulders fell. Alexandra knew exactly what button to push.

"Wouldn't it make God happy to see a family reunited?"

He glared at her, confused and trying to fight off an angry spirit. "What do you know about God?"

She cast her gaze to the floor. "Not as much as I should." She sniffed twice, and then openly wept. "I just feel so lost and alone, Adam. I don't want to go to Iraq without having a family to come back home to."

He raised his hands to clap for her performance, but stopped himself. It wasn't for him to decide if she was being genuine. The Lord knew her heart. Instead, he made a quick choice to plant a seed that might grow throughout the month that she spent in a war-torn country.

He awkwardly took her into his arms. "If you have the Lord in your heart you're never alone no matter where you go." He held her at an arms length and looked into her watery violet eyes. "Think about it, will you?"

She wiped the moisture off her face. "I will, I promise, if you'll think about taking me back."

He hesitated. Then against his every instinct, he nodded. "Okay. It's a deal."

She smiled brightly, all signs of the earlier tears gone, and wrapped her arms around him again.

He patted her back and took a step backward. "Uh, I'm going to go check on Chloe."

She returned to her coffee. "Hey, Adam, do you mind if I stay in your guest room? I want to spend as much time with Chloe as I can before I leave Monday morning."

His flat voice mimicked his spirits. "Yeah. Sure. Make yourself at home." Then he turned and dashed up the stairs.

He found Chloe in her room sitting cross-legged on her bed, brushing out her damp curls.

She perked up when he entered the room. "Hi, Daddy!"

"Hey, kiddo." He sat on the edge of her bed and patted her bare knee poking out from under her nightgown.

She sighed, a blissful expression on her face. "Isn't it great having Mom here? It's just like old times."

"You understand that she's leaving on Monday, don't you?"

Her smile fell sharply and sent a dagger straight into Adam's heart. "Yeah, I know." She looked up at him, hope dancing in her almond-shaped eyes. "Are we really gonna be a family again like she said?"

He rubbed the tension out of the back of his neck. "I don't know what the Lord has in store for us, but I trust Him."

Her freckled cheeks plumped above her big smile. "I do too."

He pulled Chloe into a warm hug. "With God leading us, we'll be okay no matter what."

"I love you, Daddy."

He kissed the top of her head. "And I love you."

"Can we invite Mom to join us for our bedtime devotion tonight?"

He forced something of a smile onto his face. "Sure."

A few minutes later the three of them were gathered on Chloe's bed reading from the book of devotions that Adam and Chloe had been using. Ironically, it was a lesson on forgiveness. As he stole a glance at Alexandra, conviction paralyzed his heart. But with the rollercoaster of emotions he'd been on over the past twenty-four hours, he was too weary to do anything about it. Finally they finished reading, and Adam knelt beside the bed with Chloe, adding his silent prayer to her spoken one.

Help me know what to do, God. I'm so confused. I'm not sure I can love Lexi again. At least not the way I . . . love Kate now. But shouldn't I try to put my family back together? I'll do whatever You want me to, God. I just have to know what it is.

"Amen," he and Chloe both said together.

Chloe hopped back onto the bed. "Will you paint my nails, Mom? Pretty please?"

"Now you're talking." Alexandra stood. "I'll get my make-up case and be back in a flash."

Adam watched her go and silently added, *Please, keep her safe, dear God, and help her keep the promise she made me. It just might be the most important one yet.*

<hr />

After a restless night, Adam got up and dressed. He hurried Chloe along, and they headed for church a few minutes early. Alexandra had made it very clear the night before that she planned on sleeping in, claiming that she needed to be well rested for her trip overseas.

That suited Adam just fine.

Reaching the church in record time, he walked Chloe to her Sunday school room, and then headed for the sanctuary. In the peaceful atmosphere he breathed a deep sigh of relief. He quietly moved up the aisle and took a seat beside the person he'd hoped to find.

Grandpa Clayton looked up from his Bible and brightened. "Good morning, Adam. You're here early."

"I needed to get out of the house."

"Still wired from winning the state championship?" He gave a low whistle that carried through the church. "That was some game."

"Thanks, but not quite. A . . . " He searched for the right word. " . . . situation has come up, and I have to make a life-changing decision. I want to do what's right in the Lord's eyes, but with this," he shook his head, "I'm not sure what that is."

Grandpa Clayton closed his Bible and set it aside. "What's the matter?"

Adam proceeded to fill him in on Alexandra's abrupt return and tearful plea for a second chance. "But I don't know if I even love her anymore."

"The Bible tells us to love everyone, even those who have wronged us."

"Got any tips on how I do that?"

"It's not always easy, that's for sure, but it helps to pray for that person. Somehow prayer changes your heart."

Adam nodded. "I think Lexi could use some prayer." He glanced at Grandpa Clayton. "She's not a Christian."

"That's something you'll have to seriously consider. Now that you are a Christian, if you become involved with a non-believer, you'd be unequally yoked, and the Bible advises against that."

Creases formed in Adam's brow. "Doesn't the Bible also instruct us to reach out to the unsaved?"

"Yes it does, and only you can decide which way the Lord wants you to go. Just keep in mind that a godly relationship is as much about commitment as it is about love. Make a choice that you can live with." Grandpa Clayton leaned in and placed his hand on Adam's shoulder. "And remember, you can't save them all."

"Shouldn't I at least try?"

"You should listen to the Lord. He'll always show you the way."

"Okay. Thanks." Adam shook Grandpa Clayton's hand, then went to claim a seat in the back of the church. He closed his eyes.

I'm listening, God, but I can't hear anything. Please help me.

By that time the trickle of people entering the sanctuary had turned into a steady stream, and he looked up just in time to see Kate walk up the aisle . . . with Nathan by her side.

That picture might have been worth a thousand words, but Adam only heard three: *Let Kate go.*

God was telling him that He had a different path in mind for him and Chloe. Adam hung his head, wondering if following God's will was supposed to be so painful.

It's for the best. He'll provide for her and Maddie better than I could. He sniffed and blinked away threatening tears. *But I was so sure . . .*

Unable to sit through the entire service watching his dreams drift farther and farther away, he slipped out of the pew undetected, made arrangements for a friend to bring Chloe home, and headed for a different sanctuary, where he knew Moses would be happy to see him.

"Kate? Is everything okay?"

"Huh?" Kate snapped her gaze up to meet her mother's and found most of the faces at the table watching her expectantly. She grinned sheepishly and glanced down at the food she'd been pushing around her plate with her fork.

"Sure. Everything's fine. I'm just a little tired. Did you ask me something?"

Kate's mother exchanged a look with her father. "We were just wondering how the Christmas pageant is coming along."

Kate nodded and pushed her plate away. "Pretty well, I think, especially given that the performance is only two weeks away."

Her mother took another small helping of candied sweet potatoes. "With all the hard work you've put into it, I'm sure it'll be absolutely wonderful."

Kate managed a lackluster smile. "Thanks."

She thoroughly enjoyed working with the children, but she'd once again succeeded in overextending herself. With teaching, leading the support group, and training for the marathon, all in addition to directing the Christmas program, she'd been burning the candle at both ends, and her wick was rapidly growing short.

Thankfully, Letisha, who'd been assisting her, had volunteered to take over this afternoon's practice several weeks ago after Nathan invited Kate to go to his office Christmas party. Unfortunately, she didn't feel much like celebrating. Her plan to keep so busy she wouldn't have time to dwell on the past had worked a little too well, and now she didn't even have the energy to ponder the miracle of Christmas. The realization brought tears to her eyes.

"Excuse me." Hastily moving away from the table, she made a beeline for the front door. Shivering as she stepped out onto the porch, she hugged herself tightly. Pastor Ben's sermon earlier that morning weighed heavily on her conscience.

"Have you let Christmas become more about you and less about the birth of our Savior?" he'd asked, and Kate sank down in her pew. "If so, this is the perfect time to get your heart right and your priorities straight."

She filled her lungs with the fresh, frigid air, and leaned heavily against the railing. "Lord, I've been so busy lately, I haven't put You first, and now I'm too weary to celebrate Your greatest gift to the world. Please, help me remember, help me *feel*, the true meaning of Christmas. Renew my strength and my spirit. Change my heart, God. Whatever it takes."

"What will it take?"

She shook her head and sighed. "I wish I knew."

Nathan came up behind her and placed his hands firmly on her shoulders. "I think a good start might be to spend time with your Bible tonight instead of with me at Doc Brewster's."

She turned and looked at him with misty eyes. "But I gave you my word."

He wrapped her in a warm embrace. "God's Word is more important to me."

She relished the comfort of his arms around her. For that reason alone she almost argued with him, but she knew he was right.

"Are you sure?"

"I just want what's best for you . . . whatever it takes."

She laid her head against his chest, listening to the steady beat of his heart while hers suddenly became light as a feather. "Thank you. For everything."

A short time later, after kissing Madeline goodbye and reminding her mother of the time to drop her off at school the next morning, Kate pulled into her garage. She carried an armload of wood into the house, built a cozy fire in the fireplace, and lit a few candles. Then she turned on the Christmas tree lights, grabbed an afghan and her Bible, and curled up on the sofa.

She intended to turn straight to the Christmas story, but her Bible fell open to the book of Psalms. Her eyes landed on a passage, and as she read it her vision blurred with unshed tears.

Restore to me the joy of Your salvation, and uphold me by Your generous Spirit.

She began to weep as she made that verse her prayer. She repeated it over and over again, and at last the Holy Spirit descended on her, bathing her from head to toe until she felt strong enough to remember again.

On a whim, she went to her entertainment center, dug in a box stashed behind a door, and pulled out a videotape marked "Christmas '06"—their last Christmas with Ryan. She popped it in.

Sitting cross-legged on the floor, she laughed and cried while she watched her sweetest memories come to life on the screen. Ryan's voice filled her living room as he filmed three-year-old Madeline tearing open her presents, and at that moment it seemed like he was right there with her. She sat glued to the television for more than an hour, allowing it to transport her back in time.

When exhaustion finally set in and her eyelids grew heavy, she realized that remembering wasn't a bad thing after all. It was a precious gift that gave her strength to keep moving on.

⁂

Kate awoke with a start two and a half hours later when her doorbell reverberated through the house. The fire had faded to glowing embers. She glanced at the clock. Ten after five. The doorbell sounded again and Kate hopped up.

"It's probably Nathan coming to check on me before going to the party." She hurried to get the door. Cold air rushed into the house, but it was the sight in front of her that nearly knocked her over.

"Adam! This is a surprise."

"Sorry to just drop by like this."

"It's okay." She held the door open wider. "Come on in."

"Thanks." He stepped into the foyer.

"So what brings you by?" She retraced her steps into the living room and added a couple logs to the hot coals before sitting on the sofa.

He perched on the edge of the recliner and rubbed his hands together. "I, uh, need to tell you something that couldn't wait."

Concern creased her brow. "What is it? What's wrong?"

"Lexi and I are going to work on reconciling our differences and possibly restoring our marriage."

She stared at him in disbelief. "Are you joking?"

He hung his head. "No."

"What . . . what does this mean?"

"I'm not sure yet. It all happened so fast. She's going to be in Iraq for a month covering the holidays so we have a little time to figure it out."

She examined him, working on keeping her emotions in check. After all, she reminded herself, they were never officially anything more than friends. But still . . . "Are you sure this is what you want?"

His weary gaze met hers. "I want to do what's right in God's eyes, and I feel like this is the direction He's leading me."

Residual emotion from earlier stung her eyes and formed a lump in her throat. She swallowed, suddenly wishing God would have led him to her. But it was too late.

He stood. "I just wanted to let you know. Chloe will probably let it slip eventually, and I wanted you to hear it from me first."

"Wait! I was actually just getting ready to read the Christmas story. Would you like to read it together?"

"Sure."

With the lights from the Christmas tree and the crackling fire casting a magical glow over the living room, they sat close together on the sofa reading from the books of Matthew, then Luke, and back to Matthew again. The intimacy of it all made it hard for her to believe that he was returning to his ex-wife.

She wanted to be angry. After all they'd been through, after she sat beside him and prayed with him the day he turned his life over to Christ, how could he choose Alexandra over her? But she couldn't be mad when he honestly thought this was God's will.

She could hear Grandpa Clayton's words from after his first visit with Adam almost three months earlier. *He's got to*

figure some things out on his own now, but he'll be back. Mark my
word. He'll be back.

Could those words be true again? She glanced at Adam
and recognized the sheer determination in his eyes.

Her heart lurched, and she knew what she had to do:
Trust in the Lord who loved her so much He came to earth
that first Christmas morning just to die for her sins . . . and
cherish this time with Adam as if it was the last they'd ever
spend together.

⁓⁓⁓

Doc Brewster lived in a large estate in an older residential
area of Harvest Bay. The gorgeous home had lots of stonework
set off by a wrap-around porch and immaculate landscaping.
It was decked out with lights and a multitude of other decora-
tions for the season, and Nathan thought it easily could have
graced the front of a greeting card.

He parked alongside the road and, holding his coat closed
at the neck to keep out the frosty air, hurried up the walk to
the front door. Doc Brewster's wife, Nancy, warmly greeted
him and ushered him in.

"Merry Christmas, Nathan! Come in, come in. I'll take
your coat and you can join the others in the living room."

"Thank you. And merry Christmas to you too."

He followed the sound of voices to an elegantly decorated
room with big windows and a large stone fireplace that
contained a blazing fire. Doc Brewster looked up when he
entered.

"Well, there's my partner in crime."

The small crowd chuckled, and Nathan couldn't help but
smile. After two months in Harvest Bay, he finally felt accepted.

He joined the group. "I'm not late, am I?"

"Nope. You're right on time. We'll be eating in just a bit. I hope you're hungry."

Nathan rested a hand on his belly. "I am now. It smells delicious."

"Good. In the meantime, help yourself to the hors d'oeuvres, and be sure to get a cup of Nancy's homemade eggnog."

Nathan crossed the room to the small table where refreshments were set out. He placed a few appetizers on a plate and ladled some of the frothy, sweet drink into a cup.

While he mingled with the staff from their office and the animal hospital where Nancy worked, he saw Denise walk in and nearly dropped his plate. She was stunning in a simple but elegant black dress, with heels to match, her hair swept up, and a dazzling smile.

Maggie entered with her, looking as pretty as ever, but he couldn't take his eyes off Denise. He found himself secretly thankful he'd suggested that Kate spend some quiet time with the Lord.

The guilt came then, poking and prodding him. He felt like a liar, loving two women and not even attempting to do anything about it. He vowed to come up with a solution soon, but for the moment he watched Denise, entranced, while she greeted the other guests. He thought his heart would stop when she met his gaze, smiled, and walked over to him.

"Hi," she said simply.

"Hi." Suddenly shy, he glanced down at his cup. "Would you like some eggnog?"

"Mmm. I'd love some."

He handed her his untouched cup and filled another one. She took a sip and looked around the room. "Where's Kate?"

"She's exhausted—mentally and physically—so, following doctor's orders, she stayed home to rest."

Denise nodded. "Good call, doctor. She's been running herself so ragged for the past few weeks that I was getting worried about her. Quiet time is just what she needs. I'll bet she's curled up with a good book."

Nathan smiled. "I'm sure you're right."

"*Hola*, Doctor Sterling," Maggie greeted brightly as she joined them.

"*Hola*, Maggie. Where's the little guy?"

"At home with Cassie."

He scrunched his brow. "Cassie?"

"Cassie Ground. She's the high school senior who watches our kids during our support group meetings. Beautiful girl on the inside and out."

He gazed into Denise's sparkling eyes. "I know the type."

After a delicious meal, they gathered in the living room once again. Doc Brewster entertained them by playing Christmas carols on his baby grand piano. Everyone sang the parts they knew and laughed and visited through the parts they didn't know. Nathan stood near Denise, drinking up her presence . . . and thinking about Kate.

When the grandfather clock in the hallway chimed nine o'clock, the party began to wind down. Denise turned to Maggie. "Are you ready to go?"

"*Si.* I miss *mi niño.*"

"I'll walk you out," Nathan said.

The threesome retrieved their coats, said their good-byes, and headed out the door. The air nipped at his cheeks and nose, but somehow he didn't notice it like he had when he arrived. Maggie quickly slid into the passenger seat of Denise's car and shut the door while he stood with Denise for just a minute at her door.

"I'll see you tomorrow morning," he said. Suddenly tomorrow couldn't arrive soon enough.

"I'll be the one up front answering the phones and working on the computer." She gave him a smile that sparked a fire in his soul.

He leaned forward then and brushed his lips against her cheek. "Good night, Denise."

"Night."

He opened the car door and she slid inside. She started the engine, pulled away from the curb, and left him standing there watching her taillights while tiny snow flakes started to fall from the heavens.

After just a second, he became aware of the bitter cold and hurried to his BMW. As he drove away, he made a quick decision, knowing the time had come. A few minutes later, when he turned onto Kate's road, he began to pray.

"God, I know you made me to give my love to one woman. All this time I thought it was Kate, but now I'm in love with Denise too. Please, God, show me the road to take. Shut and lock one door so I can confidently walk through the other one knowing I am following Your will."

He slowed down as he neared her house, noticing a strange vehicle in the driveway. It appeared to be a dark colored truck. *Maybe it's her dad's.* Moving at little more than a crawl now, he shifted his gaze to the house. The porch light acted as a romantic spotlight for a scene that made his breath catch in his throat.

Kate and Adam were standing there, holding onto each other as if it was their last good-bye.

He punched the gas hard and sped off to the sound of a slamming door and the click of a lock. The loud crack that followed could only have been one thing.

His heart.

Kate forced herself to stay in as much of a routine as possible, but it wasn't easy. The semester quickly drew to a close, adding to her workload at school. She needed to nail down monthly outings for the single parent support group, and the practices for the Christmas pageant became much more strenuous.

Somehow thoughts of Adam always seemed to sneak into her already cluttered mind and throw everything off. She hadn't seen or talked to him since the night he had come to her house, and she missed him. Some days the constant throb in her heart intensified to a sharp, stabbing pain that took her breath away, especially when she'd glance at Chloe and momentarily ponder what could have been.

Running helped. It cleared her mind like nothing else could, even when Dan joined her. She talked to him a little about Adam, but more than anything she focused on her breathing—the very essence of life—and the One to whom she dedicated it all. Day by day, He changed her physically, mentally, and spiritually. He not only healed her heart, but strengthened it as it pumped the blood through her body.

Then, on the evening of the Christmas pageant, two weeks after Adam had told her about his plans to reunite with

Alexandra, she saw him again as he sat in a pew with his parents and Kennedy. It gave her a jolt, a sudden involuntary burst of hope. But she knew he was only there to watch Chloe, and she accepted that fact.

She was okay.

Five minutes before show time, Kate and Letisha gathered the children, all dressed in their costumes and fidgeting non-stop with nervous energy, and Kate prayed with them.

"Dear God, please help this program to go smoothly. Help all the children to do their best and not be nervous. They've worked so hard, and I pray that it shines through tonight. Let their parents and grandparents be touched by their performance, and let all of us be reminded once again of why we celebrate Christmas. It's all because of Your great love."

Before she finished saying amen, the children scrambled to get in their places, except for Chloe. Kate knelt down beside her.

"Are you nervous?"

Chloe shook her head.

She adjusted the little girl's blue sash. "You make a beautiful Mary. Your daddy's going to be so proud."

Chloe's bottom lip quivered. "Do you think my mom would be proud of me?"

Kate's heart fell to her toes, and she pulled the little girl into a tight hug. "Oh, honey, absolutely." She released Chloe when the pianist began playing a lovely melody. "That's your cue."

Chloe gave her a wobbly smile and took her place on the small stage, as poised and dignified as a nine-year-old could be, gently rocking a swaddled baby doll in her arms.

Cassie Ground, standing just off stage, raised the microphone and opened the program with the song "Don't Save It All for Christmas Day."

Goose bumps popped out on Kate's arms while Cassie sang with a voice so pure and sweet about love living on if people will just give a little. Tears flowed freely down Kate's cheeks when Chloe tenderly kissed her baby on its little plastic head.

Oh, Lord, Chloe needs that kind of a mother. Please, God, change Alexandra's heart.

The hour-long program went almost perfectly. The few mistakes merely added a dose of comedic relief, as when Madeline, playing the part of one of the wise men, placed her container decorated with glitter and jewels in front of the manger, turned to the crowd and announced, "I bring a gift of Frankenstein to the newborn King!"

By nine o'clock, the set and small stage had been torn down, all the costumes put away for another year, and the empty sanctuary tidied up so no one could even tell that a children's program had taken place.

Kate plopped into a pew and sighed. "Two months of hard work, and it's over just like that."

"I kind of know the feeling."

She started, her hand flying to cover her racing heart. She turned just as Nathan reached the pew.

"You scared me. What are you still doing here?"

He sat down beside her. "Just waiting to tell you what a great job the kids did tonight. You should be proud."

Pure joy and complete satisfaction bubbled inside her, lifting the corners of her mouth. "Thanks."

"And to tell you something else."

The heaviness of his voice popped her bubbles and flattened her smile. "What is it?"

Silence filled the sliver of space between them.

"Nathan?"

"I'm seeing someone, Kate. I have been for a while now."

"Oh." She blinked twice. *Her* Nathan was seeing someone. "Is it serious?"

He met her gaze, a new, different fire burning in his eyes, and nodded. "I want to marry her."

She sucked in a lungful of air. For a moment she wondered if maybe she hadn't heard him right, but the words echoed in her brain.

"This is quite a surprise." She glanced down at her hands, at her naked ring finger, uncertain if she really wanted to know the answer her next question. "Who's the lucky girl?"

"Denise."

Of course it was Denise. Kate felt foolish for not having seen the flashing neon signs before now. "Well then, I guess you're the lucky one." She elbowed him playfully to cover up the cyclone of emotions spinning in her heart.

He chuckled. "So . . . we're okay?"

She blinked back threatening tears. "Of course. After all we've been through you can't get rid of me that easy. Besides, it just makes sense. Denise is almost like family anyway."

"Thanks."

She patted his knee. "I'd better go. It's getting late." She stood up, sidestepped around him, and slipped out of the pew.

"What are you doing for Christmas?"

"I don't know yet. I'll call you."

She hurried down the aisle and swung by the recreation room where Cassie was keeping an eye on Madeline. She thanked Cassie, grabbed Madeline by the hand, and rushed out of the church.

Once home, she tucked Madeline into bed and crawled into the safety and comfort of hers. She grabbed her Bible off her nightstand and, turning to the marked page in Isaiah, reread the verse she had come across her first Sunday back in Harvest Bay.

"Fear not, for I am with you; be not dismayed, for I am your God. I will strengthen you, Yes, I will help you, I will uphold you with My righteous right hand."

"I trust You, God. You are all I need." Tears slipped out of the corners of her eyes and landed on her pillow. "And if I never get a second chance at love, I'll be okay." She choked on a sob. "I'll be okay."

⁂

Early the next morning, the first day of Christmas vacation, Kate was abruptly awakened by the sound of her doorbell. She pulled the covers over her head and mumbled, "Go away."

When it sounded three more times in rapid succession, she kicked the covers off and trudged to her door. Looking through the peep hole, she couldn't believe her eyes. There stood Nathan with Denise right by his side.

She sighed deeply. She was honestly happy for them, and she'd gladly help them celebrate—right after she got a couple more hours of sleep. She unlocked the door and pulled it open, planning to tell them just that, but stopped short when she noticed the urgent expression on their faces.

Creases formed in her brow. "Hey, guys. It's awful early for a visit. Is everything okay?"

Nathan stepped forward. "Kate, it's Grandpa Clayton. He's in the hospital, and . . . " he shook his head, " . . . it doesn't look very good."

Kate's heart plunged to the pit of her stomach, and panic rose slowly in its place. "What do you mean? He seemed fine yesterday at brunch and even at the Christmas pageant."

Denise crossed the threshold, took Kate by the hand, and led her toward her bedroom. "Go hurry and get dressed. Nathan will tell you what he knows on the way to the hospital."

"But what about . . . "

"Don't worry about Maddie, okay? I'll take care of her."

"Okay. Thanks."

Denise gave her a sad smile, stepped out of the bedroom, and closed the door.

Dazed and confused, Kate obediently threw on a pair of jeans and a sweatshirt and stepped into a pair of slip-ons. She quickly ran a brush through her hair, then grabbed her purse.

Buckled into the passenger seat of Nathan's car, she asked, "W-what happened to Gramps?"

Nathan kept his eyes on the road. "I can't say for sure since I haven't seen him, but based on the information I got this morning from your dad, I believe he had a stroke."

"What did Daddy tell you?"

"That your grandpa went to bed right after they got home from the pageant, complaining of a headache, and this morning your mom found him unresponsive."

Kate moaned and tears spilled out of the corners of her eyes. "Poor Mom." She glanced at Nathan. "Where is she now?"

"At the hospital with your dad. They followed the ambulance over. Since Doc Brewster is your grandpa's primary care physician, your dad called me on his cell phone on the way and filled me in. I offered to come get you and take you to the hospital."

He made a sharp right onto Lake Erie Highway, which would lead them straight to Cresthaven Medical Center. She stared out the window watching the world whiz by.

"What about Liz? Does she know?"

"She's already at the hospital. She was scheduled to work a day shift in the pediatric wing. Your dad's going to go let her know what's happened once they get there."

She looked at him with pleading eyes. "Gramps had a mini stroke last April and made a complete recovery. He'll be okay this time too, right?"

"I hope so, but honestly, this sounds very serious."

She sank down in her seat under the weight of a heavy load of dread. This couldn't be happening. Not to her Gramps. Not now, just four days before Christmas.

Nathan made it to the hospital in record time and whipped his car into the first parking spot they came to. The second the engine was off, they hopped out and dashed to the entrance. The sterile hospital smell hit her instantly and turned her stomach. With her parents nowhere in sight, Kate made a beeline for the triage window.

"Can I help you?" a pretty young nurse asked.

"I'm here to see Clayton Wilbanks. He was brought in by the rescue squad."

Her expression sympathetic, the nurse said, "Yes. I'll show you to the consultation room where the rest of your family is waiting to hear from the doctor." She came around into the reception area. "Right this way."

They followed her to a partially closed door. She gestured for them to go in before retracing her steps to her station.

Summoning all her courage, Kate hesitantly pushed through the door. Inside the softly lit room, Elizabeth and their father sat together on a loveseat. Kate could tell by the traces of mascara under Elizabeth's eyes that she'd been crying.

"Daddy?" Kate forced the word past the growing lump in her throat.

Her father stood and held his arms out.

She crossed the small room and stepped into her father's embrace. After a long minute she stepped back and wiped her eyes.

"Where's Mom?"

"She's in the room with your grandpa and the doctor."

"Is Gramps okay?"

His arms tightened around her. "I don't know, Katydid. I just don't know."

Just then there was a soft tap on the door, and a doctor stepped into the room, accompanied by another nurse. Kate searched his face for any sign of positive news, but the man was a blank slate.

"I'm Dr. Parker. This is our charge nurse, Theresa. We've finished our initial assessment, and I've received the results of the CT scan we ordered."

Kate held her breath, her heart rate accelerating. Elizabeth stood and joined her and their father while Nathan waited quietly off to the side.

"Taking into consideration the information Mrs. Marshall gave me, in combination with the patient's history of a TIA and the results of the CT scan, it appears that Mr. Wilbanks has suffered a hemorrhagic CVA or stroke."

Kate glanced at Nathan, who had closed his eyes and tipped his head back against the wall.

"As I've already explained to Mrs. Marshall, basically what happens during a hemorrhagic stroke is a certain number of blood vessels in the brain burst and release blood into the area around the brain cells, which can cause a significant amount of damage. Eventually the hematoma, or pool of blood, will cause that affected area of the brain to die and the body function it controls will shut down. Depending on the size of the hematoma and the amount of time between onset and treatment, this can be a life-threatening condition."

Elizabeth cut in. "But the hematoma can be removed and the ruptured blood vessels can be repaired through surgery, right?"

Dr. Parker nodded wearily. "That is correct. Our neurologist, Dr. Khaleil, will be better able to inform you about the possibility of treatment after she completes her assessment, which will include an EEG to measure the current activity of the brain." He paused. "I pray that I'm wrong, but given the fact that Mr. Wilbanks experienced symptoms last night and remained unresponsive throughout my assessment, in addition to the results of the CT scan, it's my professional opinion that he will never regain consciousness. If I'm wrong and he does pull through, he'll have a very long road ahead of him. Please prepare yourselves for that."

A fresh wave of tears spilled over Kate's lashes. "Please, can't you do anything to help him now?"

"Mrs. Marshall provided me with his DNR papers, which are strict orders to not be kept alive by artificial means, so I'm limited."

She glanced at her father, and he nodded.

"Unfortunately, dead brain tissue can't be restored like other parts of the body can. What we can do to help him will depend solely on the level of activity in his brain, and like I said, we'll know more about that after Dr. Khaleil completes her assessment. In the meantime, we'll be monitoring Mr. Wilbanks closely for any signs of discomfort and treat it as necessary. I'm sorry. I wish I could do more."

Nathan spoke up then. "When can they see him?"

"I had him moved to a private room. Let me check on the status of that. As soon as he's situated, we'll get you folks back to see him."

They mumbled their thanks. Dr. Parker nodded and ducked out of the room.

Theresa hung back momentarily. "Is there anything I can do for you while you're waiting?"

"We'll have more family arriving any time," Kate's father said. "We'd appreciate it if you'd let them know where to find us."

She nodded. "And I'll check back with you in about half an hour. If you need anything at all, please don't hesitate to ask." She stepped out and pulled the door shut.

In the quiet, Kate began to pace back and forth across the small room, a slide show of memories flashing across her brain. The patriarch of the family, Grandpa Clayton had provided a constant source of comfort and strength, an endless supply of wisdom and stories. Feeling weak under the weight of their broken anchor, she sank to the loveseat and dropped her head into her hands.

Elizabeth sat down next to her, choking on sobs. "Kate," she said in a raspy whisper, "I'm still not pregnant. If Gramps doesn't make it, he'll never know my baby like he knows Maddie."

Kate wrapped her arm around her sister. "Shh. Don't think like that. It'll be okay. You'll see." She rocked her weeping sister, trying to offer some promise, but her words fell flat.

Thankfully, Elijah arrived a moment later and took over comforting his wife. Aunt Claire, Aunt Emily, and their husbands showed up shortly thereafter, and Nathan filled them all in on Grandpa Clayton's condition.

With so many people in the little room, Kate felt suffocated. She slipped out into the hallway. Leaning against the wall, she closed her eyes and prayed.

God, I'm scared. I've always needed Gramps, but now he needs me more. Your Word promises that You are our refuge and strength, a very present help in trouble. Please help me be strong, God. Please.

"Excuse me. Are you Kate?"

Her eyes flew open. Theresa stood in front of her.

"Yes."

"Your mother asked for you. I'll take you to her." She led Kate down the long hall and around the corner to another door. "She's in there. You can go on in."

"Thanks." Kate paused at the door, waiting for divine strength to hit her, but instead she had never felt more vulnerable. With a shaky hand, she reached for the handle, slowly pushed the door open, and poked her head inside.

Her mother sat in a chair near the head of a metal hospital bed. A big ball of emotion lodged itself in Kate's throat again and nearly choked her at her first glimpse of her grandfather.

Her mother's eyes never left Grandpa Clayton. "Come in, honey."

Knees wobbling, stomach churning, heart racing, Kate obediently pulled a chair up next to her mother's, and perched on the edge of it. Tears streamed down her face at the sight of her Gramps, lying frail and motionless against the stark white sheets. His breathing was shallow, but the slight rise and fall of his chest temporarily eased her fears.

"How are you holding up?" her mother asked, her gaze fixed on her father.

Kate wiped her eyes. "I'm okay, but how are you?"

Her mother only shook her head. Her shoulders began to shake as sobs wracked her body.

"Oh, Mom." Kate wrapped her arms around her mother.

"He's my daddy, Kate. He was there for me when we lost Mom, so strong and brave. Now . . . I don't know what I'm going to do if we lose him."

"We'll get through it together." Kate held her mother for several minutes trying to comfort her, at the same time needing desperately to be comforted.

"I always knew that this day would come, but a daughter is never ready to lose her daddy."

Kate thought about Madeline and how Ryan had left them when she was only four years old. She nodded, fighting back the urge to break down. "I know."

"If I'd only checked on him last night, maybe it would've been like before. He said he had a headache and was going to lie down. I didn't think anything of it."

"You can't blame yourself, Mom. Gramps wouldn't want that."

"You're right." Her mother wiped her eyes and took a shaky breath. "Are Claire and Emily here yet?"

"They arrived just before I came down here."

Her mother got to her feet. "I'm going to go see my sisters. Will you stay here and call us right away if the neurologist comes in?"

Kate offered her mother a weak smile. "Sure."

Her mother leaned down and kissed the top of Kate's head. "Thanks, sweetie. I'll be back soon." She placed her hand over Grandpa Clayton's before hurrying out of the room.

Alone with her grandfather in the dimly lit room, Kate scooted over to her mother's chair and leaned forward. She ran her hand over his thin hair, and then rested her head on a corner of the mattress.

"Hey, Gramps. Can you hear me?" As she expected, there was no response. "Do you remember how when I was little and I'd spend the night with you and Grandma, you'd always tell me a bedtime story? It was one of my favorite parts of staying with you." She sniffed. "Of course, the bad thing about bedtime stories is I'd usually fall asleep before I found out how it ended."

She traced the lines in the hospital gown down his frail arm. "Life is kind of like that, isn't it? Sometimes you go to sleep before you find out how the story ends." Her chin quivered and tears pooled behind her lashes. "I want you to know how my story ends, Gramps. I want you to know that I'm stronger now than I've ever been before, and so much of it is because of you. So much of who I am is because of you." She choked on a sob. "Oh, Gramps, I know it's selfish of me, and I'm sorry. You've waited so long to be with Grandma again, but I'm not ready for you to leave me yet. First Ryan. Then Adam and Chloe. I can't lose another person I love so much."

"I can't either."

She bolted to an upright position and turned toward the voice. Her breath caught in her throat at the sight of Adam standing in the open doorway, with the hallway light spilling in around him.

He stepped into the room and shut the door. "Your mom said I could come in. Is that okay?"

She nodded. Seeing him now, hearing his voice under such dire circumstances, brought on another wave of emotion.

He shortened the gap between them with two long strides and stopped at the foot of the hospital bed. "I got here as soon as I could."

She swiped at her steadily flowing tears. "H-how did you find out?"

"Denise called my cell phone while I was out exercising Moses, trying to clear my head."

She patted the seat next to her.

He moved to the chair and sank into it. When he spoke, his voice was as heavy as her heart.

"I only knew your grandpa for a few months, but he changed my life."

"Gramps had a way of making people see things in a whole new light."

He leaned forward, resting his forearms on his knees, and hung his head. "When Alexandra asked me to give her a second chance, I went to him for advice before I stopped by your house."

Kate glanced at him. "Do you mind if I ask what he told you?"

"To listen to the Lord, that He'd show me the way."

She smoothed the shoulder of Grandpa Clayton's hospital gown. "Has He shown you the way?"

He nodded. "I can't believe it took me so long to figure out that He's always been leading me to you."

"Is Chloe okay with that?" she asked, her voice muffled.

"Chloe loves her mother, but she loves you too." He met and held her gaze, his blue eyes glistening with unshed tears. "And so do I."

He took shaky breath. "I still have a lot to learn, so I could be wrong but I just can't see how it's God's will for Chloe and me to be in a situation where our hearts are continually breaking. So last night during our bedtime devotions, I got right with God. I asked Him to forgive me for the mistakes I made in my marriage, and after all this time I finally forgave Alexandra. Chloe and I prayed that He would change her heart, and then we prayed . . . " his voice cracked and he cleared his throat " . . . that you love us too, and if it's His will, you, Maddie, Chloe, and I will be a family someday."

Kate quietly wept. Less than twelve hours after she'd turned everything over to the Lord, He'd given her a second chance at love and at the very moment she needed it most.

Adam shook his head, a single tear rolling down his face. "I wanted your grandpa to know that I finally figured out that the Lord brought you into my life the day I helped you fix your flat. At the time, I thought I was helping you, but it was really the other way around. God knew that only you could help me to become a better father and coach, a better person in general. And He knew that you and your grandpa were the only two people who could lead me to Him. I've thanked God many times, but I don't think I ever thanked your grandpa, Kate. I want him to know how much I appreciate the time he spent with me."

She slipped her hand into his. "Gramps has an uncanny way of knowing things before words are ever spoken." She chuckled through her tears. "He would always say, 'A person can become pretty perceptive in eighty-seven years.' He knows, Adam. He knows."

They sat for several minutes in silence, their eyes fixed on Grandpa Clayton. Kate tried to process all the information Adam had just given her, but concern for her gramps made it impossible.

When Dr. Khaleil arrived a short time later, Kate reluctantly followed Adam out of the room to get her mother and aunts. Elizabeth reported that Nathan had gone to his office for a few hours, but three of their cousins and Pastor Ben had arrived by then, crowding the small consultation room even further.

"Why don't we go to the cafeteria for a cup of coffee?" Adam suggested.

When Kate hesitated, her father said, "You won't be far, Katydid. Someone will get you when Dr. Khaleil comes in to talk to us."

Sitting at a small table talking with Adam over a warm cup of coffee, Kate was thankful her father knew exactly what she needed. She could almost imagine that the hands of time had been turned back—before Alexandra showed up, leaving a path of destruction in her wake and before Grandpa Clayton was left clinging to life by a thread.

Thankfully, the mess Alexandra had caused could be cleaned up.

While they chatted, Adam placed his hand over Kate's. The old familiar fluttering in her chest instantly returned—a good step in the process, but she was ready for a leap.

The corners of her mouth curved upward. "By the way, in case you're wondering, the answer to your question is yes."

He tipped his head to the side. "I didn't know I asked a question."

"You prayed it, and, yes, I do love you and Chloe. Very much."

He smiled, the sparkle returning to his eyes. Before he could respond, Elizabeth skidded to a stop at the entrance of the cafeteria.

"Kate! The doctor's here. Hurry!"

They jumped up and raced back to the consultation room, arriving just in time to hear Dr. Khaleil say sadly, " . . . cherish the remaining time you have with him."

Kate felt as though she'd been kicked in the chest. A moan escaped her lips, and a tidal wave of emotion overtook her. Adam pulled her to him and rocked her gently while she wept against his chest.

Throughout the day, family and friends came and went. Jane and Ian stopped by for a while, as did Maggie and Letisha. Nathan returned after work, and then left to stay with Madeline through the night. Pastor Ben stayed with the family until after ten o'clock. Elizabeth and Elijah went home to get some sleep, and even her mother and father went home for a short time.

But Kate never left the hospital. And Adam never left her.

The next morning, Nathan brought her a change of clothes and a few toiletries that Denise had gathered for her, and Kate's emotions once again flowed down her cheeks. This time, however, they weren't tears of grief, but of gratitude. She was blessed. Sitting at the hospital while her beloved grandfather slipped further and further away, she was still blessed.

At half past eleven in the morning on December twenty-third, with his entire family and Pastor Ben gathered around him, Grandpa Clayton took his last breath. Kate's mother and aunts stood at their father's head in his final moments and tearfully sang "It is Well with My Soul." It was the most hauntingly beautiful scene Kate had ever witnessed.

She pressed her hand over her heart to try to ease the pain. She wasn't angry, didn't have the urge to cry out at the unfairness of it all. There was only a deep, heavy sadness.

When it finally got to be too much to bear, she went outside the door to where Adam and Nathan waited and collapsed into their arms. With one arm around Adam and the other around Nathan she heaved sobs from the depths of her soul until her emotional well was bone dry.

It was over.

An hour later, when Adam drove her home, she silently stared out the window. There wasn't anything left to say, and she didn't have a fraction of the energy needed to carry on a conversation.

Turning onto her road, he said softly, "I made arrangements for Madeline to spend the day at Jane's. Denise had to get back to work and, well, I just thought . . . "

He pulled into the driveway, and it hit her like a slap across her face.

"This is Gramps' house," she whispered, and new tears surfaced. Memory after memory came flooding back to her so fast she thought she might drown.

He wrapped an arm around her as they walked to the front door, but once inside, she crumbled to the floor and wept hard. He scooped her up and carried her to the sofa.

"What . . . am I going to do . . . without him?" she said between sobs. "I already miss him so much."

He kissed her forehead and rested his cheek against the top of her head. "I know, Kate. So do I, but we'll find a way to get through it together. I promise."

At that moment, in the shadow of her sorrow, a tiny ray of hope shone through.

CHAPTER
Twenty-Eight

onday morning came too quickly. Kate cried while she slipped into her black dress, pinned her hair up in a French twist, and attempted to apply her make-up. Her stomach knotted every time she thought about what she was getting ready for—Grandpa Clayton's funeral.

Big, fluffy snowflakes floated to the ground as a river of people flowed into the church. By a quarter till ten, the flower-laden sanctuary was so packed the ushers had to add two rows of folding chairs behind the last pews, and there were still people standing in the aisles. Many of Kate's friends, co-workers, and support group members were among the crowd, and she drew strength from their love and support.

At the top of the hour, the processional began, and Adam, Nathan, Elijah, and three other pallbearers carried the casket, draped with the American flag, down the center aisle while Cassie Ground sang a moving ballad that told of the hope found in Jesus. When her angelic voice lifted the words to "I Will Rise" to the peaked beams of the ceiling, the Holy Spirit moved in the church. It stirred up Kate's heart, deepening her desire for heaven.

But some days a lifetime seems like so long to wait.
Take it from this old man; it's not.

Moisture gathered behind her lashes at the bittersweet memory of the conversation she had with Grandpa Clayton just shy of six months earlier on the bench right outside the church doors. She still couldn't believe he was gone.

After the casket was in position, Adam slipped into the pew behind where Kate and Madeline sat with the rest of their family. He gently placed a comforting hand on her shoulder, and she reached up to touch his fingers while Pastor Ben made his way to the pulpit.

"We're gathered together this morning to remember and celebrate the life of a remarkable man. Clayton Wilbanks touched the lives and changed the hearts of many, including mine."

Kate couldn't stop the tears from trickling down her cheeks when Pastor Ben shared the emotion-filled story of how her gramps first introduced him to Jesus and opened his eyes to the unconditional love of Christ. When he asked if anyone felt compelled to share a few words about Grandpa Clayton, several made their way down front. The outpouring moved Kate. Her gramps was loved and would never be forgotten.

Neither would Ryan.

And somehow she would find a way to continue moving on.

Although Kate and her family had attended Christmas Eve service together, and Santa Claus left presents for Madeline to open on Christmas morning, they had all decided to wait until after the funeral for their big family get-together. By New Year's Eve, three days after they said their final goodbyes to Grandpa Clayton, they agreed it was time to celebrate their

Savior's birth. This year, Kate's house seemed the most appropriate gathering place, with Adam and Chloe included too.

Kate's mother and Elizabeth arrived early that morning to help her prepare dinner. As soon as they walked through the front door, Kate embraced her mother long and hard.

"Are you doing okay, Mom?"

Her mother offered a weary smile. "I am now. I've got my girls and my granddaughter."

"Grammy!" Madeline nearly tackled her grandmother. "Didya bring me any presents?"

Kate's mother laughed, a sweet sound after the week they'd been through. "Not yet. You be a good girl and Papa will bring them later."

"Okay! I'll be really good!"

They worked together in the kitchen, sharing their favorite memories and singing to a CD of classic Christmas carols. As to be expected, a few tears came, but more than anything, their laughter filled the house. It acted like a healing ointment for their broken hearts, and at five o'clock when the others arrived, the mood was light and cheery.

Despite Kate's best attempt at keeping the atmosphere festive, brief, unavoidable moments of sorrow came and went. When everyone crowded around the kitchen table and her father humbly took over the honor of saying the blessing, Grandpa Clayton's absence hung over them like a cloud. Gradually it evaporated as the eating and visiting began.

Kate understood that everyone needed to adjust, including her. But change was never easy, and after dinner when everyone retreated to the living room to listen to the Christmas story, her heart clenched. How many times had she sat at the feet of her family's master storyteller and listened to him read about the birth of Jesus? She adored her father, but it just wasn't the same without Grandpa Clayton there.

A lump began to form in her throat, and she quickly excused herself. She stood at the kitchen sink washing a few dishes and trying to get a grip on her emotions. Just when she thought she had it licked, she felt two strong arms encircle her.

"Are you okay?" Adam asked softly.

She nodded, contradicting her quivering lower lip.

"You aren't the only one who misses him, Kate."

"I know." She turned to face him, a tear slipping out of the corner of her eye. She wiped it away, surprised that she had any left after the week they'd endured. "The firsts are always the toughest. Each Christmas after this one will get a little easier."

He bowed his head close to hers. "Is there anything I can do to make it better for you now?"

"You and Chloe being here is enough."

He softly brushed his lips against hers, sending tingles to the deepest, most sensitive part of her soul.

She sighed and looked up into his smiling face. "That helps too."

He chuckled and laced his fingers through hers. "Come on." He led her back to the living room, where the gift giving had just begun.

It was the most fun she'd had in weeks. Excited chatter drowned out the Christmas carols still playing in the background. As soon as Kate's father passed out a present, the race was on to see how fast the paper could come off. Even her mother wasted no time in tearing into her gifts.

Before long, there were only a few presents left under the tree, and everyone started to shift their focus to the fact that a brand new year was just a few hours away. Kate sat on the sofa next to Adam, thankful for the lull, and fingered the beautiful heart-shaped locket he'd given her, wondering what the upcoming year would bring her family. She found it hard to believe that just a few years ago she had celebrated Christmas with Ryan and Grandpa Clayton. Now they were gone, but she had Adam and Chloe.

To everything there is a season. I just wish the changes didn't have to hurt so badly.

"Hey, everyone! Look what I found!" Madeline wiggled out from under the tree holding a small gift in her hands.

"Where did you find that?" Kate's father asked taking the gift from her to read the tag.

"All the way in the back."

Looking as if he'd seen a ghost, he shifted his gaze to Kate's mother, then back to the gift.

"Charlie, dear, what is it?"

Everyone turned their attention to Kate's father.

Madeline did a little dance. "Is it for me? Is it for me?"

"No, sweetie. It's for your mama." He crossed the room and handed it to Kate.

Suddenly nervous, she braced herself as she looked at the tag.

To: Katy. From: Gramps.

Her heart rate accelerated at the sight of Grandpa Clayton's unmistakable chicken scratch. She looked up at her father with questions in her eyes.

He shrugged. "You don't have to open it now if you don't want to."

Adam's arm tightened around her, providing her with a much needed source of strength. "It's okay, Daddy. I want to."

She tore open one end and peeled the paper back, revealing a small white box. Holding her breath while she opened it and peeked inside, she found a piece of notebook paper neatly folded on a puff of cotton. She took it out, set the box in her lap, and unfolded it, catching the faintest hint of her grandfather's old familiar aftershave. Her eyes already growing misty, she blinked to clear them and began to read.

Dear Katy,

Life's a journey, and you already know that it's not always an easy trip. Sometimes it seems like it's all uphill . . . or heading downhill so fast it's out of your control. There are detours and traffic jams and times when you'll break down. When you moved back to Harvest Bay, you were broken down, but I've watched you over these past several months turn your heart back to the Lord and slowly get back on the great highway. And I want you to know I've never been more proud of you."

Tears streamed down her cheeks. She frantically wiped them away, being careful not to let any splatter on this precious piece of paper.

I know sometimes you'll feel like you're making the trip alone. I did too, but one thing I learned after eighty-seven years is that love is a constant companion. When you love someone, they will always be with you—in you, beside you, behind you, above you, below you, all around you—because love never dies. The more you love, the more company you'll have on your journey. So, my dear Katy, let Jesus guide you, let love find you, and you'll always find your way home.

Lots of love forever, Gramps.
P.S. It's time for you to have this.

She wiped her face again and reread the last line. *It's time for me to have what?* She peered into the box and, on a whim, pulled the cotton out.

She gasped and her hand flew to her mouth. There was no chance of stopping her tears now. She glanced at her mother, who watched with teary questions in her eyes. Kate's hand trembled as she reached in and pulled out an exquisite antique wedding band.

"It's Grandma's ring," she breathed.

Despite the dwindling fire in the fireplace, intense warmth filled her from her toes up and concentrated in her heart. Grandpa Clayton and Ryan were both there with her. They'd always be with her because, as her gramps had said, love lived on. And now another love had indeed found her.

She turned to Adam who watched her with shining eyes, and she smiled.

Welcome home.

Epilogue

Kate took a deep breath, soaking in the electric atmosphere while she stretched her muscles.

"You ready for this?" Dan Olien asked, stretching beside her, a contagious fire burning in his eyes.

She smiled. "I think so."

"You worked hard enough for it. Now just relax and enjoy this run."

"Oh, hey, do you still need an assistant coach for the cross country team next year?"

He grinned. "You better believe it."

"I might have some extra time since my days of leading the single parent support group are numbered." She held up her left hand, and the bright sunshine reflected off her diamond ring.

He pointed at her. "You're hired!"

"As easy as that?"

He chuckled. "Well, not quite, but I'm sure there won't be a problem."

They found their places at the starting line, and just a few minutes later the sound of a gunshot split the air.

The race began.

A surge of adrenaline pumped through Kate's veins as she pushed herself to do her very best. She glanced at Dan, who could have already been far ahead but stuck right with her instead.

He'd been right. Nothing could have helped Kate learn more about herself than training for this marathon, and now she ran, knowing and loving exactly who she was. While her feet pounded on the pavement, providing a steady beat for the music within her, she reflected on the past ten months.

She'd arrived in Harvest Bay with a broken heart and a wounded spirit. She didn't have the drive to jog around a city block, let alone compete in a marathon. She survived a one day at a time, sometimes minute to minute. Through her pain and grief, she chose not to make God her ally. She'd foolishly made Him her adversary instead. A second chance at love was not only something she had no interest in; it was something she believed she was incapable of.

The Lord had certainly showed her that His thoughts were not her thoughts, nor were her ways His ways.

As the fourth mile marker came into view, Kate smiled inwardly. It was on the fourth of April that Adam had asked her to marry him. On that Easter Sunday, the day she celebrated her Savior returning from the grave, she began to live again. Her heart, now only scarred where it had been broken before, overflowed with love for the two people who made her whole, made her look forward to each new day.

Kate still couldn't help but wonder how Alexandra ever let Adam go or how she couldn't seem to see that she continuously hurt her own daughter. Kate clenched her teeth and tensed up slightly when she remembered Adam telling her about his last real conversation with Alexandra.

After she'd gotten back from Iraq, Adam had attempted to tell her that the Lord had placed someone else in his life, someone who could help him grow in his faith. She scoffed at him, told him he was wasting his time, but that it really didn't matter because she'd already decided to return to Iraq as a full-time correspondent for one of the national news stations. It was the opportunity of a lifetime, she'd said. Chloe had cried for two days.

Kate prayed diligently for Alexandra's heart to change and that in the meantime she could somehow ease the pain her absence and complete disregard caused Chloe.

With that thought, Kate faltered.

"Come on, Kate. Give 'em the business. Strong and steady, strong and steady."

She nodded at Dan's encouragement and concentrated on regulating her breathing. She pumped her arms in time to the thumping of her heart and soon got back in her groove.

At mile marker fourteen, a tiny sense of accomplishment coupled with a huge chunk of raw determination settled in her soul. She'd passed the halfway mark! It reminded her of the pride she'd felt for the single parent support group. With a little work and a lot of planning, week by week she'd seen it grow to forty plus members! Even though she was blissfully happy with Adam, it wasn't going to be easy for her to let go and step down as their leader.

The easiest transition, naturally, would have been to shift the leadership to Denise, and she would have done a great job. But on Valentine's Day, after receiving both Griffin's and Greyson's blessing, Nathan had asked Denise to marry him. It tickled Kate's heart to see the two people who meant so much to her experience true happiness and share a godly love.

Still, the Lord had put an amazing plan for the support group into motion. After witnessing Grandpa Clayton's funeral and hearing countless testimonies of how he had made a difference in the lives of others, a miracle had occurred in Maggie's heart. She dedicated her life to Christ, started attending church regularly, and vowed to be a godly example for nine-month-old Justin. She deeply desired to give back to the community that had helped her so much during her time of need, so she eagerly accepted the leadership role, with Letisha committing to serve as her assistant.

Kate thought of Grandpa Clayton then. It had been almost five months since he left them for his home in heaven, and sometimes it still sent a shock wave through Kate. She'd occasionally find herself still expecting to see him sitting in his favorite recliner or, as the weather warmed up, in a lawn chair under the big oak tree. But she knew he was with her, always with her, just as Ryan was, because love never died.

As they approached mile twenty-six, with spectators cheering from the white gates on either side of the street and the finish line in their sights, Dan pumped his fists.

"You're almost home, Kate. You're almost there."

Giddiness bubbled inside her to the point that she almost became light-headed. But when her gaze fell on a tall, handsome blond among the crowd, her mind instantly cleared. Madeline called to her from atop Adam's shoulders.

"Mama!" She waved enthusiastically. "Hi, Mama!"

Chloe stood between Adam and Kate's father. Her mother and Elizabeth flanked his other side. Even Nathan, Denise, and the boys were there.

"You go on ahead," she said to Dan. "I'll meet you at the finish line."

She veered to the left and embraced Adam as best as she could from the other side of the gate.

"I'm so proud of you," he murmured near her ear.

Her eyes glistened with tears of joy. "I love you, Adam Sullivan."

"And I love you." Then he bent down so that Kate could kiss Madeline.

"Ew! You're all sweaty, Mama!"

Kate laughed and tousled her daughter's hair. She kissed her fingertips and tenderly touched Chloe's cheek, and passed high fives around to the rest of her rallied loved ones. Then she took off again.

A moment later, with hands high in the air, she crossed the finish line, knowing that her journey was far from over. In many ways, it was just beginning.

Reader Discussion Guide

Kate Sterling

1. In what ways can you identify with Kate?

2. Kate's major conflict throughout this book is that she's broken down. Although she knows she has to move on, she doesn't want to let go. Have you ever experienced such a conflict? Who or what helped you through that time?

3. Initially Kate is afraid that since she's been away for so long Harvest Bay won't feel like "home" anymore. She soon discovers that although much of Harvest Bay remains the same, many of the people—the spirit of the town—have changed. How might this be considered symbolism? Do you think it makes it easier for Kate to adjust? If so, how? If you moved away from your hometown, what was your experience upon returning to visit family and/or friends? What aspects changed and what stayed the same? Which do you think changed more—you or your town?

4. At the end of the book Grandpa Clayton's final gift to Kate is her grandmother's wedding ring. What do you think this signifies?

5. Read Isaiah 41:10. How could this verse be used as a theme for Kate's faith journey? How could you apply it to your own personal faith journey?

Adam Sullivan

1. In what ways can you identify with Adam?

2. Adam's major conflict throughout this book is his lack of Christian faith and his inability to believe that God can love him after all the mistakes he's made in his past. Have you ever struggled with this? How did you overcome it?

3. Adam puts his trust in Kate and asks her to help him figure out what the Bible is all about. Naturally, he's upset when he finds out that she's asked Grandpa Clayton to be his mentor instead. What about Grandpa Clayton helps Adam quickly grow comfortable with the arrangement? How do you think the outcome would have been different if Kate had tried to fulfill the role herself?

4. Just a few weeks after Adam accepts Jesus Christ as his Savior, he is tested in a big way. Do you think he handles his ex-wife's sudden appearance correctly? Discuss a time when you were tested after a period of spiritual revival.

5. Read Romans 5:8. How could this verse be used as a theme for Adam's faith journey? How could you apply this verse to your own personal faith journey?

Nathan Sterling

1. In what ways can you identify with Nathan?

2. Nathan's major conflict throughout this book is his struggle with obedience. Has God ever asked you to do something that didn't quite make sense to you, including leaving a successful job or other good situation? Did you obediently follow His prompting right away, did you need Him to make it very obvious as Nathan does, or did you choose to follow your own instincts? What was the outcome?

3. When Nathan meets Griffin he immediately recognizes a wound he feels compelled to help heal. Why do you think it is so important to Nathan to help Griffin? Tell about a time when you were able to use your own personal hardship to help someone else.

4. As the story unfolds we begin to see that although God's plan is indeed to move Nathan to Harvest Bay, it isn't for the reason he thought. Have you ever thought that your path was leading you one way only to find out that God had a completely different plan for you? How did you feel at that point? Confused? Disappointed? Relieved?

5. Read Romans 5:3. How could this verse be used as a theme for Nathan's faith journey? How could you apply this verse to your own personal faith journey?